IN REMEMBRANCE OF SORROWS

A Hunter's Universe Novel
by David Michael Martin

For information contact:

Bent Briar Publishing L.L.L.P.
Denver CO 80226
www.bentbriarbooks.com

ISBNs
978-1-942665-22-9 SC
978-1-942665-23-6 eBook

10   9   8   7   6   5   4   3   2   1

Dedication

This book is dedicated in memory of the 60s and 70s ecology-now movements.

Acknowledgments

A warm thank you for my agent Laura Kathleen Sutton for patiently putting up with me over the years. Special thanks also go to BetteRose Ryan and Bent Briar Publishing for their time and effort getting Remembrance of Sorrows published.

Author Updates

For more information regarding me, the Hunter's Universe Saga, and other works in progress visit davidmichaelmartin.com.

Other Titles by David Michael Martin

Hunter's Moon
Honor and Obligation
WARPACT!
Assaultmistress Kidahin

TABLE OF CONTENTS

1
KEEPING SECRETS

Is keeping the truth to oneself lying? No. The others would smell falsehood lingering on my scent.

Too late to mention flashbacks of *Londiwe Khoza's* dead now. I accepted the invitation readily enough and without reservation. I cannot back out of the great honor given me now.

"I should not have accepted," Kidahin sang softly.

"The colony Elders asked Delwyn. He asked us, and we agreed. Who would not? You cannot back out now. Think of the honor debt they can charge you with. Your dishonor will accrue to Delwyn's character because he asked you, and us," Tialdrin sang just as softly.

Kidahin folded her orange-dappled red ears back against her short, tight red ringlets and snapped her long, red-striped, orange tail at imaginary salt flies. She turned away from Tialdrin, faced the Gracious Mistress of the Singing People, and nodded her readiness.

The Gracious Mistress frowned slightly and gave Kidahin a brief searching stare.

Smelling nothing amiss, she nodded aggressively and shifted her gaze to include the others gathered around her.

She opened her empathic mind to the pheromones drifting on the body odor of her audience, smiled brightly, and raised her arms to gain everyone's attention.

Her lips parted.

She sang an A note, clear, vibrant, beautifully supported in the alto register. The note swelled into the ritual melody. Her voice carried a harmony of delight she seldom felt since reaching adolescence.

"I love how pheromonal empathy pulls hidden motifs from a gracious mistress's voice," Kidahin sang softly in Tialdrin's elegant twitching ear.

"It amazes me how she uses tones, rhythms, melodies, harmonies, cadences, and timbres to give life to thoughts and memories and sends them out as vivid emotional imagery for us to empathize with," she added.

"Yes," Tialdrin hissed quietly. "Get ready. The Gracious Mistress and her accompanying singers are about to sing the first scenes from the Oyya Web of the spirits to guide us through this historical mission."

Kidahin relaxed and let the Song lyrics fill her ears as they painted vivid pictures in her empathic mind.

Who are we, the Eyloni, without our memories?

Who are we without our hopes, without our dreams?

We are nothing without our past, without our future; we are nothing but an arrow without a bow and without a target.

Without memories, without dreams, we are devoid of hope, and we are devoid of purpose.

Today lasts only a blink and it is gone. It is our duty to remember our past and treasure our future. This is why, so long ago, we hunted.

We, the Eyloni, know our prey. We surround the territory of the Neh'as'anni Clan, where the ni'zakhon have laid their lair. There, death stalks the land. We know the days and dreams of our People, of our Elders, and of our males and infants trapped there. But we will never let our heritage die, nor our males fall into oblivion.

Kidahin caught herself staring at reddish-yellow predawn light streaking down onto rainforest tree trunks. Golden-yellow mosses blanketed the trees from exposed roots to well into the lower branches. The faint sunbeams gave the moss orange shadows, making it appear to crawl along the gray bark. Tail-long yellow-streaked crimson leaves gave the trees a windswept look, as though nature painted the leaves in horizontal layers. The trees stood far apart, and little grew among them but sparse orange jungle grasses, a few glossy yellow plants, and an occasional scarlet, breast-high bush.

And ruts, lots and lots of ruts, ran along the ground.

Kidahin wrapped her tail around her waist, strapping her back deep into the seat as the armored personnel carrier bounced across increasingly rough terrain.

"Einstika, must you drive over every rock, log, and rut in Neh'as'anni Clan territory?" Shikararro complained, her air seat hissing as its shocks absorbed another abrupt jolt.

Einstika glared at the Eldest Huntress, and in doing so, did not see the boulder rushing towards her. Tires bounced over it, hard.

"Einstika! The tri-wheel hubs allow us to roll over occasional rocks and fallen branches, but not every one of them you see," Shikararro keened.

Einstika growled and pushed down on the clutch pedal, downshifted, and gunned the natural gas turbine engine.

"It is not my fault!" she sang. "The lidar return is corrupted. Keep in mind that the Mistress will soon hear everything we say because the radio is switched to voice-operated mode. Stop keening over nothing. I know the scrambler works because I received ground survey files. Once the speech processor syncs up, we should hear a flat monotonic voice on the cabin speakers."

"I heard that," the Environmental Interdiction supervising Mistress droned flatly over the speakers.

"Hear that, Shikararro? The A'tayotan hierarchy is listening. Hello, Mistress. The scrambler savages your beautiful singing voice. You sound like a human," Einstika trilled at insolence pitch.

"What is a—human? Do you mean someone suffering from amusia?" Kidahin sang dryly.

"I can just smell Delwyn hearing you say that!" Tialdrin trilled wistfully.

"Del-who?" Einstika sang wickedly.

Although they pulled each other's tails, they sang a note of seriousness, too. This was literally not the time to think about Delwyn, yet Kidahin could not help but think about him anyway: an affable, solitary male with a bright face and eyes that wandered and darted inquisitively as he sang.

"Kidahin, stop!" Tialdrin trilled.

"All of you have important roles to play, and I expect you to follow ritual forms explicitly. If any of you do not, I will charge you with an honor crime.

"The Territorial Boundaries of Rage and Forgiveness says rage is a teacher. Remember that and what happened here and keep that in mind at all times," the supervising Mistress interrupted.

"We know why. We came here because Hlorrithin declared all technology clans ni'zakhon for violating the Be'atika Senge's decree demanding they shut down and surrender their polluting technology. They refused, and the Be'atika Senge hierarchy declared their clans dead. Hlorrithin carries out the declaration—killing the Neh'as'anni and the fourteen clans allied with them. The Be'atika Senge's ultimatum came a week ago. We are on the edge of Neh'as'anni territory, and I can already pick up elevated electromagnetic radiation traces. What in the spirits did they do here?" Einstika sang.

"Pay attention and keep your eyes open. We are approaching the environmental disaster exclusion zone," Shikararro trilled.

The APC rolled through heavy undergrowth at a fast-walking pace. Thorns longer than fingers screeched shrilly across the cabin, scoring the orange, red, and yellow patterned paint down to bare metal.

Trying not to cause more damage to the rainforest than necessary, Einstika slowed and yanked the steering wheel hard and swung the APC into a small clearing. A gravel road made from the crushed by-products of industry crossed through the orange grasses.

Einstika turned onto the road and stepped on the accelerator.

Kidahin watched short, deep-red ferns that grew along the roadsides into the trees creep by. Orange vines climbed up brown bark. Felled understory trees covered with yellow moss littered the ground, cut down to make way for the road as it drifted through the clearing and into and around much larger trees before disappearing into the orange rainforest shade.

Einstika glanced right, her eyes dazzled by the bright coppery leaves growing among the crimson ferns.

"Einstika, turn left!" Shikararro keened.

Einstika blinked the glittering copper sparkles from her eyes and glanced through the windshield.

A large tree trunk raced towards her at astonishing speed.

Her eyes bulged.

She hit the air brakes.

"I was watching where I was going," she keened defensively over the sharp hiss of compressed air.

"Stop leafchasing," Shikararro snapped.

"I was not," Einstika trilled angrily, grinding the gears on purpose before shifting back into gear.

She drove down the road with a bit more care. Gravel sometimes caused tires to lose traction and swerve uncontrollably. The sound of driving on gravel, the treads flinging stones against the floorboards, and the soft purr of the turbine engine soothed her ears.

An hour later, the APC turned onto another gravel road, this one made from crushed purple slag. Twice as wide and well-maintained, the road gave her enough confidence to shift into high gear and accelerate. Crimson ferns along the berm and trees covered in bright golden mosses with red-trimmed orange flowers raced by in a blur.

"Should you not slow down? The road winds sharply through these trees," Tialdrin sang in warning.

"Be thankful the Neh'as'anni did not cut them all down," Kidahin trilled in disgust.

"The air looks—odd. Blurry, and it glows a pale yellow. Slow down. We do not want to hit anything, now do we?" Shikararro sang.

"I would not have hit that tree. Besides, we will not meet any Neh'as'anni traffic. They should have recalled to their elleiu trees to deal with Hlorrithin's ultimatum," Einstika sang as the APC bounced over chunks of reinforced concrete scattered across the road.

"We just ran over pieces of the Ka'tha'ma. The name means 'house of wood'. Ironic, yes? It marks the southernmost limit of the exclusion zone."

No fireside tale could match the disturbing effect the place had on

Kidahin. One moment they drove—drove!—down a wide gravel road through an otherwise beautiful arberi forest covering most of the central La'huaset valley. The next moment they drove past the obscene, washed-out pastel building drawn from the planned whimsey of a people who suffered from a defect worse than amusia.

"Hang into your adulthood knives, everyone," Einstika sang softly. "The La'huaset continental road is up ahead. It cuts straight through the rainforest valley some thirty ells wide and forty thousand ells long. It connects all the technology clans and is paved. We should not bounce around as much."

"An eyesore! It will take thousands of years for the trees to reclaim the land once we tear up the paving," Tialdrin complained.

"At least arberi trees grow faster than most," Kidahin sang.

Einstika downshifted and took her foot off the accelerator, allowing the engine to brake their speed. She shifted into neutral as the APC slowly rolled to a stop.

"Something wrong?" Shikararro trilled, curious.

"I do not trust the pavement. It is—broken up—in places, shattered even. I am shifting into eleven-wheel drive and low gear."

The APC crept forward while Einstika took a lidar scan.

"What the spirits? No scan return. I wonder why....

"No pavement! Hang on, we are going to roll down the embankment!" she trilled.

Loose items flew about the cabin as the APC tipped onto its side. Arrows spilled from Kidahin's bow quiver as the vehicle continued to roll over.

Einstika's hazard suit snagged the gearshift on the second roll. Tialdrin's healers harness slipped off her shoulder and spilled ampules down under the floorboard mats, unnoticed, on the third roll.

Shikararro smacked her head into the dashboard, tumbled onto the roof, and fell shoulder-first against the gearshift console as the APC landed upright on its wheels so hard its suspension springs bottomed out.

"Environmental Interdiction Team-one? Team-one? I have lost telemetry. Respond!" the Mistress demanded.

Shikararro, our Eldest Huntress, found the evil ailing our males and our infants. Their spirits are stolen from us.

Tialdrin wrinkled her nose as she empathized with the Song and its accompanying pheromonal fragment while giving Shikararro healer aid.

"Is everyone else okay? Shikararro?" she sang.

"Tialdrin, I am receiving corrupted radio signals from you. What is happening?" the Mistress demanded.

"Shikararro? Wake up!" Tialdrin keened.

"Leave it alone! I am fine," Shikararro growled groggily.

"My leg is pinned under the dashboard," Kidahin complained.

"At least we landed on our wheels and not on the roof," Einstika sang.

"Team-one, respond!" the Mistress repeated.

"Good to hear you, Mistress. Something jammed the lidar. We drove over a blown-out section of overpass and rolled down an embankment. The APC seems intact, thank the spirits," Einstika sang sharply.

"My leg is wedged in tight," Kidahin keened.

"Courage, Huntress. Relax the leg so I can pull you free," Tialdrin sang. "We lost everything for a few seconds, radar, lidar, radios, and lights. Even the engine stalled. Good thing the road crosses a shallow depression and not a steep gorge. Shikararro is dripping blood everywhere from a gashed temple. She cracked her head on the dashboard as we rolled over."

"My thigh is cramping. I cannot move it!" Kidahin keened.

"Cramping? Imagine that. Push down, twist to the left, and pull it out. Move it!" Tialdrin sang at imperative tempo.

"Mistress? Kidahin fainted," Einstika trilled, laughing.

"I did not!" Kidahin snarled and snapped her tail at Einstika, barely missing her quivering ears.

"Yes. Yes, you did. I can show you pictures later," Einstika sang.

"So, no casualties?" the Mistress asked.

"You sound disappointed," Einstika hissed.

"That is enough, Einstika," Shikararro growled.

"Behold our Shikararro, all discipline while her head is getting bandaged," Kidahin sang.

"Einstika, run an electrical check. See if the engine will start," Shikararro sang.

"Stay still! I cannot bandage your head while you twitch those ears," Tialdrin sang.

She showed us the vile thief, but it was just a minion of neh'tle ke'ne's'tu.

"The roll-recovery put us upright on our wheels. The engine is okay. No damage to the drivetrain, no bent frame, and no cabin damage. Navigation is—perfectly fine now. Lidar says we are about ten kamells from the T'anni River. Zooming the camera—I see a few crimson radial fern trees among the arberis and smog. Probably comes from haze, isoprene gas, and industrial pollutants mingling with dust and smoke from the blast. Gives the orange shade an—evil—phosphorescent glow. The radiation detector still points in the same direction," Einstika sang.

"Pay attention. Our mission is to investigate the source of these EM emissions and collect as much information as we can along the way. What we do here is even more important than fighting by Hlorrithin's side, strange to say. We will not stop until we know exactly what dangers he faces. Tell the Mistress about anything you deem important," Shikararro sang.

"Question. What if the radiation gets worse?" Einstika trilled.

"Our hazard suits can handle lethal doses of nuclear radiation for short periods, very short periods of time. Lethality would explain no Neh'as'anni members nearby. Hear that, Kidahin?" Shikararro sang.

"Affirm, but I will keep my bow nocked anyway."

"Mistress? We have reached hundreds of overgrown granite boulders too large to drive over. Amber grasses and sable reeds grow from soggy ground around them. The water is deep and covered with violet bladder plants and pale-yellow water succulents. I do not trust the APC as much as I do my feet. We will continue in on foot," Shikararro sang.

"Go. You have no time to waste," the Mistress urged.

"Affirm. Stop fussing with my head, Tialdrin," Shikararro trilled.

"Everyone, helmets on. Einstika, help Tialdrin. Kidahin, I will fasten yours."

"Take a deep breath, Tialdrin," Einstika sang wickedly.

"I am trusting you with my life, infant. Ow!"

"Sorry about that," Einstika snapped.

"You are nastier than usual. Is everything fine?" Kidahin asked Einstika.

"With her, nothing is ever fine," Shikararro trilled a laugh.

"Then it is good that I am the only one who hears you until we switch our suits into the radio repeater. Shikararro, everyone is ready," Kidahin sang.

"Good. I will step out first. Kidahin goes second. Tialdrin goes last. Questions?"

"None," Einstika trilled, annoyed.

Tialdrin jumped from the cabin door and landed on a clump of vermilion leaves, bent down to touch one in mild amusement, and jumped back three ells as a nightmare creature skittered sideways and regarded her warily.

"What is that?" Einstika trilled.

"Mutation," Tialdrin sang, not taking her eyes off the creature.

"Thirteen legs, normal. An ell wide, not unusual. Four ells long, also not unusual. Thorny spikes on the limbs, normal. Bright green color, normal for most prey animals. Yellow underside, not normal. Three eyes, definitely not normal. Things like this remind me why the custom of Territorial Boundaries of Rage and Forgiveness say to call the healer."

"Are you certain this is not some unclassified animal? Rainforest diversity is nearly infinite," Kidahin trilled thoughtfully.

"No. Three eyes are never normal. This is a result of environmental toxins," Tialdrin sang softly as the creature skittered back into jungle.

We must confront it and prevail to remain in the world.

"The ground around us looks clear, but be careful where you step. The trees farther ahead look safe. The mountains on the horizon and clouds look right," Shikararro sang.

"Not right enough to make me forget we are near the La'huaset Engineering Complex Technology Center, or at least near its southernmost edge," Einstika sang.

"Yes, the distant view is beautiful, but the ground here is broken up—by heavy equipment? Gouges and ruts run deep everywhere. Some larger ones overflow with jagged rocks covered by creeping plants, but not as many as the ones filled with water. Who knows how deep they go. This will not be an easy walk," Kidahin sang.

Tialdrin felt uneven rough footing against her boot soles. Like all Eyloni in general and Hunter females in particular, she hated footwear. They ruined stealth prowling. Her footfalls sounded louder wearing them than Warrior females prowling barefooted.

"It is very lonely and empty here. I feel—unwelcome," she sang.

"At least there are no Neh'as'anni La'huaset Eyloni around," Einstika noted with a subtle scowl.

"There is that. Radiation too high?" Kidahin replied with a not-so-subtle scowl.

"Good idea. Kidahin, Tialdrin, come here," Shikararro sang.

Einstika smelled Shikararro's meaning and unhooked a sensor from her suit belt. Holding it out as far as the cord attached allowed, she panned a full circle.

"No high-pitched chirps. The dial reads just over twice normal background levels. All clear, so far," she sang.

"Keep moving," Shikararro sang at imperative tempo.

They prowled over and around huge boulders covered with golden-yellow moss. One trunk, dark brown with hints of red undertones and rough, split bark, grew at a sharp slant hundreds of ells into the understory. It took Shikararro a minute to prowl around its rooty base before finding a dried-up creek, some tributary stream drained by the Neh'as'anni during landscaping. Rainforest streams, like the flooded ruts they just crossed, never dried up.

"Where is this radiation source?" Shikararro complained.

"You are two kamells away from it. It might be obscured by jungle," the Mistress offered.

"Or it might be under the jungle, which means triangulating and digging. Might I remind you we have only a week's worth of supplies? And I do not want to live in my hazard suit the whole time," Einstika growled.

"Quit complaining. Besides, you can take it off in clear areas," Kidahin sang flatly.

"The ground cover is thinning out ahead. A ridge runs through the forest up ahead. Piled up excavated dirt and long, too. Might be high enough for a good look around. Tialdrin and Kidahin will stay behind with the equipment. Einstika, come with me," Shikararro sang.

"You mean climb up that?"

"Yes. Now, Einstika."

"Affirm. Prowling through Neh'as'anni territory reminds me of a..."

"Another of your fireside tales, Einstika?" Tialdrin keened in mock-dismay

"This is a good one. I promise. I heard a rumor a few years back about the Neh'as'anni having a spaceflight program."

"No tale there. They did. They shot off a few rockets but never sent a female into space," Tialdrin sang dryly.

"Yes, they did. They figured out how to send a female into low orbit and bring her back."

"Okay, I will humor you. This was long before the Be'atika Senge issued the edict requiring the technology clans to implement environmental safeguards. By now everyone would know about it," Shikararro sang.

"Supposedly the crew missed their landing zone and ended up in Uahua'asee'a Clan territory with hungry nei'la clawing the capsule open and eating them alive."

"I know a version of this story where they landed in Ah'vou'ree Clan territory and were helped by the little sibs rather than eaten by nei'la," Kidahin sang.

"Neither one is true," Tialdrin trilled at imperative tempo.

"Not the point, Tialdrin. The point is..."

"We have reached high ground, an unstable pile of brush and rocks. Einstika, give me a boost over this—must be landscaping debris," Shikararro interrupted.

"Be careful, Shikararro. Einstika, keep an eye on her," the Mistress said flatly.

"Affirm. Shikararro, watch your feet!"

"Stop fidgeting and hold still. I do not weigh that much."

"You are overbalancing me. I do not want to fall, you know," Einstika snarled.

"Then stop fidgeting!"

"Stop rocking back and forth on my shoulders!"

"Why did we bring Einstika along?" Kidahin trilled wickedly.

"Because we could not find anyone better?" Tialdrin sang loudly.

"You know the voice-operated transmitter works fine. I can hear every word you say," Einstika growled.

"Accept it—as a compliment. Now where—do I—put my feet—next?" Shikararro sang at insolence tempo.

"Not on my head!" Einstika trilled in warning.

"Stop complaining. I cleared your head a minute ago," Shikararro sang.

"Shikararro, any luck seeing over the top?" the Mistress asked impatiently.

"Almost there. A few more ells. Most of these rocks look shattered, like blasting debris. Blasting? In the rainforest? This is evidence of widespread deforestation!"

"What fell on me? Are you trying to pull the rubble down on top of me?" Einstika keened.

This day we prepare for battle before we saw the full face of Tyreniioroneo. We sang to the spirits of the People, the powerful ones, asking for the strength and swiftness of the wind and to let us come back to our People.

"Run, Einstika. Now!" Shikararro keened.

"Wha...t?" Einstika trilled and tumbled backward reflexively as part of the ridge started to slide.

"Spirits!" Tialdrin trilled.

"Shikararro!" Kidahin trilled.

"What happened?" Einstika sang, dazed.

"Shikararro? Do not just stand there, Einstika. Help her!" Tialdrin sang at imperative tempo.

"Team-one? What happened?" the Mistress demanded.

"Part of the ridge collapsed. Shikararro fell with it. Tialdrin and I are running to her now," Kidahin sang.

"Where is she?" Tialdrin screamed.

"I do not know! She was above me when the rocks began to slide," Einstika trilled in distress.

"Focus!" Kidahin sang at imperative pitch.

"There! Near the bottom," Tialdrin sang.

"Thank the spirits. She could have been buried alive," Einstika sang.

"Come on," Kidahin sang.

"Look after Einstika, Kidahin," Tialdrin sang.

"Are you hurt?" Kidahin asked Einstika.

"No, I am fine. I jumped out of the way before the rocks could hit me. It collapsed inward and Shikararro slid along with it."

"Tialdrin, check her," Kidahin trilled.

"Not now. I am checking Shikararro. She has an injury."

"Are you safe?" the Mistress asked.

"None of us are safe standing on the ridge. Most of it looks like quarry rubble mixed with foliage and mud. They dug into the rainforest!" Einstika keened.

"Do you need a tranquilizer?" Tialdrin hissed.

"It is shock. It will pass," Kidahin sang.

"She cannot be badly hurt, can she?" Einstika keened.

"Quiet. You are not helping," Kidahin sang.

"Shikararro, you have a badly dislocated shoulder. I can pop it back into joint, but you will have limited use for a few hours," Tialdrin sang.

"What happened?" Kidahin demanded.

"I do not know. One minute I am standing there playing climbing platform, and the next rocks start sliding down and inward. Shikararro must have stepped on a key stone," Einstika sang.

"I stepped on nothing. The rubble cannot take our weight in places. I put my foot in the wrong spot is all," Shikararro snarled in disgust.

"That looks bad," Kidahin sang, frowning as Tialdrin grabbed Shikararro's arm

"Ready?" Tialdrin sang and snapped Shikararro's shoulder back into place without waiting for an answer.

"I dislocated this shoulder more times than I can count. Sometimes I can snap it back, and other times not so much. Feels numb, and I do not have a full range of motion," she sang while trying to rotate her shoulder.

"Sometimes I have to ram it against a tree, but we do not have the time. I will return to the APC. It should not remain unattended for long, anyway. I will be out of suit radio range. Once I reach the APC I can patch into the repeater connecting it with Na'di Island.

"Mistress, did you hear? I am backtrailing to the APC. Kidahin has the leadership," Shikararro sang.

"Affirm. Kidahin, continue the search," the Mistress said.

"Affirm."

"Mistress? We are ready to leave and will contact you when we have the radiation source in sight," Tialdrin sang.

"Go with the spirits," the Mistress said.

"Einstika, Tialdrin, come on," Kidahin sang and led them deeper into the central La'huaset Tribal continental jungle. She glanced up into the surrounding trees. Bright mist glowed in the early morning sunlight, shrouding orange-streaked yellow leaves.

Einstika leaned against a lone crimson radial fern tree. Arberi trees grew in abundance here. Most of them enjoyed the company of symbiotic golden-yellow lianas. Others hosted—involuntarily—green parasitic vines. They drilled spiral tendrils into the trees and sucked nutrients they could not make for themselves from the sap.

"Look!" Einstika keened, pointing through thinning jungle grasses.

"An entire swath of the valley has been cleared," she added unnecessarily.

Kidahin scowled at the yellow haze lurking above cleared, leveled ground covered with shattered orangy, boxlike buildings by the hundreds.

One of them, larger than the others by far, hovered hauntingly behind the blast-damaged buildings. The Technology Center building seemed to peer out of the early morning golden-tinged mist, an indifferent and unmistakable rectangle of reinforced concrete. Surrounded by a veil of sinister support buildings, it stood like a beige pylon guarding the source of neh'tle ke'ne's'tu.

Odd. Late dawn in Neh'as'anni Clan territory, and yet not a single figure prowled among the buildings. No female shape cast a silhouette against the tragic nightmare where faded orange shadows dissolved in an aura of golden mist, as though the sight revolted the dawn itself. Shafts of sunlight streamed down alleys and streets. A slight breeze blew through the valley and across the complex, carrying with it remnants of dust and smoke. Not so much as a single leaf rustled to break upon the silence of first light.

Years ago, visitors came to see the technological clans of La'huaset and found themselves stepping into the promise of a bright future. Large areas of jungle, sacrificed in the wake of the industrial revolution, gave way to the promise of scientific and technological enlightenment. But the subtle by-products of advancement lurked everywhere: in the water, in the air, and in the ground itself.

For two hundred and forty EST years the hub of La'huaset technological development grew in Neh'as'anni Clan territory. The name, a motto actually, meant "We are theoretical and speculative, always innovative, always creative." The name imbued the hundred or so research, factory, and Technology Center buildings with an aura of awe-inspiring mystique.

"How could they do this? These trees, thousands of years old or more, will take as long to grow back," Einstika keened.

"It is disgusting!" Kidahin trilled. "I never want to see its like again! Let me prowl down paths that lead to quiet clearings where I can rest against an arberi and ask my oyya web questions about life while enjoying the smells of catkins and vines until I fall asleep."

2
FINDING ONE'S CLAN

Shikararro told us that the only way to defeat neh'tle ke'ne's'tu was by killing it or by submitting to the Oyya Web of the spirits and seizing its essence. Whoever does this will not only free the captive spirits, but will become the bearer of its power.

Kidahin stepped out onto the low ridge overlooking the Neh'as'anni Clan industrial complex. Sunlight fell directly on ruined buildings. Several orange roofs lay shattered against the distant jungle background. She scrunched her face in disgust as fear gripped her heart. Death lurked here, and the cloying miasma made her retch uncontrollably. The foul odor wafted up from the broken pavement and shattered buildings. She gagged on a nauseating scent, smoke mingled with the perfume of flowers.

The jungle reached its highest temperature near the ground. The lack of trees, branches, and sun-filtering diaphanous red, orange, and yellow leaves made it even hotter. Eyloni lived in their megaflora elleiu tree emergent layers. Those trees sheltered thousands in high-altitude living areas much cooler than the forest floor. Even in central La'huaset the temperate rainforest grew very warm over the days-long daylight period of Elleio's orbit around the gas giant, Tyreniioroneo. The heat, worse with the entire complex open to direct sunlight, would make it a horrible place to live and work.

She stood on the precipice of coming face-to-face with neh'tle ke'ne's'tu, the very essence of environmental contamination.

Prowling with single-minded determination and alone, as Hunter females often preferred, Kidahin picked her way carefully along the edge of the vast open site. The industrial complex stretched far across the valley, and she paused several times to look down onto the crumpled pavement of a perimeter road passing below the ridge in both directions.

Her breath caught.

Rainforests covered Elleio, and neither widespread construction or buildings belonged in a rainforest. Yes, clans did have a few small buildings. They built them into naturally open spaces and designed them to blend into the surrounding jungle. Technology needed buildings. You could not smelt iron inside an elleiu tree. Seldom did anybody cut down a tree. Landscaping occurred rarely and was strictly limited to the building footprint as regulated by the Environmental Interdiction decree.

Kidahin shuddered at what she beheld.

"We must lock this place in the Dark Mistress's Abode forever!" she hissed.

The sprawling site triggered memories, ones she violently suppressed before her pheromones reached the noses of her fellow Hunters. If they empathize with her scent, they would know she was drifting away from the great honor the Gracious Mistress had granted them: a place in Hlorrithin's Song.

She concentrated on the face of Delwyn, her Warleader. She listened to the memory of his voice, and an image of him formed in her mind's eye: a handsome male in his hundreds with brown eyes and glossy black hair tinged with gray. He sang a soft, somber song in his deep voice about how humans once fought a several hundred-year battle with climate change and environmental pollution. From the human industrial revolution through when they mastered interplanetary travel, environmental damage, both global and catastrophic, wracked their planet.

She had doubted him at first, but his scent confirmed the truth of his song. Not even the Neh'as'anni went so far as to deliberately spill chemicals into the water or spew them into the air. Nor did they bury them in the ground or burn the jungle. No clan cut or burned their rainforest, spilled chemicals into their waterways, or spewed poison into their air like he described what humans had done.

But the Neh'às'anni did cut down their trees here. Their industrial activity did release small amounts of toxins into the environment. Those seemingly negligible discharges did damage Elleio life on a genetic level and altered the flora and fauna. Mutations like the one Tialdrin nearly stepped on appeared frequently now.

The toxins changed the tree-clinging mosses, made them caustic. They ate into the trees, even elleiu trees—a wood so dense Delwyn once believed he could make nails from it.

Nearly all the males, all the Comara females, and one-third of the infants died throughout the valley due to the accumulating toxins.

"This is incredible," Tialdrin trilled as she followed silently behind and just out of reach of Kidahin's tail.

"If you say so," Einstika finally snarled in disgust.

"Sorry, I was tailchasing," Kidahin admitted.

"And I smell who you were tailchasing about," Einstika trilled wickedly.

"Well...," Kidahin drawled.

"Team-one, what is your status?" the Mistress droned.

"Oh, how coincidental. The Mistress is on the radio. I wonder why?" Tialdrin sang at Kidahin, her eyes sparkling with mischief.

"Finally," Kidahin sang and snapped her tail at Tialdrin.

"Good to hear your cheery flat voice," Einstika sang at insolence tempo.

"Yes, what she sang," Kidahin added at insolence pitch.

"Mistress? We are as well as can be expected psychologically, considering where we are. Oh, we have a surprise for you," Tialdrin sang.

"We have visual contact with the likely radiation source," Kidahin interrupted impatiently.

"I have news for you, too. Shikararro reached the APC and is well. Confirm visual contact with the radiation source," the Mistress insisted.

"I need to take radiation readings along a baseline and triangulate to confirm, but I think it lies within the Technology Center main building," Einstika sang.

"Affirm. Advise when you have confirmation," the Mistress said.

The dreadful messengers arrived at dusk.

Kidahin swayed as a wave of vertigo swamped her. The sky turned dark, but it had been late dawn not that long ago. She knew from her adulthood ceremony that scene changes often happened abruptly. Then again, the busy mind often lost track of time. She swayed again, tripped, and stumbled over blackened jungle ground vines still smoldering from the massive explosion that had leveled rows of buildings hours before they entered the valley.

The setting sun cast shadows off the broken walls. Nearly every building in sight simply crumpled. A few blackened buildings remained standing. Built better or just lucky, she did not know. Artillery did not do this. Hlorrithin had to capture the technology sites intact, secure the toxic materials, and send the science to the Be'atika Senge. The shelling he authorized was directed at structures and roads. Only a coward shelled people.

One huge blast did all this damage, too. An accident? Probably a natural gas explosion. The air stank of burning plastics. Petroleum products. The Neh'as'anni used petroleum to make plastics, solvents, lubricants, and other chemicals for their industry.

The Be'atika Senge hierarchy outlawed burning coal thirty EST years into the industrial revolution. Except for aircraft, petroleum-fueled engines were outlawed forty EST years later. Even the Neh'as'anni considered fossil fuels intolerably filthy. Propane and natural gas satisfied most power requirements.

But the Neh'as'anni had reportedly developed a large-scale fission nuclear reactor to power this complex. Environmental Interdiction suspected the trace radiation in the exclusion zone came from a fission reactor, one that far exceeded lawful size.

Kidahin froze mid-step and tried to block an awful odor with the back of her hand, an automatic but futile gesture considering the sensitivity of her nose.

Burnt flesh.

The explosion had slammed shattered bodies into still-standing walls. From the ridge she saw several male bodies. They wore male adulthood volcanic glass knives at the hip. Only a few bodies wore the curving flint female adulthood knife at the breasts. The bodies called to mind a horrific image from the one place she never wanted to think about again.

The Coalition of Earth Colonies starship *Londiwe Khoza*.

Terror gripped her by the throat as shimmering bodies and parts of shimmering bodies coalesced around her. She closed her eyes for several long seconds, her heart racing as she forced one foot forward after another through swirling gray ashes until she reached her bow, lying next to a half-burned bush. Woodenly, she picked it up and gestured for the others to gaze upon the horror stretching out before them.

Einstika held back, unable to move. The seizures began, as they always did, with one. She appeared caught in an exaggerated startle. Her arms extended down, held rigid at the sides. Her face froze, expressionless. Her eyes fluttered side-to-side, wary.

Memories raced and surged as her mind empathized and focused on a fleeting image fragment and reanimated it.

She jumped into the midst of wreckage drifting around her in zero-gee: loose equipment, personal items, and bodies. Male bodies, fists and fists of male bodies, all those male deaths. *I—Kidahin?*

"Einstika? What is wrong? You spoke through your pheromones. You should not do that because it interferes with the imagery we see from hearing the Gracious Mistress and empathizing with her pheromones. You could snap yourself right out of the Oyya Web," Tialdrin sang quietly.

"Is the blast area within the source of the radiation?" the Mistress's voice interrupted.

Einstika shook her head and focused on the question.

"No, Mistress. Triangulated line-of-sight readings intersect through the Technology Center building, an ugly one, too. It withstood the shock wave with little damage. It is a large building, but I can see an airfield behind it. Part of a runway with a small propeller airplane sitting on it, too. Another one, a jet, is behind it.

"The building itself is heavily built from light tan prefabricated concrete slabs at least an ell thick. Looks very utilitarian. Probably designed to house machinery. What looked like an aerial from a distance is actually one huge tower supporting several antennas and microwave horns. I see no blast damage north and west of the airfield from here."

"Thank the spirits the Technology Center was not leveled by the blast. Otherwise everything in a ten-thousand ell radius would be covered in radioactive dust," Tialdrin keened in fury.

"Which is one reason why we stopped a thousand ells from it. I do not like being here," Kidahin sang unsteadily.

"Mistress, I am setting my camera for wide-angle zoom for pictures. Snapping now. Uploading images to you. As you can see, they built this building strong enough to serve as a bunker. It looks hostile. Prefabricated concrete slabs, and I cannot begin to imagine the effort it took them to drag the slabs here. The left side and rear remind me of a warehouse," Einstika sang.

"Let me look through your viewfinder," Kidahin sang.

"I can set up the video feed by myself. What do you want to take video of?" Einstika trilled.

"Not video. I want to take a look, and the viewfinder zooms better than binoculars."

"Oh, okay. Just do not break it," Einstika trilled in warning.

"I just want a look along the ridge. The debris is high enough for me to look for a safer way down.

"If we prowl along the ridge and avoid heavy jungle, we can get a third of the way around the complex before reaching a clear way down. The edges are steep with lots of piled loose rock. Must be rubble left from excavating the ground before they built this place. What do you think?" Kidahin sang.

"Proceed, but be careful. I do not want another falling accident," the Mistress replied.

"This is not my first time stalking an adversary, you know," Einstika keened hotly.

"This is not about you, Einstika. We are all on the same branch here. Nobody wants to risk her tail needlessly," Tialdrin sang.

"We have a lot of ground to cover. Collect your equipment and follow me," Kidahin sang.

Einstika grumbled as she picked up her gear. They were alone. No Neh'as'anni females prowled this territory, and that went against female territorial nature. She smelled no nearby females on the breeze, either.

Just the dead.

Kidahin and Tialdrin pulled ahead of her. Moving in groups vexed Hunter females. Close stalking grated against Einstika's temperamental streak. Hunters did, on occasion, prowl in groups of two or three, but she did not enjoy doing so.

Nothing in the historical songs said why Hunters were chosen for this mission. Probably the idiot A'tayotan Mistress's idea of a joke. She was a Warrior female, after all.

Einstika found the thought funny and curled her tail tip, her pons, twisting it in slow spinning circles. Delwyn called this twisting an Eyloni eye-rolling gesture, and she smiled at the thought of him.

A staccato trill nudged Einstika back on the trail she prowled.

Kidahin trilled again, her tail snapping rapidly side-to-side. Agitated, her ears twitched restlessly, alert.

The air around them turned greenish-yellow, humid, and very warm. Off in the distance stands of arberi trees stood. Farther off the stratospheric mountain range stretched across the horizon, the remnant of an eons-old asteroid impact. Between them and the arberis stood twelve elleiu trees, one of several hundred hometree groupings throughout the valley.

Elleiu trees grew tall. Yet she barely saw them behind the arberis. They stood much closer to the mountains than to the industrial complex.

So the Neh'as'anni were not insane after all, Einstika reasoned. They did not expose their hometrees to the filthy raw scar gouged into the jungle floor here. On her left, along the debris ridge, warehouses crouched like scattered fungi. The wind blowing off them carried the stench of petrol. The rainforest mist mingled with the smoke and toxic fumes as it blew past them.

It took supreme effort to breathe without gagging.

"This stuff stinks!" Tialdrin keened.

"What? You want to change clan affiliation and live here?" Kidahin sang.

"Why, that is not a bad idea," Tialdrin trilled sarcastically. "The view is gorgeous if you do not mind this running sore of modern progress burning into the ground. No thank you. Just being here makes me feel dirty."

"All of you annoy me, do you know that?" Einstika growled.

"Oh, be quiet, will you?" Kidahin sang at imperative tempo.

"Relax, Kidahin. She is just venting, and venting is good for emotional health," Tialdrin sang.

"I am not venting. I am stating a fact," Einstika trilled heatedly.

"Yes, of course you are. Stop dragging your feet through the grass and pick up the pace. We still have a few hundred ells to cover," Kidahin sang.

"Mistress, I am going to cut the channel while they argue over the next hour or two. I will switch back into the repeater feed when we reach our next watchpoint," Tialdrin sang.

"Affirm, Team-one. Shikararro reports indirect signs of movement around the elleiu trees north of you. The APC surveillance cameras cannot pick up people moving about, but she says black smoke is pouring from the chimney boles of every tree. Go with the spirits."

"Affirm," Tialdrin trilled dissonantly. So, Hlorrithin had ordered the smudge pots lit so he could flush the residents from their trees, preparatory to killing the Neh'as'anni Clan. Such a thing had not happened since the Ba'atika Senge prohibited Eyloni from making war upon one another centuries ago.

We killed them, all but one, so we could follow it and find the prohibited clan, the lair of its master prey.

Kidahin smelled the pheromones wafting around her and frowned. The Territorial Boundaries of Rage and Forgiveness said to focus on the Spirit Male as a check against female aggression. All females considered their hearts male. In that way, each carried her own piece of male everywhere she went. Just as females considered naval vessels males, so did they consider their hearts literally male.

But females also knew their spirits harbored a male component as well, their spirit males. Putting aside the fact that even considering harm to a male without honorable justification was a high-honor crime, the thought of harming a male also injured a female's spirit male.

Kidahin wrapped her tail around her waist several times and watched her pons spin in slow, tight circles. Her tail, as long as she was tall—although not quite as long as a male's ell-long tail—embraced her from hips to below her breasts.

The word 'ell' literally meant "male tail," and that comforted her.

She needed comfort. A prowling Hunter, patience personified, easily became impatient in matters unrelated to prowling or stalking. Prowling and stalking needed forest cover for effectiveness. She glanced down into the ruined industrial complex. Prowling and stalking skills would do no good in there. Now, when she most needed attunement with her spirit male, he fled from her.

"Mistress, do you hear me?" Kidahin sang into her suit mike.

"Clean and clear, Kidahin."

"We prowled along the debris ridge close enough to get a good look at the building. There is a clear path down a few hundred ells from us. A steeper one is much closer, but looks treacherous. Climbing hundreds of ells up a tree barehanded is easy. But I, for one, find climbing down unstable ground that might bury me alive not so carefree."

"I am sending pictures. You will find the view interesting," Einstika sang.

"You should see what looks like a crashed aircraft. I did not know the Neh'as'anni Clan had anything this advanced. Maybe we should give Einstika's stories a little more than fireside tale credit," Tialdrin sang.

"She said they had spaceships. This is no spaceship. It is a jet aircraft, but what type is it?" Kidahin sang curiously.

"Some kind of high-altitude hypersonic aircraft. See how streamlined it is? Long fuselage, triangle wings, and I think those engines mounted at the wing roots are scramjets. I never saw a scramjet engine so big. The four nozzles mounted below the vertical stabilizer look like—rocket engines. They mounted them in the corners of an inverted triangle and a fourth nozzle, bigger than the others, in the center. I wonder why put the bigger nozzle in the middle?" Einstika trilled loudly, curiosity flaming her interest.

"Hypersonic?" Tialdrin sang doubtfully.

"Sub-orbital capable, you think?" Kidahin sang at interrogative pitch.

"Yes, supposedly. I doubt this one ever flew, though," Einstika sang with certainty.

"Did it—crash here?" Tialdrin wondered aloud.

"Not if Einstika says it never flew. It does not look like crash damage, either. Antipersonnel mortar fire?" Kidahin sang.

"Not possible," the Mistress's monotonic voice droned flatly. "Hlorrithin would never risk targeting something that could contaminate the entire valley."

"I agree," Kidahin sang. "The holes in the fuselage are too small and confined to the wings and cockpit. Definitely not crash damage, either."

"What do you suggest?" Tialdrin asked.

"Sabotage?"

Tialdrin flicked her ears in a shrug.

"Mistress, we are moving on. Expect more pictures when we get closer."

"Keep me informed, Team-one."

They retreated from the debris ridge back into the jungle and continued on. The three Hunters stalked through heavy undergrowth faster and safer than they could scale the uneven and dangerous debris ridge. After an hour, Kidahin snapped her tail to the left and led them back up the forest side of the long, steep ridge of rainforest rubble.

"We reached somewhat more stable footing. Now what?" Tialdrin sang.

"Sling bows over your shoulders. Tie all loose items to your suit belts. Throw the supply harnesses over the ridge. They should land without damage."

"Can I bundle my equipment around your harnesses and throw them over?" Einstika trilled wistfully.

"Einstika, for the—no, you cannot," Kidahin trilled in annoyance.

"You just want to make things harder for me. I have more equipment than both of you," Einstika growled.

"How do you come up with these stupid ideas?" Kidahin trilled.

"I am a natural, I guess. Annoying is my infant name."

"I thought it was Ein," Kidahin sang at insolence pitch.

"Supply harnesses sealed and secured? Toss them over. Now, climb down without causing the ridge to collapse and bury us. The last thing we need is another Shikararro," she added.

"I claim insult!" Einstika snarled, ripping her hazard suit breast clasps open and pulling her adulthood knife from the sheath that curved around and under her neckwear-draped but otherwise bare left breast.

"You sang my infant name aloud in public!" she keened, tail swaying as she balanced-checked her footing.

"No, she did not. We are not among the public," Tialdrin reminded her.

"What?" Einstika screeched, not entirely convinced.

"Well, I suppose. Just this once. Can I go last?" she snapped.

"Of course. I will go first," Tialdrin sang.

"Good call, Tialdrin. From the middle I can grab either of you if something happens. Mistress, we are heading down the debris ridge and into the complex," Kidahin sang dryly.

Tialdrin reached the bottom and stepped onto smooth, level pavement.

"They must use a lot of vehicles. Where are they?" she wondered, glancing down the perimeter road.

"Heavy vehicles, too. Look at those reinforced concrete paving slabs. Vehicles would clutter the scene. We should not see any unless they play an important part here," Einstika sang.

"No. The road abuts the airfield over there. I would guess this is the preflight area for the airfield. See how the hypersonic jet sits on similar pavement? Mistress, the Technology Center is opposite the airfield from us. We can simply walk across the tarmac and...," Kidahin sang.

Whump.

"Did you hear that?" Einstika trilled abruptly.

"Hear what?" Tialdrin sang.

"What, Einstika?" Kidahin trilled, alert.

"A muffled thump. Look! Near the hypersonic jet. The pavement. It was smooth a moment ago, but now I see a small crater."

"Where?" Kidahin sang lightly, humoring her.

"What? That shallow hole? It was always there. Concrete does crumble under heavy loads over time. Wait. Is that a puff of smoke behind the jet?" Tialdrin sang.

Whump.

"Too small for artillery. Must be antipersonnel fire!" Einstika trilled in alarm.

"Mortars? They cannot be aiming at us. We are traditionally armed. Must be trying to take out the jet," Tialdrin sang .

"Get to cover and backtrail out of range. Try to approach the building from another direction," the Mistress ordered.

"Affirm. Huntresses, withdraw. Tialdrin, help Einstika with her stuff,"

Kidahin trilled at imperative tempo.

"I do not need help with my equipment," Einstika grunted as she shifted her awkward burden and ran.

"A'pea!" she trilled as equipment jostled out of her techmistress harness.

"Well, maybe I do," she conceded.

"Good thing I am not weak," Tialdrin sang mischievously.

"Are you saying I am?" Einstika growled.

"Quiet. We have a lot of open ground to cover. Be careful. All that techmistress stuff will pull you off-balance," Kidahin trilled in warning.

"I do not need to hear the obvious from you," Einstika snapped.

"My healers harness is not small. How about you carry it and let me carry yours?" Tialdrin snarled.

"I do not need to hear that, either," Einstika hissed.

We run for one full day under the brunt of harsh sunbeams. We are tired, but we will not give up.

The abrupt change in pheromones caused Einstika to blink in confusion. The sun? Had they really been in Neh'as'anni Clan territory for an entire orbital phase? Had the Long Night and most of the daylight period gone by so fast? Three EST days?

Of course not, she chided herself. The Song caused time to pass quickly.

"Team-one? Progress report," the Mistress demanded.

"We are climbing back onto the debris ridge and backtrailing. Treacherous as the footing is there, we deemed it safer than prowling the burnt and blasted pavement around the closer buildings, especially if someone is firing mortars. The view here is interesting," Kidahin sang, her eyes sparkling with curiosity.

"Not 'we'. I would rather take my chances on the pavement," Tialdrin complained.

Kidahin glanced at the wellnessmistress and flicked her ears.

"Are you sure about that? As tense as you smell?" she trilled.

"No," Tialdrin sang brightly. "I am not tense. Excited. I cannot wait to see what is inside the Technology building. But," she added, "I do not want to prowl through toxic areas or through mortar barrages getting there, either."

"Then hurry," Einstika sang impatiently.

Kidahin led them back the way they came, sort of.

This time they did not prowl through the jungle. Finding a clear path down into the complex meant climbing along the torn-up ridge, a continuous line of brush, grasses, heavy undergrowth all held loosely together by rocks, clay, and soil. The moist humid air and constant mist kept the woodpile wet, squishy, and slippery. Hidden holes pockmarked the ridge, eager to swallow a foot up to her crotch or a body up to her armpits.

Two hours later Kidahin called a halt.

"We climb down here. Be careful. I go first this time, Tialdrin second, and Einstika last."

"Looks like climbing down will be easier than I thought. I should review my terrain appraisal skills. I guess I am more familiar with Ushua'asee'a Clan territory," Einstika sang.

"So you prowl on tip-toes now?" Tialdrin sang at insolence tempo.

"I do not! I have nimble feet, but—Look! A sealed tunnel on that retaining wall. If it runs level and true, it should pass under the closer buildings. If it passes beyond them, it should intersect the Technology Center foundation," Einstika trilled.

"You want to go spelunking? Here?" Tialdrin squeaked and shuddered. An arboreal creature, like all Eyloni, she did not view caves as a favorite geological feature.

"Kidahin loves danger. Watch her ask the Mistress if we can go inside," Einstika sang wickedly.

"Uh—Mistress? May we explore this tunnel?" Kidahin trilled formally.

"Affirm. Shikararro reports the elleiu trees north of you are under heavy attack. The Neh'as'anni should have abandoned the industrial complex and recalled back to defend their hometrees."

"Affirm," Kidahin sang.

"I hope this is not a waste of time," Tialdrin complained as she glared over the retaining wall at the shattered ruins and smoking rubble strewn between them and the Technology Center.

She seriously wondered which path appealed to her the least and hoped the metal seal would prove impossible to breach.

3
EXILE'S NECESSITY

We fight a running battle and take heavy losses, but we can still fight. We disperse, for we must arrive in silence and prepare to face our destiny.

Tialdrin perked ears and snapped tail, deep in thought. The emotional overtones accompanying the verse put pictures in her empathic mind. Those pictures gave her and her team the emotional background of Hlorrithin and his raids on the Neh'as'anni Clan immediate and extended family hometrees scattered throughout the valley.

The theme also rooted her, Kidahin, and Einstika here, investigating an industrial site, while he fought the Neh'as'anni.

Tialdrin shook her head and shuddered. The last thing she wanted to do was dwell upon the imagery of this verse in Hlorrithin's Song.

The A'tayotan hierarchy ordered Hlorrithin to kill the Neh'as'anni and allied clans. Ancient custom said killing a clan was an ugly process. Pots of burning tar three ells wide belched thick black smoke into bellows mounted onto siege engines. Warrior females pumped the smoke into braided hoses they shoved into elleiu tree ground entrance boles. The siege Warriors pumped smoke into and throughout hollow trunks, hollow branches, and hollow fused aerial root living spaces.

Right now Neh'as'anni defenders fought pitched battles to save their males and their homes. They fought until they either suffocated or died in the fighting.

Victorious clans always offered males sanctuary and full membership in their clans. With incredibly rare exceptions, they always accepted. Males never refused female protection, and females never refused the opportunity to increase their male numbers.

But Hlorrithin declared all Neh'as'anni Eyloni ni'zakhon—outlaws— guilty of planning acts harmful to male health and causing male deaths on a continental scale.

All the hierarchies on Elleio strictly enforced the custom requiring any male who intends lethal harm to, or kills, another male, without honorable justification, shall be strangled to death with his own tail. Hierarchies passed such judgments reluctantly and rarely, and saw the death as a mercy killing. The fate of a female guilty of causing lethal harm or death to a male, a high honor crime, was too ghastly for Tialdrin to think about.

Hlorrithin told the Be'atika Senge that the Neh'as'anni Clan knew their industry risked all male lives in the central La'huaset Tribal continental valley but refused to stop polluting the rainforest anyway. This, he argued, was enough for the A'tayotan hierarchy to decree their deaths. Only hierarchies, exclusively female, could decree death penalties. No male could order the death of anybody. Yet Warpact, an exclusively male prerogative recognized by all hierarchies, governed male leadership of female fighting forces. Tradition saw battle casualties as death by combat and not by hierarchical adjudication. The worldwide Warpact the A'tayotan tied to Hlorrithin's tail granted him the one and only exception where a male could exercise quasi-death penalty powers.

The Be'atika Senge invoked worldwide Warpact in only the most dire of emergencies. As the seat of global government, only the Be'atika Senge hierarchy had male advisors. In consultation with them the Be'atika Senge declared Hlorrithin the Eleventh Hero of Elleio. They forced him to accept becoming the eleventh male to wield worldwide Warpact in the past several thousand years, the Tenth being declared several centuries ago. They charged him with leading the A'tayotan and the clans of Elleio against the Neh'as'anni and its allied clans for their role in causing an ecological disaster that was rapidly approaching a global extinction event.

Warpact gave Hlorrithin the right to command other males and their female associations. By convention, Warpact required females to follow the Warpact warleader's orders without question—more or less. Warpact gave the warleader precedence over other males in emergency situations. Females accepted—reluctantly—his right to give orders to the males they associated with. Tialdrin snapped her tail against her thigh hard enough to raise a welt. The pain helped her push thoughts of Hlorrithin and his depressing task out of mind. She had experienced the reality of mass male deaths with Kidahin and Einstika before, while aboard a human warship. This mission reminded her of that disaster.

She blinked several times, but the faint shimmering long corridor stubbornly persisted.

Like an annoying retinal afterimage, it remained barely visible against the bright sunlit pavement and stretched out ahead of them to a metal door sealing a concrete tunnel. Male bodies littered the deck, so many of them, and she suppressed an urge to keen aloud in despair when they abruptly vanished. An apprentice healer and wellnessmistress-in-training, Tialdrin knew how pheromones and music created mental scenes for her mind to empathize with.

What just happened had been faint, barely perceptible, almost like an amusia symptom—wait, what was Kidahin saying?

"Tialdrin? Did you hear me? Why would the tunnel be a waste of time?" Kidahin sang, put out at being ignored.

"This tunnel may be our path around toxic spills and crumbling rubble, and direct access to the Technology Center building," she added.

Tialdrin poked her foot at the concrete facade and then kicked the metal portal covering it. She scowled at the obviously recent addition—a padlock.

"A lock? An a'pea lock! Who would lock family members out of anything belonging to them? This is discourteous. These Neh'as'anni are—antisocial," Einstika trilled.

"Why would they lock this? Theft does not exist in any clan. The social debt theft incurs is never worth having the stolen item. Besides, everything but personal property is a public good available to all. The Neh'as'anni consider their scientific achievements public goods. Locks and doors keep nosey infants from harm or from accidentally breaking things. We keep ordnance stockpiles under lock and key, but for safety reasons having nothing to do with potential theft. Certainly no nosey infants come here. I doubt infants could manage the portal even unlocked. Maybe the Neh'as'anni added it as a precaution against incursions—us?" Tialdrin sang thoughtfully.

"No, to keep nosey tailpokers out. The padlock is simple, I guess. The eyelet welds are recent. Not normal metal, either. Must be an alloy of some kind. See the golden sheen?" Einstika sang expertly.

"Heat? The heat from welding, perhaps? Would you use heat-treated eyelets stronger than the lock itself?" Tialdrin sang.

"It looks pretty. Seems a waste using it for eyelets. As for the lock, Kidahin, give it a good smack," Einstika sang with absolute certainty.

"What?" Kidahin trilled. Did she hear her right?

"Hit the lock with your bow. As hard as elleiu heartwood is, you might actually break the lock."

Kidahin eyed Einstika. Was she serious or just annoying?

"Wait a second," Kidahin sang.

She pulled arrows from the bow quiver and set them aside. Then she pricked her ears at Einstika.

"Okay, here goes, on the padlock. she sang and swung the shortbow over her head and down.

The lock snapped open.

"Well, so much for the lock," she sang, surprised, noting there was not so much as a scratch on her bow.

"See? What did I tell you?" Einstika trilled in laughter.

Suspicious, Kidahin removed the padlock and stared at it, frowning intently.

"Oh, you think you are so strong. You did not break it. It was pushed closed by not locked," Einstika trilled shrilly.

"Well, the idea sounded good at the time. Next time you should look at something before hitting it," Tialdrin sang dryly.

Kidahin flicked her ears wide and growled at Einstika, gave Tialdrin a scowl, and retrieved her arrows. She reached out to the portal and stuck her fingers into a recessed groove set along its edge.

She pulled.

The portal swung open easily but with a slight grinding sound, like sandpaper on wood.

"Mistress, we are entering the tunnel and will let you know if we find anything interesting," Tialdrin sang.

"Maintain regular contact, Team-one," the Mistress said.

"I will leave the voice-operated transmitter on. Anything we find you will be the fourth to hear about it," Einstika sang sarcastically.

"This is not a reassuring comment. First person to hear something unusual sounds much better," Kidahin sang.

"But there are three of us and…," Einstika began.

"I get it. You do not need to explain the obvious. I understand your meaning. You are, in your annoying way, saying the Mistress is safe in the A'tayotan hierarchy hometree on Na'di Island, while we are here below the Technology Center groping blindly," Kidahin trilled in anger.

"Looks like a simple concrete tube, ten ells wide, circular, and heading off into the darkness. No light switches and no lights in the ceiling, either.

"The floor is level poured concrete, makes a wide flat path. I wonder why?" Tialdrin sang.

"Let us not keep the Dark Mistress waiting. Hand torches, everyone," Kidahin sang, switching hers on and aiming it down the dark tunnel. She started walking.

Einstika and Tialdrin aimed their torches at the featureless floor, sides, and ceiling before following after her. Nothing but faint echoes met their sensitive ears.

"The air is stale. This tunnel has not been opened very often," Kidahin sang, sniffing the air cautiously.

Four minutes later she called a halt.

"Mistress, we reached a dead end. No problems so far," Tialdrin sang.

"I have a problem. I am tired and thirsty," Einstika complained.

"I am sure you are. Take a drink from your ration bottle while we rest," Kidahin suggested.

"I am," Einstika retorted.

The elleiu trees stand before us, huge and somber. We do not know the way, but

"Focus, Einstika," Tialdrin trilled impatiently, trying to follow the Song and keep Einstika's mind on task.

"I am. I am focusing on the hatch built into the floor beneath your feet," Einstika sang smugly.

"Hatch?" Kidahin trilled.

"Do not tell me you missed it, too. Tialdrin is standing on top of it," Einstika laughed.

Tialdrin looked down at the smooth metal disk at her feet.

"She is right. I guess I am," she trilled.

Kidahin looked around and snapped her tail, wary, "I thought this tunnel would open into the Technology Center just below ground level. We should be under it by now, so why have a hatch going down?"

"Should we open it? Mistress?" Tialdrin sang at interrogative pitch.

"I see no other choice, Team-one. Go ahead."

"Good thing the handle is not locked in place, but it is recessed into the metal. The hatch is barely an ell across, a really tight space to get trapped in if we are not careful," Einstika sang in warning.

"You are paranoid. That is why we love you. Tialdrin? Open it just a crack. Try to unseat the seal so I can run a quick check," Kidahin sang.

"Affirm. Ready?"

"Yes," Kidahin barely trilled before the seal popped.

The hatch blew open violently. Swinging up on its hinges, it caught Tialdrin under the chin and knocked her to the floor.

"Dou'tu'tay! Tialdrin!" Kidahin trilled.

"It hit the helmet. Bit my lip, but otherwise, I am fine."

"Mistress, the hatch was under pressure," Einstika sang.

"I can feel bruises forming already," Tialdrin spat, the initial numbness along her jaw fading to an ache hinting of coming pain over the next few hours.

"You will live. Quit complaining," Kidahin sang.

"What is down the hatch?" Tialdrin trilled, curiosity overcoming pain.

"A stainless steel tube with rungs welded down one side. Barely large enough for one person," Kidahin sang.

"Only one?" Tialdrin trilled in dismay. "We prowl underground. Now we face a confining tube, also underground. This goes from bad to worse," she hissed.

"There is a hatch on the bottom. Take a look," Einstika sang.

Tialdrin glided up to the techmistress and looked over her shoulder.

"Uh-huh. Let us go down the hole and get it over with," she trilled.

"You first, Kidahin," Einstika sang.

"Afraid?" Kidahin teased.

"No, but I have to pass my equipment through. You go, then Tialdrin. I will lower my equipment into the tube. You pull it through, then I follow," Einstika explained with just a trace of a growl.

"Affirm. Good plan thoughtfully reasoned," Kidahin sang in approval.

"Here I go," she added and climbed into the tube.

"All clear. Closing the hatch on you," Einstika sang.

"Are you certain you can tolerate being in a hermetically sealed space?" Tialdrin sang at interrogative pitch.

"And possibly get blown out the other side like cannon shot when I open the bottom hatch? No, but this is our only option. Go ahead and close it before I change my mind."

Kidahin heard the latch snap closed. Trapped, she watched the torchlight gleam off the polished steel walls. Gritting her teeth, she reached between her feet and pulled the obvious mechanical latch.

"Opening the bottom hatch now. It looks similar to the one above me. It swings down and out of the tube. Wait—it feels locked. I see a small vent and can feel a breeze blowing up my legs. The latch will not open. I guess the pressure must equalize first."

"Sounds foolproof. No worries about power failures," Einstika sang warily.

"Well, this is of Neh'as'anni manufacture. If it does not work, just hit it really hard and it will start working again," Kidahin trilled in amusement.

"Hit it? You barely have room enough to swing a fist in there," Tialdrin sang.

"Yes, hit it. Neh'as'anni devices always fail because they are dirty and dangerous. I need more light than what the torch gives to see."

"Find any writing? Signs? Warnings?" Einstika sang.

"No, but the people working here probably drilled in airlock procedures. I know nothing. Makes me feel claustrophobic."

"Have courage, Kidahin!" Tialdrin sang.

"I hear something—hissing? A lot of hissing. Getting louder and louder. It stopped."

"Pressure equalized. Do not open the hatch yet," Einstika trilled.

"Do not worry. I am not suicidal," Kidahin sang as a loud metallic snap made her jolt.

"The hatch just clicked. Unlocked? Yes. It opens into a stairwell below me, a steep one. I have to shimmy sideways a few steps to make room for you. Can you believe it? Stairs? Tialdrin, come through and help Einstika with her equipment."

"Affirm," Tialdrin sang and dropped into the airlock.

She waited while Einstika slowly went into fits trying to pass equipment into the tube.

Tialdrin climbed back out and helped her take equipment apart. They spent even more time looking for lost parts and screws than the disassembly itself took. They passed through the airlock to the stairwell and spent more time putting everything back together.

Finally finished, Einstika and Tialdrin followed after Kidahin down the long, narrow stairs.

Einstika's mood grew worse. The tube, the stairs, and the stress of tending to her equipment sang subtle reminders of *Londiwe Khoza*. While aboard him she had pressed a life support override touch panel and almost killed herself, Kidahin, Tialdrin, and everyone else in the rescue party.

"Mistress, can you hear us?" Kidahin sang as the teammates rejoined her. Her voice broke Einstika's fixation.

"Clean and clear, Team-one. What do you see?"

The infamous stench of the monster does not weaken our will.

Kidahin empathized with the Gracious Mistress. Her pheromones infused Kidahin with a sense of purpose. The Territorial Boundaries of Rage and Forgiveness said all Eyloni must always take correct action. Hlorrithin's mission would correct the actions of the Neh'as'anni and the other technology clans. Her Environmental Interdiction team helped him by pinpointing the source of the contamination destroying central La'huaset's rainforests.

The pheromonal cue formed new mental pictures. They shifted her perspective to a new scene.

"We are in the middle of a—corridor? I am not sure, Mistress. Looks more like a circular tunnel about a forest trail wide. Concrete construction all around, looks well-fortified. Reminds me of a bunker. A pair of parallel rails bolted into the floor run its length in both directions as far as our torches shine. Kidahin is prowling in one direction and Einstika the other," Tialdrin sang.

"Look, green writing on the wall. Reactor? Spirits, a fission reactor!" Einstika trilled in alarm.

"Let me see. Yes, down the left side. Another notice, on the right, says—huh, interesting," Tialdrin sang.

"What?" Kidahin trilled.

"Some kind of symbol, a dust vortex inside a cup. Badly damaged. Someone tried hard to scratch it off the wall. The symbol below it is untouched," Einstika sang.

"A healer's mark. Their health center must be down this way," Tialdrin sang.

"Having a dedicated health center within a facility this size makes sense. They would need healers on-site, considering the dangerous materials they developed here. But why put it below ground? Trapped down here cannot be conducive to healing," Kidahin complained.

"Where to first? The fission reactor must be operating in stand-by mode. We can restore power and not grope blindly by torchlight,"

Einstika trilled cautiously.

"Fission is filthy. It contributes to the ecological disaster just as much as chemical contaminates in the air, ground, and water do. Worse, we could cause a meltdown," Tialdrin trilled in warning.

"True, but I prefer a little light. This place unsettles me, reminds me of—nevermind.

"I doubt I can make the reactor work, if it is even operational. I understand fission reactors in theory," Einstika sang.

"Theory is better than nothing. Mistress, we will camp here and rest," Kidahin sang.

"Affim, Team-one. Rest well."

"Team-one? Respond. Ten hours! You are behind schedule," the Mistress yelled.

"We hear you," Einstika sang discordantly.

"What is your status?"

"Status is groggy. Hard to sleep here. I prefer my own abode, in my own family ellelu tree. This place gives me very bad dreams, and I really need to brush my teeth," Einstika complained.

"Your heart rate is spiking," Tialdrin trilled as she checked Einstika's vitals. "What about you, Kidahin? Feeling well?"

"What? Of course I do. Why?" Kidahin trilled, puzzled. "I thought I saw something move just beyond my torchlight. At least outside the starlight is more than enough to see in the dark."

"This is a tunnel, not outside. Besides, we checked it at least a hundred ells in both directions," Einstika complained.

"Nevermind. Are you ready?" Kidahin trilled, readily dismissing her.

"Yes. We have eaten and the supplies are packed. I even used the floor as a necessary. Sorry if that sounds gross, Mistress," Einstika trilled, clearly not.

"No matter. I am used to you," the Mistress replied.

"My sense of humor gets offensive at times, or so I am told."

"So true," Tialdrin sang lightly.

Her laughter trilled to a pause as a hint of suppressed—hyperawareness?—brushed her nose. She swiveled quivering ears on Einstika with avid interest.

"All right, you two. Friendly banter aside, which way now?" Kidahin interrupted.

"Left, right, or back to the APC? I say back to Shikararro. Forgive me for stepping out of ritual character for a minute, but I feel unwell, as if I am in two places at the same time. We know there is a damaged hypersonic shuttle here. Hlorrithin could just as easily have sent a full-scale expert team poking around and not just us," Einstika keened.

"Those were not the original Environmental Interdiction Team-one orders, remember?" Kidahin sang.

"I know. I just want to go back to *Hunter's Moon*. I miss Delwyn. Spirits, I even miss Anailiatha."

"We all miss Delwyn, but only a sadistic techmistress would miss the Mistress of Sails," Kidahin sang with a tonal smirk.

"We pledged our honor to complete this mission as the Song leads. Focus.

"Mistress, you want us to check the healer abodes first, or see what is going on with the reactor?" Tialdrin sang at interrogative tempo.

"The radiation is stronger here. The source is some four hundred ells from us," Einstika added sharply.

"Check the reactor. See if you can eliminate it as the signal source," the Mistress advised.

"A decision, finally. Good, I am itching for action," Kidahin sang aggressively.

"Just do not shoot arrows at every shadow you see," Einstika trilled at imperative tempo.

"I know the difference between a hallucination and a real target," Kidahin trilled softly.

"Do you now?" Tialdrin sang with mild concern.

"The pheromones I smell from you and Einstika overlap the empathic imagery coming from the Gracious Mistress. We must empathize with her pheromones and not go off on our own," she added.

"Well…," Kidahin trilled flatly.

"Oh, nevermind. I did not sleep well, either," Tialdrin complained.

"You see them, too?" Einstika trilled.

"Mistress, we will check the reactor," Kidahin sang.

"Go with the spirits, Team-one."

"Einstika, go first. Keep checking radiation levels. Keen if they spike," Kidahin sang.

"Affirm. Oh, look, a dark tunnel, more featureless concrete and more rails on the floor. What can go wrong?" Einstika complained as she headed out.

"What about the radiation? Should it not go up the closer we get to the reactor?" Tialdrin sang apprehensively.

"The signal we followed here is electromagnetic and gets stronger the closer we get. Radiation from the uranium is nearly nonexistent by comparison, more like background noise against what we traced here," Einstika sang.

"I know about different types of radiation, different wavelengths. Are you saying the reactor is not producing both…," Tialdrin began.

"Stop. Something is up ahead, on the rails," Kidahin sang at warning pitch.

"What?" Einstika sang. She stopped and pointed her torchlight at a shadowy figure squatting across the rails.

"You are paranoid," Einstika sang as she continued forward.

"Be careful," Tialdrin warned.

"Of what? Kidahin shooting me? Spirits, Tialdrin, you…"

Einstika's voice slipped from mocking to keening laughter.

"Kidahin, come take a look," she sang and trilled louder.

"This is…," Kidahin began.

"Yes," Einstika interrupted through rising laughter. "A rail trolly, what some call a handcar. You nocked an arrow for this? At least you did not draw the coward's weapon on it."

"We can use this to save time going back. From what we know about the Neh'as'anni, I am surprised it does not have a propane motor. Manual labor sounds a bit primitive for them," Tialdrin sang.

Kidahin shined her torch farther down the tunnel.

"Looks like the end of the line. The rails dead-end next to a ramp leading up to a wide platform. I can see a door with something written on it. I cannot make it out from here."

"'Reactor. Wear Protection at all Times'," Tialdrin read.

"Radiation is well into the blue range but still nowhere near lethal. We need to take prophylactic measures to remain here more than a few hours," Einstika sang.

"I can give anti-rad shots. Open your suit injection ports," Tialdrin sang.

"Any side-effects to worry about?" Einstika trilled sharply.

"Not right away. In a few days you will feel nauseous and tired."

Tialdrin gave Einstika and Kidahin their shots first.

"Go ahead. I will give myself one and meet you on the platform," she sang.

Tialdrin injected herself and frowned at the ampoule. Only enough for three shots remained. She emptied her healers harness on the floor but could not find the other three ampoules. Gone, and without them, their stay was limited.

"So, the door," Kidahin growled.

"Yes. Open it a crack. If the radiation spikes, shut it fast," Einstika warned.

"Spirits, it will not move. Locked, maybe?"

"Try pushing it," Tialdrin suggested.

"Oh, please," Einstika scoffed. "Standard procedure calls for doors being latched and locked in emergencies. Besides, doors like this should open out onto the platform and not inward."

Kidahin leaned against the metal door and pushed anyway.

"Oh, Einstika?" she trilled.

"What the…?" Einstika gasped as the door opened into a room.

"I will tear up my Uahua'asee'a Clan learning center credentials as soon as I get back home," she snapped.

"Proof you do not know everything. The Neh'as'anni are different," Kidahin trilled.

"Wait. Wait a minute. This must be where they bring the fuel rods in. The door should pull open so it cannot clutter the hallway. If they are antisocial enough to put locks everywhere, then of all places, this is where a lock should be just to keep the unwary from wandering upon nuclear fuel," Einstika objected.

"But why is the door to the Technology Center reactor unlocked? I consider nuclear fuel worse than ordnance, and we always lock down ordnance for safety's sake," Tialdrin sang.

"Kill the torches. I am stepping into a corridor. Of course, a corridor. Just like on that a'pea ship. Two doors on each side. The corridor continues. Not a tunnel here, because I see where wall partitions are anchored into the concrete floor. Both doors are locked—no, welded shut. A caged partition blocks the corridor ahead. Some kind of security watch point, I think. The cage door is missing. Beyond the partition I see two more doors, one on the left and the other on the right. The left door is half-open, and I can see lights blinking inside an otherwise dark room.

"Tialdrin, Einstika, cover me. I am moving into the open door. Machinery, dials, and blinking status lamps fill an otherwise dark room. Most of the lamps are blue. Almost as many are green. Very few are red. Except for the status lamps, it is darker than the Dark Mistress's Abode in here.

"I pushed the door all the way open. Stepping inside," Kidahin sang quietly.

"Be careful. Do not shoot anything. You might hit something critical," Einstika warned.

"I will not. Continuing farther into the room," Kidahin sang.

She stepped deeper into the darkness and wondered what the blinking telltales meant. There were far more warning greens and caution blues for comfort.

4
THE WALL OF SILENCE

We blended into the rainforest night as the spirits taught us so long ago in the earliest songs.

"Einstika, I think this is a control room. Looks like you get a chance to blow us all up," Kidahin sang jokingly before continuing on a more serious note.

"The left wall is covered with control panels crowded with rows and columns of analog dials, digital readouts, colored status lamps, and both toggle and paddle switches. In the back left is a large crescent-shaped control console. Patch cords hang from a wall panel behind it. A beige telephonic handset and a green one hang from the wall next to the panel.

"Something bulky is slumped across the console—a body. It sits on a chair but is sprawled across the front of the console atop an elaborate keyboard. A female. Looks like she has been dead for several hours. She is wearing an ill-fitting hazard suit and—oh, spirits!"

"Kidahin?" Tialdrin trilled.

"Someone shot her in the back of the head. Shot her! With a firearm. How cowardly. I think her adulthood knife is still in its breast sheath, too. She never saw it coming," Kidahin keened in disbelief.

"But this violates social custom. Only traditional weapons are used in melee combat—knives, swords, axes. The custom applies to individuals as well as armed groups," Tialdrin seethed.

"What you say is truth. Modern weapons reveal a coward when used against a traditionally armed opponent. No sane person uses a modern weapon against a person not so armed for fear of the social debt using such a weapon would incur."

Tialdrin pricked her ears at Einstika, who stood close, petrified.

"Einstika?" she sang gently.

Einstika trilled a scale under her breath and shook her head.

"Yes, yes. I am fine," she sang distractedly. "What about her, Kidahin?"

"Blood is spattered across the console. Tialdrin, come take a look."

"What do you think happened, Kidahin?" the Mistress asked.

"Shot point blank. Why? I have no idea," Kidahin sang.

"Is the room clear?" Tialdrin wondered, glancing around the large volume.

"Yes. Clear. Sorry," Kidahin sang.

"I will look at the body. Wait here if you want," Tialdrin sang to Einstika.

"I will follow. The Mistress needs a picture for the record. Besides, if this is a control room, I need to see it," Einstika mumbled.

"She is right. Let her pass. This poor Warrior is not going to mind," Kidahin sang sadly.

Tialdrin glided up next to Kidahin, stepped lightly around her, and frowned at the body, ears twitching thoughtfully.

The dead Warrior female's ruined forehead pressed against blinking status lamps covered with blood. The bloodstained lamps gave her face a shifting macabre red mask.

"I still cannot believe it," Tialdrin trilled. "A bullet to the back of the head and not a firearm on her. Huh, the exit wound is smaller than I expected. Firearms are limited to actions against people who are likewise so armed. Guns are for firing on armed vehicles or on opponents wearing armor that render traditional weapons ineffective," Tialdrin trilled.

"Of course," Kidahin sang. "A coward hides in armor and fires a gun at an adversary from safe distances. Our APC is not armed, and its light armor protects it from jungle hazards, animals, and the rigors of driving through obstructions—or when the driver rolls it over a hillside three or four times. Is this not so, Einstika?"

"It was not my fault. Something jammed the lidar. I could not see the section of roadbed ahead missing," Einstika hissed as she glided into the room to defend herself from Kidahin's slander.

"Oh, spirits," she keened, her eyes drifting across the body.

"A small-caliber weapon did this; otherwise, the front of her head would be gone. Small weapon, too. Probably no bigger than my hand, which means a short-range weapon having no significant stopping power. A firearm this small is little better than a melee weapon. Useless at any range and incapable of penetrating even traditional armors more than ten ells away. Whoever fired the weapon gave her no chance to duel with adulthood knives or to defend herself. Dou'tu'tay, simply cutting her throat without singing a challenge is cowardly enough, but to fire a gun at melee range from behind is murder, simple and plain," she sang.

"More than murder. An execution," Tialdrin trilled as the burning memory of a shipwreck fluttered in the back of her mind.

"Yes, and a human one at that," Kidahin agreed. "A disturbing thought considering no Eyloni will meet a human for several hundred years. By tradition, executions come after conviction for killing or intending lethal harm to a male. Executions happen after a Major Consensus of females finds the accused guilty. Even if this Warrior had harmed or killed a male, no hierarchy female of sufficient rank would have called for a Major Consensus here unless the accused posed an immediate threat to other males. Beside that, a Major Consensus follows ritual form. The penalty is part of the ritual. They would have skinned her alive with her own adulthood knife and abandoned her in the rainforest, not shoot her in the back of the head from behind and leave her here."

"To me, it looks like she was sitting here minding the console when someone she trusted came up from behind and shot her. What really happened here?" Einstika trilled.

"Have courage, Einstika. This is just a theory. Do not get worked up over it," Tialdrin sang gently.

"Yes. Yes, you are right. After all, we are in a room with a gunshot body, in the La'huaset Engineering Complex Technology Center, in Neh'as'anni Clan territory. I just need a minute so I can hold the camera steady and send the Mistress a picture."

"I wonder who she was, besides a Warrior female," Tialdrin sang thoughtfully.

"A nuclear power systems techmistress," Einstika sang. "I can tell from the hazard suit and the equipment at her waist. Only a techmistress or someone of mistress social rank in a nuclear occupational specialty could operate this console."

"Einstika, take a look at these controls and see if you can restore power," Kidahin sang.

"Is this why we came here?" Einstika trilled and then shrugged. "Okay, help me lift the body off the console."

"Of course. Tialdrin, grab her left shoulder. Einstika, grab the right. I will lift her legs off the chair. Lay her on the floor," Kidahin sang softly.

Tialdrin hesitated a fraction of a second, considered Kidahin's tone, shrugged, and looped her arm under the dead techmistress's armpit.

"No rigor," she trilled, surprised. "Einstika, hold on. She is slipping sideways. Watch out, her hazard suit is ripping."

"Better you do this than me," Einstika sang as she helped put the body on the floor.

"We are the ones used to doing dirty jobs. You are a techmistress, so we do not hold you at fault if you want to step back," Kidahin sang.

"Thank you. Hey, I can see her neckwear and waistwear through the rip in the suit. She held mistress social rank, likely the mistress of power systems. She also had high hierarchy rank and was a Neh'as'anni Clan elder. And they shot her!"

"A mystery for another time," Kidahin trilled. "What can you tell us about the reactor?"

Einstika found a spray bottle full of cleaner and a rag. She sprayed the console and rubbed as much blood from the status indicators as possible.

"Well," she trilled to a drawn-out drawl. "There is some power available, but not much. Reserve system, probably batteries or a natural gas generator somewhere. I saw a design something like this. We tried a similar one in Uahua'asee'a Clan a few years ago for naval propulsion but abandoned it as unsafe."

"Meaning you can operate it?" Kidahin sang irritably.

"I think so. They followed the standardized control system layout. Fuel status reads nominal. Coolant systems are running hot. Control rods and moderator systems—the reactor faulted, and this console forced it into standby mode. The control rods are still in. I wonder what caused the fault?"

Einstika turned her back on the console and its grisly attendant to read the status lights on the wall panel.

"The fault happened in the steam turbines. A event timer recorded an unstable load and the mains spiked at about the same time as the explosion that leveled part of the complex. Power generation status—dou'tu'tay! The gas turbine emergency generator is offline. The reason? Ah, no natural gas supply. What little available electricity comes from a backup power supply. Explains all the green warning lights," she trilled, snapping her tail sharply.

"Batteries? Enough power to keep all this running?" Kidahin trilled.

"Not batteries. Well, not batteries alone. Thermocouple converters, accumulators, trickle charge capacitor banks. It looks like they cannot keep up with the coolant pump demand. When the banks fully discharge the pumps will stop and the core will melt down."

"Can you bring the reactor back online? The steam turbines can generate enough electricity to run them at full speed, yes?" Kidahin demanded.

"Depends on the fault. It could happen again. First I would have to disconnect most of the load from the transformers. If I do not, all the blast damage will surely cause another fault."

"Can you disconnect them from here?" Tialdrin sang.

"Maybe, but I have no idea what systems are damaged. I can switch everything off, power up, and then switch on the bare necessities: lights, ventilation, electric locks, and the coolant pumps, of course. It is up to you."

"Do it," Kidahin trilled curtly.

"Affirm," Einstika sang, turned, and glided back to the power distribution panel. There, she snapped breakers off by the hundreds, returned to the console, and hit the coolant system reset and waited, glaring at a series of numbers flashing across a CRT display screen.

"What do those numbers mean?" Tialdrin sang, shuddering. Standing in a room so close to a radioactive pile scared the spirits out of her.

"What?" Einstika trilled distractedly.

"Those numbers on the screen. The dials and switches below them. They look important."

"Accumulator status. Give me a minute while I get into the control computer. A'pea! The control system is locked-out. I cannot gain access. Where is the...? Ah, a magnetic card reader. Check her hazard suit. Look for a small plastic card that fits into this reader," Einstika trilled.

Tialdrin knelt next to the body, asked the spirits' forgiveness, and felt along the dead female's waist.

"Found it," she sang, pulling a small white plastic card from a pocket.

"Give me that!" Einstika trilled, snatching it from Tialdrin's hand and sliding it into the reader.

"I am in. The computer reports the reactor controls are intact. I can reboot the control program from here. Kidahin?" she trilled, waiting for permission to proceed.

"No, not yet. Can you increase accumulator output without withdrawing the control rods?"

"Maybe, if I shut off some of the systems drawing power from them. You might as well get comfortable while I look these panels over. Hopefully I can find reserve power somewhere," Einstika sang.

She stepped up to a row of blinking panels covered with breaker switches. One panel in particular drew her notice with its multiple jacks sticking out of it in a haphazard fashion suggesting they were rushed last-minute additions. Several of the long coiled patch cords hung almost to the floor, their ends plugged into the jacks in the panel.

"Kidahin, the radiation signal we traced here comes from behind this panel!" she trilled.

"What?" Tialdrin keened, backing away.

"Yes, an EM field of some kind. Nuclear radiation in the low blue range, too. Someone punched a power tap through the reactor shielding behind the console. This panel has been repurposed to emit a static field—at the floor? Keep grounded. A static discharge from it will feel like getting hit by lightning. Do not crawl under the console, either. The leakage from the reactor is equal to receiving several hundred health center x-rays at once."

Tialdrin frowned and twitched her tail in wary circles, trying to decide which frightened her more: getting electrocuted or irradiated.

"I think she tail-tied this in a hurry," Einstika sang.

"Tail-tied? I do not understand," Kidahin sang, glancing nervously at the dead Warrior's body.

"This is not original equipment. Not repair work, either. She did this, drilled a hole through a sheet of lead and tapped directly into a thermocouple converter so she could power whatever this is. But why did she want an EM static shield aimed at the floor?"

"What about the floor? Tell me what you think," Kidahin prodded.

"This—addition. I think something went wrong. I think she tried to build a high-power EM emitter, but these spare parts and panel are insufficient for generating the frequency and coverage she wanted. It did not work at the power level she wanted. My opinion, anyway."

"But why did she aim the emitter at the floor in the corner and not at the door or the radiation leak she made herself?" Kidahin trilled at interrogative pitch.

"I do not know. It did not prevent her from getting shot from behind," Einstika trilled angrily.

She reached out to the console and yanked the drawer below the keyboard open, pulled out a thick binder, and opened it eagerly.

"Well now, what is this? Schematics? No, wiring diagrams. These show the distribution of power lines from the steam turbines. Not maps, but these are drawn level by level. According to this, reactor power routes through four levels: one above us, this one, and two below. Quite spacious, too, if I read the scale right. Looks like most of the power goes to this level and level four. We might find something in those two places."

One of the console's green warning status lamps blinked nominal red.

Einstika noticed the one red dot amid a sea of green immediately.

"Mistress, I can restore power in one of two ways. I can get full power by simply rebooting the reactor and restarting the turbine control program, which should restore electrical power to normal levels. I can also reroute the power produced by the thermocouple accumulators. It will not be enough to run the mains, but it should be enough to run the coolant pumps and the lights."

"Do not risk restarting the reactor. Experts here say the best you can hope for from the accumulators is running low-current devices, mainly the lights. Try to draw power from them," the Mistress droned.

"I can do that," Einstika sang.

She stepped over to another wall panel, grabbed two vertical handles on a rack-mounted module and pulled it out of the panel.

She carried the small rectangular box to the console, set it down next to the keyboard, and returned to the panel. She pulled a second module out and set it atop the first one.

Einstika then reached into her techmistress harness and withdrew two short cables, plugged one end into each module and the other two ends into the back of the console.

"What are you doing?" Tialdrin trilled.

"Reprogramming these two process controllers. One will reroute power from the accumulators. The other is a safety buffer. It will prevent the reactor from coming online if the load exceeds what the accumulators can source."

"Oh," Tialdrin sang. She flicked a casual ear at the modules and shrugged.

"I saw that," Einstika sang. "Now you know how I feel every time you drop wellnessmistress-speak on us."

Einstika downloaded a program from the console into the two modules.

"Done. Now I hit the restart switch and confirm restart. And the modules are talking to the console. Now, I do this," she sang with a flourish as she hit the execute command key.

"And nothing happens," Kidahin sang in disgust.

"Nothing you can see, perhaps. The reserve accumulators are at zero volts right now. They have to draw power from the converters..."

A deep concussive thud shook the floor.

"Did you feel that?" Tialdrin trilled.

"Felt like an explosion," Kidahin sang, suddenly alert.

"Half the lights on this panel just turned caution blue. Does that mean anything?" Tialdrin sang at interrogative tempo.

"Oh, spirits! One of the accumulators blew out. Of course! I forgot to switch the current through the transformers. It must be done manually," Einstika snarled.

She raced to the blue-flashing breaker panel and snapped ten switches closed. Then she pulled the large blue handle on its side all the way down.

"There, that should do it," she sang in satisfaction.

"Let us hope the blast did not breach the reactor," Kidahin trilled.

"It did not. We would be dead by now otherwise," Tialdrin trilled.

"She is right about that," Einstika snapped.

Orange streaks suddenly appeared on the ceiling, followed almost immediately by blue-white flashes. They flickered like strobes for a moment longer before settling down to a glaring white light.

"The lights just kicked on, Mistress. Fluorescent ones. I hate fluorescent lights," Kidahin sang.

"Congratulations, Team-one," the Mistress praised, seemingly ignoring Kidahin's complaint.

"Congratulations, me, you mean," Einstika snarled. "You are welcome, by the way."

"Let it go. There is nothing more to see here," Kidahin sang.

"Are you sure?" Einstika trilled, sounding uncertain.

"Yes. Look around. The only way in or out is through the door we came through. The other doors in here are welded shut."

"I think they open into the reactor core and the turbine steam exchange for the generators. Radiation hazard there. I say we leave them alone," Tialdrin sang.

"I agree," Einstika seconded clearly.

"So we backtrail? To where?" Tialdrin trilled.

"Either back to the tunnel, return to the surface, and try another way in. Or we try to get in through the health center door. Maybe we can find a floor plan there. It may even show the other levels Einstika mentioned earlier," Kidahin sang.

"Mistress, what do you think?" Tialdrin sang.

"Check the health center door," the Mistress pressed.

"Affirm. Leaving the reactor control room. The hallway lights are on, too. The path we took looks much shorter with the lights on. We should reach the—in fact, I can see the health center door up ahead. Similar design to the one on the reactor control room," Kidahin sang.

"Is it open?" the Mistress asked.

"No, but the handle turns freely," Kidahin sang as she opened the door.

"Of course it does," Einstika complained.

"Ignore her, Mistress. Stepping inside," Kidahin growled and walked into a bright room filled with humming equipment blinking happily in electronic bliss.

"Dou'tu'tay! We spent time in the reactor room tailchasing for nothing," she trilled angrily.

"Why?" Tialdrin wondered.

"Take a look. This is another power-switching station. We did not have to take risks with the reactor."

Einstika read a blinking readout on the nearest wall panel.

"'Reserve Power Activation. Accumulators Charging.' I think this panel reroutes power through the accumulators and into a reserve supply," Einstika sang, intrigued.

As if listening, the transformer hum dipped in volume and the lights dimmed.

"So now the lights are flickering. This is worse than total darkness," Kidahin complained.

"Do not snap your tail at me. I added more power by reprogramming the accumulator controls, but the switches and transformers here reroute electricity into distribution lines for this level. A power surge burned out a lot of circuits, but do not expect me to rewire all this. I do not have the parts even if I knew how to fix it."

"Calm down, Einstika. Nobody expects you to," Tialdrin sang soothingly.

Einstika lowered her head, abashed at her hysterical outburst.

"I am acting like an infant. Sorry, Kidahin. I do not know what came over me. I keep seeing hazy afterimages of a warship's deck."

"You, too?" Kidahin sang in surprise.

"Similar situations: enclosed spaces, tunnels, hallways all vaguely resembling corridors. Suspicious deaths, an accident that triggers a catastrophe. I remember them, too," Tialdrin sang thoughtfully.

"But I do not *see* them," she added. "Have you been—hallucinating?"

"I hope we find no more bodies," Einstika interrupted softly.

"Real or imaginary ones," Kidahin added, just as softly.

"It makes sense having a power distribution node here. It keeps health center people from prowling to the reactor every time they want something turned on or off. Makes sense from a safety standpoint, too. Anything going wrong electrically in health center gets buffered by this station rather than blowing out the mains in the turbine room," Einstika sang in approval.

"You think they built rooms like this throughout the building?" Tialdrin sang, bored hearing more electrician talk.

"Oh, yes. If each level has equipment pulling a lot of current. They would want to switch out parts of each level without cutting power to the entire building. In fact, engineering economy insists there be stations like this one near the most energy-consuming areas. And that begs the question: why does a health center need so much power?" Einstika trilled.

We ask the spirits for the sound of the falling leaf, so none can hear us.

Stealth. Good advice, that, Einstika mused.

"Health centers draw a lot of power," Tialdrin sang expertly.

Einstika shook her head.

"Not this much," she sang and turned away from Tialdrin to glare at Kidahin as she prowled cautiously between humming transformers to a door in the far corner.

'What is it, Kidahin?" Einstika sang.

"Looks like part of a health center. I see bodies."

"Spirits, bodies? As in more than one? Bodies shot like the mistress?"

"I do not think so. This looks like an intensive care abode, a large one. It has rows of convalescent nests separated by privacy curtains. Well lit, and it has a lot of healer equipment, too. From here I see the corner of an examination table, a surgery abode, a small laboratory, and a dispensary," Kidahin replied.

"Let me see. Einstika, stay here," Tialdrin sang.

Einstika blinked furiously, trying to ignore shimmering male bodies, but they and the destroyer's barely perceptible deck persisted anyway. She glared at those dead, thinking they thought she was unaware of them.

But I know more than they think I do, she thought smugly and flattened her ears at them.

"No, I like my chances with those dead more than with these dead," she sang staccato.

"You mean the mistress? She is at the other end of the corridor. Nothing to fear there but radiation," the Mistress trilled flatly.

"I have not sent you a picture, so do not tell me what I do and do not see," Einstika snapped.

Kidahin pulled a privacy curtain aside.

"A male. His body is covered with skin rot," she trilled.

"Not shot?" Einstika trilled tremulously.

"No. He looks—pitiful," Kidahin sang sorrowfully.

Tialdrin walked around her, glided up to the next nest in line, pulled the curtain aside, and perked her ears.

"Another male. He has fungal growths on his chest and limbs as well. Remind me of skin rot, but this is not. I do not understand. Nobody gets skin rot unless they fail to take proper care of their skin. The fuzzy keratin outer layer repels water unless it becomes saturated. That is why we oil our skin daily. The fungi eating into the muscle tissue causes septic shock. Skin rot is more a Myat'ti'deep Tribal continent equatorial rainforest affliction than a northern La'huaset temperate rainforest one. They could not have caught whatever this is down here."

Tialdrin paused, put on a pair of latex gloves, bent over a body, and touched its chest.

"This body has not putrefied. The fungi grew before he died, just as limb rot does. Cause of death, I assume, is toxic shock, again just like limb rot. I doubt he was awake when he died. This would have been an agonizing death. The mistress of healers likely gave him and the others here massive antifungals and put them into medical comas. But where is she? I cannot imagine a mistress of healers abandoning patients, especially male ones," Tialdrin keened in outrage.

"Maybe they were already beyond help. She overdosed them. That would be an honorable justification for killing a male, would it not?" Einstika trilled, trembling.

"It would at that," Kidahin readily agreed.

"Oh, I feel so much better now. The mistress of healers gave them all irreversible comas and abandoned them to die here alone," Einstika spat.

It is sad this once beautiful place now harbors vile corruption.

Tialdrin, guided by changing pheromonal cues, began stalking cautiously through the intensive care abode, pulling aside privacy curtains from each nest. Every patient was male.

The moral duty of every female was to protect males, she knew. Her experiences aboard the shipwrecked human destroyer and the memory of the dead aboard him sang a counterpoint in her ears to the corruption verse just sung. The Song and her own melody rooted her mind in the scene and helped her deal with this disaster.

"Wait," she keened. "There is more. All these patients are males."

"What?" the Mistress growled. Even scrambled, the note of outrage came through clearly.

"Yes, Mistress, one hundred and one males. They all have the same skin fungal infection," Tialdrin sang.

Einstika snapped her tail in frustration.

"I would expect a facility of this size to have its own health center. But underground? And so close to a fission reactor? The potential for radiation exposure alone makes it too dangerous for males, even healthy ones. Could this have been a quarantine abode?" she trilled.

"I think what happened here was much worse than a quarantine," Kidahin trilled, suddenly both annoyed and angry with Tialdrin's casual comment. Why was she being so noisy?

"Like what, exactly? Experimental treatment? On males? I do not believe it. No mistress of healers would allow it. Tialdrin?" Einstika demanded.

"No mistress of healers would permit it. On female volunteers, yes. Never on males, even if they volunteered. I think the healers tried to help them."

"Why do you think so?" Kidahin trilled at challenge tempo.

Tialdrin glided up to the dispensary and pointed at the medications stacked behind a glass partition.

"This pharmacy is stocked with antimycotic drugs, antibiotics, and painkillers. Some of the antimycotics are potent. They took great strides to save them but failed," she explained.

"Oh, spirits—oh, spirits. A branch just hit me. We might have been exposed to the spores. This could happen to us!" Einstika keened.

"Nothing is going to happen to you, Team-one. You will be fine. This condition afflicts only males," the Mistress droned severely.

Nothing we knew could compare to the greatness of this place and the people who lived here. Their songs and ideas echoing here are all that remain of the mystery they took with them as they fled.

Einstika smelled pheromones and followed their guiding scent. The Territorial Boundaries of Rage and Forgiveness said to put matters like this to the rigors of personal rage and honor.

"That is even worse," she keened. "Our moral duty is to protect males. Seeing all this death has my mind trying to hide behind a branch that twists and turns around and down. They are DEAD. We can do nothing for them."

"You need a distraction. Why not play with one of your techmistress tools? I seem to remember you brought a portable lidar," Tialdrin sang brightly.

"So? I tried it back in the tunnel but kept getting interference. I gave up and never bothered with it again."

"You let me prowl blindly into the intensive care abode?" Kidahin trilled at insolence tempo moderated by humor pitch to soften her words.

"It is not terribly precise. Not in here, but I can take a scan now if you wish," Einstika sang.

She pulled the lidar gun out of her techmistress harness and pressed the trigger. She turned its screen to Kidahin so she could see the scan return.

"See? It might as well be showing us the Dark Mistress's Abode. This room is not even close to the shape the lidar return says it is. All the hard returns are a'pea, but at least it does show large volumes both ahead and above us and—wait. Is this a person?"

"What do you mean, a person?" Kidahin trilled.

"Spirits, are you saying there are Neh'as'anni Clan members alive down here?" Tialdrin trilled in alarm.

"Um-no, of course not. Not unless they wear something that gives a hard lidar return. It is not designed to detect people, not directly. This is just a reflected signal from one of us because we are so close to the emitter, a glitch. Sorry."

"Spirits," Kidahin cursed. "The idea of someone here is all I need."

"I know. I said I was sorry," Einstika sang wistfully.

"We are blind with ill-luck all around us. Tialdrin, keep an eye on the walls. There should be pattern transitions to let workers know where they are. Mistress, we are continuing and will call if we find anything important."

"Especially if we come across a room full of Neh'as'anni territorial defenders," Einstika growled.

"Stick your tail up your a'pea, techmistress," Kidahin cursed.

"This is not her fault. Besides, if we have a quarantine abode here, then where is the health center and its trauma abode? I think this is an annex because a health center has its own intensive care abodes. Staff should have abodes nearby. Where are they?" Tialdrin sang in puzzlement.

"Right here, I think," Kidahin sang.

"What?" Tialdrin keened, taken by surprise.

"In this door. See?" Kidahin warned.

"No, I think this is another annex. Spirits, what happened? This looks like it was overrun by a crowd!"

5
OUTLAWRY'S FINALITY

I forgot this as I looked upon neh'tle ke'ne's'tu, its mind drifting through evil and twisted dreams. So many spirits under its power, many more than just those stolen from our Clan.

Einstika twitched an ear in agreement. The teaching songs spoke of Neh'as'anni Clan technical accomplishment, but only to stress how they and their allied clans gave rise to neh'tle ke'ne's'tu, pollution sickness, and near worldwide ecological collapse.

Eyloni panpsychism saw organized systems as personalities having intelligence that focused on what they were about. Storm systems had organization and thus intelligence.

So, too, did neh'tle ke'ne's'tu. It had a mind—a corrupt and corrupting one that afflicted those around it through the technology that spawned it. Einstika halted that trail of thought and glanced sideways at Tialdrin and Kidahin.

They stood speechless at a door. It reminded her somewhat of the watertight hatches used on ships. The wheel in the middle opened it. Raised seals ran around it. Worse, it reminded her of the frame hatches on *Londiwe Khoza*.

Just thinking the name summoned a phosphorescent outline of one of his compartmental hatches. It superimposed itself over the door and filled the interior with hazy outlines of smashed equipment, personal effects, and hundreds of dead human males.

Einstika recoiled violently from the door.

"Stay here. There is no need for us to go in there," Tialdrin sang, noticing Einstika's pause.

Einstika stared tight-lipped into the room and nodded vaguely.

Kidahin stepped a tail-length into the room for a better look.

"Dead females, most of them Warriors. Thirty, all of them are health center personnel. The room itself is a shambles. All the equipment is smashed."

She stepped into the room and lifted a table off another body.

"Dou'tu'tay, this one is a male, and he did not die from limb rot, either," she trilled.

Tialdrin stepped in behind her, medically curious.

"Some kind of poison, maybe? He just dropped to the floor? Same for these females, too? But that does not explain all the damage. They must be his occupational association," she trilled analytically.

Kidahin sniffed cautiously at the air.

"I do not smell anything," she sang.

"He was the sire cairn of surgery. The Hunter beneath him was the mistress of head trauma. Their waistwear patterns tell me this, at least," Tialdrin added.

"Looks like they locked themselves in," Einstika observed, blinking her eyes furiously to rid them of the faint afterimages of another place and time.

"You think so?" Kidahin trilled at interrogative pitch.

"Someone tried to break down this door. The wall around the hatch is chipped and the upper third of the hatch itself is covered with sledgehammer dents."

"They sheltered in place here, but why?" Tialdrin wondered aloud.

"Team-one? Shikararro reports the fighting at the elleiu trees is going bad for the Neh'as'anni. Take precautions. Survivors will likely recall to the industrial complex," the Mistress warned.

"The history songs say they did not until days later," Kidahin trilled in dismissal.

"Why would they come here?" Tialdrin sang, ignoring Kidahin's slip. "The blast leveled a third of the complex. This is an industrial research site. It would serve no purpose for them to retreat here."

"Exactly," Einstika sang. "Whatever survived the blast may have military applications."

"No," Kidahin sang. "The airfield provides a means of escape, provided any aircraft still work. But fly where when they have their traditional weapons? When Hlorrithin enters the complex with the armies of all the clans of Elleio it would be better for them—honorwise—to remain in the north defending their elleiu trees than die in shame here."

"What about guns, Kidahin?" Tialdrin trilled. "If they made them here, then they have warehouses full of them."

"Not even the Neh'as'anni would do that," Kidahin sang. "The Be'atika Senge would declare them ni'zakhon, guilty of outlawry, and..."

"The Be'atika Senge did already, for ecological sabotage. They have nothing to lose," Einstika interrupted.

"Except their individual honor and respect," Tialdrin sang. "I doubt they really believed the Be'atika Senge would carry out their threat even after many warnings."

"They claimed their technology would save themselves and all of central La'huaset, but the cost was too high. They pushed their technological know-how to produce modern marvels like nuclear power and hypersonic jets and had no interest in stockpiling modern weapons," Kidahin reminded them.

"Except ones like the ambush firearm someone shot the reactor techmistress with," Einstika pointed out.

"Not in any quantity we need worry about," Kidahin sang. "Do not worry. No Hunter female throws down her bow in exchange for a melee-to-short-range gun. No Warrior female drops her knives and sword for one, either. Females would never do such a thing."

"They did it to one of their own! Someone intended on stopping the health center staff from doing something, but what?" Einstika trilled in fury.

"They must have had a minority among them," Tialdrin trilled, confused. "Group decisions require a Major Consensus because by custom we never allow majorities to control outcomes. Besides, conflict within a male's occupational or personal association is almost unheard of."

A cruel memory urged Einstika to wrap her tail around her waist several times and shudder.

"Mutiny. Delwyn calls this kind of behavior a mutiny. Just like on *Londiwe Khoza*," she sang in horror.

"Do not jump to conclusions," Kidahin snapped. "Mutiny is a wholly human concept. What about an accident, some toxic release—a leak or a spill?"

This is the evil we came to destroy.

"Door back here. Do we go through it or backtrail to the handcar?" Kidahin sang, focusing on the overpowering scent as she picked her way deeper into the room.

"I choose the handcar. I hate being underground, and I hate these walls closing in on me. How did the Neh'as'anni stand working down here? Nobody lives in a building, let alone in underground tunnels. I cannot smell the leaves, the trees, the wood. I hate this place!" Einstika trilled.

"Spirits, Einstika, why are you tying your tail in knots?" Kidahin sang softly.

"Probably locked," Einstika trilled, snapping her tail at the door in front of them.

"No," Kidahin sang in surprise as she pulled the door open.

"It opens into a very large room? Hatches run down the left and right walls, similar to the one behind us. Odd, health center staff behind us but this looks nothing like any health center facility I ever saw. Tialdrin?"

Death will come as a surprise during its sleep.

Tialdrin stepped silently around Kidahin and glided a few ells into the large bay.

She stopped abruptly, eyes wide, and turned a slow circle.

"This is a laboratory. Twelve boles in a row down the left side and another twelve down the right. They likely open into analysis abodes."

"This explains the transformer switching station we found. Analyzers in each abode and the bay equipment need a lot of electricity," Einstika sang.

"But a laboratory for what?" Kidahin trilled. "It looks—clean—too clean. Clean enough for health center work."

"This is not health center equipment," Tialdrin sang at a glance. "Something related, maybe? Prosthetics? Bionic implants? Kidahin, prowl ahead."

"You smell excited. Why? You recognize something?" Einstika growled.

"Not quite, but whatever they were doing here looks important. Are you not curious?" Tialdrin snapped.

"You are the expert in health center matters," Kidahin sang.

"I am a wellnessmistress, not a mistress of healers."

"Where should we start?" Kidahin wondered aloud.

"The analysis abodes. See if they really are analysis boles," Tialdrin sang insistently.

So curiosity was not overriding Tialdrin's caution. Good, Kidahin thought as she flipped her ears wide and snapped her tail.

Together they crossed the bay to the left wall. Kidahin stopped them at the first abode and pulled the door handle, but it remained closed.

"Locked. Of course," she sang staccato.

"Dou'tu'tay!" Tialdrin trilled as she pulled on the second abode door handle.

"What? Are you in a hurry?" Kidahin trilled as she stepped around her to inspect the third door.

"Looks like someone smacked this handle off with a sledgehammer," Tialdrin complained.

Einstika stood between them, eying the third door warily. The dim incandescent light from the ceiling lamps high above them cast the bay in dusky shadows.

"Just give each door a quick pull and be done with it," she trilled as she eyed the ceiling suspiciously.

"You are right. Tialdrin, keep going. I will go to the last door and work my way back to you," Kidahin trilled.

She sprinted to the end of the bay and pulled the handle of the door in the corner.

It swung open easily.

"Well, lucky me," she trilled at Einstika.

Einstika trilled a verbal shrug and returned to eye-stalking the bay.

The walls stretched to the ceiling. Huge air vents and pipes big enough for her to crawl through ran the length of the upper wall on both sides. A bay-spanning crane hugged the ceiling. Mounted on rails, it could roll on rubber wheels up and down the length of the bay.

"Spirits!" Kidahin cursed. "They used a'pea flickering fluorescent bulbs in the abodes. Why did they not use incandescent ones like they did in the bay?"

"Kidahin, your abode is dedicated to testing equipment. That door in the back probably leads into a storeroom. What kind of analyzer is this?" Tialdrin wondered. "This is not something a healer would use. Einstika, take a look at it."

"Why?" Einstika trilled, annoyed at the interruption.

"This looks like something found in a physics laboratory. What does it do?" Kidahin pressed before Einstika could keen an obscenity.

Einstika reluctantly tore her eyes from the shifting outlines in the ceiling and stepped into the abode.

She glared at the analyzer, a bulky two-module device sitting on a large table. She found helium hoses connecting the back of one module to the back of the table's metal skirt. Hoses and cables patched the two modules together.

She rummaged through a drawer set in the table below the analyzer and pulled out a box. She opened it and plucked out a small graphite crucible. She put it down on the tabletop, reached up, and turned the analyzer on.

A start-up menu popped up on the analyzer's CRT screen.

She read the menu options and nodded.

"Well?" Kidahin prompted impatiently.

"This is used for metallurgy. It melts a sample in the furnace module and passes the gasses to the computer in the other module. It measures the amount of carbon and sulphur in a sample of a known mass."

"Sounds boring," Kidahin trilled in disappointment.

"To us, yes. To a metallurgist, no. They probably used it to analyze that," Einstika sang, pointing her tail out the doorway at a table in the middle of the bay.

Kidahin glanced where Einstika's tail pointed and nodded.

"I think you are right," she added.

Suddenly I understand.

The pheromonal cue caught Kidahin by surprise as she empathized with it and found herself stepping through a warship's hatch. What her torch revealed caused her to stagger back and retch violently in shock. She choked down vomit.

No, she screamed in her mind. This happened to Jassalin while we were aboard *Londiwe Khoza* and not me!

The singers' cue reinforced the theme of the Song: the Territorial Boundaries of Rage and Forgiveness concept of withered trees. It reminded her that withered trees meant destruction. Rage destroyed. That was what Hlorrithin was doing now, destroying the Neh'as'anni to stop an ecological disaster.

But her memories of *Londiwe Khoza* were blending into the theme and pounding their own counterpoint to the pheromonal narrative coming from the Gracious Mistress and her singers.

Kidahin concentrated on the features of the wide laboratory bay until the narrow ship corridor faded away. She stared at the table, mentally cataloging its contents to root herself back into the reality of the scene being played out through the Song.

Another analyzer, one similar to the one in the abode they just searched, stood next to racks of bottles containing various rock samples and chemicals. Opposite the analyzer sat an oscilloscope and other electrical test equipment. A shelf bolted to the wall held manuals and laboratory notebooks. Left of the table stood a reel-to-reel tape data storage unit. The table corner next to the tape unit served as a desk for a computer terminal.

But the table's central feature, a large glass bell jar, contained a two-fisted-sized sample of a glittery metallic material.

"Some kind of metal," Einstika sang.

"Tialdrin?" Kidahin trilled, inviting comment.

"Intriguing," Tialdrin sang.

"Is that all?" Kidahin snapped.

"Almost reminds me of a disembodied brain in general shape, folds, and convolutions. Looks like someone took a sheet of gold mesh and wadded it up. Seems a touch too red for gold, though," Tialdrin snapped.

"Impressive technology. By that I mean the computer and analyzers. This setup looks—haphazard? Looks like a prototype setup. This is metallurgy testing stuff, mostly. The bottles contain acids," Einstika sang.

Tialdrin shrugged, pulled a notebook from the shelf, and riffled through the pages.

"This is about chemical research on the sample," she sang. "I wonder what they were testing it for?"

"Is this not obvious?" Kidahin trilled, annoyed.

"What?" Tialdrin trilled vaguely, consumed by her reading.

"She means the specimen in the jar sitting on the table in front of you," Einstika sang at insolence tempo.

"Oh, sorry. I got distracted reading these little handwritten details. These notes clearly refer to the sample," Tialdrin sang.

"What about it, Team-one? Describe it," the Mistress demanded.

Tialdrin leaned over the table until her nose got close enough for her breath to fog the glass.

"Well, it has an interesting structure. Never saw its like in metals before. Reminds me of fossilized tree sap, but it has a crystalline look you will never see in petrified sap."

"Just say amber. We all know petrified sap is called amber," Kidahin sang dryly.

"I see some similarities," Einstika agreed. "But this is not amber. Reminds me more of fine metal crystals, like iron pyrite. Except the color is all wrong, too coppery. The crystals are unlike anything I have ever seen before. They appear to have a grain, like fine wood. Mistress, I will send you a picture, but it will not show fine details. I think the Neh'as'anni made this stuff somewhere in this building. It looks too pure and too processed for raw ore. I wonder if it is safe to touch."

"Why touch something you never saw before?" Kidahin trilled.

"To test its mechanical properties, of course."

"I want to run a few tests myself. What do you think, Mistress?" Tialdrin sang at interrogative tempo.

"The picture you sent leads me to agree with your analysis, Team-one. How long do you need?"

"I can do the basic analysis using the equipment here. Basic chromatography takes about two hours. While the chromatograph is busy, I can conduct tests using the acids and bases I found on the table. About three hours, I think," Tialdrin sang.

"Sounds like a long wait to test what is clearly a fistful of wadded up braided copper shielding. What do you expect to find?" Kidahin grumbled.

"An understanding of what they were developing here," Tialdrin sang at insistence pitch.

"You mean besides dying from a mutated fungal infection?" Kidahin retorted.

"Thank you for reminding me. I was trying to forget," Einstika trilled angrily. "I agree with Tialdrin. We might get an idea about what they were developing by examining this metal."

"Why not just take the notebooks and the sample?" Kidahin argued reasonably. "Better yet, take the computer tapes."

"Really?" Tialdrin growled. "This table alone holds twenty-two notebooks. We would need a cart to carry all this stuff out of here. Same for all the magnetic tape reels. I say we use the opportunities given us."

"What do you think, Mistress?" Kidahin sang.

"Let them run their tests. See what they tell you before taking further action," the Mistress advised.

"Affirm, Mistress. We will proceed to testing," Tialdrin sang happily.

Tialdrin watched the printer spit several sheets of paper into a collator. Impatient, she pulled them from the vibrating basket and started reading right away, eagerly flipping pages back and forth between text and a set of graphs.

"Einstika, take a look at this!" she sang.

"Not now. I am busy watching how the metal reacts to electricity."

"It conducts, right?" Tialdrin muttered dryly, more interested in her own results.

"No. It falls apart into fractal strands when exposed to even mild currents. It reforms if I compress the strands. If I use too much force, it expands as it absorbs the compressing force."

"Meaning?" Kidahin sang, bored.

"I do not know. This is an amazing metal. I can imagine quite a few uses for it if..."

"Whatever," Tialdrin trilled, forestalling the certain list of hypothetical uses Einstika was about to recite. She picked up a probe and retrieved several of Einstika's leftover strands. She put them in test tubes, added various liquids, and put the test tubes in a rack. She clipped the rack to an agitator and watched it swivel the rack side-to-side and back-and-forth.

When it finally stopped, she released the rack and noted the color changes in the liquids.

"This material does not react to acids or bases. It appears absolutely inert. The chromatograph gives a flat line," she trilled in shock.

"Almost makes you think it is—could it be...?" Einstika stammered thoughtfully.

"It is not organic, if that is what you think," Tialdrin sang derisively.

"I know that," Einstika snapped. "I was thinking—alien, maybe?"

"As in an element not on the periodic table? Possibly. Current cosmogony theories say Elleio was a rogue that wandered near our star. The sun snagged and flung her close enough for Tyreniioroneo to capture and pull her into a stable orbit around him."

"A lot of strange stuff could have fallen onto Elleio while in interstellar space," Einstika pointed out.

"Maybe. I did get a small silica reading. But how does it react only to kinetic force and electromagnetic fields?"

"I am sure these notebooks go into surprising detail about it. Mistress, we should take them and the sample with us. Someone at the Uahua'asee'a Clan learning center can look at it when we get back," Einstika sang.

"I agree. Kidahin, move on as soon as Einstika secures the notebooks and sample," the Mistress said.

"Finally. While they do that I want to check the storeroom. I doubt it contains anything of importance, but you never know. We will have to backtrail until we find another passage," Kidahin sang, relieved they would move on soon.

It is us who Death awaits.

The Gracious Mistress's pheromonal imagery fomented feelings of doom in Einstika's empathic mind. The emotional cues should have fixed the right scene in her mind.

But memories of *Londiwe Khoza*—dead bodies, most of them males, smashed flat against the bulkhead—competed in dissonant harmony with the Gracious Mistress's imagery.

Einstika felt the group female metamind shift momentarily before the singers' emotional imagery yanked her back into character. Kidahin had said something about backtrailing? Oh, yes.

"Better to backtrail outside and try entering the building from ground level. Stalking underground is unnatural. Remaining in these plain, parallel hallways is asking for an ambush," she complained bitterly.

Kidahin paused in the storeroom door threshold.

"Yes, you have sense. I have always said so. I hated the featureless straight corridors on *Henri Edda*, hated them even more on *Londiwe Khoza*, and I hate them most here. How these Neh'as'anni tolerate them I do not understand. I wonder if living down here affects the people working here mentally."

"Mentally? As in how amusia affects everyone? Well, working underground in tight tunnels would certainly cause stress. Best we find where the alloy comes from and get out of here," Tialdrin sang.

Kidahin nodded and pushed the storeroom door wide open.

"Spirits!" she trilled in awe.

"What did you find, Kidahin?" the Mistress asked.

"This is no storeroom. The door opens out over an underground quarry capped by a concrete ceiling. I make it about thirty ells deep and a thousand ells square. The perimeter exceeds the Technology Center building footprint by at least a hundred ells on a side. Reinforced iron beams taller than me—one hundred forty-two of them—support the ceiling slabs, the intervening subsoil, and the building above."

Einstika squeezed around Kidahin for a look.

"Oh, my!" she trilled.

"Told you," Kidahin sang.

"This is impressive," Tialdrin sang, preferring to stand over Kidahin's shoulder.

"Mistress, the door opens onto a raised narrow pathway that runs the perimeter of the quarry about halfway above the bottom. Looking left and halfway down the path I see a ramp. It drops down onto the flat roof of a structure. A second ramp, perpendicular to the first, drops from the roof to the quarry floor.

"The floor is level dirt and covered with hundreds of hatches laid out in a grid pattern. I wonder why."

"This is underground excavation on a massive scale. How did they get the rubble out of here?" Einstika trilled.

"The heaped up soil and rocks making up the debris ridge surrounding the industrial complex, maybe?" Kidahin sang.

"It is awfully bright in here. Not a shadow in sight," Tialdrin trilled offhandedly

"Incandescent bulbs, big ones, in the ceiling. Explains the soothing, soft whitish-orange light. Full brightness, too. They must have a direct line to the reactor. Electric mining equipment probably pulls current directly from the reactor mains. But what is it with all those hatches bolted into the ground?" Kidahin sang.

"Too concentrated and too obvious for weapon caches. They would not bury the dead in them, would they?" Einstika trilled with a shudder.

"Nobody buries the dead, not even the Neh'as'anni. The rainforest gives life, and in death we return to the rainforest to give it life. The Neh'as'anni are environmental decadents but not abusers of the dead— the dead!" Tialdrin shrieked in cold-blooded terror.

"Oh, spirits! this is where they bury their spent nuclear fuel," she keened, backing up so fast she tripped over her own tail.

"I do not think so," Einstika sang calmly. "I know something about storing spent uranium, and this is not it."

She absently reached for the radiation detector at her hip anyway and extended the corded sensor to arm's length.

"Mid-blue range," she read from a dial on the instrument. "A bit higher than what we tracked here, but not as high as what we found in the reactor control room. Wait, I am picking up electromagnetic interference—probably from the static shield the..."

"Say again, Team-one. You are breaking up," the Mistress interrupted.

"An EM field is squelching our radios, Mistress. Do you want us to vacate the quarry?"

"Kidahin? What do you think? You have the leadership," the Mistress said.

Kidahin shook her head and snapped her tail.

"We hear you fine, but only because your signal is relayed to us via the APC repeater. Our radios lack the power. We will continue for now, but if our signal garbles, sing out and we will recall to this door and reestablish contact," she sang.

"Affirm," the Mistress said.

Tialdrin ignored the radio problem, preferring to search the floor from high ground.

"Those things stacked next to some of the hatches remind me of field stretchers. I wonder if they evacuated people to a health center."

"I am more interested in what is under those hatches," Kidahin sang.

"More of the material we found in the bell jar," Einstika trilled.

"You think they dug that out of the ground? I thought you said it was a processed alloy," the Mistress interrupted.

"Well, there are naturally occurring alloys. The Neh'as'anni probably put it through some process in the laboratory to get the results we found. They built the Technology Center above the quarry to readily exploit this resource. Seems like a lot of effort. It must have revolutionary properties," Einstika sang.

"You think the unprocessed ore is beneath these hatches? Open one up and take a look," Tialdrin trilled impatiently.

"That is a bad idea," Kidahin sang.

"But why?" Tialdrin trilled.

"Prowling into a mine in Neh'as'anni Clan territory is not my idea of fun. Bad enough being underground as it is," Kidahin complained.

"We should take a look—just to be thorough," Einstika trilled, glancing meaningfully at Kidahin.

"Fine," Kidahin conceded. "Mistress, we will remain in the analysis abode and rest before climbing down to the quarry floor. We will contact you in about twelve hours."

"Affirm. Maintain vigilance."

"Mistress? We have rested and are on the quarry bottom," Einstika sang.

"Affirm, Team-one. What do you see?"

"Pickaxes lying about—abandoned in a hurry. Floor is level compacted dirt," Kidahin trilled. Instinctive caution sang warningly in her ears.

"I see no cast-off breathing apparatus or hazard suits. Gas?" Tialdrin trilled.

"Nothing at detectable levels. Our rebreathers can handle any trace amounts. I urge caution. Neh'tle ke'ne's'tu could be lurking under those hatches," Einstika sang.

Tialdrin shuddered. The name meant industrial pollution personified. It lived——had a kind of intelligence.

"All the more why we should open one and see," she trilled uneasily.

The first of us to fall was Fitever. Her powerful spear could not strike the flesh of the enemy taking her life.

Kidahin ground her teeth as her mental perspective shifted. Fitever had been one of Hlorrithin's mistresses of battle. That she had fallen meant the final battle was underway. She ground her teeth harder as flash-frozen bodies appeared around the hatches, flickering in and out of focus.

Tialdrin, seeing nothing out of the ordinary, glided up to the quarry wall and pressed a hand against it.

"Compacted rocky subsoil. Feels dry. It should not, not underground in a rainforest valley. Water from the saturated ground should leach through the subsoil and fill the quarry. Must be sump pumps, big ones, keeping the water out. Probably inside the structure we climbed down," she sang, her melody ringing with curiosity.

Curious herself, Einstika felt the rough dry surface and nodded.

"This is compact, dense conglomerate. Hard. Rocklike. The entire complex sits atop this stuff," she sang.

"The hatches are important, not dry subsoil," Kidahin complained. "Open this one," she sang, pointing her tail at the hatch closest to her.

A determined Einstika reached down and grabbed the hatch by its handle.

"Tialdrin, grab the flange at the top. We pull together," she sang.

"Got it," Tialdrin sang. "Feels heavy. Why mount heavy naval hatches flat on the ground? Nevermind, ready."

"Not navy grade. More likely the standard security door for industrial buildings. The Neh'as'anni probably have a warehouse stacked full of them. Why pick this hatch, Kidahin? Because it is closest?" Einstika trilled.

"No. The EM field is weakest here. I do not want to get shocked by static electricity," Kidahin sang, watching them swing the hatch up, over, and back onto the ground.

"Look, a hole in the ground. Sides are coated with the same odd alloy we found in the bell jar," Tialdrin trilled mockingly.

"Not the same. Looks more like the ore it comes from. See the black crystals mixed with the metal?"

She paused for a better look.

"This hole angles down into a tunnel. I think these are the actual mine entrances," Einstika sang.

"Can you explore it, Team-one?" the Mistress asked.

"Say no, Tialdrin. This is only a hole in the ground," Kidahin trilled.

"I cannot. Mistress, I think we should take a look," Tialdrin sang.

"A'pea! Fine, I will go first, as usual. I hate these confining pathways. How humans stand such tight spaces I will never understand," Kidahin growled, growing apprehensive.

She climbed into a glittering hole that twisted down around. It vaguely reminded her of the dark emergency maintenance spiral stairway she got stuck in aboard *Londiwe Khoza* until she stepped into a brightly lit orange cave,

"Spirits. This is beautiful, like interior elleiu tree wood. The light bounces off the sides, makes them glow," she sang.

"Is it safe?" Einstika trilled from above.

"The hatchway takes a short twist down into a wide tunnel. It looks natural and not dug out. Reminds me of a gold-plated cavern. Come and see for yourselves."

"Coming. Einstika, after you," Tialdrin sang.

6
THE MOTHER'S TIE

Stanfuree showed the Warrior prowess of our Clan. Nothing can stop her strong arm and although her blows were not fatal, the enemy knew pain.

Tialdrin ground her teeth as she empathized with concurrent historical events. Warrior Mistress of Battle Stanfuree approached from the northwest to reinforce Mistress Fitever's line.

Tialdrin cursed being here with Environmental Interdiction Team-one as they poked through this filthy industrial site. While she understood the importance of their mission, the fact they did not join the battle made her feel like a coward. No doubt the original Team-one Huntresses felt the same.

The shared empathy solidified the reality of the mineshaft—made it feel more real as the view sharpened into a cavern leading through finely spun coppery gold metal. Its slightly oval width and twisting path reminded her of termite burrows.

Portable floodlights on tripods at regular intervals illuminated the length of the shaft. Its metallic walls glittered in the light. Power cables ran along metal floor panels to each tripod. A large table and a cabinet faced the wall on her right. On it sat a computer terminal.

"The lights make the walls glitter beautifully. Looks just like spun metallic amber," Einstika sang.

"I told you so," Kidahin sang.

"Why put a computer here?" Tialdrin trilled.

"Turn it on," the Mistress said.

"Of course, Mistress. Why did we not think of that?" Kidahin trilled at insolence tempo.

"No need for sarcasm, Kidahin. Mistress, it is smashed. Deliberately smashed. We could find out more, but someone is slacking on her job,"

Tialdrin grumbled.

"What? Oh, yes. Sorry," Einstika sang guiltily and began examining the items on the table.

"Mistress, the computer itself is intact, but someone smashed the picture tube. The printer is not a hard copy terminal. It has no keyboard. Printouts on the table, they read like medical text to me. This is a healer's station."

That brought a curious Tialdrin to her side.

"Einstika is correct," she sang. "I found a small dispensary cabinet filled with pills. The labels identify a variety of anti-radiation, vitamins, and amphetamines."

"Something a hard working crew would need?" Kidahin wondered aloud.

"Maybe if the environment was mildly radioactive, but I read only mild levels here—barely above normal background radiation. No sign of hazard gear. Whoever worked down here did not wear protective gear," Tialdrin complained. "This is a healer aide station, nothing remarkable in itself. Keep going. I wonder where the cables lead," she added.

"Follow them?" Einstika suggested.

"Lighted path, so we follow," Tialdrin sang.

"I will scout ahead," Kidahin sang and increased her pace into the shaft.

Tialdrin first and then Einstika followed about ten seconds apart. Several minutes into their prowl the sound of feet striking metal plates began to grate on Einstika's ears. She stopped and rapped her fist on one of them.

"This plate is aluminum," she sang.

"Loose, not bolted down. Makes a lot of noise," Kidahin growled. "Wasteful, too. Why put these here?"

"No rails, so no handcar," Einstika sang. "What about pushcarts? No need for rails, but a smooth surface means carts and not just foot travel."

"I think so, too," Tialdrin sang thoughtfully. "Concrete level floors for rails and heavy loads. Drop-in panels and pushcarts for light ones."

"Dou'tu'tay! Dead end," Kidahin cursed. "Mistress, the shaft dead-ends into an intersecting shaft. The cables lead to the right, but the left shaft looks more promising. It gleams brightly, but I see no floodlights from here."

"Follow the cables. Find out what they need all the power for," the Mistress replied.

"Mining equipment would make the most sense," Einstika sang and then hesitated.

The dark path filled her with dread.

"Are you staying here?" Tialdrin asked her, concerned.

"We do not split up. Follow me," Kidahin sang.

"Quit wasting time, Einstika. This is only a short prowl," Tialdrin sang.

Unsettling visions also teased Kidahin's eyes. She began to doubt what she was seeing and shook her head at the side effects of stalking underground and ignored ghastly memories of *Londiwe Khoza* fading into and out of sight with increasing regularity.

The visions melted into the overwhelming ambient amber glow surrounding them.

"Hold," she trilled. "Something is wrong. Either we are in the wrong shaft, or it has caved in up ahead."

"Clarify, Team-one," the Mistress droned loudly. "'Something is wrong' is not an acceptable description."

"Not a cave-in. Looks more like a dark hole ahead. Maybe the deposit ends here," Kidahin sang warily.

The three Hunters gathered around the hole and cautiously peered inside.

"The shaft ends here, and my torchlight does not hit anything. The cables lead into the darkness."

Tialdrin glided up next to Kidahin.

"Look, a light on the other side. Another shaft?" she sang.

"And they need electricity, obviously. That is why the cables go in there," Einstika sang. "I wonder why they did not set up lights in the darkness?"

"Floodlights here and floodlights on the other side. They need the lights to mine the ore. Best guess is no ore in the dark space. Wait, are those people in there?" Kidahin trilled.

"People? What people? Where?" Einstika trilled.

"Straight ahead, in the dark cavern. Look slightly off-center from the lights on the other side."

"I see nothing but glare," Einstika sang unsteadily. "You are seeing things, memories of—terrible things."

"I hate uncertainty—makes me jumpy," Kidahin complained as spectral afterimages traced vague facial outlines across her retinas.

"Nobody is here, Kidahin. The light is only glittering on dark rocks," Tialdrin sang.

"You do not sound convinced. Nevermind, I will go first," Kidahin insisted and spoke into her suit mike.

"Mistress, the shaft widens into a large dark cavern. The walls are covered with the same dark crystals we found mixed with the amber ore at the mine entrance."

"Kidahin, point your torch left," Tialdrin sang.

"Why? See someone?" she trilled apprehensively.

"Of course not. Look at the walls. This is some kind of silicate deposit. Black, glittery, and rather course-like black sand—almost like industrial diamonds," Einstika sang.

"Black sandstone? A sandstone deposit? See those picks. They ran into this stuff while mining. Did they dig this cavern out or was it naturally this way when they got here?" Tialdrin wondered.

"Probably had to dig around before finding the deposit again. Once found, they ran the cables straight through to the other side. That shaft on the other side will pass under the debris ridge surrounding the complex if it keeps going in that direction," Einstika trilled.

Kidahin listened while kicking at the cables.

"These carry more current than what mere floodlights need. Just one of them is as thick as my ankle. What did they need three for? Mining equipment? Some kind of industrial activity? More is going on here than what we have found so far," Kidahin trilled.

Phosphorescent shimmering glittered throughout the black crystal cavern.

"Hold! Movement ahead," Kidahin warned.

"Reflections, nothing more," Tialdrin sang reasonably.

"No. This did not glitter. Crystals embedded in solid rock sparkle from where they sit. This crossed in front of me."

"I see nothing. Light playing tricks in the dark. We should cross back into the lighted shaft," Einstika sang with more confidence than she felt.

"You are right. It is nothing. Keep an eye on the walls anyway. Mistress, we are crossing through the sandstone deposit."

Kidahin turned off her torch and cursed the background glitter.

"The light from both ends makes this stuff glitter just enough to ruin my night vision," she complained and clicked her torch back on.

She aimed the beam at the ceiling.

It vanished into the darkness, adding slightly to the glitter.

"Ceiling extends above us a fair bit."

She panned the beam in a circle.

"This is quite wide and uniform. This is natural. Nobody dug this out."

Not a minute later Einstika froze, hyperalert. The others continued, leaving her behind in the glittery darkness.

Dread images of a starship corridor shimmered around her, rippling like heat waves off rainforest cliffs as the voice of the Gracious Mistress of the Singing People banished them from sight but not the vaguely familiar dread entwined with them.

"This is no dug-out sandstone deposit. This is a geode," Einstika trilled.

Kidahin paused mid-step and snapped her ears in agreement.

"So? Do not dwell on it," she sang.

"Terrible coincidence, though," Tialdrin trilled. An understatement, she knew. The last time they found a geode of this size they ended up ritually executing three human males for their part in plotting to kill Warleader Delwyn.

"Are you coming?" she asked.

"Yes, yes I am," Einstika sang, relieved. The hypervigilant seizure lasted barely a few seconds. The fading hyperawareness made her jumpy. Edginess tainted her pheromones. The others smelled it on her scent. She knew it because she smelled the same chaotic emotions on Kidahin. She felt it, too, but was trying to suppress the feelings that triggered hypervigilant reactions.

Einstika focused on Tialdrin's scent. Wary feelings tormented her as well, but at least she did not struggle to control the empathic traumatic stress responses Kidahin was dealing with.

Her wellnessmistress training at least helped her deal with pheromonal empathy and the emotional mind.

"Lucky her," Einstika growled aloud.

"What was that?" Kidahin sang and then paused.

"Hold up a minute. Mistress, we reached the other side and are entering the shaft. The metallic amber looks more—refined? No sign of the dark crystals embedded here. On this side of the geode the shaft looks natural."

It was so unfortunate to lose her so soon.

The verse and its pheromonal accompaniment told them Mistress of Battle Stanfuree and her forces had been lost, a disaster because A'tayotan hierarchy battle doctrine discouraged fighting battles of attrition. Losing Stanfuree doomed them to fight a battle of attrition against the Neh'as'anni.

That thought alone infuriated her. Traditionally, the Territorial Boundaries of Rage and Forgiveness said to find resting places, which meant people had to lay their rage to rest. Their mission had been to lay the rage of the world upon north central La'huaset and its ni'zakhon technology clans.

"This stuff is simply amazing," Einstika trilled, picking at the wall with a fingernail. "Some kind of naturally occurring crystalline alloy. How was it formed? Magma?"

"Nonsense. This cavern may resemble a lava tube, but magma is molten rock, not metal," Tialdrin sang.

"Well, the Neh'as'anni did not refine this stuff down here. This must have been a fissure filled with unique metal deposits. When the asteroid hit Elleio farside eons ago, it caused volcanic upheavals here on nearside. The fissure split and lava flowed through, mixing and naturally alloying the deposit. This raw ore is what the Neh'as'anni were researching here. I can think of no better hypothesis that fits all the facts."

"Someone sounds touchy," Kidahin sang.

"Why do you think they did not make this alloy there?" the Mistress asked, ignoring Kidahin.

"It is evident to reason. When we first entered the shaft, we found an oddly textured metal with sandstone grit mixed into it. These metallic crystals closely resemble the sample we found in the metallurgy lab. If this is a metal, then it crystallizes differently under a wide variety of circumstances. It reminds me of rudimentary metalworking. The ancients heat-treated the same piece of metal at different temperatures to get a harder edge and a softer spine. It happens because the metal forms different crystal structures at different temperatures. The same thing happened here naturally with the gold, copper, and whatever alloying elements were inside the geode originally besides the black sandstone," Einstika sang.

"These walls look too regularly formed," Kidahin sang abruptly.

"Lava tubes do have unique features. You cannot think the Neh'as'anni tunneled these," Tialdrin sang.

"I know I saw someone down here."

"Spirits, Kidahin. Really? I do not want to hear this. I keep seeing dead bodies in the dark as it is," Einstika trilled.

"Not the dead, thank the spirits. Look at that and explain it, please."

"Dou'tu'tay, what is that?" Einstika keened in alarm.

"What about it?" Tialdrin sang calmly.

"Spirits, they are here. I knew it all along!" Einstika keened.

"Team-one, what are you seeing?" the Mistress demanded.

"Well, Mistress, it is hard to describe, but I see a face in the stone," Kidahin sang.

Her courage and skill would have let the rest of us survive.

"I smell them all around us. Nosey females. They are coming: Warrior females," Einstika snarled, flattening her ears against her short, red ringlets.

After what I just saw, no blinking lamp of any color can tell me all is well here.

Einstika snapped her tail in shocked reflex. That did not come from empathy with the singers. It came from her own pheromones, as if she empathized with her own emotion-laden scent mixed with the Gracious Mistress and her singers, altering the scent-linked empathy they all shared—at least momentarily.

"Forgive me," she trilled. "I thought for a moment I was with Mimiran and—Nynava—on that a'pea shipwreck again. Kidahin is right, though. It does look like a—a face."

"You are imagining things. Both of you. I see random patterns in the stone. That is all," Tialdrin sang.

"You think so?" Kidahin keened, glaring at the golden stalagmite and its vaguely Eyloni features.

"That pillar looks like it has someone encased in it," she trilled and then pointed at other pillars with her tail.

"These too, people encased in stone," she trilled softly.

"Alloy, not stone. This is the same metal we found along the shaft. The only difference is the deposits in the shaft look finely spun. This looks more—fluid—like golden, frozen mercury," Einstika sang.

"Hey, look, another computer," Tialdrin sang, snapping her tail at a table built into the wall.

"These heavy duty cables must power more than just lights and a computer," Kidahin sang critically.

"The floodlights use sodium bulbs," Einstika sang. "The cables run from the entrance to here and beyond as far as I can see, a lot of cable. Mistress? How well are you reading us?"

"Clean and clear. Why?" the Mistress promptly asked.

"Really? How odd. Good, but still odd."

"Why?" Kidahin trilled, alert.

"There should be some signal loss. We are in a tube coated with metal deposits. The APC repeater receives our radio signals and boosts them to Na'di Island. I am surprised the repeater gets enough signal. I need to think about this," Einstika sang.

"Think all you want. I am not sure it will get you closer to an answer," Tialdrin sang dryly.

"Wait a minute. I have an idea," Einstika sang.

"Will we like this idea?" Kidahin trilled.

"Wait and see."

"What are you—hey!" Tialdrin keened in warning. "Are you trying to electrocute yourself?"

"No. Remember the testing I did in the metallurgy lab? This alloy falls apart when exposed to electromagnetic fields. If I strip a wire and expose it to the alloy...."

"You are brilliant," Kidahin interrupted.

"I am not so sure about this," Tialdrin warned.

"Oh, come on. What is the worst that can happen?" Einstika sang.

"Einstika, stop. You do not know if...," the Mistress began.

"Mistress, where is your sense of adventure? Relax. I am a techmistress. I know how to handle electricity," Einstika interrupted. "I just need to get current flowing through this pillar. The alloy will either break down or melt, but it should just crumble apart."

"Well...," Kidahin trilled as every other floodlight abruptly went dark.

"You just killed half the lights," Kidahin trilled.

"You called me brilliant not ten minutes ago!" Einstika snapped.

"Before you killed half the lights down here, you mean? And I count more than a hundred pillars. You cannot free up enough bare wire to test them all without plunging us into total darkness."

"This is not a mine. This is a research site," Tialdrin trilled at imperative tempo.

"Digging in the ground for ore sounds like mining to me," Kidahin pointed out.

"One of the heavy cables feeds into a junction box on the floor. From there these wire bundles go across the floor to all the pillars," Tialdrin sang, pointing her tail at the cluster of leads running from Einstika's pillar to the nearby computer.

"These are electrodes. The instrument next to the computer is an EEG, an electroencephalograph. It records brainwave activity."

"All the more reason to try my idea on this one," Einstika sang. "When I touch these wires to the pillar, like so, the alloy should...."

"Ah! It crumbles apart into handfuls of wiggly maggot-like clumps," Kidahin trilled in satisfaction.

"The individual crystals slough off when exposed to current. Watch," Einstika sang as she brushed the wires across the upper third of the pillar.

"This is just a stalagmite of processed alloy. Why they store it like this I have no idea—oh, spirits!"

"Dou'tu'tay!" Tialdrin keened.

"I told you I saw a face in the metal!" Kidahin keened.

"Status report, Team-one. Now!" the Mistress demanded.

"We are safe, Mistress. For now," Kidahin sang.

"I want to curl up in my hometree abode and cry," Einstika trilled.

But we Eyloni know no fear and fight with valor, no matter what.

The singers strengthened Kidahin's resolve and gave her voice a dispassionate tone.

"Mistress, Einstika uncovered a body embedded in the pillar, a male. She dissolved the alloy down to his waist. Electrodes are attached to his head. He looks remarkably well-preserved, as though he was still alive. I cannot tell what caused his death."

"Suffocation, maybe? The same that killed the others? A mutated form of limb rot?" Einstika trilled.

"No," Tialdrin sang, certain. "His arms and chest look healthy, too healthy. Dead people lose their skin colors quickly. Yellows first, then oranges, and finally the reds turn light green soon after death. He looks just fine."

"This is vile. Could the other pillars have bodies in them, too?" Kidahin trilled at the same time.

Four hazy dead bodies, smashed and frozen to where the wall met the deck, clouded her vision.

"This is wrong. There is only one body here, and it is not smashed or frozen," she trilled aloud.

"The Neh'as'anni formed this alloy around him. He is not frozen. But why encase him in metal? Contamination containment? Did they put him into this stuff alive?" Einstika sang.

"Recall to the quarry," Kidahin keened at imperative pitch.

"Get out of there, Team-one," the Mistress yelled at the same time.

"How could they do that to him?" Einstika trilled as she ran. "Mistress, we are withdrawing now. This is a bad place, worse than anything I ever saw..."

"Movement ahead! Someone in combat armor. Take cover," Kidahin interrupted.

"What is that?" Tialdrin trilled.

Einstika watched as a golden figure stepped out from behind a pillar and advanced on them.

"Spirits!" Kidahin trilled. "Mistress, someone wearing combat armor approaches. She is wearing modern, actually ultramodern, battle dress. Permission to engage with firearms?"

"Attempt to evade," the Mistress insisted.

"Kidahin, do not fire. I do not think this is a person, and it is not making hostile moves!" Einstika sang.

"Yet. Move. Now!" Kidahin hissed, drew her sidearm and emptied the clip.

"Those bullets pack a punch yet did not even scratch it. Withdraw. Follow the cables back," she trilled.

A scream of despair keened after them, echoing throughout the hollow geode.

"Oh, spirits!" Einstika keened.

"What is it?" Kidahin trilled on exiting the geode into the mineshaft.

"The male in the pillar. He is alive! He is screaming, but I cannot understand what he is saying."

"No time for him now. Run!" Kidahin trilled.

Twenty minutes later Kidahin called a halt.

"We should have reached the quarry by now," she trilled in confusion.

"Catch your breath but do not count on a long rest," she added.

"What was that thing?" Tialdrin sang.

"Not sure. A defender, certainly. It blended into the pillars so well I could not tell if it stepped from behind one or out of one."

"But what was it?" Tialdrin persisted.

"Some kind of armor or alloy belting, I think. Whatever it was, it stopped bullets designed to penetrate synthetic-fiber armor," Kidahin snapped.

She paused a moment before continuing.

"And yet, she did not appear armed. The spun metal coating looked encumbering. Keep moving. That thing can blend into the surrounding deposits," she added.

"So, now what?" Tialdrin wondered.

"We abort, unless the Mistress objects."

"No abort. Recall to the quarry floor and reevaluate. Hlorrithin and his mistresses of battle have destroyed all Neh'as'anni modern weapons capability but lost two armies and their mistresses of battle in the process. He closes on them armed with traditional swords, spears, and bows and is moving into open-field battle formations as we speak."

"The Neh'as'anni were developing something very advanced here. Medical, perhaps. We did not find direct evidence of weapon development. That said, this amber alloy certainly has military potential. What if some advanced weapon system can be fired from here?" Kidahin sang.

"Kidahin!" Einstika keened at combat-imminent pitch. "Something follows."

Kidahin snapped a fresh clip into her gun and covered Einstika as they withdrew.

Thrandra and Twithora swiftly used their arrows.

Tialdrin winced. Mistress of Battle Thrandra and Mistress of Battle Twithora had begun their ill-fated assault.

"Mistress," she sang. "I recognize the twisting patterns here. We should reach the quarry hatch any minute now.

Minutes later Tialdrin slowed to a trot, hesitated, and stopped.

"Kidahin, the path ahead is blocked. Not a cave-in, either. The alloy deposits have somehow expanded into the shaft and pinched it closed," she keened.

"What? Wait, are we trapped?" Einstika trilled as pools of frozen gore appeared all around her. More partially liquefied remains slid slowly down the walls to accumulate and freeze on the deck plating.

Kidahin smelled the terror riding Einstika's pheromones. The visions they conjured in her own mind pulled her into a memory of bodies, different bodies and not collision casualties. They looked relatively intact. Her mind struggled against inconsistency. These bodies had similar wounds and combat wounds tended to randomness. These looked deliberate—executions? The dead humans on *Londiwe Khoza*. Dead males then, and dead males now. No wonder this place was destroyed so long ago.

"Kidahin, snap out of it," Tialdrin trilled. "We are trapped!"

Kidahin blinked and shook her head as the memory faded, but the feelings it brought hovered persistently in the back of her mind.

"I think not," she sang. "See how the alloy avoids the cables? Can we squeeze through?"

She glided slowly around Tialdrin and followed the cables as far as she could.

"Tight squeeze, and I see kinks and bends too tight to crawl through," she snapped irritably.

"Electricity," Tialdrin sang. "Strip a wire from the cable and do the same thing Einstika did to the pillar."

"Might not work," Einstika objected. "The pillar was small, and I dissolved about a third of it to expose the male. This much material blocking our way is on another scale altogether. Waving a hot wire against this is like whittling a stick with my fingernail. It will take time."

"Then get to it," Kidahin trilled at imperative pitch.

Einstika grunted and pulled tools from her techmistress harness. She spent several minutes cutting into the casing to expose wires, cut two of them, and stripped off their insulation.

"Hope this works," she sang softly and stretched into the pinched-off shaft as far as the loose wires allowed and touched them to the coppery alloy.

It promptly fell away in wiggly fistfuls, but not from where she expected.

Instead, the side of the shaft crumbled inward. Einstika snapped her ears, perplexed, but shifted sideways and slowly waved the wires in a circling motion at the widening hole.

The alloy fell away like grains of coarse golden sand. Within minutes Einstika tunneled three ells into the deposit, a hole barely wide enough to crawl through.

At four ells she broke into a dark, roughly parallel shaft.

"I think this leads to another hatch on the quarry floor," she sang at victory scale.

"Why go through the wall rather than the pinched-off point?" Kidahin trilled.

"I tried going forward, but the wall alloy dissolves faster, much faster. What seals the shaft looks more—refined?" Einstika sang.

"Try again. We have no idea where this shaft leads," Kidahin insisted.

"Takes too long, way too long. You seriously want to risk getting encased like that male in the pillar?" Einstika trilled.

"Fair point. Lead on. Tialdrin and I will follow," Kidahin sang.

She waited until the two cleared the narrow breach before joining them.

"This shaft bears slightly right," she sang.

A few minutes later the shaft dead-ended at an intersection.

"We reached a junction," Einstika trilled in disgust. "Dou'tu'tay, I was hoping for a straight path out."

"I see light down the left path," Tialdrin trilled.

"Both left and right. One is just much brighter than the other," Kidahin pointed out.

"Which way?" Einstika trilled.

"Right. Going left will bypass the quarry," Kidahin trilled at insistence pitch.

Thirty ells into the shaft she thought she heard the soft, whispery sound of light rain on leaves.

"Tialdrin, Einstika. When I say run, do it."

"Spirits!" Einstika trilled under her breath. "That cannot be rain. Not underground."

"Team-one, status update!" the Mistress demanded.

"Run. Do not look back," Kidahin trilled, ignoring the A'tayotan Mistress.

"What is behind us?" Tialdrin trilled.

"Not behind, it sounds like it is all around us. Run!" Kidahin keened at imperative pitch.

The floor sprouted a golden stalagmite right in front of Kidahin.

She drew her sidearm and fired into the smooth golden pillar.

"Spirits! It leapt out of the floor," she trilled.

"Not out of the floor. It is the floor. This is some kind of auxetic material. It shrinks and compresses when absorbing impacts," Einstika sang.

"It looks unstable. Could the Neh'as'anni make a weapon out of this?" Tialdrin trilled.

"Of course!" Kidahin sang.

"No. That does not explain the male in the pillar!" Einstika trilled.

"Of course it does—antipersonnel. Encase the enemy in metal."

"Then why the electrodes?" Tialdrin objected.

"Einstika, why are you stopping? Get away from it!" Kidahin trilled at imperative tempo.

"No, and put that coward's weapon away," Tialdrin sang.

Einstika had indeed stopped. An idea born of inspiration came as if from the spirits themselves.

"Be calm. It is not making threatening gestures. This cannot be solid alloy. I think this is another encapsulated male," Einstika sang.

"What is happening, Team-one?" the Mistress screamed frantically.

"A metallic shape came up out of the floor. Einstika is getting a closer look," Kidahin sang as she pulled her sidearm and took aim—just in case.

"Easy, Kidahin. It is not attacking," Tialdrin trilled.

"Just standing there. Why, I wonder. It looks twisted—mutated," Einstika trilled.

"Mutated? It could be toxic. Get away from it, Team-one," the Mistress ordered.

"See? We have our orders. Fall back, slowly," Kidahin trilled.

"A'pea you, Kidahin. You, too, Mistress. We cannot let this thing slip away. Mistress, this thing looks like an effigy, as if made by someone who never saw an Eyloni before. It solidified into a figure. The anatomy is there, but the proportions are off. I wonder how it sees," Einstika sang analytically.

The misshapen golden figure stepped forward.

"Mistress, it is moving. On feet this time," Kidahin sang, maintaining her aim.

"Do not shoot. Whatever happens, do not shoot."

The figure knelt and extended arms to Einstika.

"What is it doing? Surrendering?" Einstika sang.

"You think so?" Tialdrin trilled, clearly not convinced.

"Well, just look. Does this look like a fighting stance? It wants something," Einstika sang.

"Be careful," Kidahin warned.

"I am careful," Einstika sang unsteadily.

"It has not moved," Tialdrin sang critically. "It does not breathe. It reminds me of a translucent version of the same alloy we found in the bell jar. Einstika, do you still have it?"

"I do, why?"

"It is the only thing we have it could want."

"Good point. Should I give it to—it?"

"Yes," Tialdrin sang. "I think so."

"Well, I suppose—okay. Mistress, I am placing the alloy sample into the hands of a mutant male," Einstika sang as she dropped the sample into the outstretched amber hand.

"And nothing happens," Tialdrin sang irritably.

"Wait. Look again," Kidahin sang as she watched the sample melt into the outstretched hand.

"Spirits. It absorbed the sample into itself. This is amazing. We need a science team here!" Einstika sang.

7
THE DISINTERESTED MOTHER

But arrows cannot kill neh'tle ke'ne's'tu.

"The science teams came later, Einstika. You know this," Tialdrin sang.

"I know my history songs as well as you do," Einstika trilled. "But if I had been there, I would have sent in a team of techmistresses and not the Team-one Environmental Interdiction team they did send."

"Enough!" Kidahin sang. "You know none of the techmistresses were sent in early. Pay attention and stay in character. It is hard enough for me to do that as it is without you distracting…"

Garbled static blasting from their hazard suit speakers interrupted Kidahin mid-rant.

"Say again, Mistress. I did not catch that," Einstika sang into her suit mike.

"That did not come from me," the Mistress replied promptly.

A second blast of garbled notes screeched from their speakers, longer and more varied this time.

"What is that, a warning?" Kidahin asked Einstika.

"Powerful transmitter or very close to us. I cannot find a direction to its source. My best guess is below us—down where we found the mutant male."

"I have doubts about that being a mutant. I doubt even more that it was male. Better possibility is some kind of remote-operated drone," Tialdrin keened.

"Dou'tu'tay! These a'pea Neh'as'anni La'huaset Eyloni are cowards," Kidahin trilled.

"Quiet, Kidahin. Listen. It is speaking again," Einstika sang.

"Staccato beat, and with so much dissonance I cannot understand it.

Yet I can almost imagine an accompanying melody that would clear the static," Kidahin sang.

"That is it!" Einstika sang as she pricked her ears at Kidahin.

"A voice processor," she continued. "Something like the scrambler linking us with the A'tayotan Mistress on Na'di Island. It probably uses a similar technique to the one that turns her voice monotonous."

"I do not think the scrambler should take all the blame," Tialdrin trilled in laughter.

"What are you trying to say?" the Mistress said dryly.

"This may be some kind of autonomous perimeter defense unit," Tialdrin replied innocently.

"Doubtful. Perimeter defenses sing a simple 'get out' in the clear. No one garbles a warning," Kidahin sang.

"Not if it alerts defenders to an intruder presence—such as us," Einstika sang.

"Looks at this!" Tialdrin keened, pointing to the walls. "They are shifting around us."

"A drone runs on electricity. The current is triggering the metallic alloy lining the walls. Any simple impact will cause it to contract and swell, effectively entombing us here. Just like it did to the male we found embedded in the pillar," Einstika trilled.

"Recall back to the tunnel handcar, now!" Kidahin keened at combat-imminent tempo.

"Team-one, what is happening?" the Mistress yelled.

Kidahin ignored her. Something made from the same wall material was advancing on them, hugging the churning wall for cover.

She drew her sidearm, aimed right of the advancing drone, and fired one shot.

Garbled speech screeched from the walking horror.

She ignored it and concentrated on the metallic-amber device as it advanced.

She squeezed the trigger slowly and methodically until she emptied the fourteen-round clip. With each bullet's impact the amber alloy coating the drone swelled slightly, absorbing the impact.

"Einstika, the bullets make the skin swell when they hit."

"Auxetic materials do that. Mistress, are you hearing this?" she trilled into her mike.

"Backtrail immediately to the tunnel entrance. Get outside and swing around to the other side of the building. Find a ground-level door and get in that way," the Mistress demanded.

"Affirm. Everyone, recall to me and follow!" Kidahin keened.

"Two hours and still no handcar, Kidahin. This is not the right tunnel," Einstika complained.

"It is," Kidahin sang brightly. "See? The handcar is up ahead," she added, snapping her ears forward.

"I want a rest," Einstika complained as she slowed to a walk.

"Rest on the handcar while Kidahin and I do the pumping. Once on the handcar you can start taking your equipment apart so it can go through the airlock," Tialdrin sang.

"No. Too easy to lose a screw or some small part while moving," Einstika sang irritably.

"Oh," Tialdrin sang.

Kidahin scowled at the handcar. The last time she saw it she nearly shot it with an arrow, but now she wanted to embrace it like a long-lost lover.

"We rest here. I trust this tunnel more than the blast-damaged buildings outside," Tialdrin sang.

"A good idea," Kidahin sang and then froze as phosphorescent retinal afterimages flashed across her vision. For a brief instant the tunnel shimmered, losing its round concrete tube appearance as it became a blue and burnished stainless steel corridor aboard *Londiwe Khoza*.

She blinked and the vision vanished.

"Something—no, forget it. I thought I saw—nevermind. Get some sleep," Kidahin trilled.

"I will eat first," Einstika trilled shakily.

"You sound unsettled, Einstika. Why?" the Mistress asked.

"I keep seeing—impossible things."

"Me, too," Kidahin sang softly.

"Have you decided on how you want to proceed?" the Mistress asked.

"Not yet," Kidahin sang, cursing the Warrior female and her scrambler-rendered flat voice.

"Do we take the handcar back to the steps leading to the airlock, or do we continue down the tunnel?" Kidahin asked as she stretched herself awake. Two hours was too short a nap.

"And then what? Go left, right, or back to the APC? There is a lot of technological development going on here. Let Hlorrithin deal with it," Einstika complained.

"Hlorrithin soon faces the fight of his life," the Mistress reminded them. "And besides, I told you to get above ground and approach the building from the left side."

"Kidahin, what is happening? You are worrying me," Tialdrin sang softly.

"I know. I cannot help it. I know what happens here from the history songs. This feels different. Something is wrong. I cannot get a feel for this place, as if the tunnels and rooms are shifting locations around us. It makes the hair on my pons stick out."

"I see that," Tialdrin sang dryly. "But you feel something else. I smell it in you scent."

"Just as we reached the handcar, for a moment—the time it takes to draw breath—I thought I was back on *Londiwe Khoza*."

"The shipwrecked human destroyer? I guess that makes sense. These buildings do have an almost human feel about them, and no Eyloni builds like this even in our time. Do you just remember that ship, or are you experiencing traumatic stress…?"

"Team-one? Did you reach the end of the tunnel?" the Mistress demanded.

Kidahin deliberately turned the repeater off.

"Spirits, but I am hating that Warrior right now," she keened loudly before switching the repeater back on.

"We will ride the handcar to the exit," Kidahin growled as she and Tialdrin began rocking the hand pump.

"Wrong direction," Kidahin grumbled. "Wait for the wheels to stop and pump in the opposite direction."

"Wait," Einstika trilled. "We are not going back to the stairs?"

"No. The ground above us slopes down. We should find another portal-sealed tunnel entrance going this way."

"Or a dead-end," Einstika snapped. "I hope you are right so I can keep my equipment in one piece. I do not trust the airlock. How far this way do you think the tunnel goes?"

Kidahin happened to point her torch forward just in time.

"Slow down before we hit the stop block!" she keened as the portal rushed toward them.

"We reached the entrance, Mistress. The portal is not locked and opens easily. Looks like we rode to the far right of the building. We are on pavement next to a retaining wall. Tialdrin, Einstika, follow me.

"Mistress, broken ground, crevices, and reinforced concrete rubble surrounds us. Even taking a wide sweep around to the other side of the building means climbing over a lot of rubble."

They passed shattered buildings, backtrailing several times to find a safe path.

"Mistress, we are between two partially collapsed buildings that look unstable and ready to collapse at any moment. The safest path is to prowl to the perimeter and climb the debris ridge and come in from the airfield side and behind the building."

"Speed is paramount, Team-one. Take the fastest path."

"The fastest path means climbing over and down toppled walls. I am not going through that!" Tialdrin keened.

"Do not be an infant. Fine, I will go," Kidahin trilled, annoyed.

"No, let me," Einstika sang. "I am lighter than either of you, so just rig a harness and lower me over the collapsed wall. Pull me up if the wall below it cannot support my weight."

"I like this idea less than Tialdrin does," Kidahin complained. "The safer path is to walk a quarter-way around the complex and come in from the opposite direction."

"Let me do this. Loop a rope through my techmistress harness," Einstika sang.

"Rope? You? Who needs rope? Any of us can climb anything," Tialdrin sang.

"Almost anything. The tallest tree and the steepest cliff are natural and stable. Even landslides stabilize over time, but blasted buildings are not natural and I doubt they settled much in a few days. You cannot rely on it, and I am sensible enough to know I cannot trust anything artificial."

"Me, too, which is why you do not hear me laughing," Kidahin sang as she looped the rope around the harness and tied it. "Put this on, hang onto the rope, and I will lower you down."

Einstika nodded and jumped over the toppled concrete wall and hung there, looking down.

"The rest of the wall shattered and buckled as it slammed into the building next to it. Lots of stress fractures, too. I can jump through some of them. Only the reinforcing rods kept the concrete from crumbling to dust. Spirits, this looks like impact damage."

"Artillery fire?" Tialdrin wondered.

"Not possible. Shelling cannot hit the exact same spot every single time. This looks hammered."

Einstika listened, shrugging in doubt. The incidental motion sent her spinning lazily.

Her foot struck the wall at an angle.

It promptly crumbled into dusty rubble, taking her with it.

"Einstika!" Tialdrin trilled as the rope whizzed through her fingers.

"Pull me up!" Einstika keened as the rope snagged on a twisted metal rod.

"Dou'tu'tay!" she keened, choking and sputtering as she dangled wildly in a cloud of dust. "I am fine, just fine. The rope snagged. I see a piece of wall on the ground below me. Looks like it fell onto a road cut into the hillside. Can you lower me onto it?"

"Does it look safe?" Tialdrin trilled.

"I think so. It covers the road like a bridge. Looks like the road goes around the Technology Center building. Must be how they get vehicle to the airfield from here. Big cracks below. I can see clear to the pavement so no rubble under it. Climb down and see for yourself."

"What else do you see?" the Mistress asked.

"Oh, I am fine. Thank you for asking," Einstika growled.

"What do you see?" Kidahin sang impatiently.

"Blasted walls and pieces of roof. Wait, I found a split in the wall wide enough to jump down to the road below."

Einstika untied the rope from her techmistress harness and jumped through the especially wide crack.

"Okay, some rubble down here but the road is otherwise clear. It leads out of the embankment and toward—oh, these are new, "she trilled.

"What is new?" Kidahin trilled.

Tialdrin gave the rope to Kidahin and climbed down over the twisted reinforcing rod. From there she jumped onto the section of shattered wall. She eyed the crumbling split Einstika jumped through warily. She cautiously stepped over bent reinforcing rods and watched Einstika prowl below.

"I see what you mean—treads pressed into the dust," she sang.

Kidahin landed next to Tialdrin and looked down.

"Landscaping vehicles, if I am not mistaken. Footprints next to them, booted footprints at that, heading toward the airfield," she sang.

"I wonder what this place is really all about," Einstika growled.

"Only two options present themselves: a technology development center or a command center for the combined defense forces of the Neh'as'anni and their allied technology clans," the Mistress growled.

"True. Either one explains erecting buildings on this scale," Kidahin sang.

"Wait. Why assume this place has anything to do with defense forces? Every clan has territorial defenses, and the Neh'as'anni have no territorial ambitions. They always gave their technology away freely because they consider their advances as public goods. That is why it has been so hard to recover Neh'as'anni technology and get it under the Be'atika Senge's control," Tialdrin sang.

"And it stands to reason they built this place for the public development of social technology, does it not? The Neh'as'anni pushed their industrial base beyond all reason and before any environmental impact studies could be completed," Einstika sang.

"Look at these tracks," Kidahin interrupted. "This footwear has soles. You rarely see that even in combat."

"Who wants to wear footwear? Bad enough when I have to take mine out of the carry sack and put them on when we suspect contaminated ground. They make my feet hurt," Einstika complained.

"Wearing footwear would depend on what they were developing here. Technologies based on fossil fuels and nuclear fission are overgrown with hazards. What more hazards might exist when new technologies are being developed?" Tialdrin trilled rhetorically.

"We will soon see. The road branches just past the building. Looks like the main road leads to the airfield, but I see a fork that branches behind the building. See it? And there is a door down there, too," Einstika sang.

"How close are you to the building?" the Mistress asked.

"A few hundred ells from it," Kidahin sang offhandedly.

"Minutes away, and we are standing out in the open," Tialdrin sang excitedly.

"We need to get out of the open. Besides, I want to see what they have been building here. Can you read what the sign on the building says?" Einstika trilled.

"Not from here. Should be a door below it, though," Kidahin sang.

Without any doubt, their brave spirits will find their path to the Oyya Web of the spirits.

The verse and the pheromonal odor accompanying it told them that by now Thrandra, Twithora, and their archers had fallen.

"Well, this is not entirely unexpected," Einstika trilled, scowling at the writing on the front of the building well above her head.

"No door, but this is clearly a research center if the writing is any indication," she added.

"'*New Dawn*'," Tialdrin trilled. "Sounds pretty, and given the sloppiness of Neh'as'anni environmental compliance measures, I mean ominous. How are we getting inside?"

"Are you blind?" Einstika trilled at insolence pitch. "We go through the door just around the corner."

"That is green. Probably an emergency exit," Kidahin trilled.

"What other door do you suggest?" Tialdrin trilled mockingly.

"What about the door further down the left side?" Kidahin suggested.

"Too far down, and I think it opens into an addition and annex of some kind. They probably park the excavation vehicles there. Who cares about construction equipment?" Einstika sang

Tialdrin twitched an elegant ear at Einstika.

"The annex is big enough to store excavation equipment, but no vehicle is getting through that door. It is just a way in without having to go around back to where they drive the vehicles in. We are not here to look at construction vehicles. Besides, this door is closer—if we can open it," Tialdrin sang.

"Agreed," Kidahin added as she reached out to pull on the obvious handle.

The door remained frozen in place.

"Solid. Something holds the door in place," she trilled.

"Like a lock, you mean?" Einstika trilled at insolence pitch.

"Do you see me singing laughter? Tialdrin, help me pull," Kidahin keened.

"Wait, Kidahin. I see writing next to the lock," Tialdrin sang.

"This emergency exit can only be entered from here using a code issued by the sire cairn of research," Einstika read aloud.

"Dou'tu'tay," Kidahin cursed. "So much for an easy way in. Maybe I can shoot the lock apart."

"Or let me do what I do best and have a go at it with my tools," Einstika sang.

"I was pulling your tail," Kidahin laughed.

"Uh-huh. An electric lock, but no power. Makes it harder," Einstika sang as she rummaged through her techmistress harness. She pulled out and sat next to her a set of small screwdrivers, a spool of insulated wire, a pair of needle-nose pliers, a battery, and a small binary-number generator.

"Give me about an hour," she sang and leaned into her work.

"Just be careful," Kidahin sang.

"And take your time," the Mistress advised. "You never know what an invalid code might do."

"Thanks a lot," Einstika snapped.

Almost to the second of her estimate the lock clicked.

"And open!" Einstika sang.

"Well done," Kidahin trilled.

"About time," Tialdrin trilled hastily. "Open it and get inside. Those dust clouds behind us look wrong."

Kidahin glanced over her shoulder and frowned.

"Fighting," she trilled offhandedly.

"Come on," Tialdrin trilled. "The door, remember?"

"I pulled the handle. It still does not open. You said it was open," Kidahin trilled accusingly.

"Unlocked," Einstika clarified. "Seal looks hermetic. This is likely an airlock hatch."

"For what? Some kind of laboratory clean room? Maybe the entire building is hermetically sealed. Differential pressure? Maybe the air has to equalize first."

"True," Einstika trilled. "But unless the system is purely mechanical, the air pressure will not equalize…"

"Let me try again," Kidahin interrupted and grabbed the door handle.

Einstika's ears caught it first, a fine low-pitched whistling.

"Wait!" she trilled and began palming the wall near the door until she felt jets of air brush her skin.

"This is a vent. I thought it was ornamental at first," she sang.

"I can hear it. Escaping air," Tialdrin sang.

"So the air inside is not stored? They just vent it? Why? Excessive use means the building must have stored air. Otherwise it would lose safe air every time someone used the door," Kidahin sang thoughtfully.

"I doubt it," the Mistress said. "I can think of no reason why they would seal the entire building. I can imagine specialized isolation rooms. The door probably opens into one of them."

"I see your point, Mistress," Tialdrin sang. "The color suggests this is an emergency exit."

"Hey, the venting has stopped," Einstika sang.

"Which means the air pressure has equalized. Can we open it now?" Kidahin trilled impatiently.

"Of course. The higher internal pressure kept the seal intact. Remember when Tialdrin got hit on the chin by the airlock hatch? Forcing this door open would have blown it off its hinges and probably kill anyone in its way."

Kidahin gripped the handle firmly, ready to pull when Einstika's words penetrated her poorly veiled impatience.

"Are you sure it is safe to open?" she asked.

"Of course."

Kidahin pulled slowly, and the door swung open effortlessly.

"Welcome to the New Dawn Technology Center," she sang and stepped inside.

"Small room, but nothing like the one-person airlock we found below. Come on in and close the door," Kidahin sang.

"Done," Einstika sang, closed the door, and looked around.

"Spirits, it is dark in here," she complained.

"Look away. I am shining my hand torch on the floor."

Kidahin aimed her torch at the floor and watched dull yellow light gleaming from the shiny orange tile. It gave the room a dim orange glow.

Tialdrin twisted around Kidahin to look at the door on the far wall.

"Even I can open this," she sang as she examined the doorknob and lock.

"A much simpler pressure management system is used here. It is empty now, but who knows what they used this clean room for. Watch your suit seals, especially the ankle seals. Keep in mind that this technology is generally filthy," she warned as the door clicked loudly.

"That means room pressure has equalized with the interior," Einstika sang.

Tialdrin scowled at the lock.

"I see it. solenoid-driven bolt. It has retracted into the wall. It is unlocked. Opening slowly. No lights inside," she warned as Kidahin unsnapped her holster.

"I doubt any amber-coated drones are wandering around here, so stop waving that coward's weapon around."

"We call them coward's weapons now, but we did not do so as much in Hlorrithin's time," Kidahin sang as she pushed Tialdrin aside.

"Follow me," she sang.

"Wait while I take a scan," Einstika trilled.

"Why?" Kidahin trilled. "You said the lidar just as likely gave a scan of the Dark Mistress's Abode as it did any open areas down here?"

"That was true then, but not necessarily now. Now that we are above ground and far from the reactor and those tail-tied electromagnetic fields and photon emissions I should get a better scan."

"Oh, spirits! Go ahead," Kidahin trilled.

"Affirm. Well, the EM emissions are causing some interference but trace ultraviolet light looks like drizzle falling across the scan. I can see wall returns. Lots of open volume around here," Einstika sang.

"Obviously," Kidahin trilled, getting more impatient. "Hallways and rooms are open spaces. Mistress, we stand in a rectangular room two ells wide and three long—completely empty, too. The floor is a nice soft orange patterned tile. Concrete walls have been painted in the same blended orange shades, beautifully done. Tialdrin is at the door across the room from me. Come on, let us go."

Einstika ignored Kidahin and squinted up at the ceiling.

"Fluorescent lights in the ceiling. Off, of course. I do not know if that pleases me or not. Some of the bulbs are broken. I wonder why," she muttered aloud.

"Shock wave from the blast?" the Mistress asked.

"Maybe," Einstika allowed. "But I think powerful current surges blew them out."

"Pay attention and follow me," Kidahin sang. "Tialdrin, wait here while Einstika and I check the hallway.

"Mistress, the hallway goes left some thirty ells. It goes right only three or four ells.

"Both ends have doors. The right hallway dead-ends into one of them. The two doors at the end of the left hallway go left and right."

"Turning right takes you to the front of the building. I want you in the interior, so go left," the Mistress said.

"Affirm. Einstika, go right and check the door."

They advanced into the hallway. Tialdrin stepped into the doorway to keep an eye on them.

"Unlocked," Einstika sang, opened the door, and gave the space beyond a quick glance. "Just an empty, closed-off section of hallway."

As she closed the door she noticed a list posted on the back of it.

"Found something," Einstika trilled.

Tialdrin glided up next to her and read the posting.

"This is a schedule for prophylactic tasks," she sang.

"Prophylactic tasks? As in cleaning duties? Something maintenance might do?" Einstika trilled.

"Yes. These tasks are not something a mistress of healers would concern herself with. The paper has a bloodstain on the corner, just a drop, and a mistress of healers would never tolerate this."

"Probably a glass cut," Einstika suggested, pointing her tail at the broken glass on the floor.

"Broken bulbs. Someone got hit by flying glass when the bulbs blew out," she sang.

"Or tried to change a bulb," Tialdrin sang, snapping her tail at the fixture above her.

Tialdrin moved her torch closer to the ceiling and shadows melted away.

"See? Blood on the socket. It looks fresh, but it is dry."

"I wonder if the blood belongs to the same person who scribbled this below the schedule," Einstika sang.

"Scribbled what?" Kidahin sang as she returned from the other end of the hallway.

She looked over Tialdrin's shoulder and squinted at the schedule.

"Terrible handwriting—written in negation scale—probably a hastily scribbled 'do not open' or 'keep out'. Someone's idea of a joke? Why put a keep-out sign on the wrong side of the door? Not important. Come look at the doors I found."

They followed her to the end of the hall.

"This door is welded shut," Einstika sang, pointing at the door on the right with her tail.

She knelt to examine the door on her left.

"This one is not locked or welded," she sang, running her hand flat against the door.

"Bent here, like something heavy rammed it from the other side. It is just jammed in its frame. Give it a good kick," she sang.

"Stand back," Kidahin warned and kicked the door.

Nothing.

"It is locked," Kidahin trilled accusingly.

"It is not," Einstika sang.

"Come on!" Kidahin trilled and smacked the door with open palms.

It remained closed.

"It is locked, I tell you," she trilled in warning pitch at Einstika.

"No. I checked. The bolt is not engaged. This is a solid door. Ram it."

"What? You expect me to overbear a door?" Kidahin trilled, snapped her ears at the door, and slammed her shoulder into it.

No match for her assault, the stubborn door banged open and swung inward.

"Nice hit," Tialdrin sang with admiration.

"Dim light inside. Incandescent light bulbs? Not enough power to run them," she complained.

Kidahin pushed the door wide open and stepped into an assembly area.

"Clear, follow me. Spirits, this thing looks more impressive up close," she sang.

"We should not be surprised by Neh'as'anni aircraft technology," Einstika trilled, likewise awed.

"Tell me what you see, Team-one," the Mistress demanded.

"We found another scramjet. Einstika, send a picture," Kidahin sang.

"Affirm."

8

THE MOTHERLESS MOTHER

I can only honor their courage by stabbing the fatal blow.

"This is incredible engineering," Einstika sang in awe. "After looking at the scramjet up close I can safely say they got it working. See the jet parked in front of it? It must be three times the size of the scramjet. Look at its tail section. See its shape? An exact silhouette of the scramjet. They used it to carry the scramjet."

"But why use a jet to carry another jet when they can simply fly the smaller jet? Why use one jet to carry another?" Kidahin trilled, puzzled.

"Because the scramjet is more than just a hypersonic aircraft. It really is a suborbital shuttle. They use the larger jet to carry it into the lower stratosphere. There they release the shuttle. The shuttle then fires its scramjets and flies until the oxygen drops too low for the scramjet engines. Then the rocket engines fire and send the shuttle into suborbital flight. This is magnificent if it works like I think it should."

"I wonder why they left it here. I would never leave a key technological advancement behind," Kidahin sang.

Einstika prowled around behind the shuttle and glanced up at the vertical stabilizer assembly and frowned at the rocket engine bells.

"Here is why," she sang. "One of the four engines is missing. They either removed it for repairs or did not have time to install the fourth engine. Weight and aerodynamics would be wrong with the engine missing for it to fly on scramjets alone. Suborbital flight would be impossible without all four engines."

"That does not quite answer my question. They could have mated the hypersonic jet to its transport jet and taken off. I would have," Kidahin complained.

"Maybe whatever happened, happened too fast? And I do not mean the initial blast that devastated a third of this complex. I think something bad happened in the tunnels, bad enough for someone to shoot a nuclear techmistress in the head from behind regardless of the cowardice such an act displays or the social debt it incurs," Einstika snapped.

"Injured instinct," Tialdrin blurted flatly.

"What about it?" Einstika trilled.

"The Territorial Boundaries of Rage and Forgiveness warns us that injured instinct foments dishonorable acts of rage."

"Like what?" Kidahin trilled. "I cannot imagine anything causing a female to ignore her instincts, turn, and run. Even a female blinded by fury keens in challenge and slashes with her adulthood knife."

"What if the nuclear techmistress was shot by a male?" Tialdrin trilled.

"Never sing that again!" Kidahin threatened, struggling to restrain the anger driving her to pull her adulthood knife and challenge Tialdrin.

"Everyone knows males are inherently safe except when they are away from female pheromones for too long. We protect and defend them. We often say males are strange, but that is a tail-tug we tell them. But the truth rides on a male's scent and grabs us by the nose. That techmistress would have smelled his scent, empathized with its emotional content, and immediately known his intent well before he drew the coward's weapon."

"I agree with Kidahin. Anything else to add?" the Mistress asked.

"This warehouse serves the Technology Center exclusively. They use the rear third or so to assemble prototype aircraft. The Neh'as'anni built this place heavy, like a bunker. Poured concrete floor, tall walls, and pallets of crates stacked around us explain the tow-motors and hydraulic hand carts. I see a cargo lift along the wall next to the shuttle. This cargo lift is big enough for a tow-motor, maybe two of them. Shaft goes down, obviously, a long way down, too. Looks like thirty or forty ells deep because I can see the platform on the bottom of the shaft," Tialdrin sang.

Einstika reached around Tialdrin to punch the obvious up button.

"No power. We cannot bring the platform up and ride it back down," she trilled.

"Why would we? Lifts move equipment, not people. The door next to the lift shaft should be the way down. Einstika, open it and take a look," Kidahin sang.

Einstika snapped her tail, flipped her ears at Kidahin, nodded, glided to the door, and abruptly stopped.

"What is that?" she sang.

"What is what?" Kidahin trilled, annoyed.

"Behind us, next to the wall, surrounded by stacked crates by the door leading back into the main building. Looks like a small all-terrain vehicle to me."

Tialdrin sprinted up to the crates for a look.

"Nice design," she sang. "I wonder if it works."

Einstika glided up to her.

"Crates are too heavy," she sang and started climbing over them and down onto the small vehicle.

"It is an ATV," she trilled excitedly. "Electric, too. Unbelievable. The Neh'as'anni make dirty fossil-fuel-powered rotary-driven internal combustion engines. The Be'atika Senge ordered them to convert to natural gas and electric vehicles years ago."

Einstika snapped the power switch on.

The dash screen lit up immediately.

"Battery gauge reads only half a charge, yet it looks new—never used.

"Engine? This green button is the engine switch. The dash legend says the engine, motor is more correct since it is electric, is in low gear and ready to operate.

"The screen is flickering. A'pea thing must have a loose wire or a short somewhere…," she grumbled and smacked the dash in frustration.

And yelped in alarm as the ATV lurched into a crate and began shoving it slowly but with gaining speed at Kidahin.

"Dou'tu'tay!" Kidahin swore as she easily side-stepped the careening crate.

"Sorry. I am sorry. I did not think hitting the dashboard would actually work. I should have set the brake first."

"Or shifted it out of gear?" Kidahin growled.

"Climbing down an open shaft surrenders the high ground. Take the side door down. Once there we can set a watch and get some rest. Mistress? Do you mind us taking a break?" she added.

"Not at all," the Mistress said.

"Affirm. Tialdrin, come with me. Einstika, get out of that thing and bring your equipment to the door. Mistress, we will report when ready to continue."

"A few hours will be more than enough," Tialdrin sang, relieved.

Einstika dawdled, unwilling to leave the ATV just yet. The warehouse fascinated her more than anything potentially hiding below. The warehouse layout was supremely efficient. She admired engineering economy at work. Putting a hanger in the rear for prototype development made logical sense, too. Using the hangers on the airfield meant carting supplies to them from the warehouse—highly inefficient.

The supersonic transport and its shuttle payload took up two-thirds of the warehouse hanger. Equipment and both completed and partial assemblies filled the last third, leaving little room to work while the transport jet remained inside.

Einstika abandoned the ATV, turned, and noticed an uncanny symmetry in the stacked crates nearby. Ignoring the others, she walked up to and stepped around the crates and gasped.

Rows and rows of crates stacked floor to ceiling occupied a roughly cubic volume, all uniformly spaced within a metal scaffold structure.

Einstika stared at the pallet storage and retrieval mechanism in awe. Rack-and-pinion axles and gears moved a pallet lift fork to any one of hundreds of pallet locations within the stacking cube.

She glided up to the obvious control station and found a row of indexed slots filled with rectangular punched cards. A card reader sat next to the index slots and was electrically connected to a process controller. Cables ran from the controller to motors mounted to a series of lift fork platforms. Inserting a card into the reader apparently told the controller which fork to send where within a specific row and column. The fork then retrieved and brought the requested pallet to the station.

"This device is ingenious!" she trilled.

Kidahin glanced at her, left Tialdrin to continue exploring the landing of a narrow shaft, and glided over to see what technical junk Einstika was fawning over now.

"No electricity? Too bad. Come on, time for us to go down the hole again," she sang.

"Affirm," Einstika trilled wistfully.

"Mistress, it has been twelve hours. How do you read me?" Kidahin sang.

The suit speakers remained silent, not even static crackled from them.

"I turned the radio repeater off, remember?" Einstika trilled in laughter. "Switching on. Repeater is synching up. I have a signal. Try again."

"Affirm. Mistress? Team-one checking in."

"I hear you clean and clear. What is your status, Team-one?" the Mistress said.

"It sounds so good to hear your reassuring flat, mechanical voice again," Tialdrin sang sarcastically.

"I hate sleeping down here. Why did we not sleep in the warehouse? On ground level? I get bad dreams down here," Einstika complained.

"Me, too. They do not feel like dreams, though. Spirits, they remind me of the traumatic stress flashbacks I had months after we left *Londiwe Kh...*," Kidahin paused. Her role here should not summon traumatic visions from the far future.

"Mistress? Ready to proceed," Tialdrin sang.

"First, tell me what you see," the Mistress insisted.

"We climbed down a narrow shaft about thirty ells deep running parallel to the lift shaft. I am facing an entrance to a big storeroom. Makes sense because my earlier lidar scans found large open spaces down here. We just woke up and ate, so not much else," Einstika grumbled.

"Well, I found an artificial necessary down the hall," Tialdrin sang.

"An artificial what?" the Mistress asked.

"Necessary. It looks just like one. Contoured wooden bole, water trickling through it. Made out of ceramic, I think. Warm water, too. Keeps it at body temperature. Comfortable to use, too."

"I will file your observations under disgusting. Anything else?"

"And using the floor for a necessary down here is not disgusting?" Tialdrin keened rhetorically.

"Entering the storeroom," Kidahin sang as she gave Tialdrin a pained look.

"It looks clear, going in," she added seconds later.

But my arrows were few and weak, the Gracious Mistress sang.

That meant they would take heavy casualties soon, Einstika knew.

"This is a continuation of the stacking mechanism above us," she sang aloud. "See where the pallet fork comes down through the ceiling?"

She glided over to an open crate and looked inside.

"They keep food here. Here, Tialdrin. Catch!" Einstika trilled as she tossed an object at her.

Tialdrin snatched the object out of the air and looked at it.

"E'bato? In a can? *Eww*. Do not expect me to eat this."

"Why not? I heard the Neh'as'anni found a way to preserve and store food. Why bother? The rainforest provides fresh food all the time for anyone who needs it. Why pick excess food just to pack it into cans?" Einstika sang.

"Environmental contamination?" Kidahin trilled thoughtfully. "Maybe the surrounding forest is already contaminated. Neh'tle ke'ne's'tu corrupts leaves, fruits, nuts, and roots."

"Could be, but even thinking about it scares me to death. No wonder the Be'atika Senge called upon Hlorrithin to destroy the Neh'as'anni. They are an abomination to the natural environment," Tialdrin sang.

"I can imagine another reason for preserving food," Einstika sang.

"Such as?" Kidahin trilled.

"The shuttle. If they can fly it into a stable orbit and maintain it for a few days, then the flight crew would need food. There is no forest in space, after all," Einstika sang.

"But in cans? Why not dehydrate the food and wrap it in plastic?" Kidahin trilled, perplexed.

"Plastic packaging is lighter than aluminum cans. Means they would have to carry more water, and water is heavy and—oh, look at this. Tialdrin, catch!" Einstika sang wickedly.

Tialdrin snatched the can out of the air and read the label.

"Canned malutha berries? *Uhg!* Even the sound of it is disgusting," she trilled.

"Tialdrin, come here. Hang back, Einstika," Kidahin trilled.

"Why?" Einstika trilled.

"Blood on the floor over here. You might faint on us," Tialdrin sang in humor melody.

"You are not funny," Einstika growled and glided up to Kidahin, glared at Tialdrin, glanced down at the blood on the floor, and stepped back.

"The blood looks wrong—unrealistic—not spatter or drops," she sang.

Kidahin twitched her ears, agreeing.

"Bloody. Smeared, I think, as if someone crawled through briars," she trilled.

"Not briars. Head wound. Bled on the floor while crawling," Tialdrin sang.

"Looks messy, but head wounds bleed a lot even from minor wounds. Looks like someone pushed a blood-stained mop down the hall...," Einstika trilled.

"No," Tialdrin interrupted, eying the blood with distaste. She glanced at Kidahin and snapped her tail.

"Someone with a head wound crawled through that door," she sang.

"Mistress, we can follow the blood or look elsewhere," Kidahin sang.

"Secure your ground first," the Mistress advised.

"Affirm. The warehouse down here takes up a lot of space and stores quite a lot of items. The open areas are relatively clear. Give us twenty minutes to check all the blind spots," Kidahin sang.

Einstika prowled along a line of stacked crates to a break between them and paused.

"Tialdrin, Kidahin? I found a door."

Tialdrin got there first and glared at the door suspiciously.

"Read what the sign says," Einstika trilled, pointing at big green letters stenciled across the door.

"'Restricted Access'? Any door implies that already, so why bother with a sign? Doors are an affront to privacy and courtesy unless used to warn people that something inside is dangerous," Tialdrin sang.

"I hate doors, and this place is full of them," Kidahin grumbled.

"Open it," Einstika sang.

Kidahin scowled. "Yes, of course," she trilled hesitantly.

"What?" Einstika sang. "You are the combat specialist here. You check the door first. If locked, I will open it."

"This door looks somewhat like a submersible hatch. No handle? It pushes open?" Kidahin murmured as she shoved the door, to no effect.

"Might as well shove the wall. Locked from the other side. No latch or release on this side and no exposed hinges either. It has to push open."

"Can you open it, Einstika?" the Mistress asked.

"Not with what I have with me. There is no lock to force open. No way to get into the latch mechanism from this side. Tamper-proof, but I could blow it open if I had explosives or cut the latching mechanism out if I had a torch. Might be a torch in the hanger end of the warehouse."

"Mistress?" Tialdrin sang. "I think we have no choice but to loop back and investigate the other door."

"She means the bloody trail door, Mistress," Einstika complained.

"No kidding, Einstika?" the Mistress sang dryly. "Proceed."

"Affirm," Einstika sang and perked her ears at Kidahin.

Kidahin swatted her tail at Einstika close enough for its ringlet-covered pons to just miss her cheek. Kidahin spun her pons in rapid, tight circles to emphasize her annoyance.

"I thought you preferred looking through crates of food," she sang.

Tialdrin trilled a snicker and added, "She might at least sample a canned snack."

"I am not *that* hungry," Einstika snapped. "But canned food probably tastes better than field rations."

Kidahin smiled. "There may be some truth there," she agreed.

"Mistress, we reached the bloody trail door."

"Be careful, Kidahin. The assailant may still be inside."

"Affirm. Tialdrin, Einstika, keep alert while I go through first."

She pressed her hand against the door.

"Huh, unlocked. Figures. Going in and looking around. I see. Oh, spirits!" Kidahin keened and froze.

"Tialdrin, Einstika, there is a body here. Looks desiccated. Naked, but not bloody. A male, and he cannot be the one who made the blood trail. He looks pitiful," she trilled, heartbroken.

"Dou'tu'tay! What is this?" Tialdrin trilled sharply.

And I never was the best of archers.

Einstika shuddered, knowing he would soon enter dire combat. And the verse sang truth: he, like all males, was no great archer. Hunter females shot bows better than other people. Warriors shot adequately, but except for firing longbows in support of infantry, they preferred infantry. Like Warrior females, males excelled in melee combat. In fact, males were incredibly crafty and dangerous melee fighters.

"Einstika, send the Mistress a picture of everything in here. Now," Kidahin trilled.

"Affirm," Einstika sang, struggling to shake the feeling of impending doom as she stepped between two rows of stacked steel capsules.

"Spirits, what do you think these things are?" she trilled as she panned a camera down the wide path.

"Looks like ordnance. Unlawful ordnance at that. Cruise missiles, maybe?" Kidahin trilled sharply.

"What am I seeing? A health center morgue?" the Mistress interrupted.

Einstika reached the rows of burnished, stainless steel capsules stacked three high in tiers. Each capsule sat lengthwise, one end mounted into a niche on the wall. The stacked capsules sat recessed an arm's length further into the wall than the ones below them. They filled the room on both sides, leaving a wide central space for moving capsules about, for individual capsule support equipment, and for walking space.

Tialdrin shoved Einstika aside to get a better look at a capsule. Long and narrow, the ends poking into the pathway had trapezoidal noses with glass tops facing the ceiling. Each glass neatly framed the face of an occupant. A control panel and display sat on the lid below the window.

"Mistress, I think these capsules are used for cryogenic sleep. This is impossible, according to what science I know. Any person can be frozen solid easily enough, but waking them up is something far different. Water inside the cells forms crystals upon freezing. Those ice crystals lacerate the cell membrane. All you get when the person is thawed is a mush of dead tissue," Tialdrin trilled, paused in awe, and continued.

"The Neh'as'anni must have solved this problem. If true then the range of possible healer applications for this technology is almost endless. If they can reverse the freezing process and revive the sleeper then all the environmental damage the Neh'as'anni have committed over the course of two centuries can be forgiven. A mistress of healers needs to examine these bodies in a lab setting before any conclusions can be made, of course. I estimate at least four hundred capsules are here," she sang.

"What happened to the body on the floor?" Kidahin trilled. "He is clearly a male. Why does he look shriveled up and so dry? A thawed body is watery. He should have—rotted."

"Seal failure, perhaps?" Tialdrin speculated.

Einstika returned from examining another capsule.

"Each one is connected to an elaborate life support system. These people were put into the capsules alive. I am certain of it," she sang, paused, and then frowned thoughtfully.

"I wonder if they were experimenting with long-term space travel life support systems," she added, sounding intrigued.

"Do not be ridiculous. Why travel in space? To what purpose is there in space travel?" Kidahin sang rhetorically. "Even if we went into space, we certainly would not let males go with us and endanger their lives for no reason or gain," she scoffed as she noticed a break in symmetry.

"See that? A capsule is pulled partway out of its wall niche. Do you think he got out of it on his own, walked a few ells, and died?"

"I was wondering about that myself," Tialdrin sang. "I will check it while you go look in the other capsule windows. Can you see what they are wearing?"

"These two males are bare-chested, but that is normal for males," Kidahin sang.

"This lid's latches have been forced," Einstika sang.

"Kidahin, she is right. This one was opened from the outside. The occupant is facedown. Einstika, help me pull the lid open," Tialdrin sang.

"The lid swings on hidden hinges. Makes sense for a hermetically sealed tube. Ready. Tialdrin? All right, here we go, brave Team-one opening a cryogenic capsule. Oh, spirits. Kidahin, this is a male, too. I think the body on the floor was the original occupant."

I was alone, the last of several thousand strong.

Kidahin shuddered and struggled to remain in character. The endgame approached. He gained victory, but victory killed him in the end.

"This male wears a hazard suit. The male on the floor is naked, just like the others. He is not—dehydrated—like the one on the floor, either," she trilled shakily.

"And his skull is staved in," Tialdrin keened in outrage.

"Truly an honor point crime, because nobody kills a male. Even for an honor-point death penalty, no male is killed like this," Einstika keened as fury summoned a pheromonal memory. She unwittingly empathized with it as her memory of Jassalin's scent flooded her mind, forcing her to see horror from Jassalin's point of view.

She was looking up at a hole in a deck-access lift of a human warship. She fell through that hole. The lift doors across from her were closed and bent in its frame and blocked by a pile of misshapen frozen human bodies.

"Not without honorable justification," Tialdrin trilled, watching Einstika warily. The techmistress's pheromones, strong, nearly masked the scent of the Gracious Mistress and her singers.

Einstika smelled like she was struggling with some powerful flashback having something to do with Jassalin. After a moment she continued.

"Even when justified, he must be strangled and not beaten to death," she added.

"He looks middle-aged," Kidahin trilled in puzzlement. "He likely popped the seal and threw the original occupant on the floor, hoping to save his life."

"An act of desperation. Surely he saw how the body looked while pulling it out. What about the others?" the Mistress asked.

"Each capsule has an identification number stenciled on it," Tialdrin trilled.

"Control numbers for experimental fodder?" Kidahin keened, outraged, and then swooned slightly as memories of *Londiwe Khoza* overwhelmed her. That disaster she did not want to think or talk about. So many male deaths. She trembled and could not stop shaking. She did not want to experience the deaths aboard that ship again.

"That is a wild theory," Tialdrin sang distractedly, worried. Kidahin's pheromones smelled like Einstika's had minutes ago. The scent swamped the singers' empathy linking them with the Song.

"No female would ever experiment on males," she continued. "There is no evidence of anything like that happening."

"These capsules are evidence enough for me," Kidahin trilled aggressively.

"No, wait. Think about it. Males are rare because their birthrates are less than ten percent of all births. This is true worldwide, is true on all ten tribal continents, and is true in all clans. The Neh'as'anni are no different. Killing off their own males is the same as killing off their own clan, familial suicide. What if they brought them here to receive a cure? Would they not do so if the victims were too contaminated to remain in the clan health centers? But this does not look at all like any health center I ever saw before. We do not have enough evidence to start snapping tails at theories. We must find the truth," Tialdrin sang.

"Not our mission," Kidahin trilled. "We came here to find the source of the radiation signal and report back."

"Which we did," Einstika snapped. "I do not mean to pull your tail, Kidahin, but there is more to this place than a reactor leak—as if fission radiation was not bad enough. The static shield the dead mistress rigged in the control room proves this. I think she did so to prevent that odd metallic amber alloy from reaching into the building from the mines below. There is something going on with that material. Remember the male we found encased in it? Does it have anything to do with these people? Hlorrithin needs to know if that alloy poses a danger. A few low-resolution pictures and our radio logs tell him nothing helpful. If we can find an administrative center, we might learn more."

"Einstika is right, Kidahin," Tialdrin sang while patting down the capsule occupant's hazard suit pockets. "I found something, folded paper with writing on it."

Tialdrin paused to unfold the paper.

"This handwritten note is hard to read. The ink is blotchy and smeared along the creases. Water made the ink run, which means he probably thawed and refroze at least once before the power failed for good."

"So?" the Mistress asked.

"Well," Einstika trilled thoughtfully. "This technology works, otherwise, they would never put so many males into cryogenic sleep. The cooling system failed, but no healers remained behind to correct the fault. The system reset itself, freezing at least some of the occupants again. Some of them may even be revivable. At least the dead died peacefully."

"Except for him," Kidahin sang sarcastically, pointing at the facedown male with the crushed skull.

"Nothing more we can learn here. We should go," Tialdrin sang.

"Wait," the Mistress interrupted. "Read what the letter says."

"Oh, of course," Tialdrin trilled. "Hard to read enough words for it to make sense. Wait a minute. He addressed this to whoever found him. A precaution—he knew the head wound was serious. He calls himself a sire cairn, but I cannot make out his occupation. His occupational association turned against him. He warns something about stopping the research. No, not stopping. He wants it paused, does not say why. The materials—no, the substances—are safe. I think he means the amber alloy. That is all. Too much water damage."

"His occupational association turned against him? Females almost never turn against a male. He must have killed their honor somehow," Kidahin trilled.

"So it seems, but we cannot know for sure. Do not jump to conclusions," Tialdrin warned.

"If his experiments killed males, then all females have an honor-point duty to save them and strangle him with his own tail!" Kidahin trilled at imperative pitch.

"I want to leave," Einstika trilled, gesturing with her tail at the door in the back of the room.

"Not through there," Tialdrin sang. "That is where they prepared the males for freezing."

"Then we backtrail to the other door," Einstika sang, turned, and left.

Kidahin twitched her ears quizzically at Tialdrin and followed Einstika to a familiar door.

"We cannot get through this without specialized equipment," Tialdrin sang.

"Agreed. Look around. This cannot be the only way down," Kidahin sang.

"Look at this," Einstika sang.

"Look at what?" Kidahin sang.

"This is a lift platform. Probably used for the food storage area. See that door next to the lift?"

"More bodies in there?" Tialdrin trilled, shuddering.

"Small door in the corner? I doubt it. Probably a small room," Einstika sang as she opened the door and looked inside.

"Thought so. Small room filled with transformers and breaker boxes. This supplies electricity to the cryogenic systems and this lift."

"Let me see," Kidahin trilled as she stepped around Einstika.

Tialdrin poked her head in last, looked around, and snapped her tail in agreement.

"Yes," Einstika sang calmly. "A power distribution node, but it looks different from the ones in the tunnels. Automated, computer controlled, with a lot of redundancy built in. Tialdrin? Read the breaker labels aloud while I check the control console."

"Affirm. These switches turn on and off life support, ventilation, air temperature, lights, refrigerant purge—whatever that is—and other obscure stuff. The big, blue lever must be the breaker for the reactor mains."

"Not surprising," Kidahin trilled. "This equipment and the equipment we found below uses a lot of electricity. Explains the need for a large, dangerous, and illegal fission nuclear reactor. These Neh'as'anni are ecological saboteurs."

"The display here shows current power levels. Little power is available, but I expect this because the reactor is offline," Einstika sang.

"These switches have all been turned off, and the control computer disconnected. I think I can tap into the accumulators from here and restore power to some low-power devices—lights at least," she added.

"I found the door locks, lift controls, and other security systems on this panel," Tialdrin sang

"This makes no sense," Einstika trilled. "The room was unlocked, but from here anyone can shut off anything on this floor—the cryogenics systems. Yet they locked everything else or welded doors closed. What happened here?"

"Can you restore power to the whole building from there?" the Mistress asked.

"No. I need to reboot the reactor control systems. This console does not have access privileges to the reactor, but I can switch into the accumulators to get the lights on at least," Einstika sang and snapped three switches closed and watched analog dials rise as the accumulators bled power from the stand-by reactor. She glided over to the panel near Tialdrin and ran a finger down a row of breakers, snapping a few of them closed.

"Hey!" Kidahin trilled some distance away.

"What?" Tialdrin sang.

"Nothing, it is nothing. Flickering fluorescents make me jumpy. I thought I saw someone, just a trick of the light. Oh, I went back to the capsule room but found nothing more," Kidahin sang as she entered the room.

"That male would not have shut the cryogenics systems down and then climbed into a capsule. Someone else did it, but why?" Tialdrin trilled.

"No blood here, so it could not have been him. Someone switched the power off after he entered the capsule. He did not kill these males, thank the spirits," Kidahin sang.

"So now what?" Einstika wondered aloud, sounding edgy. Being so close to mass male casualties churned up horrific memories long repressed.

9
THE STRONG MOTHER

But I knew what I must do.

Einstika recoiled in horror. The verse she just heard and smelled reminded her of Hlorrithin's pending death.

He would die because a mistress of battle had remained behind and so did not lead her archers in the endgame soon to occur somewhere between the airfield and the elleiu trees to the north.

Mistress of Battle Shikararro.

Because of her, Hlorrithin died. Would die, Einstika corrected as she wrestled with an overpowering instinct common to all females.

Male endangerment.

A male in danger increased female physical endurance and intensified adrenaline surges. Together they multiplied a female's physical strength and resolve. Heightened resolve altered her mental state and fueled an intense combative fury the reasoning mind found hard to ignore.

Just knowing a male faced imminent danger could rouse the instinct, but smelling danger in his pheromones all but blinded females to the danger a male faced.

Male pheromones also countered the instinct by calming and reassuring. The scent of a male who felt safe also stopped females from blindly fighting to exhaustion or death.

Einstika felt a slow-burning fury as pheromone-driven visions of wreckage, blasted equipment, scattered personal items, and bodies—fists and fists of them, appeared around her.

Male bodies.

Einstika knew Kidahin saw them as well because she smelled anger on Kidahin's scent.

This was all Shikararro's fault, instinct screamed at her.

Rage filled Einstika. The Boundaries of Rage and Forgiveness said clan rage was the branch upon which ni'zakhon, outlawry, depended. The Boundaries cut a trail for people to gather and destroy outlawry because it posed a threat to all people.

"Einstika? You hear me?" Tialdrin trilled with concern.

"What?" Einstika snapped, her rage draining away thanks to the kind, sympathetic thoughts riding Tialdrin's scent.

"Oh, I am sorry," she added, calmer. "I was asking a question when—nevermind. Can we take the lift shaft down? I want to avoid the cryogenics room if possible."

"Mistress?" Kidahin sang.

"Try a different door. I doubt the cargo lift drops below the foodstuffs storage area."

"Affirm, but first I have to go back into the cryogenics room and put the male we found in a more dignified position. I want to close and seal the capsule containing the male with the crushed skull, the sire cairn, as well," Kidahin sang.

"Thank you. I appreciate that. It is not the bodies themselves so much as why they are here at all," Einstika trilled, distraught.

"Bad things happen all the time, just not that often to males," Kidahin sang from the distant cryogenics room.

"I know this, but I never considered the Neh'as'anni as savages hiding under a thin skin of civility," Einstika yelled back.

"We should have expected this by their blatant indifference for the serious environmental damage their technology was causing. This alone told us they were uncivil," Tialdrin sang.

"Be calm, Tialdrin," Kidahin trilled, her voice louder as she drew closer to them.

"Show me this door you found," she sang.

Einstika led her to a familiar sealed door.

"This door? What about it? We talked about this already. It cannot be opened with the tools we have. What do you want to do? Return to the warehouse and look for pickaxes?" Kidahin trilled.

"Never thought of that," Einstika trilled at mocking tempo. "I prefer sledgehammers and wedges myself, good old-fashioned physical labor."

"You? A techmistress? You prefer hard work?" Kidahin trilled, laughing.

"I do not, but sometimes simple tools solve problems in cases where technology is wasteful or inadequate to the task," Einstika sang. "In such cases I follow the Techmistress's Root."

"The what? What does that mean? Hit the door futilely until it buckles? This door will never yield to brute force."

Einstika snapped her ears a 'no' and continued.

"The Root says the best solution is likely the simplest one and is the taproot of—like—everything in engineering practice," she added.

"We will never open this without explosives or a torch. A pickaxe would only scratch the finish, and a sledgehammer would just dent the metal. No wedge is going to spring this door open," Kidahin sang flatly.

"Why bother? What lies beyond it? It could be pressurized," Tialdrin sang.

"No hermetic seal here," Kidahin scoffed, pointing at the seam with her tail.

"What do you think is behind it?" the Mistress asked.

"No idea. A sign on it says entry is restricted, but does not say why," Tialdrin sang and then paused.

She canted her ears, reached out and touched the sign.

"Wait. This is paper, not paint. Glued paper, someone did this last-minute to stop people from opening the door. Maybe to stop entry into the lower levels," she added.

"I wonder why," Einstika sang.

"Any number of things for all we know," Tialdrin sang.

"Let us find out. Could be important," Kidahin trilled.

"Important enough to risk our lives?" Tialdrin trilled.

"Mistress? Any suggestions?" Kidahin sang formally.

"Return to the warehouse and get whatever you need to open that door."

"Affirm," Kidahin sang. "Einstika? You admired it—the warehouse. Take Tialdrin and look for tools while I set a watchpoint here and..."

"No need," Einstika interrupted smugly. "Remember the Techmistress's Root?"

"What about it?" Kidahin trilled impatiently.

"While I was in the cryogenics power room flicking breakers for the lights, I also snapped off the electric locks on this level."

"So?" Kidahin trilled at interrogative tempo. "Do you see a doorknob, latch, or handle here? Even unlocked, we cannot release the latch from this side."

"No need to," Einstika sang. "Just push."

Kidahin glared at Einstika for several seconds, pivoted on her heels, leaned into the door, and pushed hard.

The door opened. Rather reluctantly, or so Kidahin thought.

"Dusty," she sang. "Rarely used. Must be a service chase for the lift shaft."

"Just opening the door unsettled the dust. See how it just hangs there? No air circulation, but at least I can see through it well enough," Einstika trilled.

"I go first," Kidahin sang and stepped over the threshold.

A ceiling light flashed on, and Kidahin flinched.

She froze a beat before trilling a scale of angry notes, her heart hammered staccato.

"Repeat that, Team-one," the Mistress demanded.

"We can cook," Kidahin sang sharply. "I am in a big room filled with pans and lids. We found a service chase leading into the rear of a nutrition center. All the lights work, too."

"The door opening probably toggled a switch," Einstika trilled and bent over to examine the door frame.

A minute later she shook her head.

"No switch here. My guess is a motion sensor. More fluorescent bulbs casting dim, fluttering light. Distracting, and it hurts my eyes. A nutrition center does make sense here. Food storage is close by," she concluded.

"Clever layout," Tialdrin sang. "They prepare the food here. This follows the placement of a ground-level outer aerial root abode, the ones across from the hall of voices in any elleiu tree. If the similarity holds, we should find a hall of voices since it serves as a communal dining and meeting area."

"Uh-huh," Einstika grunted, more interested in examining the machines set against the wall. She found the simple controls on a dishwasher absolutely fascinating. A loud crash startled her, and she leapt sideways, landing next to an oven.

"Dou'tu'tay! A'pea!" Kidahin swore.

"What happened? Kidahin?" Tialdrin trilled.

"I bumped into a stack of dinner plates. They fell over, obviously. Shattered almost every one of them. Noise scared the dou'tu'tay out of me, too. Why make dining plates that can break? Wooden plates are better and do not break. These look like some kind of glazed ceramic, porcelain maybe. Why waste the material and energy firing clay plates? Faster and cleaner to carve and polish deadwood into plates than to make them out of ceramics. This is wanton wastefulness for no obvious reason."

"Cleanliness," Einstika sang. "This dishwasher control sets water to boil. Boiling kills germs. Porcelain would survive boiling water and detergents better than wood."

"Do you need healer aide?" Tialdrin sang to Kidahin, trying hard to keep trilling laughter out of her voice.

"No, the plates fell away from me, but be careful walking around them. The pieces look sharp, and I see fine slivers everywhere."

Kidahin stepped over to another door, opened it, and looked inside.

"Another door here. It opens into a landing overlooking a square shaft going down. A ramp drops from it to the corner, makes a tight turn, and drops further down to another landing on the adjacent wall. I think they continue on around and down the shaft. Parallel rails run from the kitchen through the door and on down around the spiral."

"Rails? See any handcars to shoot at?" Einstika trilled laughter.

"No, none," Kidahin snapped. "The rails look the same as the tunnel ones, but I doubt anyone can pump a handcar up these inclines."

"Let me get a look," Einstika trilled as she stepped around Kidahin.

"Impressive. They can move prepared food from the nutrition center kitchen down to the communal dining abode below. Strange, I expected communal eating next to this room and not down a level. Why build further down rather than straight across?"

"I would never live here even if the pathways and rooms followed an elleiu tree perfectly. We always lived in trees, from pre-sentient times to modern times. We never lived on the ground, let alone in caves," Kidahin trilled in disgust.

"Me either," Tialdrin sang at imperative tempo.

"So below is the dining abode? How does this help us?" Kidahin trilled.

"We know what is at the other end of the ramp," Einstika sang.

"You do not. Go down and see for yourselves," the Mistress demanded.

"Affirm," Einstika sang excitedly.

"Tialdrin? Stop staring at that oven and get moving. Follow us and keep close," Kidahin trilled. She turned and stepped between the rails and followed them down to the adjacent wall landing. She continued on down and around to another landing and continued on around and down to the fourth landing that sat directly below the entrance above.

"These landings are supports for the ramps," Kidahin sang as they stood before a closed door.

"This should open into the communal dining abode. Eating down here sounds nauseating in my ears," she growled.

Tialdrin reached for the door and pushed.

"Unlocked. Ready, Kidahin?"

"Open it," Kidahin sang.

"A'pea! Dark, really dark in there. No lights but a few weak, flickering incandescent bulbs. The whole room is dark enough for the flashes of light to ruin my night vision. Makes it harder to see, distracting. Thank the spirits they are not fluorescent bulbs. I am putting my back to the lights to get a better view. Okay, I see rows of tables, enough to feed a few thousand people all at once, just like the hall of voices in a hometree."

"What would three or four thousand people do here?" Einstika trilled.

"Research, a lot of research," Tialdrin trilled.

"Follow me. Keep vigilant. A dark space filled with flashing lights makes ideal cover," Kidahin warned.

They wandered cautiously for several minutes before reaching the far wall and another door.

Was I not responsible for the spirits of the males? Of the infants?

The pheromonal cue accompanying the verse set the upcoming scene. Right now Hlorrithin realized the duty he owed to the People superseded the duty he owed to females to keep his rare and valuable male self alive. Einstika twitched ears and shook her head, trying desperately to understand the imagery clouding her mind's eye. She saw Hlorrithin marching with the O'un Tu Clan female army.

Shikararro was still holding her archers in reserve, and Einstika could not remember why. Shikararro returned to the APC with a dislocated shoulder, but she could still direct her archers through the A'tayotan using the APC's radio. The A'tayotan hierarchy did, after all, direct all military forces on Elleio—except for the Neh'as'anni and their ni'zakhon allies, of course.

"A sign on the door reads, recreation center?" Tialdrin sang, perplexed.

"And what, exactly, is a recreation center?" the Mistress yelled, disbelief ringing in her otherwise flat, speech-processed voice. "How can anyone exercise or relax in an underground vault, under a building, and within an industrial complex? What does it look like?"

"Another large room similar to the dining abode. High-relief wood paneling looking like the interior of an elleiu tree covers the walls and ceiling. Looks like the fused aerial roots inside a tree at a casual glance. Nice orange shades, too. Large bole openings run along the left and right sides. Reminds me of upper-branch abodes. The floor, polished wood paneling, matches hollow interior branch pathways, but the floor space is too open and flat for a tree pathway. I am walking alongside a wide strip in the middle and down the length of the room covered with nests, seats, and plants—living plants at that. The arrangement along the strip staggers to accommodate a wandering stream trickling through it. I see a small waterfall halfway down from where I stand," Kidahin reported.

"Anything else?" the Mistress asked.

"More tables and chairs."

"Kidahin, wait. What is that, over against the wall?" Einstika sang, pointing with her tail.

"I see it, them. Cutting torch tanks, two of them. Left here for some reason. Repairs, maybe?" Tialdrin sang.

"The door near the airlock is welded shut," Kidahin trilled.

"Not using this thing," Einstika trilled, certain.

"Why not? What if someone prowled around down here welding doors shut and then released the buhnnie extract into the air system…"

"Kidahin," Tialdrin interrupted. "I found more doors. Several of them, in fact. These wall abodes look like decorated room entrances."

"So?" Kidahin sang.

"They look like upper canopy shops."

"Shops? I cannot imagine living here, let alone working or shopping here," Kidahin trilled. "And yet these people lived here and not in their own family hometrees."

"So it seems," Tialdrin sang, likewise puzzled.

"Kidahin?" Einstika trilled from the far right corner. "I found an ascending path leading to another door. The high-relief paneling matches the texture of a tree's main pathway leading from the forest level toward the vantage. The lowest main branches split from the trunk there, so we should find a Watch there."

"Climb there and see if you can open it," Kidahin trilled.

"I did. It is locked, secured by an odd mechanical lock. Looks like you need a cryptogram to open it. I can remove the faceplate and get into the mechanism—um, wow. This thing is really arcane."

"Arcane, how do you mean?"

"This thing is intricate, full of miniature gears. Really complicated precision work, too. Mechanism contains a hundred gears or more, fine machine work, and only about the size of my forearm. It reminds me of a spring-driven timepiece. A row of ten wheels lets you dial a number or letter marked on each wheel. Thumbing the wheel to any letter moves the gears inside."

Einstika paused to remove the thumbwheel chassis.

"No stepper motor or magnetics inside. Nothing needing electricity. This is purely mechanical, and I hate mechanical devices as much as I hated taking mechanical engineering courses at the Uahua'asee'a Clan learning center. Digital electronics is the branch to the future. I have to bypass this thing and—oh, a'pea!"

"What? What happened?" Kidahin trilled, racing up the pathway.

"The tumblers drop through barbed slots if the cryptogram is wrong. Once they fall through the bolt, they foul the lock, making it impossible to open. Ingenious device. I have to pull the tumblers out through holes in the gearbox using needle-nose pliers. If I pull wrong, all the tumblers drop. This thing is made from hardened steel. No torch will cut through to the bolt," she trilled.

"I can barely see inside it. You barely have enough room to get the pliers in there. I was hoping I could help," Kidahin sang as she and Tialdrin set the tanks down behind Einstika.

"This does look something like a pathway into the upper tree, if you use a little imagination, anyway," Kidahin added.

"A lot of imagination, you mean," Tialdrin trilled. "What about the lock?" she asked Einstika.

"And, open!" Einstika sang and then pulled the door open.

"Look at that," Tialdrin sighed.

Kidahin blinked, impressed in spite of herself.

"This looks more like an elleiu tree interior pathway than a hallway. See how it branches off into two trails ahead that spiral upward?" she sang.

"And after that the resemblance fails," Einstika trilled in disappointment.

"Doors," Tialdrin spat, seeing what Einstika was glaring at.

"Welded shut and buckled outward from the other side. My guess is an explosion," she added with an ugly hiss.

"Maybe," Einstika sang. "Certainly no sledgehammer did this. Now what?"

"Cut it open," Kidahin sang.

"No!" Tialdrin trilled. "What if the air is contaminated?"

"Cut a small hole and take a sample. Switch to rebreathers and let the hazard suits filter out any toxins," Einstika sang.

She paused and looked over her shoulders.

"You brought the tanks and hoses but not the torch. Find it. At least buhnnie is easy to test for. So are low oxygen, carbon monoxide, and carbon dioxide levels. Tialdrin, can you test for anything more exotic?"

"Only a few simple toxins with what I have with me," she sang distractedly.

"What is the matter with you? Not feeling well?" Einstika trilled, concerned.

"No, I am fine, perfectly fine."

"Find that cutting torch so I can get started."

"Already done. I found it on the floor not far from the tanks. Do you need any help?" Kidahin asked.

"No. I can put everything back together. Did you notice the gauges? No? Fuel is down half and the oxygen is down two-thirds."

"Is there enough, you think?" Kidahin trilled.

"Not for both doors," Einstika trilled, her melody ringing with disappointment.

"Mistress? Which door do you suggest?" Kidahin sang.

"The one you think leads to the vantage. A vantage and its down-facing watch control access to the upper branches and the males' safes in any hometree. As the strategic center of any elleiu tree, I would put a command center there."

"Me, too. Einstika, cut open the one bearing to the right. If this pretty pathway mimics the interior spaces of a hometree accurately, then I would expect the left path to lead into the emergent layer residence abodes."

"Sound reasonable, but I urge caution. I mean, just how far would they go to mimic a hometree underground?" Einstika warned.

Tialdrin watched Einstika light the torch. Suspicious, she switched her suit radio to the privacy channel.

"Mistress? A word, please."

"Affirm. Privacy channel switched in and on scramble. Go ahead," the Mistress said.

"Are you talking to Einstika and Kidahin on another channel?"

"No, why?"

"They seem distracted, as if listening to someone. I see it in their body language. They hesitate, as if hearing something. They act—I cannot explain it. Preoccupied, maybe? The Song does trigger distracting memories, but this reminds me of traumatic..."

"Stop right there. Do not climb out onto a limb on this. The historical Team-one had its share of doubts, too. We know from the history songs that Einstikalin had suspicions, but Tialdrinaha did not."

"I know this," Tialdrin sang. "I think they are talking to someone."

"They are probably discussing the mission."

"Good point, but if so they are discourteous by leaving me out of it. Their hesitations, their stances, warn me they are—or think they are—talking to someone else."

"According to the teaching songs only Team-one made it to where you are, so who else can be there?"

"I do not know, but that is the point. I think something is wrong. Something about their scent interferes with the scent-linked empathy we share with the singers. I think they see pheromone-induced visions unrelated to history as I remember it."

"You are an associate healer barely out of wellnessmistress training. You are imagining things," the Mistress sang in the Gracious Mistress of the Singing People's voice.

She paused a beat and then sang a verse from the Song.

"Submit its will," Shikararro's counsel echoes in my ears.

Her beautiful voice enhanced the emotive power of her pheromones that created the mental reality surrounding them. The Song and its imagery reminded Tialdrin that right now Shikararro was giving the A'tayotan Mistress an update from the APC. The A'tayotan called her updates mission-critical. And yes, history proved just how critical those updates had been, but staying with the APC prevented Mistress of Battle Shikararro from fighting alongside Hlorrithin.

"I must be imagining things," Tialdrin complained irritably and abruptly cut the privacy channel.

"Stand back," Einstika warned and yanked the door open.

"Welcome to the vantage," she added.

"Einstika!" Tialdrin keened, realizing she had been leafchasing. "I needed an air sample first."

"Yes, sorry about that. I got absorbed in my work. You said nothing, so I kept cutting."

"No matter now," Kidahin sang as she stepped through the open door.

"See anything?" Einstika sang, curious.

"Big room. Lots of furniture. Hand torch does not even light up the far wall. Let me check something. No, it is nothing but a trick of the eye. No one here, either. I hate these a'pea flickering fluorescent lights. Eyes adjusting, getting a better look now. Clear, come on in."

"You said furniture?" the Mistress asked.

"Yes, chairs, tables, bookcases, and nests. Circular tiered seating drops into a depression in the middle of the room. Very comfortable looking seats, too."

"But the focal point is bare wooden floor. What did they use this for?" Tialdrin wondered aloud.

"Hand-to-hand combat training? More than enough room to demonstrate moves and countermoves," Einstika suggested.

"So what is that thing clustered in the center? Cover? No, it looks more like an odd cluster of—spotlights?" Kidahin sang.

Einstika scowled at the cluster. "Not spotlights. Looks more like cameras? No," she cursed and snapped her tail in self-annoyance.

"This is a planetarium projector," she trilled. "They used it to project starry night sky in here."

Kidahin saw a rippling shimmer off her left and spun around.

"Tialdrin, what are you doing?" she trilled.

"Admiring the ingenuity of these people. The projector is elaborate, too elaborate for just projecting a simple night sky. This is astronomical study quality. I wonder, could they have a telescope on the roof? We should explore this room, set a watch, and get some rest."

"Agreed," the Mistress said. "Call me when you leave that room."

"Mistress? Twenty-two hours have passed. How do you read me?" Tialdrin sang.

"Clean and clear, Team-one."

"If this room corresponds to a vantage, we can reach a residential area from here if the internal elleiu tree pattern holds. One ascending pathway leads to something a sign calls 'Administration'. A second and steeper path leads off into the residence abodes, we think…," Kidahin sang.

"We are running low on rations and water," Einstika interrupted. "We cannot stay much longer before we must backtrail to the foodstuffs in the storage area."

"What Einstika is suggesting is that she prefers returning to the APC for food over eating the canned food they stored here," Tialdrin clarified.

"A'pea that. Our immediate concern is choice. Which path do we take? The one labeled Administration or the one leading to the residence abodes?" Kidahin sang, scowling at Einstika and Tialdrin.

"Try Administration first. Maybe we can find evidence for the purpose of this place," Einstika sang.

"But exploring the residence abodes might provide answers from the residents' point of view," Tialdrin sang.

"You are pulling our tails away from Administration. Why?" Einstika trilled accusingly.

"What? What make you say this?" Tialdrin sang calmly.

"Maybe you should tell us."

"What is wrong with you, Einstika?" Kidahin trilled.

"Nothing. It is nothing. I am—imagining things. Suggestions, Mistress?"

"Administration. I care about their purpose, not their living arrangements."

"Administration it is, then. I hope we do not regret this," Einstika trilled.

"Why should we regret this?" Kidahin sang curiously.

"I do not care how familiar these pathways seem. They feel wrong to me—flipped around. The idea of building pathways that copy elleiu tree branches underground throws my senses off."

"This place gives me bad feelings. Listening to you does not make me feel better," Kidahin sang as the lights faded. "Oh, thank you for turning off the lights. Oddly, I feel better in the dark down here."

"No problem. Just watch where you aim that filthy sidearm of yours. You might shoot me by mistake."

"I will not," Kidahin sang in laughter.

"Are we going or not?" Tialdrin demanded.

"Coming," Kidahin sang. "Mistress, I am taking the right pathway. It leads up and around a short curve and into a tack-welded closed door."

Kidahin glanced at Einstika.

"Can you cut this open?"

"Why not just give it a push?" Einstika suggested with a trilling giggle.

"Why? You think I can shove a welded door open?" Kidahin trilled, snickering.

"No. They welded this from this side. I got enough fuel to cut these eleven small welds. I still cannot believe someone sealed them in. What happened here?"

"Focus. Can you cut it open or not?" the Mistress demanded.

"I can. I do not want to, but I can."

"Then do it and stop wasting time," Tialdrin trilled.

"Why? Why do you want to get in there so bad?"

"Just what does that mean, Einstika?" Kidahin trilled.

"She is talking to someone!" Einstika keened.

"Who else can I talk to? There is nobody here but us," Tialdrin sang reasonably.

"How do I know for sure? It is just—there is this signal…"

"And you think Tialdrin is talking to it?" Kidahin sang.

"I, yes. Yes, I do," Einstika trilled.

"You are leafchasing fantasies," Kidahin sang.

"I am not having an empathic breakdown!"

"Of course you are not. You are tired and stressed. We all are," Tialdrin sang soothingly. "Just open the door. The sooner we get in, the sooner we can leave."

"Affirm. You are right. I do not know what I was thinking. Give me two minutes—done. That was easy enough. Welcome to the New Dawn Admin—Dou'tu'tay!" Einstika trilled.

"Spirits! Look at that," Kidahin trilled.

"Dou'tu'tay," Tialdrin echoed.

"What do you see?" the Mistress demanded.

10
BAD MEDICINE

And fighting its formidable power, I discovered how to achieve such a feat.

Kidahin paused at the door and twitched her ears. That verse of the Song warned them that Hlorrithin was closing on the complex from the north and would catch the Neh'as'anni between his forces and the debris ridge behind the airfield.

"Well? Going to open that door or just stare at it?" Tialdrin sang.

"Just leafchasing," Kidahin sang, giving a pheromonal shrug. She shoved the door open and looked into a broad hallway. Doors ran down both sides of it, all of them having keypads below simple pull handles.

"This cannot be an administrative center," Kidahin grumbled.

"This wall paneling looks remarkably like the inside of an elleiu tree branch pathway. I think these are residence abodes," Tialdrin sang.

"Abodes do not have doors. A door implies distrust of others and violates courtesy customs," Kidahin objected as she reached out to tap on the nearest keypad.

"Dead, no power," she sang.

Einstika glided around her and tried a second keypad.

"This one, too," she sang. A note of inspiration trilled in her ear. She grabbed the handle and pulled it towards her slightly.

It opened easily.

"Unlocked. Makes sense. A power failure would otherwise trap the resident inside," Einstika sang as she yanked the door wide open. She paused for the fraction of a second courtesy required before entering another's abode.

And she immediately jumped back into the hallway.

"What?" Kidahin sang.

"A body. Now we know what happened to them," Tialdrin trilled, staring at a contorted body crumpled on the floor.

"Warrior female," she added unnecessarily.

Einstika stepped around Kidahin to try another door. She pulled it open.

"There is a dead Hunter in here. Similar body position, too."

Kidahin opened a door on her left.

"Another dead Warrior. Her body is in the same violently twisted spasm. Likely they are all dead by similar means," she trilled.

"Indeed," Tialdrin agreed.

"There is a dead male in here!" Einstika keened from another doorway.

"Notice anything obvious about them, Tialdrin?" Kidahin trilled at interrogative pitch.

"I do," Tialdrin trilled.

"What do you think? Buhnnie?"

"Indeed, and I am sure they did not all eat buhnnie fruit at the same time," Tialdrin sang.

"I do not see any bitten-into fruit. No, atomized buhnnie fruit extract, I would guess. Probably sprayed into the air vents," Einstika sang.

"Yes," Tialdrin agreed. "The Neh'as'anni likely put it in the central air system as a contingency measure."

"What kind of contingency would call for mass suicide?" Einstika trilled.

"A last resort? If New Dawn got overrun? Those cryogenic capsules filled with dead males would anger the general female population once they found out.

"Treating males suffering from mutated limb rot is one thing, but I doubt they would tolerate cryogenic research on them. They probably did not know about whatever they were doing to the male we found encased in the amber alloy mined below us. Someone anticipated getting overrun by their own clan members."

"Then again, Hlorrithin is coming for them. They probably patched a canister filled with buhnnie fruit extract into the air system to kill invaders—us," Tialdrin trilled.

"No, we opened too many doors without triggering a buhnnie discharge. Besides, safeguarding the building from intrusion means they would have wired triggers into doors. We walked through an outside door without getting gassed in the first room we stepped into. No, someone living here did this—killed their own people. And they did it long before we climbed over the ridge into the complex. I do not know if it was released before or after the explosion that took out most of the buildings, but it was not done for defensive reasons.

"This was no mass suicide, either. I know a few common airborne agents that kill immediately. Someone wanted them to suffer. Buhnnie kills in an agonizingly slow manner," Kidahin sang, gestured them out of the hall and closed the door.

"Take this path. It should lead to the administrative center," Einstika sang.

"Mistress? Any ideas?" Kidahin sang.

"Did you see anything useful in those abodes?" the Mistress asked.

"No. Every abode likely contains at least one dead resident. I doubt there is anything useful here. Hundreds of abodes here means we lack the time to check them anyway.

"The signs we found are confusing. Scent marks paths better than signs, and these people knew where the paths go," Kidahin sang.

"Maybe they simply identify the pathway's location and not where they lead? No matter, continue prowling," the Mistress said flatly.

"If these ascending pathways mirror an elleiu tree, then this path should continue into a vantage," Einstika sang.

"Which one? There are two doors up there. One is open, which makes sense since no door blocks entry into a vantage. Does anyone see a problem here?" Kidahin trilled.

"The door is not welded shut?" Tialdrin sang.

"Exactly," Kidahin sang. "Stand back while I...."

"Oh, please. I am getting tired of your a'pea thinking. We are the only ones alive here," Einstika interrupted.

"Wait! Where are you...?" Kidahin keened.

"Going inside. Exploring," Einstika sang aggressively. "Ah, I found an antechamber. In an elleiu tree this would be a males' safe, but this is wide open and not a maze of aerial roots. They put a watch point here instead."

"I smell reactive aggression on you, Einstika. Why?" Tialdrin trilled.

"I see two more doors ahead," Einstika trilled, ignoring Tialdrin. "One is open just a crack. I will check it first."

"Be careful," Kidahin warned.

"I think I fully understand how lifeless this place really is. The dead cannot hurt us if we do not—spirits. Oh, spirits. I was wrong. Mistress, you need to see this," Einstika trilled hysterically.

But I had only one chance.

The Territorial Boundaries of Rage and Forgiveness taught the necessity and danger of persistent rage, a rage that refused to go away when a person, or a People, could not let go of it. The safe trail around persistent rage led to the Rite of Forgiveness.

The empathic nature of Eyloni meant the emotions of others were only a sniff away. The customs of privacy and courtesy demanded a person ignore what she smelled on another's scent unless that other voiced it aloud. Giving voice or action to thoughts raising social debts placed an obligation on the insulted person to set the offending matter aside for a time, withhold punishment, forget the offense, and abandon the social debt owed her.

However, if a person said what was on her scent or otherwise acted on it then she incurred a social debt. Social penalties included dueling to first blood drawn or to death, banishment for days to weeks, loss of social rank or even hierarchical rank in one or more member societies or hierarchies, or the silent treatment lasting for hours to months.

The Rite of Forgiveness exclusively addressed assaults against civility and did not address crimes against morality. Moral crimes assaulted one's own or another's honor. The hierarchies prosecuted honor crimes immediately and ruthlessly, and were never forgiven. Honor crime penalties usually demanded the extreme range of social debt penalties but often demanded the death penalty. The honor crime of causing intentional harm to or death of a male without honorable justification always incurred the death penalty.

"Well? Is it clear?" Kidahin finally grunted, growing impatient with Einstika's leafchasing.

She stepped around Einstika and into a large circular room meticulously crafted unto the likeness of an elleiu tree's vantage.

A group of obviously dead people sat around a large wooden table. Above them a sculpted, high-relief ceiling appeared open to the sky. A lamp provided simulated sunlight beaming through vermilion, crimson, and yellow variegated leaves.

Fused aerial root paneling ran around the room from ceiling to the polished, soft mellow-orange wooden floor. The table, beautiful beyond description, was cut from a cross-section of a trunk. Polished to a deep orange, she could see individual growth rings from where she stood. Seats of the same polished wood surrounded the table. Above and behind it hung a flat display screen several ells across presenting a map of the La'huaset Tribal continent. Twenty glowing points scattered across central La'huaset matched the locations of the Neh'as'anni and their allied technological clans.

Red identified the few clans still resisting. Blue showed clans in decline. Green marked those clans destroyed by Hlorrithin.

Kidahin scowled at the bodies, Hunters and Warriors, frozen in grotesque sitting positions.

"We found the New Dawn administrative command center," Kidahin sang.

"You did?" the Mistress yelped. "Einstika, set up a video feed and send pictures of everything."

"Affirm, Mistress."

"Describe what you see while she sets up, Kidahin. Why do you think this is a command center?" the Mistress asked.

"Their rank earring hoops have a lot of accomplishment webs, honor knots, and mission beads woven into them. Every female here has a rank that exceeds yours, Mistress. So many high-ranking females together convinces me this was the Neh'as'anni supreme military counsel. I think they were in the process of a Major Consensus discussion when someone poisoned them."

Kidahin paused. Someone was missing—and his absence frightened her.

"Mistress, their sire cairn is not here. Why?"

"What about the male we found with the smashed skull?" Tialdrin trilled at interrogative pitch. "He was a sire cairn. We assumed his occupational association was the research staff. What if he was holding Warpact here? Did he assault their honor by abandoning them? Or did they assault his honor by rejecting and killing him? Remember the letter we found?"

"I do," Kidahin trilled and pointed her tail at the bodies. "This is buhnnie poisoning."

"I agree. Look how powerful the seizures were. Their fingernails dug right into the tabletop. See how deep the scratches are?" Tialdrin sang analytically.

"I will check the other door while you search the room. Maybe something remains for us to find," Einstika trilled impatiently. She grabbed the handle and flung the door wide open.

"A good idea, but I doubt we will find anything useful. Whoever poisoned them would have taken anything important. See anything, Tialdrin?" Kidahin sang. She turned to look at what Tialdrin was doing and froze.

"Nothing here. I agree with you. Anything of value was taken hours ago."

Kidahin ignored Tialdrin as male bodies floated around her. She struggled to ignore them. Moral duty demanded she save them, so why was Tialdrin more interested in poisoned females, and a medically detached interest at that? Tialdrin was Assault Team-Two's moral theorist, so why was she not putting theory into practice here?

A'pea Tialdrin. At least Einstika had the scent of someone with the right moral view.

Hyperarousal drove Kidahin's self-confidence and rising aggression as she wondered why Tialdrin was suddenly indifferent about the mission.

Spirits of the O'un Tu Clan, give me light feet!

"Mistress, I found a mainframe computer in here," Einstika trilled.

"Can you log into it?" the Mistress asked.

"No. These flickering fluorescent lights tell me the voltage is too low. They keep kicking on and off. Wait, I found the breakers for this room. Let me flip these switches."

"Well done, Einstika," Kidahin trilled as the bulbs flashed on and remained on.

"Yes. They have enough electricity now because I turned the computers off," Einstika sang.

"Why did you do that?" Tialdrin sang, curious.

"We cannot transmit files to the A'tayotan from here even if we had the power to run everything. I need a whole team of techmistresses to make sense of this system."

"We do not have the time. Hlorrithin is northwest of us and needs those files to stop a global environmental disaster," Kidahin keened as she searched the room.

Two mainframe computers, each waist-high and longer than a lab table, dominated the middle of the room. Four reel-to-reel magnetic tape drives stood against the far wall. Four CRT display workstations with dedicated keyboards sat on the left. Directly in front of her squatted a printer big enough to accept paper sheets as wide as she could spread her arms. Its built-in keyboard meant it could be used as a hard-copy terminal.

A free-standing, wheeled cabinet housing a multi-disk hard drive memory unit about chest-high looked too big to put arms around. A power cord and data cables tethered it to the right wall.

No computer expert herself, Kidahin knew it was a hard drive unit simply because she could see the stack of disks under a clear plastic bubble atop the unit.

"Why not just take the hard drive unit and forget the computers?" Kidahin suggested.

"I think so, too. The hard drive is used for bulk archival storage. The tape units swap blocks of code in and out of core memory so the computer can run programs larger than its memory capacity. Looks like someone will have a lot to carry," Einstika sang wickedly.

"Who, me?" Kidahin trilled.

"Yes, you. You too, Tialdrin. Come here and get a feel for what we have to push around for the next few hours."

"Dou'tu'tay, Einstika. Just take it apart," Kidahin trilled.

"No, not unless I have to. Look, those casters have brakes. Can you release them?"

"Of course," Kidahin sang, feeling much better now that they were making measurable progress.

"Dou'tu'tay, this thing is bulky," Tialdrin complained.

"Will its size pose a problem?" the Mistress asked.

"It depends on what you mean by problem," Einstika sang.

"She wants to know if we can get it back to the APC intact," Kidahin trilled.

"Precisely," the Mistress confirmed.

"I think so. I am more worried about getting it out of here, over rubble, and through the jungle. Let me send you a picture so you can see the size of it," Einstika sang.

"It does look unwieldy," the Mistress admitted. "Those little wheels will not matter once you leave smooth tiled concrete floors behind."

"Agreed. I am hopeful about the amount of data stored in this unit. I think it could hold more than a gigabyte."

"Who cares? We have to push or carry this thing out of here and back to the APC," Kidahin sang.

"Where Shikararro is doing nothing while Hlorrithin risks his life," Einstika spat in disgust.

"Exactly. Why are we safeguarding this piece of junk while males risk their lives?" Kidahin trilled.

"We never abandon males, any male," Einstika added, furious.

The hate Einstika voiced caused Kidahin to glance out the open door. On the command center floor lay dead bodies, a hundred or more, all males. Movement flashed in the corner of her eye, and she staggered backward in retreat and slammed into the hard drive unit.

"Kill the lights," she sang. "Someone is alive out there."

Einstika froze. Yellow afterimages filled her eyes with visions triggered by Kidahin's powerful warning pheromones. Desiccated bodies drifted near the door. She glanced from body to body, saw movement, and focused on the fuzzy outline of a retreating female figure.

"Kidahin, wait. Stop!" Tialdrin trilled.

"Kidahin, she is killing them!" Einstika shouted over Tialdrin. "She is the reason why Hlorrithin dies!" she added, scowling at Tialdrin.

"Who is?" Tialdrin trilled at interrogative pitch. "No one is here but us."

Kidahin unsnapped the holster at her hip and pulled her weapon, aimed, and fired.

"Team-one, I hear gunshots. What is happening?" the Mistress demanded.

"Kidahin, stop!" Tialdrin trilled again.

"Shoot her!" Einstika keened.

Kidahin aimed at the fleeing Hunter's head and emptied the clip.

A ricochet grazed Kidahin's leg, and the momentary pain distracted her. The Eldest Hunter and the bodies immediately disappeared.

"I shot her in the head. I am sure of it," Kidahin panted.

"My leg hurts," she added in afterthought.

"A ricochet," Einstika sang.

"Someone was there!" Kidahin trilled.

"I thought so, too. But when you started shooting I lost sight of her—them," Einstika trilled uncertainly.

"She has a gun of some kind, one not of Environmental Interdiction issue. I am the only Hunter authorized to carry a firearm here. She may have found one in the warehouse. Thank the spirits she did not set explosives. With all the mining below there must be explosives around here somewhere," Kidahin sang.

"I saw nothing but Einstika trilling and you aiming—at nothing," Tialdrin sang calmly.

"Your scent tells me you are thinking too much about *Londiwe Khoza*," she added.

"Shove that wellnessmistress nonsense off a branch and use your healer skills to do something about her leg," Einstika trilled.

Tialdrin scowled but turned to examine Kidahin.

"Fine. Let me see it," she sang, pricking her ears at Kidahin.

"Mistress, we need a few minutes to treat Kidahin's scratch and patch her suit," Einstika sang, watching Tialdrin carefully.

"This is a mere flesh wound, nothing more. The bleeding has already stopped, but you need a few sutures or it will start bleeding again," Tialdrin sang after a few minutes.

"Just patch it so we can get this a'pea hard drive back to the APC. Mistress, have you heard from Shikararro?" Kidahin growled.

"No. What she does is not your concern. Getting the data back to us is. I am sending regular reports of your progress to Hlorrithin. Your prowling and discoveries have put him on the path to victory. By his order I am recalling you. Get that data to us now!"

"Affirm, Mistress," Kidahin sang, her hyperarousal draining away as news of Hlorrithin's continued safety shoved the last of the emotional dread of dead males aside.

"Dou'tu'tay, I feel cold," she complained.

"Reaction to the wound," Tialdrin sang offhandedly. "And you are finally calming down. Enjoy feeling cold while you can, because once we get moving, you will heat up again, and these sutures will start itching."

"Mistress, we are ready to leave the administrative center," Einstika sang.

"Wait. Do you hear that?" Kidahin sang.

"Oh, spirits. Again? There is nobody here," Tialdrin trilled in frustration.

"Quiet. This sounds, different. Like scratching, or clanking. Like something metallic dragging our way," Kidahin trilled.

"Get out of there, Team-one. You may have Neh'as'anni forces returning. The pictures Einstika sent me make it clear they could use the Technology Center building as a rallying point even if nothing inside is of any help to them," the Mistress said.

"Shikararro should have stopped them from coming," Kidahin cursed.

"Nevermind her. Go!" the Mistress yelled.

"Affirm," Einstika sang. "Tialdrin, are you finished suturing that little cut yet?" she trilled, still watching her suspiciously.

"I am…," Tialdrin began.

"Then quit leafchasing and help me with this cabinet. The quickest way back is through the lift shaft and up the service ladder," Einstika trilled.

Tialdrin grimaced and then growled. What Einstika said did not sound right, but history was in the telling. After centuries of retelling the same story over and over again, minor details became fuzzy. That did not matter much as long as the Song continued to track their historical roles.

"Kidahin, hurry up and head back to the lift shaft," Einstika trilled.

"I am trying to. I see it up ahead. I can already see the rungs set into the wall. How do we carry this thing while climbing?"

"Thread a rope through the cabinet first and then climb to the ground level. Wait for Tialdrin to join you. Then both of you pull it up while I keep it from bumping into the rungs or slamming into a wall. Move!" Einstika urged at imperative tempo.

"Kidahin, climb faster," Tialdrin sang.

"I am trying to. I think I tore a suture. The a'pea thing is bleeding again. I need a new bandage when we get up top."

"Mistress, we are recalling back to the warehouse and will contact you when we get there," Einstika trilled.

"Affirm, Team-one."

Two and a half hours later Einstika turned the voice-operated transmitter back on.

"We have reached the warehouse. The hard drive unit is still with us and undamaged. It got stuck in the service shaft, but we freed it without having to take it apart," she sang.

"I think something is moving down there," Kidahin warned.

"Not again!" Tialdrin sang.

"Dou'tu'tay! What the a'pea is that? Kidahin, shoot it now!" Einstika trilled.

Kidahin drew her weapon, aimed down the lift shaft, and fired repeatedly.

"What is that thing?" Einstika trilled.

"Not some memory from *Londiwe Khoza* this time. I did not get a good look, but it was person-shaped. I emptied a whole clip into it. Wait here while I reload."

"That a'pea female you shot at. She must have let it out of the lower levels. That, or she is wearing body armor," Einstika trilled.

Tialdrin hesitated at Einstika's mention of another female. What other female? An empathic figment in Kidahin's mind? Why was Einstika humoring her? The object in the shaft below looked real. Well, as real as pheromonal empathy could make anything look real here.

"Your shooting scared it off," Einstika sang.

"I doubt it," Kidahin sang in warning.

"Recall to the APC with that data storage unit!" the Mistress snarled.

"We will not go anywhere very fast dragging this cabinet. Our hazard suits slow us down as it is," Einstika growled.

She shoved the cabinet hard and it rolled across the smooth warehouse floor until it bumped against a wooden crate, the same crate the all-terrain vehicle had nearly rammed into Kidahin hours earlier.

"Load it onto the ATV. We can drive through the small side door next to the big rear door they use to bring the jets in and out of here," she sang.

"Probably locked," Tialdrin sang.

"Of course, to keep people from getting in, not to stop us from getting out. Kidahin, open it while Tialdrin and I tie this thing on top of the ATV."

"Affirm," Kidahin sang.

"The cabinet will not fit on the roof," Tialdrin warned.

"It will fit, but barely. You sit on it and tie yourself to it, otherwise you might tumble off."

"Me? Why me?" Tialdrin objected.

"I am driving. Kidahin will jump in the passenger seat as I pass her."

"I do not like this idea," Tialdrin complained.

"Too bad," Einstika sang as she put the ATV in low gear and flipped a switch.

"Hang on, Tialdrin," Einstika added as the ATV lurched forward.

Einstika drove to Kidahin. Behind her a coppery-gold shape climbed out of the shaft.

"Hurry! An amber-alloy armored figure just cleared the lift shaft," Kidahin trilled. She charged the closing ATV, jumped into the passenger seat as it passed, grabbed the roller bar, and wrapped her tail around the small seat as Einstika sped through the open door.

As soon as they cleared the building Kidahin heard distant singing coming out of the north behind the airfield.

"Antiphonal challenges," she snarled and gnashed her teeth. Antiphonal singing projected mockery, and mockery fomented rash action.

"Hlorrithin is goading them. Shikararro and her archers must be fighting with him," Einstika sang.

"No," Tialdrin sang. "She is directing her archers from the APC. Remember your history? Shikararro helps Einstika interface the...."

"Shut up!" Kidahin trilled. "We cannot use objective knowledge while in subjective time. We must follow history as prompted by the Gracious Mistress and her singers. We will...."

Kidahin hesitated as dead males covered the pavement everywhere she looked. She had a mission to complete: trace a radiation signal to its source and capture whatever information they happened to find.

But she could not ignore those bodies. The data stored on the hard drive would save them all.

"We cannot let them capture us. Einstika, turn left and follow the pavement back to the retaining wall. Drive around the rubble and continue southwest to the perimeter road. Maybe we can find a gradual slope up and over the debris ridge to a trail back to the APC," Kidahin trilled.

"Affirm."

Kidahin scowled. Saving males mattered more than any other consideration, yet Einstika hesitated. Spirits. What was wrong with her, anyway?

Einstika held her anger in check, but it was so hard. It fought her reason as she smelled thoughts of dead males on Kidahin's scent.

And what was wrong with Tialdrin? Why take Shikararro's side in this? She did nothing, *nothing*, while males died!

"The dou'tu'tay batteries just died," Einstika growled after forty minutes of driving. "Climbing up the ridge and over undergrowth drained them fast."

"How far are you from the APC?" the Mistress asked.

"Less than a thousand ells by my reckoning. Putting the ATV in neutral and pushing it sounds better than carrying the hard drive," Einstika grunted.

"Not for long. Sooner or later we will run across something we cannot push wheels over. Maybe we should open the top and take just the disks with us. Surely the A'tayotan techmistresses can install them into one of their own hard drive units," Kidahin sang.

"No," Einstika trilled. "The disk coatings are scratch-sensitive. Hlorrithin needs this data right away, which means figuring out how to interface the unit with the APC on-board computer. I lack the expertise, which is why we needed a senior techmistress."

"Shikararro is a senior techmistress? Well, that figures," Kidahin trilled in dismissal.

"You did not know?" Einstika trilled heatedly. "I guess it does not matter, now. Her shoulder injury snapped the branch off that plan. By now she has rejoined her archers at the airfield."

Together they pushed the ATV some three hundred ells before it bumped into a vine too big to roll over and too embedded into the undergrowth to move.

"Well," Kidahin drawled. "Now we carry. Soon we will be home."

"On our way home, you mean. Home is another three-day drive in the APC. At least it is roomier than the ATV," Einstika sang.

"I recognize this rise. We left the APC just beyond those trees," Tialdrin sang, relieved.

"It does look familiar," Kidahin agreed.

"Mistress, we will reach the APC within the hour," Einstika sang.

Kidahin and Tialdrin hoisted the hard drive onto their shoulders.

Einstika led the way as she absently wondered why the Mistress did not reply.

Kidahin and Tialdrin complained as the off-balance cabinet tended to slide off their shoulders at every chance.

Einstika topped the rise first and saw the armored personnel carrier, right where they left it.

"APC in sight," she sang unnecessarily.

"Stow the a'pea thing, get in, and get out of here," Kidahin sang.

"Affirm," Einstika trilled. "Come on, Tialdrin. Help me get this thing through the door. Kidahin, Tialdrin and I will hold it level while you grab and pull it across the back seat."

"I do not think it will fit back there even if we lay it sideways," Kidahin growled.

"Dou'tu'tay," Einstika cursed. "I may have to stand it next to the APC, connect the power and data cables, and download the data here before we can leave."

"Maybe we can unbolt and pull out the back seat?" Kidahin sang hopefully.

"What about the thorax supply compartment? We used up most of what we brought with us. It is nearly empty now," Tialdrin suggested.

"Might work, but we cannot connect it and download its files from there," Kidahin sang.

"Wait! Do not open the compartment. Let me do a security check on the APC first," Einstika warned.

"Oh, spirits. I forgot to check for sabotage before I opened the cabin door. Thank the spirits I did not turn anything on," Kidahin confessed.

Einstika made a quick and thorough check and sighed.

"Kidahin? Come look at this."

"What is it?" Kidahin trilled as she glided up to the techmistress.

"A nice security precaution. Shikararro ran a detonator circuit through the supply compartment. A clever one, too. Makes sense. She could not risk leaving the APC unattended, so she sabotaged it."

"What did she do?" Kidahin sang at interrogative tempo.

"Patched a sensor into the starter solenoid. Rather than turning the starter motor on, it triggers a blasting cap on the thorax natural gas fuel tank. I can disarm it in about ten minutes," Einstika sang and grumbled about having to make sure the firing circuit was not rigged to go off if tampered with.

"I am surprised she did not sabotage the engine compartment," she added as she worked.

"That would have been too obvious," Shikararro sang.

The three Hunters spun at the sound of her voice.

"This smells wrong," Kidahin sang. "Why are you not with Hlorrithin?"

Shikararro gave her a quizzical look.

"I am not supposed to. Remember your history? I am overseeing the recovery of Neh'as'anni technical data, which was far more important than anything else," she sang.

"Then help us load this thing into the supply compartment," Kidahin trilled. *More important than Hlorrithin?*

"No. We need to make data cables and power cords and get this thing up and running," Shikararro sang.

"We are doing this here? Now? While Hlorrithin takes a beating at the airfield?" Einstika keened in anger.

"I will drive, Einstika," Kidahin trilled warily. "If these disks are as sensitive as you say, then bouncing down jungle trails will cause the read-write heads to scratch them."

"I know," Einstika sang in the same wary tone.

Kidahin watched the three load the cabinet into the compartment.

"Einstika, can you make the cables you need while I drive?"

"Yes, but you will have to stop when I am ready to connect the hard drive to the computer."

"Affirm. Get in, everyone," Kidahin sang.

"Running systems check. Systems nominal. Computer is up and ready to accept external data storage. Start the engine, Kidahin," Einstika sang.

The natural gas internal combustion turbine engine turned over immediately.

I cannot fail now!

Victory pheromones filled Einstika's nose. Now was the time for Hlorrithin to strike the final blow.

But he would die because Shikararro did not return to his side in time.

Pheromonal fury reeked from Einstika as a traumatic stress flashback filled her eyes with red lights and hundreds of dead bodies frozen solid. No! Red meant safe. Green meant danger. We found bodies not frozen. They are intact. I do not understand it, but their rigor is consistent with buhnnie poisoning.

Einstika's pheromones overpowered Kidahin. The history songs said Team-one stayed here until the files had been downloaded.

Or did they?

Kidahin pushed the clutch pedal, shifted into neutral, hesitated again, and shut the engine off.

"Kidahin? What is it?" Tialdrin trilled in concern.

"Nothing, Tialdrin. Nothing at all," Kidahin sang, paused a few seconds.

"Einstika? Do it."

"Yes, Kidahin. Shikararro, I claim a point of honor against you for cowardice in the face of the enemy," Einstika keened.

"What?" Shikararro trilled.

Einstika, already grasping the handle of her flint-bladed adulthood knife, pulled it clear of its breast-hugging sheath and cut Shikararro's throat.

11
KEEPING APPEARANCES

"Einstika! What have you done?" Tialdrin keened hysterically.

"Nothing, why?" Einstika sang innocently, cocked her ears quizzically, and began twisting her pons in slow circles as she admired the adulthood knife in her grip.

She smiled vaguely at its sharp, clean, black and red flint blade and felt an immense sense of pride.

"Why did I draw my knife? There is no threat and the blade is still clean, see?" she sang and thrust the knife in Tialdrin's face.

"You violated history!" Tialdrin keened. "Shikararro did not die during the Battle of Withered Trees, let alone by your hand. You committed an honor crime. Spirits, the Gracious Mistress will charge all of us with honor crimes!"

"What are you singing about, honor crimes? Why would she do that?" Kidahin trilled impatiently.

"For this!" Tialdrin trilled, snapping her tail at Einstika's flint blade and pointing at the rear seat before noticing it was empty.

Empty?

She froze in mid-rant, dropped to her knees, and frantically searched under the back seat for the body she knew was there.

Kidahin glanced away from the windshield long enough to frown at Einstika. "What is she looking for?"

"I have no idea," Einstika snapped, the prideful regard she felt for her adulthood knife rapidly fading. "I heard her leafchasing after Shikararro and something about not dying during the Battle of Withered Trees."

"Of course she did not die then," Kidahin sang, annoyed at stating the obvious. She sighed, twisted around in the driver seat, and glared at Tialdrin.

"Shikararro lived to send captured data to Hlorrithin and then rejoined her Pathwalker archers with the help of Environmental Interdiction Team-one. What does Shikararro, or Hlorrithin for that matter, have to do with anything?"

"I—I thought I saw Shikararro sitting next to me. I saw Einstika turn in her seat and cut Shikararro's throat," Tialdrin trilled, suddenly uncertain.

"Oh, really?" Einstika growled. "And just where was she sitting? On my lap? We barely have enough room in here for us and our equipment. And how do you suppose Shikararro got here when she died hundreds of years ago? What did we do? Go back in time and get her?"

Tialdrin snapped her tail several times and twisted her pons around in tight frustrated circles.

"No," she retorted nastily. "I think I saw a scene from the Song of Hlorrithin."

"A scene from—as in a reenactment of the Song of Hlorrithin? Memorial celebrations like those involve many people," Einstika scoffed. "I would certainly remember getting an invitation to join in a celebration involving thousands of people."

"I know, I know. But I can almost remember hearing dialogue prompts through pheromonal empathy."

"I do not hear singers, and they sing the historical scenes into existence. Nor do I smell singer pheromones or feel like I am in scent-linked empathy with them. What I see here does not even look like a scene from a teaching song concerning the Battle of Withered Trees. Look around and you will see we are not in some historical setting," Kidahin sang at impatience tempo.

Tialdrin desperately did not want to shove the good sense Kidahin made off the branch. Ready to drop the matter, she was about to agree when a whispering rhythmic beat brushed her ears.

"Do you hear that?" she trilled.

"Hear what?" Kidahin sang.

"Maybe she hears Hlorrithin keening for her help," Einstika scoffed.

"I never heard Hlorrithin, and I never heard Shikararro, either," Tialdrin sang.

"What do you hear, then?" Kidahin trilled dryly.

"Singing."

"You do?" Einstika trilled, spreading her ears wide and listening for the slightest hint of music. "If ritual singers are singing an emotional reality for us to experience, then we should all hear them. I hear nothing. Do you hear anything, Kidahin?"

"I hear nothing except you two leafchasing after fantasies. I do feel strange emotions. Every time I wrap my tail around them they slip free. Can you tell us what you hear?" Kidahin sang, smelling growing certainty in Tialdrin's intoxicating body odor.

Tialdrin ignored Kidahin least she lose the thread of melody murmuring in her ears.

The spirits come to us through sound, through music that vibrates the chest and excites the heart. They come through the drum and voice. They cause us to remember what substance we are made from and where we come from.

The ancient songs say that the skin or body of a drum determines the person or thing called into being. Some drums are journeying drums transporting the drummer and his listeners to various places. Other drums are powerful in their own ways.

The Territorial Boundaries of Rage and Forgiveness tells us rage teaches, calls for healing, belongs to the Spirit Male, and demands correct behavior. Personal rage and honor stand among withered trees. When it cannot find a resting place, it injures instinct. Clan rage and persistent rage summon the Rite of Forgiveness, which requires setting the matter aside for a time, withholding punishment, forgetting the offense, and abandoning the social debt.

"I hear someone singing about setting this matter aside for a time," Tialdrin finally trilled.

"As in the Rite of Forgiveness? What matter should we set aside? You cannot mean setting aside our mission. Spirits, Tialdrin, I keep seeing dead bodies from *Londiwe Khoza*. They look so real I can barely concentrate on anything else. Do you hear the Song of Hlorrithin, too?" Kidahin trilled at interrogative tempo.

"No, but I think we should set the *Londiwe Khoza* deaths aside. Their influence on our pheromones is a distraction. Someone is singing from the Wisdom of the Clans, and she keeps repeating how the Territorial Boundaries of Rage and Forgiveness are managed in social life," Tialdrin sang.

"Wait, I hear something new," she added.

This is the most beautiful dawn I can remember.

"Now she sings from the Song of Hlorrithin, a verse well into the Song, too. She is singing in imperative pitch and in harmony with the Wisdom verses. I can barely hear her, almost like she is singing from inside a hollow elleiu tree branch up in the canopy. You cannot hear her?" Tialdrin trilled in frustration.

Einstika and Kidahin exchanged furtive glances and snapped their tails no.

"I hear nothing," Einstika added. "Sing what you hear," she trilled impatiently.

"This is the most beautiful dawn I can remember," Tialdrin sang in triple-part harmony, repeating the rhythm exactly as she heard it.

Tialdrin's singing voice and her pheromones conjured mental visions about the dawn and its many meanings. The dawn heralded the end of Elleio's Long Night. Beloved by everyone, it promised new beginnings. The dawn rose slowly in service to all. It was a source of hope and happiness.

And yet Hlorrithin would never see another dawn after the final battle. A cool predawn breeze gusted over the three Huntresses as they watched the dawn break above the trees.

The first rays struck the canopy. Bright oranges and reds sparkled through huge diaphanous leaves and blended through layers of leaves to a dominating orangy shade hitting the trail. Auroras flashed across dim blue gaps in the canopy.

Auroras often appeared just after sunset and just before sunrise, but in central La'huaset they sometimes flashed throughout the Long Night in concert with magnificent lightning from the vast electrical storms common then. Green, magenta, and pale yellow streamers would sometimes even shimmer in the daylight like pale rainbow wraiths in the northern sky.

"This is a beautiful dawn," Einstika admitted, twisting her pons in lazy circles and thanking the spirits for the comforting view.

"I do not know what you are hearing, Tialdrin. But it must have inspired you to think about the Song of Hlorrithin. Your scent paints the most beautiful visions of dawn in my mind, a good beginning for our mission," Kidahin sang.

"Spirits, the troop transport just dropped us off and here we are leafchasing after the dawn," she added with a trace of annoyance.

Kidahin switched the main power from standby to operate and rocked the control collective side-to-side and up-and-down to get a feel for the feedback from the golden auxetic muscles driving the small light armored vehicle's eleven insect-like legs. Satisfied, she pushed the collective forward slightly and the LAV lurched ahead in a slow, rhythmic crawl down a brightening narrow trail.

The rainforest pulsed with ocher and pastel vermilions and crimsons with subtle scarlet blotches. Hints of yellowed orange, yellow ocher, and sunburst yellow streaks broke up the predominating reddish orange. Branches and trunks ranging from off-white through beige sienna to burnt rusty orange appeared and disappeared. Yellow-green mosses sprouting large black flowers clung to the branches closest to the trail. Windshield-high orange ferns crowded the path on both sides. Above, yellow-orange pale light filtered down through layers and layers of colorful leaves, each leaf big enough to cover the LAV like a tarpaulin.

The drivetrain thrummed as legs scrabbled over ferns and pale yellow ground vines. They grew among and under the orange ferns. Most vines grew wrist-thick, but some grew waist-thick across the trail. Ground vines like those made most wheeled-vehicle travel here dangerous if not nearly impossible.

Tialdrin's comments, wheeled vehicles, and Hlorrithin pinched a nerve in Kidahin's pons as she scowled at the passing trees. Fossil-fueled wheeled armored personnel carriers were used in Hlorrithin's time. They saw limited use during the Battle of Withered Trees.

But leg-driven, fusion-powered light armored vehicles came much later. Delwyn compared them to an Earth insect called a carpenter ant. He said they looked remarkably alike: three-segmented, black, eleven legs. Scale the exoskeleton up, put the reactor in the abdomen, the leg drive auxetics in the thorax, and the cabin in the head. Even the dual driver and gunner cockpit canopies resembled the insect's compound eyes. Both even had mandibles.

Kidahin stared at burnt-orange mosses and thumb-sized black blossoms creeping by the windshield. They made the rusty bark look long-dead and rotten. The rusty soil, not dusty, was not really damp, either. That trilled a sour note because the rainforest, always damp, should be wet if not squishy.

Kidahin smelled black blossoms and got a nose full of Einstika's anger-laced pheromones at the same time and began leafchasing after her intriguing scent as the trail shimmered and shifted before sharpening back into focus. Male bodies covered the trail, and she wondered how she could avoid crawling over them. The scattered corpses made the forest look like the scene from a battlefield right out of ancient times.

"Kidahin, do you see them?" Einstika keened in horror.

"I do. I know why Tialdrin thought about the Song of Hlorrithin."

"Oh?" Tialdrin sang, curiosity drawing her away from the unnaturally dry trail.

"Yes. Hlorrithin saved people, females generally and males specifically, and the environment from an ecological disaster. We must save males from dying…," Kidahin paused as the battlefield carnage summoned words from a Delwyn song.

He often sang about the spirits. Humans saw them changing form when they traveled from tribal continent to tribal continent. On the European Tribal continent they assumed female forms. Delwyn habitually gave the formless and androgynous spirits individual genders and personal names. The song honored spirits called *valr kjosa*.

One of these spirits, called *Female-in-Armor*, loved strife, wore armor and shield, threw stones while running, hurled spears while running, displayed Warrior-female strength, healed others like a surgeon-in-battle, and carried the honorific Driver-of-Victory. The song told a story about how she and spirits like her chose the battle-dead and took them to Vallr-holle, the human Oyya Web.

But on Elleio people sang the dead into the Oyya Web. The spirits did not come and take them there like they apparently did on

Earth.

The Assault Team-Two mission directive to save males had nothing to do with preparing a Death Song ritual place for Delwyn to sing them into the Oyya Web. Yet dead males, fists and fists of them, covered the trail as if waiting for their corpse-chooser spirits to take them.

Kidahin's eyes glazed over and the bodies blurred. She blinked several times, yet the bodies remained fuzzy and indistinct, like places or faces half-forgotten.

She growled, wondering what was making them look fuzzy. They fell where they died and should stand out against the grass and the forest background. Instead, they faded into the grasses as if they grew around and through the bodies.

Maybe their clothes made them look that way. Humans had a peculiar habit of wearing clothing to excess. Counting the clothed bodies, Kidahin found about a fist of human male bodies for every hand of Eyloni ones.

She clutched her ankles with one hand and pulled them into the seat under her and keened. Shuddering, she gripped the collective with a twitching right hand.

All these male bodies in one place at the same time made no sense. Kidahin closed her eyes but could not wipe what she felt from her empathic mind.

"It is our duty to save males," Tialdrin keened at imperative pitch.

"This is why we are here. We must reach the fall-back point to prevent this from happening," Einstika trilled. "Thank the spirits this beautiful dawn has come."

Kidahin cringed. What was she singing about? Bodies surrounded them, but as the sunlight streamed into her eyes their outlines blurred as fungi-covered knobby branches crawled steadily past the windshield. Kidahin frowned at them and leafchased after drifting thoughts.

***

Kidahin climbed up into a twisting fused-root path in one of her Uahua'asee'a Clan extended family elleiu trees. She hurried up the hollow interior to an emergent-layer branch. Driven by an irresistible scent, she stepped into the branch and ran up the tree, passing several small boles, abode entrances, leading into the personal living spaces of those living in this branch. The scent-markings of hundreds covered the upward-spiraling pathway, but only one mattered now.

"Aplilin," she trilled happily.

Aplilin, best friend and steadfast lover for over two years now, lived here.

Prickly wariness swept through Kidahin. She shook the feeling aside as thoughts of Aplilin stalked her. The hollow emergent layer branch and its amber-orange path dimmed slightly when she reached Aplilin's abode, poked her head into the dim bole, looked around, hesitated for a second, and stepped inside.

Lover or not, the customs of courtesy and privacy demanded this polite way of entering the abode of another person.

Hearing no challenge nor expecting one, Kidahin stepped into the abode and prowled quietly against the hollow log interior wall. She paused briefly to glance into side openings that led into storage spaces, workrooms, the necessary, and the dining area.

Impatient, she glided across the central living space in eager anticipation of reaching the sleeping nest and its occupant. Large amber eyes widened in desire as she saw her sleeping lover lying curled among the several cushions and pillows they had shared many times.

Kidahin stopped at the nest and watched Aplilin sleep.

Aplilin immediately snapped into a sitting position.

Startled, Kidahin jumped backwards across the living area to within ells of the abode entrance, wary.

"Kidahin?" Aplilin trilled and stood up, twisting slightly to give Kidahin a stunningly suggestive profile pose.

Kidahin stared at the beautiful Huntress. Muscular for a Hunter female yet quick and lithe, Aplilin easily matched the strength of many Warrior females yet retained the artistic, rhythmic grace of a Hunter. Her physical presence projected an aura of recklessness, valor, attitude, and aggression.

And she adored Delwyn. Every time mating season came around she stalked him relentlessly. In fact, during the last mating season she pushed Mistress of Sails Anailiatha off the Warleader's Watch just to gain a few ells head start.

Mating with Delwyn never brought them infants. But this never stopped them from sharing mating empathy with their favorite male.

Kidahin smiled softly and gazed upon her lover. Like Delwyn, Aplilin had a stubborn tail and rarely bothered to think matters through. She likely thought she could force conception through sheer strength alone.

"Kidahin, come to me," Aplilin trilled suggestively.

Desire swept through Kidahin. In both mating and in pleasure seeking, females twined tails and enhanced their shared empathic contact through scent. Low male numbers meant females twined tails with one another and often with more than one female at the same time to enjoy pleasure and shared intimate companionship. Both Kidahin and Aplilin enjoyed occasional intimate company with other females, but they sought each other out consistently and often.

Aplilin stood, naked but for the adulthood knife strapped around and under her left breast and the military rank earring and its webbed, beaded, and knotted golden hoop hanging from the short gold chain in her left lower earfold.

"Well?" Aplilin sang as she glided silently up to Kidahin and stopped, all but touching.

"Yes," Kidahin stammered. "It is me. Did I wake you?"

"No," Aplilin sang. "I waited for you. Come twine tails with me."

"I cannot. I am on a mission. How are you not with me?" Kidahin trilled, staring longingly into Aplilin's amber eyes.

Aplilin snapped her ears violently at Kidahin.

"You play a historical role in the Song of Hlorrithin. The remembrance ritual collapsed and you are lost in the Oyya Web. You, my Kidahin, are leafchasing after fragmentary visions you and Einstika create through shared empathy."

Kidahin leaned back, flattened her ears against her short crimson ringlets and spun her pons—not in prelude to suggestive foreplay—but in warning.

"No! Saving as many males as I can before the disaster kills them takes precedence. Dead males cover the ground like rotting buhnnie fruit impaled on im'ahailee blades. They are everywhere. Tialdrin is right: it is our duty to protect males."

"Come to me," Aplilin urged, her tail twisting invitingly. "Twine tails with me. Rubbing our pons together will trigger pheromonal memories and trilling pleasure. Our empathic sharing will overpower the visions you share with Einstika and Tialdrin and snap you out of the Oyya Web."

Kidahin yearned for her lover, but Aplilin was the fragmented vision she had leafchased into being.

"Forgive me, my Aplilin. I cannot turn my tail and run from males in need—not even for you," Kidahin keened, turned, and jumped through the bole threshold and back onto the upper canopy hollow branch. Her bare feet barely brushed the amber pathway before it vanished.

***

Kidahin leaned back into the driver seat and sighed. Being with Aplilin felt so real, and she looked out the windshield at nearby rolling hills to distract her thoughts.

They flattened out to the north. Dense jungle grew tall around the narrow trail. Densely clustered trees and clumps of tall grasses matching her skin shadings grew even thicker and close enough to brush against the passing LAV.

The air, hot and humid, turned hazy. Landmarks faded and blended into the vague orange of jungle-blindness. Pastel vermilion, amber, scarlet, and crimson leaves turned the dawn into an overwhelming yellowed-orange shade. It overbore the brighter reds and oranges.

Branches covered with golden mosses threw shimmering auras around crimson arberi leaves. The leaves in turn broke up some of the predominating orange shade. Mosses hanging from branches sprouted fist-size black blossoms. Beautiful as it was, Kidahin kept a wary eye on the increasing number of deep-green parasitic vines on the trail. Worse, the number of faded yellow-green dead or dying branches increased as well.

"This ground is too dry," Tialdrin complained.

"Um," Einstika grunted in agreement.

"At least we will not get stuck in mud," Kidahin trilled offhandedly as she drove into a meadow of amber grass. She pulled up alongside a long line of spindly, tan trees.

Tialdrin smelled their rich resin scent and sighed.

"Permaleaf trees. They grow near water. I smell them but not the water," she complained.

LAV mechanical legs drummed rhythmically as they scrabbled over large purple clinkers. They covered the trail in increasing numbers as it wandered among several crimson radial fern trees. Many of the trees' twenty-four-ell-long branches had snapped at the midpoint and sagged to the ground, their deep crimson fading to light green as they died.

The LAV skittered over more cobalt boulders, but the farther it crawled the smaller they became.

"This looks more like an old road than an animal trail, but no road has been built in several hundred years," Tialdrin trilled.

"Probably a remnant of a reclaimed roadbed. This valley once belonged to the Neh'as'anni and their allied clans," Kidahin sang stiffly.

The scattered rocks turned broader and flatter. The path took on the color and texture of an old lava flow. The trees thinned out until only buhnnie trees dominated.

Sprinkled among the buhnnies stood granite boulders, remnants from some landslide. The boulders stood like sentinels set upon both sides of the trail. The overgrowing scarlet mosses and orange ferns gleamed in the bright dawn. Beautiful scarlet four-lobed leaves grew around the base of each granite monolith.

The legs changed pitch as they struck slabs of sheared limestone partially buried in the dry, rust-colored soil. Buhnnie trees grew close to them and all around the granite rubble.

Kidahin growled at the trees, their stubby branches, their few leaves, and their huge oversized green fruit. Too much fruit, she realized.

Tialdrin watched the forest creep by. Red mosses grew on the boulders at breast height along a strip as wide as her hand could span and down the rocky wall without a break. The mossy band blinked redly at her, and she dropped her gaze to the im'ahailee passing underneath the LAV. A grassy plant, im'ahailee leaves could slash through gloves with ease. The smell of buhnnie fruit made her mouth water. They smelled edible but were poisonous. The green rinds warned everyone to avoid them. Buhnnie killed by interfering with nervous system synapses and caused the body to contort into grotesque shapes. It was a horrific and painful way to die.

"This is wrong," Tialdrin trilled in distress. "Buhnnie and im'ahailee grow in sparse patches. They do not grow in broad swaths. That red moss reminds me of a blinking panel, something like the flashing red battle status panels running down the corridors of—of *Londiwe Khoza*."

Tialdrin gasped and shuddered. *Londiwe Khoza*, the dead humans came from him. Their deaths happened on his decks, in space. Why then did she see his dead crew scattered across the forest?

A sudden deep emotional shock nose-blinded Tialdrin just long enough to free her from Kidahin and Einstika's enthralling scent. They and the LAV turned transparent orange, and through them she saw a large gathering of females sitting in a complex branching pattern.

***

"Tialdrin?" a familiar voice sang.

"Mimiran?" Tialdrin trilled warily.

The golden-orange dawn flared briefly and softened into the soothing amber of an elleiu tree abode. It did not, quite, smell like a living tree, which meant it was a simulated abode aboard the Compact warship *Hunter's Moon*.

Tialdrin sat on a nest pillow in the middle of the living area. Across from her sat a Warrior female: Mimiran, Mistress of Inner Strength and resident surgeon-in-battle.

Tialdrin stared at Mimiran in wide-eyed wonder, belatedly realizing she sat in one of several counseling abodes Mimiran used throughout the Health Center.

"You were singing something about our moral duty?" Mimiran trilled in no-nonsense imperative tempo.

"Was I?" Tialdrin sang. "I think I mentioned it to Einstika, but..."

"But what?" Mimiran prodded. "Our moral imperative is to protect males. You told me this once."

"I remember. You changed the subject to something about social customs being involved when we allow males the freedom their autonomy demands. You then attacked my argument concerning morality issues holding the high ground over civility issues."

"Yes," Mimiran agreed. "What else did I tell you?"

"You said I was a rational and intuitive empath and could serve as a wellnessmistress," Tialdrin sang.

"Indeed. You are a healer's assistant now. You apprentice in wellness counseling under my guidance and have been for two years now. What does your training sing to you right now?"

Tialdrin gave the pheromonal equivalent of a shrug.

"I expect better than mindless leafchasing from you," Mimiran scolded in typical loud, impatient Warrior fury.

"Think back to your adulthood ceremony. What warnings did you hear from your immediate family females before they sang you into the Oyya Web?"

"Ritual singer empathy creates a subjective mental reality. Minor differences in each singer's pheromonal imagery gives the vision quest an open-ended depth," Tialdrin sang.

"Correct," Mimiran sang in approval. "But what did they warn you about?"

"Ignore blind trails. Do not prowl down them. Stay on the path they sing for me," Tialdrin sang. What point was Mimiran trying to make?

"Also correct," Mimiran trilled, paused, snapped her ears, and whipped her tail in Tialdrin's face.

"Think about what I taught you. Tell me what is happening to you three right now," she demanded at imperative pitch.

Tialdrin snapped her ears and growled at Mimiran.

"We are in a light armored vehicle, four of us, I think. I do not know why I keep thinking four when there are only three of us. We share pheromonal empathy while traveling, but I think we somehow lost contact with the singers. But if that really happened then the Oyya Web would have ejected us back to consciousness."

"Indeed," Mimiran agreed. "Tell me. What happens when you prowl down a side trail while in the Oyya Web?"

"A side trail is a fragment, a random mental scene, a figment. It can come from the strong emotional thrust of a ritual singer or, rarely, from the emotional tailchasing of the female experiencing an Oyya Web vision quest. Fragments often backtrail and loop into the quest plot because the empathy between her and the singers is strong. But a figment can arise independently from the intended quest and become circular and self-sustaining. Anyone caught in a figment may not even suspect or realize it. She becomes trapped in her subconscious mind, usually irrevocably trapped," Tialdrin sang as a tremor of doubt rippled through her body.

Then her resolve solidified, and she continued.

"But I am not alone. Kidahin and Einstika are with me," she trilled defiantly.

"But what are you doing?" Mimiran demanded.

"Driving through the forest to save thousands of males from dying!" Tialdrin trilled aggressively.

"Which males? How do you know they need saving?" Mimiran trilled reasonably.

"All males," Tialdrin sang. "Eyloni and human males," she quickly added.

"Human males? Really?" Mimiran keened imperiously.

"Yes! The humans aboard *Londiwe Khoza*," Tialdrin trilled, paused, and glanced around Mimiran's abode and frowned in confusion.

"Wait. That—is wrong. *Londiwe Khoza* is a shipwreck in space. How can we drive through a rainforest to reach a shipwreck on an asteroid?"

"Einstika and Kidahin have traumatic stress caused by the dead males they see. They tailchase after a figment that leads them on a mission to save the New Dawn males and prevent Hlorrithin from dying. The empathy you share—their pheromonal imagery and your empathy for them—pulls you by the tail into a fragment that does not backtrail or loop into the vision quest."

"I think you are more likely the fragment trying to draw me away from our mission," Tialdrin countered craftily.

"If you think this then you must admit you are in a vision quest. What ritual could include hundreds of dead males?"

"The Death Song ritual Delwyn sings for Nynava and the humans who died aboard their warship," Tialdrin keened in outrage.

"Delwyn sang that ritual before you even began associate healer training with Mistress of Healers Allohindra. I missed it because I broke nearly every bone in my body and was in a regeneration chrysalis in Health Center. I doubt his song created empathic imagery of an LAV crawling through La'huaset rainforests. Tell me, have you met Nynava yet?"

"No, but....," Tialdrin paused, confused.

"Listen to your wellnessmistress training. You know how traumatic stress affects female pheromonal empathy. Come to me. Twine tails with me. Empathize with my scent."

"Yes, Mistress," Tialdrin sang, stood up, and walked into Mimiran's embrace. They entwined tails, and Tialdrin felt the thrill of intimacy. The faded orangy Kidahin, Einstika, and the LAV abruptly vanished. Then Mimiran and her counseling abode vanished as well.

"Kidahin, do you want me to drive? Do you need to rest?" Einstika sang.

Kidahin yawned and nodded wearily. "I can use a break. Spirits, I am afraid to close my eyes."

"Me, too. I keep seeing things—horrible things," Einstika admitted. "About an hour ago I swear I heard Mimiran singing a song she taught me two years ago. I heard two voices, both hers. They sang at the same time. One sounded close, but the other sounded hollow and distant. I thought I was leafchasing because it reminded me of a Delwyn word."

"A Delwyn word?" Kidahin trilled, curious. The mention of Delwyn shoved weariness off a branch, her interest piqued.

"Yes," Einstika trilled. "*Jinx*, the word he uses when pointing out when two people sing the same word at the same time."

Jinx summoned a vivid memory of Mimiran, and Kidahin laughed.

"Jinx bothers Mimiran," she trilled.

"Mimiran tailchases after pheromonal imagery when it raises questions in that mistress-of-inner-strength mind of hers. The pheromonal taint in his scent associated with jinx worries her for some reason. Merkrida said Mimiran was overreacting. She asked Merkrida if she thought he meant it," Einstika sang.

"Meant what, exactly? That singing the same word at the same time summons ill-luck? Or that singing the word itself repels ill-luck summoned by the coincidental speech?"

"I do not know," Einstika admitted. "Still, I cannot get Mimiran out of my head."

Kidahin trilled a sympathetic note and returned to leafchasing about Aplilin standing in profile.

She sighed. Aplilin. Combative, having a reactionary sense of valor and dedicated, Aplilin often charged recklessly across the brittlest branches, jumped onto the weakest leaves, and prowled onto the most treacherous trails. The very thought of her summoned a sense of resolve.

"I am wide awake now. I can drive for a few more hours. Thank you for asking," Kidahin sang.

Einstika flipped her ears wide and then perked them at Kidahin by way of reply, turned back to the windshield, and saw Mimiran staring at her.

***

"What does your nonverbal social synchrony tell you right now?" Mimiran trilled at interrogative pitch.

"Mistress?" Einstika sang respectfully as a briefing abode aboard a troop transport solidified behind the Mistress of Inner Strength.

"What is Kidahin feeling?" Mimiran pressed.

"Confidence, Mistress. Her humor is rather dry for a Hunter female right now. Oh, she is more impatient than usual. Why?"

"And how do you rate yourself?" Mimiran trilled, ignoring the question.

"Myself?" Einstika echoed angrily. "What do I have to do with Kidahin, Mistress?"

"Nothing. I am asking you to assess yourself."

"A waste of time. This mission pulls my tail. I feel like Kidahin and I are tailchasing—doing something to no purpose. I feel unusually aggressive, too. Spirits, Mimiran, I feel like Hollfara sounds when she lectures down at people. I keep having bouts of furious impatience, but that is only because I want to complete the mission. Kidahin and I are of one mind in this. Her confidence inspires me. It pulls me into pheromonal unity with her."

"One mind to do what?"

"Save those males from dying by the thousands," Einstika keened with rising impatience.

"Which males, exactly?" Mimiran pressed.

"Dou'tu'tay, Mimiran. Are you dense or just uncaring?"

"Tell me what males you are trying to save!" Mimiran keened at imperative pitch.

"The males dying in the forest!"

"Eyloni males or human males?" Mimiran demanded.

"What difference does it make?"

"All the difference, Einstika. What males and how did they die?"

"How did they die? Are you being morbid? Some died in a huge industrial explosion, some died in a forest battle, and a great many died aboard their warship. The survivors are waiting for us to save them."

"You are in a small light armored vehicle. How many survivors can you bring back with you?" Mimiran trilled.

"All of them!" Einstika keened incoherently.

"Einstika, you said it yourself. They are dead. They died long ago. Think about this," Mimiran sang in her most persuasive rhythm.

"No. They live. They need us to protect them. Kidahin is certain of it!"

"You have never been a blind follower. You push against a team leader when you have something contrary to add. You have tangled Kidahin in your tail more than once before," Mimiran sang desperately.

"I never oppose Kidahin in matters of strategy. I love her and she loves me. She sees the mission clearly, and I am not going to kill thousands of males like I almost killed Assault Team-Two aboard *Londiwe*

Khoza."

"Yes, Einstika, *Londiwe Khoza*! Think about him. Remember why the society of Assault Team-Two names you their ritual Wild Mistress. You are not thickheaded like Aplilin. Listen to me and consider this. The mission Kidahin is undertaking is what Delwyn calls a fubar and a snafu. You know what he means by those words. He sings them over the combat address system often enough, almost as much as Anailiatha sings a'pea every chance she gets," Mimiran urged.

Einstika half-listened as Mimiran began to sing the mind song they sang together for the first time while riding in a troop transport. No, flying in a troop transport? No, riding in an LAV to *Londiwe Khoza* and his doomed male crew?

***

"No. The mission to *Londiwe Khoza* happened in the past. This is now," Einstika keened as the cockpit, right windshield, and buhnnie trees slammed into being around her.

"Of course this is now," Kidahin sang confidently. "When did you think it was?"

"Mimiran and her ideas about Delwyn's jinx word got to me. Our mission to the human shipwreck happened two years ago."

"Yes, so?" Kidahin agreed.

"So we cannot be rescuing those human males now."

Kidahin glared at Einstika with ear-dipping contempt.

"This is obvious. They died aboard their warship. He hit an asteroid, remember? An asteroid is in space. We are in a two-seated light armored vehicle and driving in a rainforest. Spirits, Einstika, you must be tired. And you wanted to drive while I slept?"

"If you feel up to driving, then go right ahead. I have complete confidence in you."

Kidahin unwrapped her tail from her seat and lashed it around Einstika and gave her a reassuring squeeze.

"*Vi e'ta ka nabi*," Kidahin sang at combat-imminent tempo. A favorite phrase of Aplilin's, it meant now was the time to part the branches.

Kidahin squeezed Einstika harder and sent loving pheromonal thoughts to her. Einstika was a wonderful occasional lover, an accomplished fighter, and an excellent teammate. But she had nothing on the immense physical presence that was Aplilin. A weaponmistress and demolitions expert, she excelled as an infantry prowler.

"Einstika, please do not take this wrong because I love you, but why are you on this mission?"

Einstika wrapped her tail around her stomach in layers over

Kidahin's tail and twisted her pons around Kidahin's.

"I volunteered," Einstika sang. "I am sure of it. Why? Are you having second thoughts?"

"Of course not, but I cannot remember why we need a power plant techmistress."

Einstika absently rubbed her pons against Kidahin's and thought about it.

"Reactor," she finally trilled, certain. "I have to shut down a reactor."

"A reactor? Here in the middle of the jungle?"

"I think so, otherwise the Mistress of Battle would have assigned Jassalin or Aplilin and not me."

"That makes sense," Kidahin sang brightly.

12
THE SELF-MADE STRANGER

Einstika wiggled deep into her seat. Dissatisfied with the fit, she wrapped her tail around the seat and her waist and pulled herself deeper into its soft contoured cushions. She fumed silently at Kidahin's lapses in leadership and the inconsistencies in their mission.

She knew the *Londiwe Khoza* males were not a part of the mission because they died nearly two years ago and hundreds of light-years away. The males killed by neh'tle ke'ne's'tu died centuries ago on Elleio, also hundreds of light-years away. Males did not die in large numbers now because the Be'atika Senge's prohibition of war had kept the peace since the Battle of Withered Trees. The male population numbered about one in forty, and only a continent-wide disaster could kill a large number of them.

Yet the rainforest certainly looked like they were somewhere in the central La'huaset Tribal continent.

Her techmistress mind had been leafchasing after nuclear reactors. What did a'pea nuclear reactors have to do with anything? Orbital power stations beamed energy to surface collectors, but some Clans used small boron fusion reactors to provide electricity to their industries. Large-scale reactors did not exist on Elleio and had not since Hlorrithin shut down the Neh'as'anni industrial fission power plant.

Einstika asked herself for the millionth time what she was doing here. Nothing made sense, and that is Kidahin's fault. Everything is Kidahin's fault. No clan puts a boron reactor in the middle of the jungle. Boron generators took up little space, true enough. Take four light armored vehicles parked side-by-side and stack that many three high and you have an idea of size. Clans built them close to or inside of their technology centers. They did not build them in the middle of the jungle.

Environmental Interdiction would never allow it even if there was a valid reason for doing so.

And what did shutting down a boron generator have to do with saving anybody? Who needed rescuing from whom? How did cutting power to a clan's technology center help matters? The Mistress of Battle would have told us something this vital.

Einstika tightened her tail and squeezed herself deeper into the contoured seat and pouted. Spirits, I should remember such a briefing. I am the techmistress here, and I would have to shut off the power.

I remember no briefing, and I think we never had one. Kidahin apparently thinks we did or does not care why we are driving in the middle of the jungle.

Einstika growled softly. Kidahin often ignored important details, especially those not tactically relevant to her goals. But Kidahin also never forgot why a teammate was included. Being with her lent support to the vague notion that a reactor was their target.

But why? Clans shut down their reactors from time to time for maintenance and refueling. Still, shutting off the electricity to save many males defied reason.

Could a boron reactor melt down? Spew radiation? No. They were not like the fission reactor operating in this valley generations ago.

Oh, spirits. I recognize this valley from history songs. The Neh'as'anni and their allied clans lived here.

Einstika drifted off into leafchasing after fragments of a past where she turned power back on rather than shutting it off. No. She saw herself drawing electrical power from a reactor and diverting it to something else, something aboard *Londiwe Khoza*.

No, it could not be so. They drove through a La'huaset jungle on Elleio and not through a holographic jungle on *Hunter's Moon*.

And they certainly were not driving down bare utilitarian corridors of a shipwrecked human destroyer.

But Kidahin should know what was going on. An assaultmistress always knew everything about a mission. The Mistress of Battle told an assaultmistress everything relevant to the mission.

Einstika heard Mimiran singing in her ear. Mimiran? So, the Mistress of Inner Strength came with us. But when, exactly?

Or did she just imagine hearing the Warrior Mistress?

Einstika gripped the armrests and squeezed until her knuckles turned pale orange. Mimiran sang a derogatory refrain about being a blind follower.

Einstika did not follow anybody blindly. Yes, she rarely opposed Kidahin in matters of strategy, but she did often suggest tactical alternatives. Jassalin yanked Kidahin's tail over strategy, but it was her place to do so as the second-in-leadership.

The scent of Mimiran's lingering pheromones stressed that she not remain a blind follower. Her scent summoned words telling Einstika their mission was a fubar and a snafu. The raw emotion attached to those Delwyn words brushed against leafless branches in Einstika's naturally male-hyperaware mind.

Everyone aboard *Hunter's Moon* knew what Delwyn meant by those words. Fubar meant mating nonstop until it lost all meaning. Snafu meant futile mating had become routine. Delwyn sang them when he meant someone was doing something to no purpose: tailchasing. Or when someone was thinking about something to no purpose: leafchasing.

Mimiran's scent called out with insistent pheromonal urgency, and it said she was leafchasing and tailchasing after figments.

Einstika tried to empathize with Mimiran, but she lost the scent and those Delwyn words before the empathic link could form.

Einstika watched as the undergrowth grew up and around the road to form a tunnel.

She leaned forward and scowled at the twisted brown, orange-yellow, and yellow brush as it appeared to wrap around tall weathered, pitted, and crumbling granite boulders lying along the roadside. Relics from some ancient avalanche, the enveloping undergrowth looked like it was trying to consume them.

The *plop-splot* of LAV legs hitting saturated ground and sinking slightly before withdrawing from clinging mud distracted her from a morbid thought: the rubble reminded her of ribs poking through the sad remains of a desiccated chest.

The sounds of mud and metal on stone. Einstika growled and shook her head. She snapped her ears forward at the muddy ground. Rains, mists, and artesian springs soaked the ground. It was a rainforest. Leg-driven LAVs could crawl over squishy ground, roots, and vines that obsolete wheeled vehicles could not. And legs did not leave ruts or get stymied by rough terrain like wheels did.

"Wheels. Nobody uses wheels in the jungle, not in living memory anyway," she muttered aloud.

"What about wheels?" Kidahin sang.

"Oh, nothing. Just leafchasing."

Plants grew slow on Elleio. It took a century or more for the jungle to recover from wheel rut damage.

Wait. Did not damaged forests have something to do with the mission? She stared at the passing jungle for clues.

Water rippled across the trail ahead. Amber grasses and sable reeds grew in and near the roadside. Violet bladder plants floated placidly in deeper water anchored to nearby pale-yellow leaves which poked above the water nearest the reeds. Ragged trees grew behind them. Their leaves hovered hauntingly behind the standing water. Their resin-scented sap stung her nose.

The leaves looked blurry yet barely ells from the mid-morning sunlit trail.

Einstika snapped her ears wide in surprise. Sunlight? Here? How? She could not see the sky because the surrounding undergrowth completely enveloped the trail. It should filter the sunlight down to dim, pale-orange shade.

And yet she saw full morning sunlight beaming down on the trail. Loud clattering yanked her from leafchasing. LAV legs banged into and stepped over many large cobalt rocks. The trail lost its natural forest wandering as it straightened out and turned gravelly.

The scattered cobalt rocks gradually became clinkers and then crushed slag as musically whispered verses tickled her ears.

The young spirits left joyful laughter as they flew away. The males' spirits blessed me with songs I never heard before.

The light they left in their parting was a gift to face the darkest night that, without doubt, waited for me ahead. I did not have long to live.

Einstika knew those verses. They came from the Song of Hlorrithin. A disjointed glimpse of rocky cinder roads shimmered onto the trail. She clenched her muscles and braced herself and waited for the LAV to roll over and tumble down an embankment.

But the expected embankment never appeared on the relatively flat jungle.

Einstika missed the scent of Mimiran's guiding pheromones. Did she abandon her? Would thinking about the Song bring her back?

Those verses mentioned spirits. The spirits who sing existence into existence live in the Oyya Web. But the young spirits in the verses belonged to dead people. They, like the spirits themselves, took the form of metaphysical water vapor. Indeed, in the say'ta've language the phrase *ki'to'eyloni* meant "water people." Changing pitch and tempo shifted the meaning to *spirits*.

Music carried a dead person's spirit to a state of being where it condensed and rained onto the Oyya Web. The exhaled moist breath of joyful singing during a Death Song ritual sent them on their way. The spirits who sing existence into existence lacked gender, which meant the male spirits in the verses belonged to dead males.

She frowned, her ears flat against her head. If the young spirits and the male spirits flew away, then they already rode the melody of their death songs into the Oyya Web. They were long dead. Nobody remained for her to save.

Mimiran knew this, knew they were leafchasing after figments as they tailchased their way down this trail to—where? And how long? At least two hours. When did she eat last?

Einstika looked away from the windshield and the now suspect jungle. Eyes roving for any distraction, they fell on the lidar.

"Impossible!" she trilled.

"What is impossible?" Kidahin sang curiously.

"The lidar shows the trail barely thirty ells wide and going off into infinity ahead and behind us!"

"That is stupid," Kidahin snapped. "Do you hear what you are singing? The trail just extends beyond lidar range. Take a few seconds to look around and you will see the trail is less than thirty ells wide."

"It is not just the trail. The lidar does not pick up anything more than a few ells on either side. It should at least show ground clutter beyond the trail!"

"Why does this matter? Our mission is forward, not to either side," Kidahin sang reasonably.

"*Jinx!*" Einstika keened at imperative pitch. "I heard Mimiran singing that we were leafchasing and tailchasing here! We must stop and figure out why we are here."

Kidahin smiled at the Delwyn word he sometimes used to point out ill-luck and sighed. She missed Delwyn. The powerful emotion distracted her enough to begin puzzling over Einstika's concern when a hauntingly familiar muted melody interrupted. The harder she tried to empathize with the music the quieter it became until it disappeared.

Kidahin shrugged thoughts of it and Einstika's leafchasing concerns aside, but the effort exhausted her.

The inherent musical nature of all Eyloni made the deliberate disregarding of music stressful. They thought in melodies. Internal dialogue amounted to melodies. Kidahin tried explaining it to Delwyn when he mentioned hearing voices in his head. He thought in his native language and rarely in concepts. She explained how she rarely thought in say'ta've. She thought in concepts expressed by melodies. He understood because he likened her thinking process to what he called jingles: short mnemonic-purposed melodies.

She snapped her ears. Enough of this. Clearly Einstika cannot see the tree because of the forest. She was not a strategist. Who she really needed was Aplilin. She was no strategist, either. But she got things done. Maybe Aplilin could help her remember details from the briefing. Random fragments jumped at her until one surged forth in revealing clarity.

"Einstika, the briefing never mentioned a reactor or a power plant, yes? Most of the wounded we encounter should be females, but we must expect a number of males, the sire cairns who fought with them."

"We should not see many male losses because we rarely let males do anything really dangerous. We do dangerous things for them, so unless a male has no choice he does not fight," Einstika trilled in agreement.

"And yet males are crafty and deadly fighters. They often match Warrior strength and exceed the endurance of Warriors or Hunters. Only Comara have nearly limitless endurance," Kidahin sang. She paused and turned thoughtful. What else? Oh, the combat-action reports.

"I think the mistresses of battle survived the first assault. I know they complained about APC combat ineffectiveness against enemy countermeasures," she added.

"Neither side broke combat tradition, Kidahin. Think about it. The social stigma of breaking tradition kills honor and makes the breaker a ni'zakhon. Bows and arrows, knives, spears, shields, swords, and other allowable melee and missile weapons are used in set piece or open field battle. This always wins the honorable victory, just as custom and tradition demand. Modern weapon usage remains restricted by law to actions taken against technological targets."

Kidahin grunted. This was why the smart assaultmistress orders her APC into the combat zone quickly and rapidly deploys her team before the vehicle is fired upon.

"We will make an initial security sweep through the combat zone on foot. I do not trust these new visual and thermal cameras any more than I trust this APC. It just does not make sense to drive a wheeled vehicle through jungle terrain. Instead of improving surveillance drones, the A'tayotan should come up with a vehicle that walks over jungle hazards."

"I agree," Einstika sang readily and then paused in confusion.

She sat in a wheel-driven armored personnel carrier, but she clearly remembered sitting in a leg-driven light armored vehicle mere moments ago. The echo of clattering legs banging on stone pavement still rang in her ears.

"Prowling is preferable to staring at a screen and wearing headphones," Kidahin continued blithely. "Instinct does not appreciate technology like it does the nose, eyes, and ears. Cameras and microphones only give a narrow and quick assessment of the immediate area. But as techmistress, you should scan the combat zone before we leave the APC."

Einstika leaned back into the headrest and shook her head.

"Kidahin, something is wrong here. I know I was sitting in a leg-driven LAV only a few minutes ago, but now I can feel tire vibrations through the floorboard. This mission is—fubar. We should sing for a Major Consensus on how to proceed. Once we can tail-tie our minds around what Mimiran was saying we can..."

"No," Kidahin sang flatly, contradicting all custom and courtesy regarding female decision making. "We will make contact with the Mistress of Battle soon. She will give us an on-site update on the local threats."

Privately and being careful not to let doubts seep into her pheromones and tip Einstika off, Kidahin wondered why for the spirits' sakes did the Mistress of Battle assign Einstika to her. If wounded males needed saving, then she needed a healer and not a techmistress. A healer's ward on the APC shielded it from hostile fire because healers, except for their adulthood knives, never carried weapons or fought unless in self-defense.

Einstika sat quietly, stewing in her fury for good reason. Seeking a Major Consensus was the fruitful vine upon which all female conflict resolution blossomed. Refusing to consider a Major Consensus tail-slapped the face of female civility. Kidahin would never push tradition off a branch no matter how angry or distracted she was unless—Mimiran was right.

The ancient songs say that the skin or body of a drum determines the person or thing called into being. Some drums are journeying drums transporting the drummer and his listeners to various places. Other drums are powerful in their own ways.

The Territorial Boundaries of Rage and Forgiveness tells us rage teaches, calls for healing, belongs to the Spirit Male, and demands correct behavior. Personal rage and honor stand among withered trees. When it cannot find a resting place, it injures instinct. Clan rage and persistent rage summon the Rite of Forgiveness, which requires setting the matter aside for a time, withholding punishment, forgetting the offense, and abandoning the social debt.

One phrase in particular rang loudest in the clear singing voices.

Withered trees.

Withered Trees named the last battle Hlorrithin had fought while caught in the midst of neh'tle ke'ne's'tu. But the name did not come from the ecological disaster surrounding him at the time but from the ancient Wisdom of the Clans. Within the context of the Wisdom song the name Battle of Withered Trees reminded everyone the battle was fought to satisfy personal rage and honor.

"You are not a blind follower," Mimiran insisted. "You are the Wild Mistress. Rage fills you, drives you to seek revenge, pushes you to draw the adulthood knife and keen in challenge at Death. The Wisdom of the Clans says both the Territorial Boundaries of Rage and Forgiveness and the Rite of Forgiveness compel you to set this matter aside and withhold punishment."

Einstika heard the wisdom in Mimiran's words and forced herself to ignore Kidahin's rich, overpowering scent swirling around her nose. Severed from their shared pheromonal empathy she fell like mist headlong into the Oyya Web of the spirits.

***

"Wake up!" Kidahin yelled over the mesmerizing rumble as the single-seater six-wheeled tactical command carrier bounced over the rut-filled narrow path.

How embarrassing! Barely two hours into the mission and here she was already leafchasing to the tune of tires running over vines and roots.

She yawned and glanced at the instrument cluster mounted above the steering wheel, snapped her ears and glanced through the windshield again, and snapped her ears in disgust at the a'pea metal seam joining the two a'pea glass plates. The dou'tu'tay thing ran down the windshield slightly to the right. Only a fingernail wide, it blocked her view. How the A'tayotan hierarchy could approve the design baffled her. Why not put a single a'pea plate of armored a'pea windshield glass and forego the metal obstruction?

Trill!

Kidahin stomped her bare foot on the brake pedal reflexively and glanced at the flashing lidar screen. She shifted into neutral before the engine could stall and popped the door window open to listen.

Nothing. Well, the engine idled whisper-quiet.

The lidar chirped another warning.

"Dou'tu'tay distracting windshield," she sang.

Trill!

Kidahin glanced at the lidar and then looked out the windshield in disbelief.

The trail had opened into a wide clearing covered with breast-high orange grass. The blades rippled in waves as lazy gusts brushed through the branches of a few nearby arberi trees.

Twelve distant solid returns following a ragged line across the lidar screen had triggered the warning tone. Twelve elleiu trees stood in a broadly scattered arc across the scan return background. The trees beyond the clearing blocked them from her sight. Elleiu trees grew three to four times taller than arberis, so the elleius were far away.

The lidar gave her a distance certain, but thoughts of distance faded as she realized they held the high ground for a battle in progress.

The lidar showed forces moving in open-field combat. They fought using traditional weapons and in the traditional manner.

Kidahin shifted into high gear and raced recklessly through the clearing and down a narrow jungle path. Soon enough she found Hunter archer teams on her right firing wave after wave of sheaf arrows. In front of them Warrior pike teams rushed the home tree defenders.

The moving tactical command carrier simply vanished around Kidahin, leaving her standing in tall vermilion grass mid-prowl into a solitary stalking sweep near the main entrance bole of the closest elleiu tree. She held a shortbow equipped with a bow quiver and eleven arrows.

The reddish-orange and yellow-variegated patterns of her skin blended into the surrounding vermilion grasses and crimson arberi leaves. She pricked her ears forward and nodded to herself and smiled at the bow. It felt good in her hand.

Close-in assaults on defenders under cover called for shortbows because they could shoot in melee-to-short range. Longbow archers fired flight arrows in long-range ballistic volleys, but shortbow archers could draw and fire sheaf arrows at targets as close as an ell away.

Kidahin keened a high-pitched ten-note challenge so incredibly harsh the two enemy Warriors guarding the central entrance bole flinched. One of the two startled back and smacked her head against the low-hanging aerial roots behind her.

Shrieks and wails assaulted Kidahin's ears as she advanced. The smell of fear rode high amid shouts of rage. Bare feet padded through tall vermilion grass, close. The defenders fought well cursing and panting. They knew their doom approached, yet they fought as females always had in defense of their territory.

Siege engine fires roared to life. Warrior pike teams halted the advance to pump thatch-woven bellows within the siege engine nearest her. Smudge pots belched forth thick black smoke into long woven hoses. She could smell a faint hint as it streamed from tiny gaps in the weaves. The foul, low-grade tar smoke clung to her and her fellow shortbow archers. Bad enough to breathe it from a distance, but far worse for the gagging, pumping Warriors.

Kidahin tried her best to ignore the oily smell and keened for her hand of archers to hold the high ground for the siege engine Warriors, the bellows, the smudge pots, and the thatched hoses. The Warriors needed time to force the filthy smoke into the enemy hometree's low ground entry points. Black, sooty, greasy smoke soon filled hollow passageways. Thick and cloying, it brought the defenders down gasping and choking.

Kidahin smelled her fellow shortbow archers and fell into scent-linked empathy with them. She set her stance, nocked an arrow, drew it back, and aimed as female pheromones filled her head with emotionally charged words.

"Run, you filthy Neh'as'anni Clan! Run!" she keened aloud harshly as she fired two arrows back-to-back, hitting the two Warriors about to spear the bellows team.

A shod cudgel made a sickening hollow smack against a nearby head and startled Kidahin into making a reflexive evasive twist that saved her life. Spinning halfway around and extending her bow arm she pulled the already nocked arrow to her cheek, aimed along an imaginary line from the flint arrowhead to the target, and fired.

From the corner of an eye she saw a bellows Warrior swing a lead-shod club into the side of a male's head and he dropped to the ground, half his forehead shattered. Stringy gore splattering across the ground hung in strings from the long blades of beautiful vermilion grass.

The Hunter fighting alongside him keened in despair as the Warrior brought a backswing around and across her jaw, shattering and ripping it and half of her throat out as well. A second Hunter heaved a spear into a bellows Warrior, pinning her to the siege engine.

Kidahin fired another arrow, hitting the spear-throwing Huntress through the throat.

"Die, filthy Neh'as'anni female," Kidahin trilled harshly and cringed as her heart hammered. Her heart, her personal piece of male, thudded a warning: trilling made her a target.

Yet the Song drove her to trill the challenge aloud again.

Smoke tore at her lungs. She gasped for air and struggled to stifle a coughing fit. The spear pinning the Warrior had punctured the bellows and black smoke streamed from the hole. She coughed her lungs dry as the remaining Warriors pumped nonstop. They needed her and the other archers to cover them while they worked. Kidahin knew her valor here would help determine who would win the victory.

She followed a second Hunter shortbow assault team. They climbed into the tree's outer fused aerial root structure and rushed into a small exit bole on the lower tree.

"Switch to air!" a Warrior assaultmistress keened.

Time to breach and invade the lower tree. But first the Warriors had to pump fresh air into the tree. The cooler air forced the crippling smoke farther into the upper tree and also gave the assault teams cleaner air to breathe.

"Hurry!" the assaultmistress keened as she left the Warriors and leapt through the bole threshold.

Kidahin signaled her shortbow team to follow and jumped into the breached bole. They landed amid gasping mouths and twanging bowstrings. A Neh'as'anni female screamed. A second one shrieked as a Warrior smacked her down before driving a short sword into her chest.

Kidahin heard a male singing fortitude to the defenders.

A sire cairn.

"Do you hear that?" Kidahin trilled harshly.

"I do. Where is he?" Einstika sang grimly.

"Close, very close. Sound carries in elleiu trees because the branching hollow pathways resonate over a wide range of notes. He is singing from the Vantage in the crown or from a males' safe near it."

"He sounds closer than that, but I do not smell him. Spirits, it is darker than the Dark Mistress's Abode in here," Einstika complained.

"Wait, I see him!" Kidahin keened, drew back on her bow, aimed, and fired an arrow.

"Mistress Shikararro," a Warrior sang out. "We have killed all the

Neh'as'anni females in this tree!"

"Good," Shikararro's voice sang, her voice oddly flat and unnatural.

Radio, Kidahin realized. She knew that voice. Radio contact meant Mistress of Battle Shikararro was not personally leading the assault.

"Well done," Shikararro's voice continued. "Organize Hunter prowlers and send them to search the local jungle for escaping infant males and their infant female associations. Offer them asylum and sanctuary with our clan in accordance with all custom and tradition."

"Affirm, Mistress!" the Warrior trilled.

Kidahin, slow to come out of battle frenzy, paused in confusion. Eyes wide open, she turned around in a slow circle. The glow of burning torches, the smell of smudge pots, and the sight of the siege engine dominating the background froze her in mid-turn. She pressed ears flat against her short red ringlets and whipped her tail side-to-side in broad swipes.

I have just killed a male!

She stepped back and twisted around searching for Einstika just as the techmistress drove a spear through her heart.

***

"Where are you, Kidahin?" the Wild Mistress sang at imperative interrogative pitch.

"I am—in what was Neh'as'anni Clan territory. What happened? Einstika?"

Kidahin felt like she was prowling down two overlapping trails at the same time. The more familiar one led through memories of her as assaultmistress and leading Assault Team-Two. The least familiar path stumbled through entwining visions of Assault Team-Two and flashbacks from being the second-in-leadership for Environmental Interdiction Team-one.

The second path led to a name.

"Shikararro," Kidahin trilled. The name annoyed her, sounded harsh in her ears, grated on her nerves.

Why?

Twanging shortbows, shrieking screams, and keening challenges trilled from figures fighting desperately in what looked like a pheromonal image from a preadolescent history song.

A scene from the Battle of Withered Trees stalked her.

Oh, spirits. Hlorrithin fought in this battle not far from here.

Kidahin glanced down at the spear splitting her sternum and traced the shaft back to Einstika. Her hands still strangled the shaft in slow motion, her murderous glare focused on the piercing spearhead and not her target.

Kidahin felt no pain, which confirmed the notion she prowled through the pheromonal fragments of a teaching song.

And yet it smelled so real. It felt real, too. But empathic sharing worked that way. The singers sang up the emotions needed to fix the scene in the mind. Choking on siege engine smoke made a teaching point about the assault on Neh'as'anni trees, but suffering combat wound pain did not. Everyone learned about the past by empathizing with passed-down emotional memories of important events.

But singing enhanced empathic learning. Singers intimately familiar with the event sang while focusing on the memories they themselves had learned in the same manner. Singer pheromones established the empathic link and called forth the shared mental visions, but the singing kept the theme pure and drove the plotline forward. Yet she did not hear singing.

At a loss, stymied, and furious, Kidahin stopped struggling, slowed her breathing, and pointedly ignored the impaling spear. Glaring at Einstika, Kidahin flexed her long, four-jointed fingers and balled them into fists and jumped back and clear of the spearhead.

"This is not fair!" she screamed in abject fury.

"Maybe you should try something a bit more sensible," a melody of trilling voices sang in dripping contempt.

"Like what, Einstika?" Kidahin snapped as she pivoted away from the lethal spearhead to glare vicious hatred at the treacherous techmistress frozen in mid-thrust.

"We are not Einstika," the melodious voices sang.

"This is wrong. Memories of historical battles have nothing to do with my mission. I am *not* a speared corpse on a battlefield!"

"*Ki*, Kidahin," the melodious voices trilled approvingly.

Kidahin dodged around Einstika and never noticed the fatal wound in her chest had vanished.

"No," the voices sang. "You are not dead. You do not belong here. You still hold the high ground for the male fighting on the low ground. He still fights, but he will lose if you remain here."

"You speak of Delwyn!" Kidahin trilled.

"Perhaps. Then again, perhaps not. But either way your concern is with one male and one male only."

"I am sent on a mission to save many males and not just one," Kidahin retorted.

"If this is so then what are you doing here?" the voices demanded.

"I am leading a team sent to rescue males," she sang.

"Where are they?" the voices trilled at mocking tempo.

"Einstika is here. She—she—killed me with a spear thrust...," she sang, her voice dropping by octaves into silence.

"So you are dead?" the voices trilled in mock-astonishment.

"I must be," Kidahin trilled tremulously.

"Why did your Huntress teammate stab you?" the voices sang in a crafty inflection.

"I—because I killed a male," Kidahin trilled, uncertain. Killing a male called for being skinned alive with her own adulthood knife and not stabbed in the heart with a spear.

"You never killed a male, ever. We know this because his spirit would cry out to us if you had."

"You are the spirits," Kidahin sang.

"We are who are," the voices admitted.

"Help me save the males I am sent to save."

"There are none to save. You know this," the spirits sang flatly. "You are in the Oyya Web, just as you were here during your adulthood ceremony. As we told you then, we tell you again: you must reach the high ground."

"What do you mean? I see dead males on the ground all around me."

"No, you do not," the spirits keened at imperative pitch. "You are merely tailchasing after mindless low-ground strategies and leafchasing after memories best left with us. Remember what we asked you about holding the high ground?"

"I do. Battle on the low ground is folly while the high ground remains unsecured."

"Yes," the spirits agreed. "You and your two Hunter companions are held captive on the low ground by your strength of will while you tailchase after insurmountable low-ground hazards. Who did you send to secure the high ground for you? You are an assaultmistress. A worthy assaultmistress sends prowlers into the high ground to secure it first. Who did you send?"

Kidahin floundered in confusion. The spirits sang truth. An assaultmistress led twenty females, and she led Assault Team-Two. But she and Einstika had just fought in a battle that felt more like a ritual reenactment of the Battle of Withered Trees than any teaching song could match.

Or maybe not. Einstika would never attack an Assault Team-Two Huntress without cause because she and every Huntress in Team-Two belonged to the same extended families. So where had they gone? They would have never abandoned any male.

A vile stench crept across the battlefield, not siege engine smoke this time. Hundreds of dead bodies lay rotting among amber blades of grass. Kidahin recoiled and retched violently into a gagging spate of dry heaves. The continuous retching broke the empathic connection between her and the spirits. The rotting casualties, the smell of carnage, and the battlefield itself vanished, replaced by the idling tactical command carrier waiting next to her, cab door still hanging wide open.

***

Kidahin stared at a scattered arc of elleiu trees off in the far north. She reached for the open door, grabbed a climbing rung, and swung into the driver seat.

Her eyes never left the black smoke belching from their crowns. Perversely, it clung there, a stubborn sooty mist. Smoke usually rose on hot air, but smudge pots burned a low-grade mud-like tar. It made thick cool smoke, not much warmer than the air around it. The smoke tended to remain near its source for hours unless pushed away by moving air. Smoking out elleiu trees was an ages-old battle tactic not used in centuries, except once. Hlorrithin used it during the Battle of Withered Trees.

Hlorrithin. Kidahin leafchased after the name, but no sooner than she reached a liana of clarity it slipped from her grasp.

"Hlorrithin," she sang aloud and shuddered. She stomped on the clutch, shifted into gear, yanked the steering wheel to the left, popped the clutch, and stomped on the accelerator.

"South," she sang with renewed clarity. The males who needed her fought in the south.

The tactical command carrier raced down a well-maintained gravel road with few twists and turns. The rainforest blocked distant landscapes, but the occasional gaps ahead gave Kidahin some doubts so she checked the lidar.

A spotty smear stretched across the screen. It rested at ground level about a fingernail high. The blurry details meant it was either moving or its density changed along its length. At hundreds of ells long, she doubted it was moving, which meant changes in density: like brush piled up some twenty to forty ells.

A berm, maybe? Some defensive ring made from what? Ripped up jungle?

Curious, Kidahin switched the lidar to scan a wide forward-facing sector. Doing so reduced flank and tail range but increased forward range and resolution.

The irregular berm jumped in size on the screen. It still lacked fine details but did confirm her initial identification: a berm. It stood over forty ells in some places but barely twenty in others. It traced an uneven gradual arc that bent around to the south.

She reset the lidar and folded her ears flat against her short red ringlets. Some persistent nagging worry sang just out of hearing that the berm was important somehow.

Trill!

She shifted the tactical command carrier into neutral and let it roll to a silent stop. She muted the lidar warning tone, shut the engine off, and listened to the whispering gentle breezes brush her ears.

The lidar bloomed with crawling fuzzy patches. Several of them floated below and around the berm: combat teams on the prowl.

She felt a surge of clarity and shuddered. She pushed the clutch pedal, started the engine, and shifted into low gear.

Trill.

She ignored the muted warning tone this time. The males she sought were fighting near the berm. Immeasurably tired, she yawned, looked down, and frowned at the instrument panel. One screen remained dark since the mission began some two hours ago.

The staccato rumble of tires on rough road sent her into leafchasing about the screen. It displayed video from cameras mounted on ear and tail drones.

Kidahin hit the brakes. The wheels locked up and the engine stalled.

"Stupid," she snarled. "I could be flying an ear or tail all this time. An ear's basic camera sees better than a lidar return."

True. A solitary Hunter sitting in a tactical command carrier used the drones so she did not have to abandon the vehicle to prowl security sweeps. She typed a query into the drone piloting system and waited. The screen came alive and reported the advanced radio and video ears and tails were ready for launch. The screen also reported the vehicle's low audio and thermal countermeasures were in stealth mode.

An ear flew itself and radioed anything its microphone picked up. But a tail needed a pilot, and she could not fly one and drive at the same time.

The thought of sending out an ear to listen for males in distress appealed better than driving down every road in Neh'as'anni territory searching for them.

"Wrong!" she keened. Techmistress Einstika should pilot drones. She knew how to make an efficient use of them.

So, where was she?

13
SELF-EXILE'S BOON

Kidahin started the engine, shifted into low gear, released the clutch, and nudged the tactical command carrier forward at a hesitant crawl.

The idling engine threaten to stall as it labored; yet she kept her foot off the accelerator.

"Doubt kills," she muttered to herself. The sensible and practical female maxim rang hollow in her ears. The welcoming rainforest setting made the warning sound doubly prudent.

She bumped the accelerator with a timid foot, and the tactical command carrier lurched deeper into the La'huaset Tribal continental jungle. Hundred-ell-tall orange radial ferns and spindly succulent hardwoods draped in golden mosses loomed over the narrow animal trail as she drove. Knee-high Comari-hands with their single, half-ell wide pale yellow leaves grew among the trees.

The engine labored, threatened to stall. She tapped the accelerator again and lurched on.

Gravel crunching under tires snapped her alert.

"A gravel road? How can there be a road here? They are relics from a horrific past. No clan has built a road in centuries," Kidahin growled aloud.

She saw a large o'ka'me colony creeping towards the windshield, and her mouth watered. The reddish-brown and earthy smelling mound of moss vaguely resembled a bloody brain.

But it was edible.

She hit the brakes, jumped from the cab, and gobbled handfuls all the while glancing about wildly, wary. Still chewing, she dashed back into the cab, shifted into gear, and continued south at a slightly faster speed.

Kidahin frowned at the rainforest. It looked more and more alive the farther south she drove. Oddly, the trees and grass seemed to pulse in blended ocher pastel vermilions, ambers, and scarlets. Familiar patterns appeared in the variegated yellowed-orange, yellow-ocher, burnished gold, and sunburst yellow creeping vines and hanging lianas. She knew these landmarks, recognized ones nearly covered by layers of undergrowth. She could not recall when she had seen them before. Sometime recent because what she saw matched the patterns of the leaves in her memory perfectly: no new growth, no change in light, no change in shade.

She considered the faded, vaguely hazy orange shapes hiding just beyond trees that were themselves draped in yellow mosses. The moss glowed like auras in the streaming sunlight.

No elleiu tree towered above her. Indeed, she had not seen one since leaving the siege engine battle up north.

Golden mosses spotted with large black blossoms dangled from branches and overhanging vines, brushing the windshield as she drove under them. So did the infrequent few deep-green parasitic vines.

Kidahin smiled, knowing the mosses were trying their vegetable best to strangle the predatory greenery.

She turned into a clearing filled with hundreds of breast-high orange ferns. Tires crunching over rusty, blue-black gravel sapped at her awareness and lured her into mindless leafchasing. Barely aware, she drove through patches of bare soil spotted with large, low-hanging dull-red ferns, some even turning coppery-orange. Orangy-yellow vines crept up tree trunks. Scarlet entangling undergrowth hugged the ground around them.

A stout trunk jumped into her view, startling her and banishing leafchasing thoughts.

She spun the steering wheel wildly, oversteered, and nearly hit a pile of cut saplings shrouded in yellow mosses.

She yanked the wheel hard, stomped the accelerator, and regained the gravel road. Shifting into low gear, she made a point of taking the time to see details and shove remaining leafchasing thoughts out of her head.

Kidahin frowned slightly at the faint glowing tint covering the forest. It looked wrong, too yellow, more yellow than what the backscattered leaf-filtered sunlight should allow. And where did the ever-present slightly bluish haze of isoprene go?

A verse from a history song provided a likely answer, and her stomach clenched in reflexive horror.

"This is smog!" she keened.

She glared into the smog and by doing so did not see the approaching intersection until the front tires hit a low concrete barrier. She bounced sharply in her seat.

The engine stalled as the back tires hit the curb, leaving her partway in the lane of the intersecting wide and paved commercial road.

The pavement filled Kidahin with disgust. At least the gravel road more-or-less flowed with the landscape, rather like an animal trail. But the pavement mercilessly cut through the arberi trees. No jungle grasses grew between the paving slabs, either. That meant it saw frequent use.

The pavement put her on edge, and she turned to warn Einstika before remembering she was alone.

She glanced at the lidar. The scan return showed fuzzy patches moving along the bottom of a long berm-like structure up ahead.

What was a berm doing in the middle of a rainforest? She doubted what she saw. That was bad.

Doubt kills. It killed just as surely as an incautiously placed foot. What was she seeing here?

Kidahin pulled over and shut off the engine. Stumped, she reached for the instrument panel and flipped a switch, put on a headset, and watched as the lidar screen displayed a panoramic view from atop the cab.

She reached for the flight control yoke next to the screen and launched a small drone, an ear. She flew it in a series of overlapping circles above one of the fuzzy patches and listened.

The camera aboard the ear gave her adequate visuals for flying, but not good enough for detailed ground observations. Yet the screen showed a prowler unit cutting through the undergrowth. Nothing came over the headset but the faint background hum of propeller wash.

Kidahin knew that solitary Hunter stalkers and even the somewhat noisier Warrior triads could silent-stalk. What little noise they made sounded natural in a rainforest full of subtle sounds. But large groups magnified even natural sounds to unnatural levels. Vehicles, whisper-quiet, hummed with a mechanical regularity easily heard by the discerning ear.

"Kidahin? I have a status update for you," Mistress of Battle Shikararro sang over the cabin speaker.

Kidahin jumped in her seat hard enough to smack her head against the cabin dome light.

"Mistress? You are alive?" Kidahin keened in wild relief. Einstika had not killed her?

"No. The spirits are speaking to you from beyond the jungle. Of course I am alive. What did you think? Nevermind. My Pathwalker archers have eyes on a Neh'as'anni force. I lost contact with two forward stalker teams sent in to make an assessment. Send one of your tails in to scout the area immediately forward of the berm and keep in mind that an Environmental Interdiction team is somewhere inside the complex attempting to secure the Technology Center, capture any Neh'as'anni for interrogation, and intelligence gathering. They have a priority classified mission, too. If they cannot complete it, they will evacuate and head north to the perimeter road and follow the ridge to the northbound commercial road. Keep them in mind."

"Affirm. Should I close on the berm and attempt to rejoin the Pathwalkers?" Kidahin trilled.

"No. Conceal your vehicle off-road and send the tail out. Do a high-ground survey first and then fly over the berm outside edge before transmitting what you find back to me. I want a complete report on our movements, the Neh'as'anni movement, and an idea of how the roads in and out of the airfield look."

"Affirm," Kidahin sang, feeling much better. Shikararro lived! For some odd reason the notion of the Mistress of Battle being dead had trilled in her ears for hours.

Maybe she remembered it wrong. Maybe Einstika was dead?

Kidahin drove a few hundred ells over smooth paving stones before turning off-road into a clearing and drove into a stand of arberis, steering around several more until they surrounded her with yellow-variegated crimson leaves.

She shut off the engine, reached for the control yoke, and this time launched a tail. She flew the larger and better-equipped drone off her left flank and into the canopy, dodging branches as she weaved between crimson leaves longer than she was tall.

She flew the tail barely three hundred ells before it simply stopped transmitting sound, picture, and talkback telemetry.

Shot down? That made the most sense. Her heart began hammering a staccato beat against her breast.

Kidahin replayed the video feed, paying close attention to the telemetry data.

She saw nothing, and the telemetry gave no evidence suggesting that the tail had been shot down. The data should show in-flight damage before the tail broke up and a crash trajectory if it had not broken up.

But the telemetry read like the tail had simply winked out of existence, here one second and gone the next.

Sudden hyperawareness dumped an adrenaline surge into Kidahin's bloodstream, and her heart raced as she prepared for an aggressive defense. She would complete the task set by the Mistress of Battle, but she needed answers. She launched a second tail and flew off her left flank at an angle that would intercept the point where the first tail vanished but at a tangent. The drone's cameras and microphones saw and heard nothing when it arrived: no trees, no sky, no ground, no rustling leaves, no snap of twigs, not even the whisper-quiet hum of the drone's propeller wash. She banked the tail and flew back over her hiding spot and over her right flank slowly until she saw nothingness ahead.

"This makes no sense. How can there be nothing at all on the left or right beyond three hundred ells?"

Kidahin banked away from the gray void and flew over the paved road to the intersection where she had stalled out. The camera showed a similar sea of slate-gray nothingness a mere stone's throw from the gravel road.

"I am being surrounded!" Kidahin keened and slammed the yoke forward and flew the tail down the paved road towards the berm.

The closer she flew to it the more detailed and expansive the rainforest became. The telemetry confirmed she had already flown several thousand ells and the view above the canopy seemed to go on forever. The canopy glowed with life. It radiated an aura of arboreal health. But why? The trees looked normal, yet different—more real. The drive from the siege engine battle to here had also looked, sounded, and smelled normal.

Well, no. Not really. The rainforest throbbed with intensity, but the trees she drove through on the way here looked—what, exactly? Dull? Flat?

"No. Stagnant. There was a listlessness, almost as if the forest was calling out to the spirits, begging them to give it purpose," Kidahin trilled.

She leaned into her seat as the tail overflew the berm and picked up some of Hlorrithin's skirmishers on patrol. They were preparing to breach the berm.

Two scenes called out to her. Hlorrithin's Warpact and the female armies supporting it moved with an impressive and subtle purpose. Yet glaring all around them were the magnificent bold colors and calming sounds of the rainforest, the berm, and the northwest edge of the airfield. Both smacked her with a sense of realism. The people moving through the jungle undergrowth gave the scene a dynamic and real quality completely lacking since she left the siege engine battle.

Kidahin glanced through the windshield at the surrounding arberi leaves. Oddly enough, the jungle video streaming from the tail looked more alive than the arberis growing next to her. She watched more of the high-quality camera video as the tail tracked the scouts from above as they prowled the berm.

"Time to fly a stealth pass," she muttered and banked the tail and dropped just above them and zoomed the camera for a better look.

She zoomed in on the neckwear and waistwear the Hunters wore.

"Now I can see who and what you are," Kidahin sang and then trilled a giggle. Delwyn would have no clue what the identifying colors and patterns on their neckwear and waistwear meant beyond the basics all males were allowed to know.

Compared to humans, Eyloni wore next to nothing. Humans wore strangling and restricting uniform clothing to excess. Their clothing proclaimed status with all the subtlety of a flash, a bang, and a scream. Yes, rank and status mattered in Eyloni social life. Females fussily observed both down to the smallest detail so to not give offense. Yet the signs of rank and status except for the bold statement an adulthood knife and the male-awarded earring webs, knots, and beads made were otherwise as subtle as they were obvious.

Kidahin carefully studied the prowlers' waistwear patterns and colors. They declared an older Hunter as a member of the La'huaset Tribe and the O'ni'da family belonging to the O'un Tu Clan. The loincloth hanging from it reflected her relatively high social rank and clan status. The colorfully beaded neckwear pattern gave her hierarchy and standing within it. The obvious knapped flint adulthood knife curving around and under her left breast declared her an adult, of course. The braided waistwear ties gave away her social title, a mistress of arms.

Kidahin blinked at the long, hideous black scar running from the Huntress's ample left breast to hip. It alone identified this Huntress better than her skin color patterns did.

"Zalzadrin, the Mistress of Arms aboard our warship. What is she doing here?" Kidahin sang softly.

"She plays a part in the Song of Hlorrithin ritual reenactment of the Battle of Withered Trees, just as you do. You must remember!" Aplilin's voice trilled at warning tempo.

Kidahin smiled fondly as she imagined hearing Aplilin. But Aplilin was not here.

Kidahin snapped her tail and zoomed in for a look at the other prowlers and stalkers. She read signs of status on their waistwear as well. Hlorrithin should begin his assault soon. He held the worldwide Warpact. Hunters and Warriors from all ten tribes followed him here, and yet these females wore La'huaset tribal colors and either O'un Tu or Uahua'asee'a Clan patterns.

Kidahin sighed, relieved. This at least made sense among several things that had not been making sense lately. Clans formed armies from their female populations and were led by their sire cairns. Warpact required those males to honorably surrender their autonomy to Hlorrithin, but even in Warpact rarely did different clans mix within the same combat teams.

Her relief soon turned to boredom from watching the prowlers move down the ridge.

She flew the tail over them, squinting at the video stream until she saw the obvious: this was no berm in the strictest military sense because it lacked uniform height and thickness. This ragged line of ripped soil, rocks, and mangled jungle was merely a long ridge of debris dug up from when the Neh'as'anni cleared the ground for their buildings.

From above the debris ridge she found several breach points already held by Hlorrithin.

Frustrated and angry, Kidahin flew the tail back and landed it on the roof.

"Why did I just fly a tail above Shikararro's archers? Her request makes no sense. Her perimeter prowlers certainly know more about the debris ridge by simply being there than I can see through a camera."

As if in answer, Kidahin saw a hazy vision of Shikararro sitting in the front passenger seat of a long-obsolete armored personnel carrier rather than a modern tactical command carrier.

Her imagination at work? Yes, of course it was. Shikararro was prowling with her archers, yes?

Kidahin saw her reflection in the instrument panel and froze.

Spirits. I look older than Zalzadrin and I am wearing more accomplishment webs, honor knots, and mission beads in my rank earring than I have a right to.

"Dou'tu'tay!" Kidahin trilled, her heart beginning to pound again.

Altering male-awarded military rank was a high honor point crime recognized by all hierarchies as a death penalty offense.

What else had changed? She glanced down at her waistwear. The underthong tie colors declared her a Mistress of Scouts.

"I am not a Mistress of anything. I am merely an assaultmistress. If I was a Mistress of Scouts then I would be on the ridge with my stalkers and prowlers.

"A'pea this. I do remember leading a team here!"

The tactical command carrier dissipated like a puff of smoke, leaving her standing atop torn branches and tangled undergrowth on the ridge exactly where she saw a stalking Huntress minutes ago.

Kidahin ignored the abrupt change in scene. Her vehicle already forgotten, she knew only that she was a solitary scout. Her mission was to prowl along the ridge. She reached the top in minutes and gazed into a yellow haze that clung to the surrounding trees.

Below, the perimeter road hugged the inside edge of the excavated debris. Across the road the industrial complex disappeared into the yellow-tinted haze.

Kidahin glared at the complex with its streets and orangy boxlike buildings. Righteous wrath and loathing choked her. Beyond the contaminating, golden-tinged, early morning haze she could barely make out the blackened outline of the beige Neh'as'anni Technology Center. Inside hid the source of neh'tle ke'ne's'tu, an environmental contamination so subtle and deadly its sinister call of promised technical innovation nose-blinded those who fell under its alluring scent. These people and this place once promised scientific and technological enlightenment but instead delivered death to tens of thousands of males, thousands of Comara, and hundreds of Hunters and Warriors—a death more gruesome even than buhnnie poisoning.

She stepped up to the edge of the ridge for a better look. The view felt familiar, and yet it did not. Backwards? Reversed? Something about the point of view seemed wrong.

She always saw patterns because all Eyloni used patterns to recognize the leafy skin colors of other people and to prowl through the colorful rainforest without getting lost.

"I saw this from a different vantage point. I saw it from somewhere on the other side of the Technology Center building, from well inside the industrial complex."

She gazed above a line of toppled buildings barely visible in the mist.

Then a memory keened at her. She had prowled in front of the La'huaset Engineering Center of Operations Technology Center. She saw the warehouses in the mid-ground and the hangers and airfield behind them with the ridge she stood on right now in the far background.

Sour smoke mingled with the scent of flowering trees stung her nose. The stench made her stomach lurch. She fell to the ridge mildly nauseous and forced her heaving gags to stop.

Had she inhaled the scent of neh'tle ke'ne's'tu? Had she already fatally contaminated herself?

Kidahin stood and glided away from the edge to prowl along the narrow winding trail as it followed the perimeter road below towards the runways and the closest hanger.

Kidahin struggled as she climbed over mounds of debris. She had to pause several times to watch what the Neh'as'anni were doing.

She felt something amiss and turned to focus into the distance and waited until the obvious finally snapped its tail in her face.

The torn ridge rubble meant nothing tactically, but the crumpled pavement below did. Both the nearby runway and the perimeter road were shattered, even pulverized in places. Paving slabs had buckled from the roadbed as though punched from below ground. No aircraft could take off now. No doubt the other runways had similar damage.

Still focused on the road below, Kidahin tripped over coils of blackened jungle roots and vines ripped up when the jungle was cleared and pushed onto the ridge.

She twisted into a graceful recovery and caught a glimpse of bright sparkles coming from the distant leveled buildings. Broken windows flashed shafts of brilliant sunlight back across the complex. Still-standing buildings beyond them glittered in the dawn.

The sour scent grew stronger as it drifted apace with her. She shied away from it, but it already triggered a memory that dropped her to her knees as it dredged a name from a disaster.

"*Londiwe Khoza.*"

"Our mission to the shipwrecked human destroyer is our shared past, my Kidahin. What you see before you now comes from our shared historical past. Did you notice how the Neh'as'anni have dug in across the airfield? You are out of position. Go to New Dawn!" Aplilin's voice whispered insistently in her ear.

"What in the spirits is a 'new dawn', Aplilin?" Kidahin keened, glancing wildly about for her lover. She neither saw or smelled the strong, muscular Huntress. Impatient, Kidahin pushed thoughts of Aplilin aside and stepped back onto the narrow path.

It rose and fell along a jagged line, becoming an obstacle course filled with rocks and tangled, twisted branches mired in slippery molds and mosses.

Kidahin spun her tail rapidly to keep balance but stumbled several times anyway, distracted by Aplilin's disembodied voice singing "New Dawn" over and over again in her ears.

New Dawn? Why did that name bring feelings of despair? All those males died aboard *Londiwe Khoza* two years ago.

"Of course!" Kidahin keened, finally grasping onto the slippery vine twisting through her memories. These dead males came from her recent past, but the Battle of Withered Trees happened centuries ago. The siege engine assault on the elleiu trees was an image from a teaching song she learned as a preadolescent.

Below, the Neh'as'anni were moving onto the perimeter road.

Kidahin snapped her ears at them. They certainly were not a memory. This felt too real for recalled pheromonal empathic learning. Teaching songs put a person off the trail as an observer, but this felt more like taking part in the action as it happened.

In fact, it felt just like being in scent-linked empathy with the family females during my adulthood ceremony. While in the Oyya Web I ignored their warnings and forced my own path through the mental imagery until I met the spirits themselves.

Kidahin frowned. No, rituals followed a series of scenes having beginnings and endings. Time did not flow normally in ritual empathic visions.

"I remember taking part in the opening assault of the Battle of Withered Trees with Einstika, but Einstika is not here now. And where is Tialdrin? Oh, spirits. I am stalking through my own leafchasing mind. I must have imagined the tactical command carrier and the drive here."

But after a moment Kidahin snapped her ears in violent denial.

"No, my imagination is not at work here. If I played a minor role in the reenactment of the elleiu tree assault, I would have been expelled from the Oyya Web when Einstika killed me."

Kidahin mentally retraced her path back to when she received the status update from Shikararro.

"She sent me here to surveil the left flank of Hlorrithin's forces. But those forces are her Pathwalker archers. She already knows what is here. Wait, she said an Environmental Interdiction team was executing a priority classified mission. But why tell me about it?"

Doubts buzzed her ears like salt flies as the forest faded away.

Kidahin wore a hazard suit. Startled by the sudden confining clothing, she tumbled over the ridge and into tangles of orange thorny brush. Uprooted long-dead briars snagged at her arms and legs, arresting her downward plunge as dead male bodies sprouted among the grasping thorny vines like pale puffy gourds.

Panic gripped her, and she averted her eyes.

"After what I just saw, no blinking lamp of any color can tell me all is well here," Einstika's voice trilled hollowly.

"There are four dead bodies smashed and frozen to where the wall meets the deck," Hollfara keened from some great distance.

"What blinking lamp? What wall and deck? Where are you? Einstika? Hollfara? I do not remember you being here!" Kidahin trilled.

But Einstika she remembered being here. This was all her fault.

Enraged, she spun on bare heels and climbed like a Warrior was wont to do, shoving aside encumbering undergrowth until several interwoven stems snagged around the holster at her hip.

Kidahin's eyes froze on the revolting coward's weapon. Nobody carried firearms anymore. Indeed, no Eyloni had carried one since Hlorrithin's time.

"Oh, spirits. Aplilin is right. I remember now," she keened.

"I am participating in a bimillennial celebration ritual commemorating Hlorrithin's victory. Physically I am sitting in the Singer's Grove and caught in a pheromone-induced vision quest, but in my mind I am playing out a historical role in the Battle of Withered Trees. Something must have happened to sever the empathic link between me and the Gracious Mistress and her singers. But what? Only a powerful emotional thrust can smother pheromonal empathy during a ritual.

"I have been drifting aimlessly through random mental scenes. No ritual participant noticed me so far, but even if they did, they would think I am nothing but a pheromonal prop placed here by the singers for them to interact with, just as I am interacting with this central La'huaset jungle right now."

Bright mist glowed among sunlit-shrouding orange-streaked yellow leaves. An arberi tree stood out from the mist, its outline noticeable only by the green parasitic vines growing up its trunk and along its main branches. Near it stood another arberi, its branches clearly visible from the golden-yellow lianas hanging from its crimson branches. Golden-yellow mosses covered its gray bark. Those leaves screened the dawn's rays down to reddish-orange shade. Scarlet brush, golden vines, and vermilion grasses less than an ell tall grew among them.

And it was all her own mental hallucination.

It looked real because she expected it to look real. Prowling through it took as much time and effort as did prowling through the real thing. Cut off from the Gracious Mistress's empathy meant the surrounding jungle and the debris ridge came from her own memories of the central La'huaset rainforest added to the historical imagery she remembered from the preadolescent teaching songs.

Too bad she could not imagine a clearer path, but pheromonal imagery did not work like that. Because she *knew* this forest, she could not disbelieve or misremember it somehow.

Kidahin keened an obscenity and took the time to step gracefully through the entangling undergrowth towards a sturdy trunk growing through the ridge at a canted angle. The reddish-barked sentinel, draped in pale yellow moss, seemed determined to hold the encroaching debris back from consuming the forest.

She passed the trunk and prowled another hundred ells to a second one, a dark brown one laced with red undertones. Heavy ground-moving equipment had shattered it, and it still looked rough and split.

She prowled the ridge, brushing aside swaying yellow vines from branches rustling above until the ridge turned slick with stones worn smooth by flowing water. A creek or river had been scraped from the forest floor and piled up here.

Kidahin snapped her tail in disbelief and glanced at the sidearm at her hip. Its use, considered cowardly *no matter what* in her time, was grudgingly allowed in expressly limited situations in Hlorrithin's time.

She tailchased an all-consuming question: how could she simply wander off and get lost in the Oyya Web? She should have remained in a scene created by the singers.

"I thought I had better discipline than that!" she keened aloud.

"This is not a question of discipline. This is a matter of traumatic stress," Aplilin sang insistently.

"Aplilin! Are you with me?"

"I am always with you, my Kidahin."

Kidahin felt an ethereal tail wrap around her waist. She considered what to do next.

A person could wander through pheromonal imagery and never know she was trapped in her own head. Scenes became self-generating when anyone empathized with her own pheromones to the point of excluding the scents of the females singing the Oyya Web scenes she was supposed to empathize with. The empathic visions became enthralling. But seeing the coward's weapon and leafchasing through memories had somehow opened her mind to the love she felt for Aplilin.

Now she had to reenter the ritual reality. That meant she had to hear the Gracious Mistress singing, and she had to smell her pheromones. Empathizing with the Gracious Mistress and her singers should pull her mind back into the ritual imagery.

But why could she not hear or smell the singers now? They would have helped Aplilin reach out to her empathically because she was not some fragment of memory she leafchased into existence.

So, how do I find the Gracious Mistress?

"I need to find a scene where Einstika, Tialdrin, and I reenacted the actions of the historical Environmental Interdiction Team-one. But first I need to figure out why I can not hear the historical script being sang to everyone in the ritual or smell the pheromonal cues coming from the ritual singers.

"All those male deaths aboard the human warship, obviously.

"Traumatic stresses from *Londiwe Khoza* must have somehow distorted the subjective ritual reality," Kidahin concluded nastily. It makes sense if the male deaths from Neh'as'anni environmental contamination and from the medical experiments in New Dawn triggered them. No, not a trigger but favorable conditions. We all knew Hlorrithin dies soon after the battle. Knowing that planted the seed in Einstika's mind. I think she was seeing the bodies, too. Did she assume that Shikararro's absence from the APC contributed to Hlorrithin's death?

"This is not your fault, Einstika. I felt the same way," Kidahin trilled.

So now what? How can I escape this self-imposed mental trap? I am caught between scenes in a ritual construct.

But in ritual, the plot is a timeline of interrelated scenes. I would have to reenter the plot at a scene prior to the one where we violated history.

"So I only have to find the right scene at the right time and undo whatever it was we did that caused us to kill Shikararro," she trilled, snapping her tail.

That might get her back into the plot, but after she fixed whatever went wrong she still had to reenact the remaining scenes to the ritual end.

A daunting task. Several thousand people played parts in the Song of Hlorrithin ritual, all of them sharing pheromonal empathy with the Gracious Mistress and her singers. When Einstika killed Shikararro the empathic shock ejected us from the plotline, stranding us in a fragment of mental imagery.

Kidahin wondered just how much time she had. She knew the Song of Hlorrithin was a long ritual lasting about a week, but in the mind the events spanned about a month. Time in rituals shared features with time in dreams. Dreamed events could span hours, days, or even years in a single twenty-minute dream. A dream about a ten-minute event could last for hours. A centuries-long epic event could last only a single sleep cycle. Time was mutable here, subjective, and did not hold to the rules of cause and effect. Scenes popped in and out of existence, an affront to continuity.

"This explains my bad temper. If Tialdrin could smell me now, she would say I am no different than Hollfara, who talks at people and not to them," Kidahin sang wryly.

"Think about Shikararro!" Aplilin's voice insisted at imperative tempo.

Kidahin perked her ears forward and then flicked them wide apart.

"What about her, Aplilin? She gave me the leadership after dislocating her shoulder. She returned to the APC and watched the Neh'as'anni defend their northern elleiu trees."

But wait. Say Einstika blamed Shikararro for Hlorrithin's pending death. Could traumatic stress alone push her to kill Shikararro? I knew Shikararro doing nothing was historically wrong. Einstika knew it, too.

"The A'tayotan Mistress told us Shikararro rejoined her archers, which was what the historical A'tayotan mistress believed at the time," Kidahin sang aloud.

She knew historically that Team-one should not have found an abandoned APC. Shikararro should have drove until she intercepted Team-one on a paved road.

"Finding the APC abandoned triggered Einstika's traumatic stress response, a response she felt necessary to save Hlorrithin's life. I smelled her pheromones, empathized with them, and got pulled into her belief. My empathic reinforcement pushed her into challenging and then killing Shikararro.

"Her death collapsed the ritual around us because her death runs counter to historical fact. Empathic shock expelled us from the ritual plot.

"The teaching songs say Shikararro told Hlorrithin how to submit neh'tle ke'ne's'tu to his will. Her early death would prevent him from doing so."

Kidahin wrinkled her nose. Today, neh'tle ke'ne's'tu meant environmental catastrophe, pollution sickness, and filthy technology in general. But in Hlorrithin's time it referred specifically to Neh'as'anni technology, the Neh'as'anni themselves as a pejorative, and the tail-tied belief their filthy technology would ultimately save Elleio from rampant birth defects and imminent ecological collapse.

"Hlorrithin did submit neh'tle ke'ne's'tu, but he had help from Team-one," Kidahin sang reverently and gave the rainforest a subtle smile. Shikararro helped him by holding her Pathwalker archers in reserve near the ridge opposite the airfield. She also helped Einstika with the hard drive unit they took from New Dawn. Without Shikararro, Hlorrithin would still win the battle.

"But," Kidahin cautioned herself, "the A'tayotan mistresses of saga agree he would have failed to stop the radiation leak from contaminating all of central and eastern La'huaset. Most of the people would have died, and he would have died before capturing the Neh'as'anni space technology. The mistresses clearly teach that we would never have bothered to develop spaceflight without the Neh'as'anni base research."

But wait. Shikararro played a pivotal role in history. Her early death would have suspended us between scenes while everyone else continued to act out their parts. Yet the ritual cannot end because it needs Shikararro to complete her role.

"The singers are trying to draw us back into the ritual plotline. My hearing Aplilin proves it. I remember the history songs now, which proves it, too."

So what happened to Tialdrin?

Kidahin gave her thigh a sharp snap of tail to help her focus.

Tialdrin wondered why we lost contact with the A'tayotan Mistress. I think she was the only one who still remembered we were in a ritual reality.

Traumatic stress was rare in females. Communal pheromonal empathy blunted the shock of distressing events. The greatest stress a female ever experienced was a male death in which she either felt powerless or was truly powerless to prevent. Kidahin knew pheromonal empathy was a rational aspect of female life. A female experienced traumatic stress only when she believed she could have made a difference.

"But," she snorted. "Belief often leafchases after the irrational. We empathically drew on our collective self-generating pheromonal visions. Tialdrin's wellnessmistress training allowed her to notice something was wrong with the empathic narrative. She became aware of the Gracious Mistress and that pulled her into a scene from the Song of Hlorrithin.

"Einstika and I lost her scent and immediately forgot her, which freed us to wander deeper into our own self-created visions.

"And every time I recognized a scene from the Song of Hlorrithin it slipped away, replaced by visions of dead males."

Around her dead human male bodies appeared as if summoned. They were buried along the ridge in the undergrowth stretching out ahead until they vanished into the yellow-tinged haze.

14
PASSING STRANGENESS

The gory visions triggered seizures. They usually began like an exaggerated startle reflex: her arms held rigid at the sides, face frozen in tense wariness, and eyes fluttering side-to-side. The visions, the memory, and the emotions then combined to trigger instinctive rage keyed to saving males at any cost. The overreaction summoned more flashbacks. Even the memory of it threatened to pull Kidahin back into the self-created subjective nightmare from which she had just escaped.

The Territorial Boundaries of Rage and Forgiveness offered a branch she could grasp: it demanded she forget all social debts. She flattened ears against her short crimson ringlets in denial. Male-killing was not a social debt. It was an honor-point offense and an unimaginable one at that.

But her righteous anger was social in nature. She needed to kill the fury associated with the memories of *Londiwe Khoza* and his dead—sing it into the Oyya Web of the spirits.

Only by singing a Death Song ritual could she lay the debt aside. But people sang Death Songs for the dead. For whom could she sing a Death Song for? Warleader Delwyn sang the Death Song for the *Londiwe Khoza* dead almost two years ago. Death Song rituals relied on social participation. Could she even sing a meaningful Death Song by herself?

And custom required a male to sing the lead in any Death Song unless one was absolutely unavailable, an impossibility in everyday social life.

But right now she stood apart from social life, the Song of Hlorrithin playing out in the recesses of her empathic mind. The scenes and every person here existed as pheromonal figments sent to her mind through the scent and music of the singers.

The flashbacks came from her subconscious mind, as did the several side-scenes she wandered through.

Delwyn was the key.

Intimately familiar with him, his music, and his scent, Kidahin summoned a mental picture of him: an affable and solitary male with a bright face and eyes that wandered and darted inquisitively. She considered the motifs living in his Death Song and imagined herself gazing down a shallow angle onto the Singer's Place on Ibeetu. Delwyn stood there with his drum ready and the Society of Hunter's Moon sitting around and behind him in a tiered branching pattern. He faced a distant mountain peak, looking up at it from a shallow incline. From memory the Place of Mourning sprouted amid a grassy amber meadow. Sunset hit the distant summit, spraying prismatic rays from frosty peaks in a riot of sparkling colors.

Delwyn beat his drum as the refracted light combined with the setting sun.

Kidahin followed his dirge beat as it built into a melancholy melody. The dull central La'huaset Tribal continent scene faded into the background, replaced by the vibrant and living forest of the distant moon Ibeetu.

Rainbows flashed above Delwyn. The setting sun bathed the peaks in yellow light. The clear light-blue sky framed shimmering auroras as they whipped across the sky like disembodied green and yellow tails.

Kidahin looked for the Mistress of Songs and saw Aplilin standing in her place.

Their eyes met.

Aplilin perked her ears, signaling ready. Kidahin felt both the beat and the encouragement of her lover.

The tempo changed. It was time.

She sang from the Rite of Forgiveness about forgetting the social debt. She sang in honor of the humans who died on *Londiwe Khoza*.

She sang in remembrance of the sorrows endured by the People leading up to the Battle of Withered Trees.

She sang in memory of Hlorrithin, the Eleventh Hero of Elleio.

And she sang for the joy of finding peace and rest.

As the last note faded she heard the Gracious Mistress.

I am at peace. My duty is fulfilled.

The ritual neared its end and Kidahin still remained trapped in a stubbornly persistent side-scene. Yet the themes of being at peace and of having a duty fulfilled rang in her ears.

Forget the social debt.

"Time is mutable here, my Kidahin," a disembodied Aplilin trilled softly.

What about it? Time in rituals flowed like it did in dreams. Reenacting historical events spanning months in just a few weeks meant eliminating pesky notions of causality and cause-and-effect sequences. Going back in ritual time was possible. Simply return to the scene she reenacted prior to the event and set it on the correct path.

Kidahin thought about Einstika and Tialdrin as she resumed prowling. They remained lost to her, beyond reach until she caught up with them in a scene from the ritual past.

***

The edges of leaves and grasses sharpened and their colors bloomed as life swept into the rainforest scene with the coming of Hlorrithin's forces.

Kidahin could not reenter the ritual plot without risking getting caught up in the scene being reenacted. Better she find a scene she reenacted just before Einstika killed Shikararro.

But which scene? Before they found the APC abandoned, sometime after they found the hard drive unit.

Leaving the warehouse annex and driving south broke with the historical narrative.

What made them drive south?

Reentering a past scene meant finding it and stepping into it as the singers called it into existence. But finding a specific scene beginning or ending while outside of the ritual plot meant not only reaching the scene but waiting for it to animate. Only then would her present self merge with her reenacting past self and pull her into the ritual timeline.

Then all she had to do was convince Tialdrin and Einstika to drive north.

***

The airfield hummed with life now. Old scenes no longer needed lost their vitality and faded from the shared empathic reality as events moved on.

Kidahin knew she had to reenter ritual time sometime before the ATV left the annex.

"The scenes for Hlorrithin's assault on the airfield remain. They and the scenes around them are safe, but prowling too far from New Dawn increases the risk of stepping into a vanishing scene. Losing contact with the ritual reality traps the empathic mind. If the ritual ends before I can reenter the corrupted past scene the mental imagery fades away leaving no way back to conscious awareness. The ritual cannot be suspended without stranding all participants in their subconscious minds.

"If I prowl along the path taken by the historical Team-one and listen for the plot-driving melody then I can wait until I hear the right verse, empathize with it, and drop into the scene," Kidahin reasoned aloud.

She sat on a large rock wedged between two splintered trunks and considered likely scenes. Her knowledge of history and the scenes she appeared in suggested several choices.

The scenes from the Battle of Withered Trees came from empathic visions encouraged by the Song of Hlorrithin. The Song set the ritual theme. The best trail must begin with first singing the entire Song and then considering the historical scenes it memorialized.

Kidahin began.

> Who are we, the Eyloni, without our memories?
> Who are we without our hopes, without our dreams?
> We are nothing without our past, without our future; we are nothing but an arrow without a bow and without a target.
> Without memories, without dreams, we are devoid of hope, and we are devoid of purpose.
> Today lasts only a blink and then it is gone. It is our duty to remember our past and treasure our future. This is why, so long ago, we hunted.
> We, the Eyloni, know our prey. We surround the territory of the Neh'as'anni Clan, where the ni'zakhon have laid their lair. There, death stalks the land. We know the days and dreams of our People, of our Elders, and of our males and infants trapped here. But we will never let our heritage die, nor let our males fall into oblivion.
> Shikararro, our Eldest Huntress, found the evil ailing our males and our infants. Their spirits are stolen from us.
> She showed us the vile thief, but it was just a minion of neh'tle ke'ne's'tu.
> We must confront it and prevail to remain in the world.
> This day we prepare for battle before we saw the full face of Tyreniioroneo. We sang to the spirits of the People, the powerful ones, asking for the strength and swiftness of the wind and let us come back to our people.
> Shikararro told us that the only way to defeat neh'tle ke'ne's'tu was by killing its essence. Whoever does this will not only free the captive spirits, but will become the bearer of its power.
> The dreadful messengers arrived at dusk.
> We killed them, all but one, so we could follow it and find the prohibited clan, the lair of its master prey.
> We run for one full day under the brunt of harsh sunbeams. We are tired, but we will not give up.

We fight a running battle and take heavy losses, but we can still fight. We disperse, for we must arrive in silence and prepare to face our destiny.

The elleiu trees stand before us, huge and somber. We do not know the way, but the screams of the captive spirits guide us through the darkness of the Long Night

The infamous stench of neh'tle ke'ne's'tu does not weaken our will.

We blend into the rainforest night as the spirits taught us so long ago in the earliest songs.

We ask the spirits for the sound of the falling leaf, so none can hear us.

It is sad this once beautiful place now harbors vile corruption.

Nothing we knew could compare to the greatness of this place and the people who lived here. Their songs and ideas echoing here are all that remain of the mystery they took with them as they fled.

I forgot this as I look upon neh'tle ke'ne's'tu, its mind drifting through evil and twisted dreams. So many spirits under its power, many more than just those stolen from our Clan.

This is the evil we came to destroy.

Death will come as a surprise during its sleep.

Suddenly I understand.

It is us who Death awaits.

The first of us to fall was Fitever. Her powerful spear could not strike the flesh of the enemy taking her life.

Stanfuree showed the Warrior prowess of our Clan. Nothing can stop her strong arm and although her blows were not fatal, the enemy knew pain.

It was so unfortunate to lose her so soon.

Her courage and skill would have let the rest of us survive. But we Eyloni know no fear and fight with valor, no matter what.

Thrandra and Twithora swiftly used their arrows.

But arrows cannot kill neh'tle ke'ne's'tu.

Without any doubt, their brave spirits will find their path to the Oyya Web of the spirits.

I can only honor their courage by stabbing the fatal blow.

But my arrows were few and weak.

And I never was the best of archers.

I was alone, the last of several thousand strong.

But I knew what I must do.

Was I not responsible for the spirits of the males? Of the infants?

'Submit its will', Shikararro's counsel echoes in my ears.

And fighting its formidable power, I discovered how to achieve such a feat.

But I had only one chance.

Spirits of the O'un Tu Clan, give me light feet!

I cannot fail now!

This is the most beautiful dawn I can remember.

The young spirits left joyful laughter as they flew away. The males' spirits blessed me with songs I never heard before.

The light they left in their parting was a gift to face the darkest night that, without doubt, waited for me ahead. I did not have long to live.

I am at peace. My duty is fulfilled.

Only the spirits of the O'un Tu knew what laid ahead for me.

But the dreams and hopes I knew that day gave me the strength to stand against any evil.

Kidahin finished and then paused. The Gracious Mistress had already sung "I am at peace. My duty is fulfilled." Two verses remained before the ritual ended. The singers spent on average two hours singing the bridging refrain between verses. So from the singers' point of view the Song, and therefore the ritual, would end in another four hours. But for the participants joined in ritual empathy the historical reenactment continued for a full day, about half of a Delwyn day.

She had an EST day to reenter the ritual, shove Einstika and Tialdrin down the historically correct path, and reenact Kidahindrallin's courageous actions to their conclusion.

The ritual spanned events lasting a full month, and she had only a day before those events concluded.

"Einstika and I got pulled into playing Twithora and Thrandra at the siege engine scene. I can go back and get her first," Kidahin sang aloud.

"No, my Kidahin. The subconscious lacks the capacity to sustain more than two independent scenes involving the same person at the same time. You were below New Dawn with Einstika placing the alloy sample in the drone's hand then," Aplilin whispered at warning tempo.

Kidahin snapped her ears in absentminded agreement and picked another scene.

"What about when we found the handcar in the tunnels?"

"No!" a disembodied Aplilin trilled at imperative pitch. "The singers lose continuity when they shift from earlier to later tunnel scenes. The difference is subtle, but the differences have faded away."

"We left the tunnels and climbed over ruins. I can return to where Einstika used a rope to drop onto the airfield service road next to New Dawn," she sang.

"You were there more than once, too. Einstika stabbed you with a spear at the elleiu tree battle then. You cannot waste time trying to find Einstika and Tialdrin. You must find the appropriate scene having them in it. Think, my Kidahin! You must return to a scene before Einstika kills Shikararro," Aplilin growled sharply.

"We found the shuttle with the missing engine in the warehouse annex. Everything—well, almost everything—we did there was historically accurate up to when we left in the all-terrain vehicle," Kidahin sang.

"You must stop Einstika from taking the wrong turn. But do not go back too far. Once you reenter the ritual reality you must assume Kidahindrallin's role and follow the plot to its end," Aplilin pointed out.

"I will return to the command center and wait for them there," Kidahin snapped impatiently.

"No," Aplilin objected softly. "Mimiran says your exposure to the dead there triggered the traumatic stress flashbacks."

"But we found the hard drives there, and the Gracious Mistress sang Hlorrithin's plea to the O'un Tu spirits then."

"Mimiran agrees," Aplilin cautiously allowed.

"I can stalk them until they leave the command center and follow them back to the annex."

"Absolutely not!" Aplilin trilled angrily. "You fired the coward's weapon at a flashback figment there."

"Antiphonal challenges came from the airfield as Hlorrithin began the final assault. Tialdrin gave us a history lecture then, and I remember a flashback," Kidahin sang.

"Yes," Aplilin agreed. "Get there after the flashback and reinforce Tialdrin's line of thinking. Tell Einstika to drive north to the airfield."

"Affirm," Kidahin sang.

Aplilin's ethereal presence left Kidahin.

Kidahin planned her route to New Dawn. She would arrive sometime after the Gracious Mistress sang about the spirits of the O'un Tu Clan giving Hlorrithin light feet and before she sang about him not failing. In theory, the ritual plot should sweep her back into the ritual present. But just as males were strange, so too was time in the Oyya Web. Duration varied and did not follow cause and effect. Time backtrailed and looped in the ritual reality.

Kidahin twisted her tail idly to keep her balance as she climbed down the ridge to the perimeter road. The slippery footing kept her focused, yet she slipped on moldy logs halfway down the slope anyway.

Impatient, she leapt over several tail-lengths of tangled debris and tumbled gracefully to the ground.

Combat forces moved ahead of her: Neh'as'anni. She could not risk getting pulled into the ritual present here and get drawn into the assault on the airfield.

Kidahin continued angling across and down the ridge, singing her progress to the tune of a song that celebrated Hunter prowess.

I am a Hunter female.
A Hunter places her feet like this. A Hunter sticks her tail out like this. Hunters stalk. Hunters prowl.
I am prowling and stalking.
It is best to be a Hunter female because we prowl like no others.
Hunters do not like people near us with their noises while we stalk.
I have something I must do. I dance around a shattered bole. I smell scents drifting all around me. I see an animal trail dropping under a hollow branch.
I feel the breeze on my face.
I jump onto the narrow path and prowl down a long, twisting ridge.
I feel the sun on my face, yet leaves block my view.
More scents ride the breezes. I know the way. I can smell the living scent. I smell females all around me, nosey females. Hunters prowling alongside Shikararro's archer scouts.
I smell others coming, Warrior females from Hlorrithin's breaching force.
The leaves brush against me as I pass through the concealing brush. They hide me.
The breeze is against my face. They cannot smell me.
The Warriors are prowling.
I press up against a torn branch twisting and turning around and down into the ridge.
I smell prowling Hunters close ahead. I silent-stalk onto a much narrower path, a trail barely a footprint wide as it drops down a steep angle.
Thank the spirits I feel the uneven rough footing on my bare feet. Not slippery, this trail is good for climbing.
A Warrior stands nearby.

Kidahin sighed. Singing focused her mind as she twisted through thorny coils without so much as a snag down to the perimeter road and realized she prowled too close to the pending battle.

She hugged the overgrown rubble shrouding the roadside and withdrew a few hundred ells and then sprinted across the road and continued over several ells of leveled heavy gravel to the nearest runway.

Standing on open flat ground and exposed, she ran south to the cover of empty, washed-out, shattered buildings. Nothing historically important happened here now, so most of the industrial complex south of New Dawn was slowly fading away.

The dull emptiness served as a constant warning not to remain in fading scenes least they vanish and pull her into oblivion with them.

Shattered buildings and rubble piles came into view, with New Dawn looming far off her right shoulder. She darted down a side road angling between warehouses before turning head-on towards New Dawn.

Kidahin saw the green door on the right side of New Dawn. She could open the door, cross the clean room, enter the hall, and walk to the annex.

As she watched, the door slowly turned dull gray-green. She paused, tempted.

Why not? The door was part of the building.

New Dawn looked dull and abandoned—empty—but it did not fade as she stared at it. It remained for the final battle, a prop needing a scene to breathe life into it. Her presence alone could not animate it because the singers did not sing historical action here until later in the Song of Hlorrithin.

But many scenes nearby, around, and in New Dawn witnessed multiple historical events from different points of view. Some of those points of view happened only once and faded away even as the main scene remained. New Dawn and the surrounding airfield scenes, although dull and empty now, saw action leading up to the final battle. They would not vanish from the singers' empathic metamind until the ritual ended.

Kidahin froze as if hearing the snap of a twig and cursed.

She came so close to killing herself.

The path to the green door and the door itself never saw historical action after Team-one entered New Dawn through the clean room. Their entry happened early in the Song, and no later historical scenes happened here. She came so close to walking into a vanishing scene, into what Delwyn called a "you cannot get there from here."

She ran.

"Hurry, my Kidahin. You must reach the warehouse annex before the Gracious Mistress sings Hlorrithin's plea to give him light feet!" Aplilin trilled faintly.

Kidahin froze again.

"How do I get inside without alerting Einstika and Tialdrin or violating Team-one's historical actions?" Kidahin keened desperately.

No helpful Aplilin bothered to answer.

The Neh'as'anni used most of the warehouse annex for prototype assembly. About half the size of New Dawn, it easily contained the suborbital shuttle and its supersonic transport. The end abutting New Dawn itself warehoused supplies drawn upon by the research teams. Team-one drove out an annex side door towards the rear of the building. No one paid more than a passing glance at the hanger door in the back.

Kidahin sprinted around the annex to the closed hanger door.

It hung from a two-piece rail. She tugged at the obvious handle.

"Locked," Kidahin trilled.

The keyhole took a key as big as her hand, probably one made of bronze or another metal strong enough to lever a latch or bolt without snapping.

Where was Einstika and her tools when she needed her?

Kidahin scowled, drew the coward's weapon, held it at an angle point-blank to the keyhole, and fired until she emptied the fourteen-round clip.

As the last hollow staccato clap faded she examined the ruined lock. The bullets shattered the pressed metal cap holding the core in place. She spent several minutes prying the mechanism free and tossed it to the ground, stuck a finger into the hole, and felt around for the latch.

She found it and pushed up hard. She pushed the heavy locking bar out of the hole in the concrete floor and struggled to hold the latch as she slid the door open.

She let go of the latch and heard the rod scrape along the concrete floor as she pulled the door open wide enough to step through.

Inside, she pulled the door closed and prowled cautiously up to the hypersonic suborbital shuttle.

"This technology let us pursue space-based manufacturing, matter-antimatter fusion, and the warships that keep our males safe from threats like the Ni'zakhonii," Kidahin sang in a melody laced with both admiration and revulsion.

She skipped briskly through the annex to the entrance into New Dawn itself and hesitated. This door was jammed last time she was here. Now it was already open, so Environmental Interdiction Team-one was already here and prowling below.

Perking her ears at the open doorway, she heard faint singing.

The heart-aching dullness drew life from the Song as the Gracious Mistress sang.

Spirits of the O'un Tu Clan, give me light feet!

Somewhere below, her subjective self was congratulating Einstika for stopping the lights from flickering. They would find the hard drive soon. Einstika would complain about hauling the unit back through the ruins and then the flashbacks appeared. Kidahin remembered firing the coward's weapon and getting hit by a ricochet.

But Tialdrin saw no flashback or the shadowy female figment.

Gunshots echoed hollowly from the lift shaft.

"A scene break approaches, my Kidahin. Step into your subjective self at the scene break," Aplilin whispered hauntingly at imperative tempo.

Scene break? What scene break? They would start climbing the lift shaft any minute. Wait, climbing and wrestling the hard drives took the historical Team-one a few hours. Nothing relevant happened during that time, so the singers skipped to the scene beginning where Team-one stepped out of the lift shaft and into the annex.

Kidahin backed into the shaft entrance and waited.

Colors brightened and sharpened. Sounds whispered and rang. Vitality returned as the subjective ritual present rushed into the scene. Her objective self merged with her subjective roleplaying self, locking her into what was now the ritual present.

Kidahin stepped into the annex.

"Mistress, voice-operated transmitter is back on. We are in the warehouse. The suborbital shuttle is on my left. We have the hard drives with us. They only got stuck once," an oblivious Einstika sang.

"Wait," she added. "I think something is moving in the shaft below us. Dou'tu tay! What is that? Kidahin, shoot that thing, now!"

"Shoot what? Some flashback figment?" Kidahin sang calmly.

"A what?" Einstika trilled at interrogative pitch.

"This is a figment pulled from our memories of *Londiwe Khoza*," Kidahin sang patiently.

"Oh, really? You were shooting at a figment?" Einstika trilled doubtfully.

"So that is why—I knew this might happen," Tialdrin trilled.

"Focus, Team-one. Figments? What are you singing about? Stop wasting time and get those hard drives to the APC!" the Mistress demanded.

"We are not going anywhere fast dragging this thing with us. These constricting hazard suits slow us down enough as it is," Einstika trilled and shoved the drive cabinet in frustration.

It rolled forward until it bumped into a nearby wooden crate.

She scowled at the crate for some time.

"Einstika! I am not pushing this thing by myself," Tialdrin complained.

"Wait, Tialdrin. Help me put this thing on the ATV. We can drive it out the side door next to the big back door they use to bring the jets in."

"What if it is locked?" Tialdrin scoffed.

"Locked to keep people from getting in, not for keeping people inside from getting out. Kidahin, look for a latch. It should be a simple bolt. Open the door and wait while Tialdrin and I tie this thing down."

"Affirm," Kidahin sang.

"It will not fit," Tialdrin warned.

"Yes, it will. Barely. Sit on it while I tie it and you to the ATV with some rope," Einstika sang.

"Me? Why me?" Tialdrin objected.

"Because I will drive and Kidahin will jump in as I drive through the door."

"Oh," Tialdrin trilled.

"Are you ready?" Einstika keened at Kidahin.

"I am. Will we fit in that thing?"

"Barely. Get ready. Here we come."

Einstika switched the motor on, shifted into gear, and squeezed the hand throttle gently.

"Hang on, Tialdrin," she trilled.

"Why? This is not so bad at all."

"Hang on, anyway."

"Affirm."

"Mistress, we are leaving the Technology Center building."

"Affirm, Team-one," the Mistress replied.

Kidahin waited impatiently as Einstika turned and headed for the open door. She jumped into the passenger seat before Einstika could hit the brakes.

"Go!" she sang.

Einstika nudged the ATV through the open door. She heard distant singing coming from behind the airfield and tapped the brakes until the ATV stopped.

Hlorrithin's forces sang antiphonal challenges. Antiphonal challenges mocked. They goaded the Neh'as'anni into taking rash actions.

"Hlorrithin is close, probably on the other side of the debris ridge by now. Shikararro and her archers should be with him," Einstika trilled heatedly.

"Her archers are, but she is not," Tialdrin sang. "She directs them from the APC. Remember your history? We intercept Shikararro before she rejoins them."

"Team-one knew they would intercept Shikararro from the time she dislocated her shoulder and returned to the APC," Kidahin gently reminded her.

"I know this," Tialdrin shot back warily. Something in Kidahin's scent seemed to suggest they had not known. Why did she have doubts? The teaching songs clearly showed Shikararro in the APC intercepting them in the ATV.

"Kidahin, are you well?" she trilled softly.

"What? Oh, yes, I am. Why?"

"Your scent. You are anticipating—dread?"

"I am sorry. I keep expecting dead human males to appear at any moment."

"Please, spirits no," Einstika implored. "I kept thinking about them so often since the mission began that I imagined seeing them from time to time."

"Me, too," Kidahin admitted.

"We should turn right and head for the runway, yes?" Einstika sang at imperative interrogative tempo.

"Yes, of course," Kidahin stammered in surprise.

"Neh'as'anni forces defend the debris ridge behind the airfield. You should drive down a runway and continue across the gravel to the perimeter road," Tialdrin added helpfully.

Kidahin snapped her ears at Tialdrin and then spread them wide. Tialdrin and Einstika were giving her less trouble than she expected. How did they so easily avoid the historical mistake they made the first time? Aplilin helped her return to the annex lift scene. Had she or maybe Mimiran sent them back to the same scene, too?

"Take the northeastern runway, Einstika. It is only three hundred ells from the perimeter road," Kidahin sang.

"Affirm."

Kidahin squirmed impatiently and ground her teeth. The shattered pavement demanded careful driving, but Einstika took care to extremes.

"You will not break an axle by hitting pieces of broken pavement," Kidahin snapped.

"A'pea the axle. Sharp jolts might cause the read-write heads to hit and scratch the magnetic coating on the hard disks. Scratches could make them unreadable."

"But what happens when we run out of road?" Tialdrin trilled.

"Ten commercial roads pass through the surrounding ridge. One of them leads northeast. It should be clear because the Neh'as'anni forces retreated to the west."

"Sounds too easy. We simply drive out?" Tialdrin sang in disbelief.

"That is the way they went," Einstika trilled.

"Are you sure about this road out of here?" Kidahin trilled.

"Very sure, thank the spirits. I cannot imagine driving this thing over the ridge and into the rainforest. Simple wheels need animal trails, paths, or relatively clear ground. They cannot clear dense undergrowth, and even trails inevitably cross fallen branches and thick ground vines. Driving over them without tri-wheel axles would be impossible. Even pushing through undergrowth alone would drain the battery long before we reached the APC."

"This is true," Kidahin sang.

"What about when we reach the road, Kidahin? The APC is not where we left it," Tialdrin complained.

"Shikararro should be driving northwest by now and will soon cross the north commercial road. Means we are out of radio range for now. We get the hard drives to her, and we take the APC to Hlorrithin," Kidahin sang dryly.

"Not quite," Einstika sang. "Shikararro and I will interface the hard drive to the APC on-board computer. I will wire the drives into APC power and make data cables for the computer interface. Shikararro will write a data transfer program that breaks the drive security protocols and copies the files into memory."

"Shikararro is a techmistress?" Kidahin trilled wryly.

"Yes, of course she is. You did not know? The A'tayotan told me during the mission briefing. We were supposed to find and disable the security protocols and shut down the radiation source we tracked to New Dawn. If we could not stop the radiation, we were told to capture computer files and download them to the A'tayotan."

The debris ridge dropped abruptly on Kidahin's left.

"There, the northbound road, turn!" she trilled.

"I see it. Hang on, Tialdrin. This will feel like you are going to tip over," Einstika warned.

"Then slow down. The hard drives and the ATV will roll on top of me, not you!"

"Listen!" Kidahin keened, her ears twitching. "Do you hear it?"

"Hear what?" Tialdrin growled.

The roar of a thousand challenging contact calls burst through the silence as Hlorrithin's forces dropped over the ridge behind the ATV.

"The final battle is upon us. We must hurry," Kidahin sang.

"Mistress, we are on the northbound commercial road. Where is Shikararro?" Einstika sang over her hazard suit radio.

"She cannot hear you. The repeater is in the APC, remember? If you could talk to her, then you could also reach Shikararro," Kidahin sang.

"We should be close enough," Einstika objected.

"Kidahin, can you hear me?" Shikararro's voice trilled over their suit speakers.

Einstika gave Kidahin the stiff-tail look and keyed her radio.

"We can. Where are you?" Einstika trilled.

"Following an animal trail more north than west and will cross the road in another hour or two. I will fall out of radio range again. Where are you, exactly?"

"About to turn onto the north commercial road. We found an all-terrain vehicle. We found a hard drive unit."

"Keep driving. When I reach the road I will drive south to you."

"Affirm," Kidahin trilled.

Victory pheromones filled her nose as the Gracious Mistress sang the final battle scenes into existence.

I cannot fail now!

15
REMEMBRANCE AND CONTINUANCE

A muffled blast and shock wave struck the ATV a glancing blow hard enough to lift its left tires off the pavement.

"Dou'tu'tay! Do something," Tialdrin keened from her makeshift seat atop the hard drive cabinet.

"Concussive strike," Einstika sang as the ATV dropped back onto all four tires.

"Fired by whom?" Tialdrin wondered, gripping the ropes tying her and the hard drive cabinet to the roof so tightly her knuckles turned pale orange.

"The Neh'as'anni, of course," Kidahin snarled.

"Maybe. The northwest-bound road goes through the ridge near the airfield. Hlorrithin may have ordered the ridge collapsed to block the road, or the Neh'as'anni did so to keep his forces from reaching the airfield," Einstika sang.

Kidahin snapped her ears no. "The Neh'as'anni retreated to the airfield ahead of Hlorrithin. They collapsed the ridge to delay his pursuit. I never did understand why he did not come down this road and flank them," she complained.

"He could not and you know why," Tialdrin sang heatedly.

"Yes, yes. I know—the reactor. Still, Shikararro could have sent her Pathwalkers down this road to the perimeter road and flank them."

"Shikararro has to meet us, remember? She should already be here," Einstika grumbled.

"Give her time," Kidahin sang. "A wheeled vehicle creeps down rainforest trails. We can move faster than she can right now."

"Not for long. The battery is running low. It was never meant to supply current for hours at full speed," Einstika trilled.

"How much longer?" Kidahin sang.

"Forty minutes and then we either walk or wait."

"Shikararro is somewhere on our right flank. Do you want to stop here and wait for her?" Kidahin sang.

"No. We close the distance so I can get a quicker start on wiring the hard drive into the APC computer," Einstika sang.

"I think the Neh'as'anni made those cryogenic tanks for some kind of spaceflight life support system but ended up using them to keep their males alive while they sought a cure for the jungle rot they all had," Tialdrin blurted.

"So? Do you think this excuses them? No, someone turned the capsules off, killing them. Remember the letter we found? What about the bodies in the residence abodes and in the command center?" Kidahin trilled.

"Kidahin, I have reached the road," Shikararro's voice crackled over the radio. "Where are you?"

"Heading north on the same road. Einstika thinks we are well south of you. How is your shoulder?"

"I rammed it against a tree four or ten times to pop it back into place. It is stiff and lacks a full range of motion. I am turning south onto this a'pea Neh'as'anni road. I do not see you yet, but I am picking you up on lidar. Expect me in about twenty minutes."

"Pull over, Einstika. We can untie the hard drive and get it ready before Shikararro gets here," Kidahin sang.

"And me, do not forget about me," Tialdrin complained.

Einstika pulled over, and by the time they finished freeing Tialdrin from the ropes Shikararro was pulling up beside them.

"Unwieldy looking thing," she sang, glaring at it.

"Very. The weight is off-center. Can you help us set it on the ground?" Kidahin sang.

"Of course," Shikararro sang and grabbed the cabinet with her good hand. Together they lifted it off the ATV and set it down on its locked casters.

"Pull it up to the driver side door," Shikararro sang.

"It will not fit in the cab," Kidahin sang.

"I need it as close to the computer as possible," Shikararro sang.

"Why?" Kidahin asked, curious.

"Cable lengths," Einstika sang.

"What about them? The auxiliary power cable is more than long enough," Kidahin snapped.

"A'pea the power cable. Ribbon data cables are never much longer than my tail because the port buffers supply little current," Einstika trilled as she examined the hard drive port connectors.

"How much time, do you think?" Shikararro trilled, twitching her ears.

"It depends," Einstika sang. "The APC interface port and the auxiliary power port are easy enough, but the hard drive connectors are not standard. I will bypass the drive port connectors and solder directly to the controller circuit board. Three hours, maybe, assuming I make no mistakes. Then everything gets *wei es ta tau*."

"'Tied up in high branches?' Why?" Shikararro trilled.

"I do not know the operating voltage," Einstika sang as she removed several screws, carefully slid the rear panel aside, and sighed in relief.

"These components give me some idea of voltage. The auxiliary power port can provide adequate AC voltage and current. I will have to guess the cycles-per-second, which can be dangerous," she warned.

"Why? It might explode?" Kidahin trilled and backed up a few ells.

"What? Of course not. Low voltage causes digital circuits to glitch. If they glitch the read-write heads could erase data from the disks."

"Can you prevent this?" Shikararro trilled at imperative interrogative pitch.

"I think so. I can disconnect the drive heads from the circuit board, get the voltage right, solder the wires back onto the circuit board, and turn the power back on."

"And hope to the spirits it works?" Kidahin demanded.

"Well, yes," Einstika admitted.

"Do it," Shikararro sang.

"Why are you not programming whatever needs programming?" Kidahin trilled at Shikararro, giving her an impatient glare.

"I can do nothing until Einstika finishes," Shikararro snapped.

"I am finishing right now," Einstika sang as she plugged a cord into the APC auxiliary power socket and flipped a switch.

"Yes!" she trilled in triumph.

"Yes, what?" Kidahin sang. "All I see is a red light."

"Red means the hard drive is powered up and ready. Low or high voltage would give a green warning light," Einstika sang.

"Plug in the data cable," Shikararro sang.

Einstika did so and handed the other end to Shikararro.

"Spirits, please do not let this dou'tu'tay thing glitch the computer," Shikararro trilled and plugged the cable into an auxiliary data storage port.

"Well?" Kidahin trilled.

"The computer recognizes the hard drive."

The read-write heads clattered loudly.

"What is it doing?" Kidahin trilled, jumping back three ells.

"Resetting the read-write heads. See? The disks are spinning up to speed," Einstika sang.

"Dou'tu'tay!" Shikararro cursed.

"So it is not working after all," Kidahin growled.

"It is working, but the computer cannot read the disk format," Shikararro sang.

"A security measure?" Kidahin wondered aloud.

"No. Format determines how data is written onto a disk."

"Can you do anything about it?" Kidahin pressed.

"I can run a program used to recover corrupted files," Shikararro sang grimly.

"But?" Kidahin trilled, noting Shikararro's warning tone.

"The program reads a disk track-by-track and sector-by-sector, reconstructs the files, reformats the disks, and writes the files back onto the disks."

"It destroys the files as it recovers them?" Kidahin keened warily.

"It does. I have no choice."

"How long will it take?"

"A few hours," Shikararro trilled.

"Hours? Put it in the equipment storage compartment. We can drive while the program recovers the files," Kidahin sang.

"No!" Shikararro and Einstika keened together.

Shikararro glared at Einstika but focused on Kidahin.

"One hard bounce while the program is reading or writing a disk could cause the heads to strike the disk surface and scratch it. A scratch will corrupt the file, maybe even make it unreadable."

"The A'tayotan Mistress will not like us sitting here twisting our tails waiting," Kidahin trilled.

"It cannot be helped. You and Tialdrin go prowl a perimeter sweep while Einstika and I stand here staring at this thing like a pair of sun-struck eo'ons."

"Affirm. Tialdrin, come with me," Kidahin trilled.

"You know we will not find anything," Tialdrin sang.

"I do, but they would have made a security prowl because it is always wise to do so," Kidahin sang.

"Why waste the time? We know the Neh'as'anni recalled to New Dawn right after the Battle of Withered Trees," Tialdrin sang.

"Would you rather watch Shikararro and Einstika?" Kidahin sang.

"No, techmistress details bore me," Tialdrin sang wryly.

"Techmistresses love screws, wires, and circuits. The only thing I care about is getting those files uploaded to the A'tayotan for analysis," Kidahin snorted.

"The A'tayotan will probably spend days prowling through them only to find the recipe for e'bato in a can."

Kidahin gave her a disgusted look and snapped her tail at a crimson flower.

Tialdrin watched the shattered flower's petals fall to the ground in an interesting pattern and sighed.

"It feels so—empty—here, no motion but ours, no sounds but ours, and no scents on the air but ours," she complained.

"The forest will look, smell, and sound alive the moment we rejoin Shikararro and Einstika," Kidahin sang reassuringly.

"I know how scenes work here," Tialdrin sang quietly.

"Indeed," Kidahin trilled as they stepped through the thick undergrowth and onto pavement. "We prowled farther south than I thought," she muttered.

Distant rumbling echoing out of the southwest sounded like an approaching thunderstorm. Tialdrin frowned at the noise and twisted her tail idly.

"I know no storms hit during this battle," she trilled.

"Those are explosions, not thunder. Demolition blasts, I think," Kidahin sang.

"Kidahin, where are you?" Shikararro's voice sang over the radio.

"On the road south of you."

"Return at once," Shikararro trilled.

"Affirm, acting," Kidahin sang.

Kidahin and Tialdrin appeared from behind the APC and found Einstika and Shikararro standing next to the hard drive, their tails snapping.

"It is not done yet?" Tialdrin hissed.

"It is more than half done," Einstika snapped.

"I lost a third of the files during recovery. They are gone forever, no hope of getting them back," Shikararro snarled.

"You erased the files?" Kidahin keened incredulously.

Shikararro lightly touched her adulthood knife and spun on Kidahin.

"This thing stores data in a nonstandard format. Files are stitched and woven together. The recovery program reads the data and restores the weaves from individual stitches to make new files. Sometimes the program makes wrong guesses," she trilled.

"Have you read any of the intact files?" Kidahin pressed.

"No. The computer copies the recovered files into a queue for uploading. File recovery is almost done, but uploading the files to the A'tayotan takes longer."

"We have to sit here and wait for them to upload?" Tialdrin trilled impatiently.

"No. We upload through the broadband radio channel to a radio repeater. The repeater sends the files on to Na'di Island and the A'tayotan hierarchy," Einstika sang.

"Why not send them over the direct channel we have with the Mistress?" Tialdrin wondered.

"We talk to the Mistress on an amplitude-modulation frequency that skips off the ionosphere. It is too noisy and lacks the bandwidth for high-speed digital transfers," Einstika sang.

"If you can send the files over the APC radio, why are we not leaving?" Kidahin trilled.

"We are sending files now," Shikararro sang.

"We cannot leave until the last recovered file is copied from the hard drive to the computer," Einstika trilled, growing tired of explaining technical details to non-technical people.

"Oh," Kidahin sang.

"Einstika, disconnect the hard drive and get in," Shikararro trilled at imperative tempo.

"Finally," Einstika trilled.

"Destroy the hard drive," Shikararro added.

"Easy enough to do," Einstika sang. She grabbed a wrench and smashed the clear plastic dome, shattering the stacked disks inside into shards.

"Good enough. Get in. We have other important work to do," Shikararro sang.

"Such as?" Einstika trilled as she slid into the driver seat and started the engine.

"Mistress A'londra wants me to hold my archers in reserve along the ridge facing the airfield."

"What for? Nothing can fly off those damaged runways. They should be using the tarmac as a forward staging area," Kidahin sang.

"I am sure this is happening right now," Shikararro sang.

"Then why hold your archers back?" Einstika trilled.

"You found something useful in the files?" Tialdrin wondered.

"I did not, but the A'tayotan is expecting to."

"We are hours away," Einstika trilled as the APC bounced through jungle undergrowth.

"Find more animal trails," Tialdrin sang.

"Zir'con trails are wide but nei'la and eo'on trails not so much. Animal trails run more or less north and south. Driving west means rolling through thick entangling jungle. I am heading northwest into the arberi tree forest. Once there I can drive faster," Einstika sang.

"But driving north is going out of our way," Kidahin objected.

"But quicker over the long prowl. Good thinking, Einstika,"

Shikararro sang.

"Driving around these trees feels like flying after creeping through the jungle," Kidahin sang as the surrounding scenery shifted to an arberi forest.

Shikararro flicked her ears in agreement and glanced at a blinking message on the computer.

"File upload almost done. Thank the spirits," she trilled softly.

Kidahin frowned at a line of trees up ahead.

"Turn left. We should be going southwest by now. Picking our way through dense forest will slow us down," she sang.

"I think those trees follow a river bank," Einstika sang.

"It cannot be the T'anni River. The surrounding mountains feed several tributaries. This is likely one of them. Are you thinking about driving downstream to the northwest-bound road? Can we do so without getting stuck?" Shikararro trilled at interrogative pitch.

Einstika flicked her ears in agreement and snapped her tail enthusiastically.

"The APC floats and the two base tires on each hub can handle a creek bed. If the base tires drop into pits or hit snags the hubs will lock and the tri-wheels will roll over them," she sang and slowed to a stop, blocked by the thickly overgrown line of trees.

"I need to take a look. Get out and stretch your tails," she added.

"Good idea. Kidahin, take Tialdrin and prowl a perimeter sweep while I kick the tires and check for damage," Shikararro sang.

Kidahin flicked her ears in agreement and looped her tail around Tialdrin's waist.

"Follow the creek upstream a few hundred ells and swing back around through the jungle. I will go downstream, do the same, and meet you back here," Kidahin sang.

"Sounds good to me."

Einstika pushed through the scarlet vines and the vermilion grasses towering above her. Water lapped gently, close enough for her to smell its crisp dampness. She stepped out onto the south bank of a rather large creek. Clear shallow water flowed slowly downstream an ell below her feet. The muddy bottom gleamed in the sun.

"It looks about ten ells wide and maybe an ell or two deep at most. I am sure there are deeper and shallower spots," she sang loudly and began prowling downstream. "I do not see a gap wide enough to drive through," she added.

"Tialdrin will find a suitable spot," Shikararro trilled reassuringly.

"Of course she will," Einstika sang at mocking tempo, swayed side-to-side, doubled over, and violently emptied her stomach into the placidly flowing water.

"What was that?" Shikararro sang.

"Nothing—it is nothing. Wait, I see movement on the opposite bank, stealthy movement. Much too stealthy for zir'con or nei'la and too deliberate for eo'on," Einstika sang softly.

"Neh'as'anni skirmishers?" Shikararro sang quietly.

"I think so," Einstika whispered and withdrew into the tall grasses. "Yes, I see a Warrior triad moving downstream. They are stalking the creek. Any closer to it now and they will start wading."

Shikararro quietly brushed up against her.

"I can pick them off, real easy," Einstika sang under her breath, drawing her bow.

"Why bother? What can they do? Stab the APC?" Shikararro sang.

"They can follow us. What if they climb on the roof and smash the antenna?"

"Good point," Shikararro muttered, nocked an arrow, and drew her bow. "You shoot the left. I shoot the right. We both shoot the middle," she murmured.

Shikararro fired first, Einstika a half-breath later. Both Warriors dropped instantly. Shikararro fumbled an arrow as Einstika snapshot the third Warrior. She missed, and the Warrior tumbled into grassy cover with a nearly Hunter-like agility.

"Dou'tu tay shoulder!" Shikararro trilled.

"Beautifully executed tumbling evasion," Einstika sang, impressed.

Shikararro listened a moment and snapped her ears.

"She did not sing a contact call. She is alone and knows it," she trilled, paused, looked up at the sky, and keened a contact call.

"We are not going after her? Four Hunters pursuing one Warrior? It will be quick and easy," Einstika trilled.

"She is not worth the time lost running her down," Shikararro sang as Tialdrin and Kidahin arrived in response to her call.

"Warrior triad. We dropped two," Shikararro sang in answer to their questioning scent.

Kidahin glared at the opposite bank.

"I found a trail wide enough," Tialdrin sang.

"Good. Lead Einstika to it."

"Affirm," Tialdrin sang, spun on her bare heels, and prowled slowly back the way she came.

Einstika started the engine and waited for Shikararro and Kidahin to get in. She turned right and followed Tialdrin down a narrow eo'on trail through tall fiery fluorescent crimson ferns.

Einstika cringed at the thought of her tires grinding the magnificent plants into the ground as Tialdrin stepped aside to point her tail at a narrow path between the trees.

When Tialdrin saw Einstika nod, she ran to the passenger door and slid into the seat.

"The bank drops an ell into water another ell deep," she warned.

Einstika snapped her ears impatiently and drove through the ferns, over the bank, plunged into the water, turned with the downstream current, and ground her teeth as her stomach growled loudly.

"Is that your stomach growling, or are you grinding gears again?" Kidahin sang.

"My stomach hurts. The field rations no longer agree with me," Einstika snapped.

"Me, either. Thinking about food makes me nauseous," Kidahin sang.

"Driving downstream is even better than dodging around arberi trees," Kidahin trilled.

"Much faster," Einstika agreed as her stomach somersaulted with every little bounce. "Neh'as'anni love roads. I do not understand why they did not build one going east and west."

"They did, the La'huaset intra-continental road. Oh, and the file upload is finished, if anyone cares," Shikararro sang.

"About time. The intra-continental road is well south of us, below the industrial complex. We are north of it and about twenty to thirty minutes from the bridge," Einstika trilled.

Kidahin stared out the window at yellow water reeds. Crimson ferns and arberi boughs lined the creek on both sides.

The windshield wipers swept away random splashes churned up by the tires. Muddy clouds billowed downstream ahead of them. Kidahin stared blankly at the cloudy water and did not see the gleaming white concrete bridge until it dominated her view, burning a dazzling afterimage into her eyes. She blinked several times to clear her vision and scowled, not impressed.

Concrete pillars held a simple concrete slab twenty ells long about an ell above the water. Low concrete barriers ran down both sides. What for? To keep people from falling off the sides? No one was that inattentive, not even the Neh'as'anni.

"A'pea thing looks like bleached bones," Einstika trilled.

"Why build this thing? Why not build the road up to the shallows and set paving stones on the bottom? The water can flow over them. Who cares if the tires get wet?" Shikararro trilled angrily.

Einstika let off the accelerator and shifted into neutral.

"Why did you do that?" Tialdrin sang, curious.

"I am looking for an easy way out of here."

"Turn left and drive," Kidahin suggested at insolence tempo.

"Spirits, you are brilliant. Why did I not think of that?" Einstika trilled hotly.

"Worried about the incline?" Shikararro asked.

"I am," Einstika growled. She turned to glare at Kidahin.

"You remember what happened when we reached the intra-continental road overpass? I do not want to roll the APC upside-down into the water," she trilled.

"Turn parallel to the bridge and drive up the bank," Tialdrin suggested.

"It does seem that obvious, yes?" Einstika sang, staring at the bridge.

"But?" Kidahin prodded.

"Notice the slow current under the bridge? How it wells up and rotates? The water is deep there. We will sit at an angle."

"The current can push us over?" Shikararro trilled.

"No, but it can shove us up against the bridge. Grinding against it as we drive out will slow us down. The drag will pull us into the bridgehead."

"Once the front tires are on the bank you can steer away from it," Tialdrin trilled.

Einstika snapped her tail in frustration and glared at Tialdrin.

"The creek bed was probably dredged to sink the pillars on stable ground. The bridgehead and retaining wall extend underground and act as an arch to support and anchor the bridge in place. The tires might dig into the ground and strike the retaining wall. Think of driving up against a tree. The tires spin and we go nowhere."

"Drive up at an angle first and then cut back parallel to the road," Kidahin suggested.

"That might work," Einstika trilled.

"Why not turn around and drive upstream to a better spot?" Tialdrin sang.

"No," Shikararro trilled. "No backtrailing upstream. It will take too long to push through the forest to regain the road."

"But it might be faster in the end," Kidahin sang.

Shikararro scowled but nodded.

"You are right," she spat. The idea of backtrailing felt like a retreat to her.

"Fine," Einstika sang. "Let me get turned around."

"Team-one, report your status," the Mistress's voice said from the cabin speakers.

"Now she speaks?" Einstika trilled in disgust.

"It has been some time since we last heard from her," Shikararro agreed. "Mistress, we drove down a creek to a bridge on the northwest commercial road. The bridgehead has potential hidden obstacles. We are heading back upstream a few hundred ells to find a better way up the bank," she sang.

"No. Get out of the creek now and drive to our staging area with all due speed. You will rejoin your Pathwalker archers. Kidahin now has the leadership of Environmental Interdiction Team-one. I will have access codes downloaded to your computer soon. They should allow Kidahin to unlock reactor controls, building central power, research labs, and the cryogenic storage and revival systems."

"Affirm, Mistress," Shikararro sang.

"Mistress? It will take Team-one some time to prowl back through those tunnels," Kidahin warned.

"You will enter the building. Mistress of Battle A'londra will give you a list of items to access and shut down using the protocols recovered from the hard drive files."

"Affirm, Mistress," Kidahin trilled.

"Why us?" Einstika trilled as she pulled the APC parallel to the bridge.

"You have experience with Neh'as'anni electronics. You have specialized hazard equipment. And you are acclimated to the building," the Mistress said.

"Acclimated?" Einstika sang.

"Radiation exposure. Remember the shots I gave you?" Tialdrin sang softly.

"Of course. Do they last this long?" Einstika trilled.

"Long enough," Tialdrin sang. "Spirits, we have not been here for weeks."

"No, but several days at least. I thought antirads lasted no more than a day or two per shot," Kidahin sang.

"A few days, true enough. They make you violently sick after a week or two. We will get another shot when we arrive," Tialdrin sang evasively.

"But?" Kidahin trilled, smelling something vague in Tialdrin's scent—worry? Guilt?

"That explains my stomach pains," Einstika interrupted. "I am ready, Shikararro," she added.

"Get us out of here," Shikararro growled.

Einstika drove forward until the front tires reached the steep bank.

"Here we go!" she trilled.

Tires dug into the clay, and the APC bounced up the bank and slid sideways until it hit the concrete retaining wall. The tires dug down into hard compact soil and lost traction. The hubs locked and the axle bounced up as the tri-wheels engaged.

The APC shimmied violently against the retaining wall and then surged halfway up the bank.

"Almost out," Einstika sang as the tri-wheels bit irregularly, slamming the APC hard against the bridgehead.

The right middle tri-wheel bit down into something hard and

unyielding. The axle tried to jolt down, up, and forward at the same time—and snapped.

The bouncing abruptly stopped.

"Dou'tu'tay! A'pea!" Einstika keened.

"You broke an axle," Shikararro accused.

"I do not need to hear the a'pea obvious," Einstika hissed in outrage, opened the door, jumped out, and slipped on clay to the gap between the tri-wheel and the bridgehead.

"Dou'tu'tay!" she keened.

"She sounds like Anailiatha," Tialdrin breathed in Kidahin's ear.

Kidahin stifled a chuckle.

"What happened?" Shikararro keened.

"We hit a spur sticking out of the retaining wall below ground."

"The tri-wheel should have pulled the axle over it like any other log, boulder, or pit," Shikararro objected.

"The spur jammed against the hub," Einstika trilled, crouching to get a better look.

"So?" Shikararro sang.

"Each tire sits at a point on an equilateral triangle with the hub in the center serving as a gearbox. When the bottom two tires lose traction the hub locks to bring the third tire down to lever it over large objects or tire-sized pits.

"I know how they work," Shikararro keened. "Why did this one not work?"

"The a'pea spur hit between the leading base tire and the apex tire. It drove the lead tire down below the spur. The hub locked the gimbal to let the three tires roll as one wheel. It tried to lever the axle over the spur. The torque snapped the axle. Normally the APC can run with one broken axle, but the spur is wedged firmly between the lead and apex tires. We cannot push the APC free. Backing up will not work, and I do not have enough clearance to get in and remove the wheel and hub."

"We have to walk?" Tialdrin trilled.

"No, we prowl at pursuit pace. Do not give me the stiff tail, either. It is nothing to pursuit prowl for a few hours," Shikararro sang.

Tialdrin jumped from the cab down onto muddy orange grasses, followed by Kidahin.

Shikararro keyed the radio. "Mistress? We broke an axle and are proceeding on foot from the bridge."

"Disable the computer and destroy all stored data. We are not like the Neh'as'anni with their many roads and vehicles. We have no spare transport to send for you. I will tell A'londra to dispatch a hand of your archers and have them escort you to her."

"No. Hlorrithin needs them more than I do."

"Hlorrithin will insist. Your three teammates are vitally important to what A'londra is planning," the Mistress said.

"What do you expect me to do with a hand of archers? Have them carry us?" Shikararro growled.

She snapped the microphone off, opened the door, stepped onto the running board, and reached under the dashboard. She flipped a green switch. Immediately the smell of burning circuits filled her nose. She climbed up to the roof and jumped onto the bridge. She looked down the road and snapped her tail at imaginary salt flies as an uneasy shudder crawled through her.

Prowling in straight lines defied all instinct, but right now it sounded better than stalking through jungle terrain. If only they could climb into the canopy and jump from tree to tree. Hunters tree-hopped through dense canopy faster than they could prowl through jungle. Unfortunately they would soon leave the arberis behind, and the amber-brown everleaf trees replacing them fell short of one another farther than even a Hunter could jump.

"Kidahin and Tialdrin, prowl along the left shoulder. Einstika, you and I will prowl along the right shoulder. Let us go!"

Einstika glanced across the road at Kidahin, behind at Tialdrin, and then forward, alert. Hlorrithin's Warpact held the surrounding territory, but territory held did not mean territory safe.

Pursuit pace fell between a jog and a slow run. It let a prowler or stalker keep up with a fleeing target without overtaking it. Anyone in good health could pursuit prowl for an EST day, but Hunters often pursuit prowled for almost two EST days. Males and Warriors snagged their toes in grass after a day, but the Comara females—indefatigable—easily prowled at this pace for an EST week.

Shikararro wanted no stragglers. A Neh'as'anni Huntress in a tree might loose an arrow, and isolated targets were safer and easier to pick off.

"How long, do you think?" she asked Kidahin.

Kidahin flicked her ears as she settled into an endurance rhythm. Her bare heels smacking on hard pavement almost immediately triggered a rippling spasm of stomach cramps.

"About eleven hours," she sang as they subsided.

"Eleven?" Tialdrin trilled.

"We drove northwest into the arberi tree forest. The creek took us more west than south," Einstika sang from far behind Shikararro.

Tialdrin glanced over her shoulder at the distant Einstika.

"Are you well?" she trilled.

"I am now. I vomited my ration. This jogging is not sitting well with me," Einstika sang as she closed the distance.

Distracted, Tialdrin did not hear the subtle rush of grass slipping between toes closing on her left. The knife sliced so swiftly she felt nothing until her intestines spilled onto the road.

"Tialdrin!" Einstika keened and charged the Neh'as'anni Warrior.

Shikararro and Kidahin spun in one swift twist, nocked arrows and drew bowstrings, and fired snapshots.

Tialdrin struggled to hold onto her guts and dropped to her knees.

The Warrior dodged Shikararro's arrow. Einstika's pierced her hand, knocking a gleaming steel combat knife from her grip.

She drew her flint adulthood knife and lunged for Einstika, slashing with the strength only a Warrior female could summon.

Einstika blocked the blow with her bow. The knife struck the bow quiver and cut the bowstring, knocking the useless bow from her grasp and spinning her around. She drew her adulthood knife and sliced a diagonal deep into the Warrior's back from shoulder to hip.

The Warrior cursed and tumbled gracefully into the roadside jungle cover.

"Tell me what to do," Shikararro keened as she knelt beside Tialdrin.

"Nothing," Tialdrin gasped, still on her knees clutching her guts to her abdomen.

"Even I know this is simple surgery. You are an associate healer. Tell me what to do," Shikararro snarled.

"Find the antishock, antiviral, antibiotic, and antipain ampoules in my healer harness. Find an IV bag and cut it open. Irrigate the wound. Wrap it with loose gauze and keep the intestines wet," Tialdrin gasped, panting rapidly.

"We can do this. Kidahin, pack gauze around the wound. Splash an IV bag on the guts. Einstika, put an IV in her arm if you can," Shikararro trilled.

"I know how!" Einstika snarled.

Shikararro jabbed a syringe into Tialdrin's chest.

"Antipain is in."

"The IV, antiviral, antibiotic, and antishock are in," Einstika sang.

"That was the Warrior we both missed," Einstika trilled savagely.

"You think so?" Shikararro sang softly as she wrapped Tialdrin's abdomen in layers of loose gauze.

"I remember her skin color patterns," Einstika sang and leapt to the roadside to vomit her stomach empty.

"Seeing serious wounds is unsettling," Shikararro sang sympathetically.

"Seeing blood does not bother me. My stomach is twisting like it has its own tail."

"Want to trade? My bowels gurgle and I soiled myself three times as we ran," Kidahin complained.

"The antirad shots?" Shikararro trilled.

"It is too early for the side-effects to hit. We did not eat or drink anything while in the exclusion zone but the supplies we took in with us," Kidahin sang.

"What about the air? Remember how it smelled?" Einstika sang in disgust.

"Radiation?" Shikararro trilled.

Kidahin snapped her ears no. "Not if the antirads work and we received the right doses."

"We should hunt down and kill that Warrior," Einstika trilled.

"No. She is an assault prowler, a melee fighter. Warriors do not use shortbows, and she has no longbow. If she had one, she would have shot from a distant tree and not charged us with a knife," Shikararro sang.

"What do we do now? Carry Tialdrin and keep our noses to the wind?" Einstika growled.

"We stay here," Shikararro sang.

"That makes sense. The Warrior can attack us if we move," Kidahin sang.

"We wait with arrows nocked until my archers arrive," Shikararro sang grimly.

"However long that takes," Einstika grumbled.

16
LOVING ONE'S SPIRIT

The Pathwalker archers finally arrived. Four of them lifted Tialdrin onto their shoulders and jogged back the way they came, while their assaultmistress reported to Shikararro.

"We must hurry. Mistress A'londra wants you to give Hlorrithin cover fire when he begins his advance," she sang.

"Why the hurry? New Dawn must be secured before she will let him anywhere near it."

"A'londra says she needs these two," the assaultmistress sang and pointed her tail first at Kidahin and then at Einstika.

"Why? A'londra is Hlorrithin's Protectress and Mistress of Battle. She never leaves him for long," Shikararro sang.

"No, she does not," the assaultmistress trilled.

"But?" Shikararro stammered, not believing her nose.

"Yes!" the assaultmistress confirmed and turned envious eyes on Einstika and Kidahin.

"You get to fight alongside Hlorrithin himself!" she gushed.

"I doubt it. He is too busy," Kidahin sang, dismissing the idea outright.

"Busy, yes. More likely A'londra will meet you, tell you what she wants, send you on your way, and rejoin him," Shikararro sang.

"What about Tialdrin?" Einstika trilled in wild hope.

"I doubt she will be out of surgery by the time you meet A'londra," Shikararro sang.

"Rejoin your hand and keep your nose in the air for an ambush," she told the archer assaultmistress, turned, and ran after the joggers.

"Affirm," the assaultmistress sang and followed her.

Kidahin and Einstika both expected the sudden sprint and followed them. At assault closure pace they quickly passed Tialdrin and her four bearers.

It did not take long for running on hard pavement to jostle Kidahin's stomach into a frenzy. Her bowels gurgled a frantic warning. Without breaking her stride she untied the underthong from its waistwear straps and violently eliminated.

"We are here," Shikararro sang.

"Obviously," Kidahin growled dryly, more thankful for a settled stomach than the abrupt change in scenery.

Hands of Pathwalker archers gathered around Shikararro and caressed her with their tails in welcome.

"The sire cairn wants you with him right away," one of the archers sang.

"Now?" Shikararro trilled resentfully.

"Yes, Mistress. He left Hlorrithin about an hour ago and wants to discuss a battle plan with you."

"Fine," Shikararro trilled to a sigh. Males could be so—infuriating.

She stepped between Kidahin and Einstika and wrapped her tail around them in a touchingly intimate embrace and then silently rejoined her archers.

Clashing swords and twanging longbows muted by distance brushed Einstika's ears. "The Neh'as'anni fight in the traditional manner after all?" she trilled, perplexed.

"Using modern weapons in personal combat is dishonorable," Kidahin reminded her.

"The Neh'as'anni destroyed vast swaths of their forests, contaminated their home territory, experimented on helpless males, and sent neh'tle ke'ne's'tu onto tens of thousands of males, infants, and Comara. Hlorrithin declared them ni'zakhon. They must be removed from the world. They ignore honor and cast centuries of tradition aside," Einstika spat.

"The Neh'as'anni remain Eyloni—The People. They cannot be less than The People anymore than we can. The first songs tell us to give a defeated clan's surviving males and infants sanctuary after its females have been killed. The first songs predate the Be'atika Senge's decree outlawing war among the clans and between the tribes by several thousand years. No female facing death would ever risk the survival of her clan males and infants."

"Kidahin and Einstika? I am A'londra," a melodious voice interrupted.

Both Hunters froze mid-step and stared at the Warrior blocking their path.

Her beauty seized Kidahin by the tail. Tall as a Hunter and twice as muscular, A'londra reminded Kidahin of Aplilin. Aplilin looked more like a tall, lean Warrior than the Hunter female she was. Aplilin would closely resemble A'londra had she been born a Warrior female.

"Well?" A'londra trilled impatiently.

"Yes, Mistress?" Kidahin sang, impulsively glancing out of social habit at the status symbols the Warrior wore.

The rank earring and its many multicolored webs, knots, and beads hanging from A'londra's left lower earfold declared the highest military rank Kidahin had ever seen. Her neckwear necklace and its several knotted strings of multicolored beads draping loosely down her huge bare breasts proclaimed her high social status. The braided waistwear underthong ties cutting into her muscular hips identified her as a Mistress of Battle, a Protectress, an O'un Tu Clan elder, and a La'huaset Tribal Elder. The color patterns on her short loincloth revealed only to female eyes her high standing in the hierarchies.

"Stop staring and come with me," A'londra snapped.

"Yes, Mistress," Kidahin and Einstika trilled and followed the Warrior.

A'londra stopped when they reached the perimeter road. She glared at the runway, the tarmac far behind it, and the fighting going on between them.

"You have captured the hangers?" Kidahin trilled, watching the female ranks fighting along a line halfway between where she stood and New Dawn.

"Not all of them."

"Oh," Einstika sang. "Why are we here? Shikararro sang something about going back into New Dawn."

"I hate this name. New Dawn, indeed. New disaster, you mean," A'londra snapped. "Nevermind. We will punch through the Neh'as'anni soon and enter the Technology Center building."

A'londra glared at Kidahin until she had the Hunter's full attention.

"You entered this building once before?"

"Yes, Mistress, from a door on the far side. Why hurry? The Neh'as'anni prowl down the rotten branch of a battle of attrition."

"No clan has fought another in centuries, but the art of war doctrine still remains a part of our tradition to this day," A'londra stated flatly.

"'Never fight a war of attrition'," Einstika quoted melodiously.

"Correct," A'londra sang in approval and focused back on Kidahin.

"The radiation signal you traced here is getting stronger. We must stop it before it sterilizes the entire valley."

"The Neh'as'anni probably occupy the New Da—ah—the

Technology Center," Einstika sang, stumbling at A'londra's sudden hateful glare. "Why have they not shut it down themselves?"

"I do not know. I do not understand the Neh'as'anni or the motives driving them," A'londra confessed.

"I do," Kidahin trilled.

A'londra gaped at Kidahin in shock, at a loss for words.

"Not their motives," Kidahin corrected hastily. "I think they cannot shut the reactor down. Someone killed everyone in the—Technology Center—using buhnnie. I think nobody knows the security codes, and we took the hard drive containing backup copies. Maybe they want to retake the building and shut the reactor down themselves," Kidahin trilled.

"We have the codes, and I am not going to radio them to the Neh'as'anni and hope they do the honorable thing. Those codes may also unlock unlawful weapon technology like the amber alloy the A'tayotan says you found," A'londra trilled.

"Which is not a weapon in and of itself," Einstika growled.

"Anything having weapon qualities is a weapon waiting in ambush. We cannot worry about it now. Get whatever you need to reenter the building and be ready to go in forty minutes," A'londra sang, spun on her bare heels, and glided away from them with the rhythmic grace few Warriors could match.

"Forty minutes? What can we do in forty minutes?" Einstika keened.

"You can come with me," an imposing Huntress sang from behind them.

They spun around on the speaker.

"Mistress Healer?" Kidahin sang.

"Follow me," the Healer trilled at imperative tempo.

"We have little time, Mistress," Einstika trilled hesitantly.

"A'pea your little time," the Healer snarled. "You entered a fission reactor control room. You exposed yourselves to radiation, and to only the spirits know what else. I must examine you."

Kidahin ground her teeth. Unlike males, females could refuse healer care. "There is no time, Mistress. Thank you for your interest in our health," she sang.

"I am Hlorrithin's Mistress of Healers. Exposing him to you two may risk his health. I will not clear you for combat until I examine you. Decide upon your honor and not your right of refusal."

"Hlorrithin will not prowl anywhere near us," Einstika objected.

"Perhaps not, but Mistress A'londra will. Wherever she goes, he is not far behind. You will likely come within knife-throwing range of him, even if only momentarily. I will not risk his life. Follow. Me. Now," the Healer demanded.

She led them to an articulated vehicle. Doors had been cut into its side, one near the rear tires and another near the front end. A'londra flicked her tail at the door by the tires and stepped through it and on into the soft-yellow hollow log interior.

Medicinal odors gave the trailer's purpose away immediately.

"This is a mobile health center," Kidahin trilled in surprise.

"Yes, my own design," the Healer sang proudly as she led them down a narrow center aisle, brushing curtained abodes as she passed. She stopped, pulled a curtain aside, and snapped her tail at the examination table inside.

"Sit on the table. Einstika, you first. How do you feel?"

"Well enough, I guess. A bit tired from running. Yet I do not feel quite myself, either. Eating upsets my stomach, makes me nauseous. I threw up a few times."

The Healer trilled sympathetically as she held out a diagnostic scanner and walked a slow circle around Einstika.

"You have elevated radiation exposure," the Healer sang. "Except for the nausea, how is your appetite?"

"I am not hungry."

"When did you eat last?" the Healer pressed.

"Several hours ago, but I am not hungry," Einstika repeated defensively. The Healer shoved a small jar into Einstika's hand.

"Go to the necessary and fill this."

"I do not have to use the necessary," Einstika objected.

"Fine. I have an enema bottle right here."

"That will not be needed," Einstika trilled hastily, bolted through the curtain, and flew down the aisle to the necessary.

"And you?" the Healer asked Kidahin.

"I am not hungry, either. My stomach feels fine, but my bowels are loose."

"I see," the Healer trilled sourly and aimed the scanner at Kidahin.

"You also have elevated radiation exposure. How close did you come to the reactor?"

"We entered the control room but not the reactor room itself."

"Oh? Tialdrin gave you iodine, K-factors, and antiradiation shots at regular intervals, yes?"

"She handed out iodine and K-factor pills with our rations. She gave us shots before we entered the exclusion zone. She gave a few more while we were in the New Dawn building," Einstika sang as she returned with her sample.

"Obscene, the Neh'as'anni giving so deadly a place such a beautiful name," the Healer growled. She shoved a sample jar in Kidahin's face and sent her to the necessary.

Einstika surrendered her jar and watched the Healer add things to it and place it in an analyzer.

Kidahin returned and surrendered her jar.

The Healer prepared the sample and put it on top of the analyzer and waited for the machine to finish its analyzing. It chimed, and she read the number flashing on the screen. She withdrew Einstika's sample and replaced it with Kidahin's.

"You have mild radiation sickness," the Healer told Einstika.

"Give Einstika a K-factor IV," she told an associate healer.

The analyzer chimed again, and the Healer read a far bigger number.

"You have moderate radiation sickness," she told Kidahin and ordered the associate healer to prepare an IV.

The associate healer put the IV in Kidahin's arm, but the Healer opened the drip rate to its maximum and squeezed the IV bag as she glared at Kidahin.

"This direct exposure to neh'tle ke'ne's'tu will cause you much pain over the long run. You should never go anywhere near that place again. Stay here and accept further treatment. Techmistress Einstika can do A'londra's bidding."

"Einstika and Tialdrin, yes?" Kidahin trilled hopefully.

The Healer closed her eyes, pain tainting her scent.

"Radiation sickness stopped her blood from clotting properly. She bled out during surgery. I am sorry," the Healer sang and wrapped her tail around Kidahin in shared sympathy.

"I can do this by myself," Einstika trilled, feeling lost without Tialdrin.

"I will never let you go alone," Kidahin sang gently. "We know what to expect, and you cannot be in two places at once."

Kidahin canted her ears respectfully at the Healer.

"I am advised of my condition. I respectfully decline your proposed treatment," she sang formally.

The Healer snapped her tail violently, sweeping the countertop and knocking everything on it across the floor.

"Clean this up!" she trilled at another associate healer.

"You are worse than a male patient!" she keened furiously at Kidahin.

"Thank you for the compliment," Kidahin sang, remembering how often Delwyn resisted Mistress of Healers Allohindra's ministrations. Everyone knew males made horrible patients.

The Healer was still growling about the arrogance of all patients when A'londra poked her head through the curtain.

"Kidahin, Einstika, we must go," she trilled.

"Wait a few more minutes, Mistress A'londra. I am giving them healer treatment," the Healer interrupted.

"Treatment? For what? They cannot fight?"

"They say they can, but I have advised them against it," the Healer spat.

"Can you do this?" A'londra trilled at imperative interrogative pitch.

"We can!" Kidahin and Einstika sang.

"See? They say they can," A'londra trilled.

She grabbed Einstika by the shoulder and pitched her through the open doorway. She jumped beside Kidahin, yanked the IV from her arm, and shoved her out as well.

"Follow me. We go to the Mistress of Arms next."

A'londra led Kidahin and Einstika back to the perimeter road and the assault teams staging there.

Kidahin squinted at the battlefield. Hlorrithin had pushed the Neh'as'anni back until they were within a few thousand ells of New Dawn. But in so doing, he spread his forces wide to prevent the Neh'as'anni from flanking them. Pathwalker archers fired on the Neh'as'anni from shattered buildings and street rubble.

"Delwyn calls this 'urban warfare'," Kidahin whispered tonelessly in Einstika's ear.

"I call it cowardly warfare," Einstika trilled under her breath. "They must know they cannot win," she trilled aloud.

"Battles of attrition are wasteful and pointless," A'londra sang.

"I never saw so many infantry in one place," Einstika trilled.

"Yes, this is an entire mobilized body of ten-thousand females. They drive a wedge into the Neh'as'anni. Shikararro's Pathwalker archers give them cover fire. Once they clear a path to the Technology Center building you two will open the rear door. We will hold the building perimeter while you and four assault prowler hands occupy critical areas."

"And then do what?" Kidahin sang.

"Once the perimeter is secured I will fold my tails around Hlorrithin and escort him through the critical areas. Understood?"

"Yes, Mistress," Kidahin sang, wondering if the lock was still shot apart.

"Do we prowl with the assault teams?" Einstika trilled.

"No. They will secure the ground floor. You will describe the critical areas below the building to the Assaultmistress leading them. The other assaultmistresses will send out watch triads and solitary prowlers. Once they are in place you two will split up. Einstika and the techmistresses will take the reactor control room. You and the healers will take the cryogenic vault and save as many males as possible."

"Affirm," Kidahin sang.

A'londra gave them identical green file folders.

"These folders contain lists of codes and matching control numbers recovered from the files Shikararro sent to the A'tayotan. Sensitive information is often terse, and these files are no different. Even worse, data loss randomly deleted portions of the files," she sang.

Einstika grimaced as she riffled through the pages in her folder.

"A lot of text is missing in the reactor protocol section," she complained, snapping her tail angrily at imaginary salt flies.

"The A'tayotan believes the Neh'as'anni deliberately deleted some of the text. You mentioned a techmistress who was shot dead in the reactor control room. Maybe they shot her for tampering with the files," A'londra trilled.

"These codes came from the hard drive we took from the command center mainframe. The techmistress was killed in the control room. I doubt the control room computer has access privileges to the mainframe. Whoever shot her probably tampered with the control room in some way," Kidahin growled and glanced through the papers in her own folder.

"The cryogenic revival procedure looks complete, but I am no healer," she added.

"You will take the healers to the cryogenics areas, step aside, and touch nothing unless they tell you to," A'londra warned.

"They are all dead," Kidahin trilled sadly. "Whoever killed them most likely killed everyone in the command center and the residence abodes as well. Only the spirits know why."

"I think someone objected to the continuing development of their spaceflight technology. The section on spaceflight is quite detailed. What I am reading is amazing science, almost fictional," Einstika sang.

"A'pea space flight!" A'londra snapped and spat-grimaced. "Take them and go," she told the ranking Assaultmistress.

"Come with me," the Assaultmistress sang. "The final battle begins now."

"*Vi eta ka nabi*," Kidahin trilled and smiled, remembering fondly that 'time to part the branches' was Aplilin's favorite contact call.

The Assaultmistress shoved wandering thoughts about sight-seeing off the branch as she prowled around two jets and under a suspended engine. Prowling inside of any unnatural structure and especially this building made the crimson hairs on her pons tingle.

"Where to first?" she trilled testily.

"The door beside the lift shaft," Kidahin sang, pointing her tail at the shaft door.

"Does this lead to the reactor level?"

"No. I do not think we can get there from here," Kidahin keened.

"That is a Delwyn saying," Einstika trilled a chuckle.

"How did you get to the control room?" the Assaultmistress demanded, in no mood for humor.

"Underground tunnels," Einstika trilled distastefully.

"One tunnel is a few hundred ells in front of the building. It meets a second one running perpendicular to the building and exits about a thousand ells off to the building's right flank," Kidahin clarified.

"Which means both entrances are currently in Neh'as'anni-held territory. The reactor powers the industrial complex. The Neh'as'anni would not go outside the building to a tunnel for routine access. This building is the focal point for all the industrial research done here. There must be a direct path to the reactor from here. Describe in brief detail the paths you stalked from the time you entered the tunnels until when you left this building," the Assaultmistress sang.

"We entered the concrete tunnel. Dust made the hinges grind as we opened the portal door," Kidahin began.

"The dust came from nearby collapsed building rubble," Einstika added.

"Indeed?" the Assaultmistress sang. "Continue, but skip over the minor details. I do not care about things like dusty hinges."

"Affirm. The tunnel dead-ended ten minutes into our prowling. A hatch in the floor there opens down into a stainless steel one-person airlock."

"Under this building?" the Assaultmistress trilled.

"Absolutely," Einstika sang.

"The bottom hatch opens into a deep narrow stairwell that leads to a door in the side of the perpendicular tunnel. Parallel iron rails bolted into the floor run its length. We turned left and prowled up to a handcar sitting on the rails at another dead-end. A ramp on the right leads onto a platform with a large door. A sign posted there warns people to wear protection," Kidahin sang.

"The rad-counter picked up radiation well into the blue range," Einstika trilled.

"This is the medium hazard range, yes?" the Assaultmistress sang.

"It is," Kidahin agreed. "The door opens into an antechamber. The first two doors, one left and the other right, are welded shut."

"Welded? Why?" the Assaultmistress trilled.

"I do not know about the right door. Radioactive material storage, maybe? A sign on the left door says it opens into the reactor room," Einstika sang.

"A cage runs across the antechamber," Kidahin continued. "The security door in the middle of it is missing. We found two more doors, one left and the other right."

"The left door opens into the reactor control room," Einstika blurted. "The Warrior shot in the back of the head is there, slumped across a control console. Her neckwear and waistwear identify her as a Neh'as'anni Clan elder."

"Shot?" the Assaultmistress keened in disbelief.

"Yes, with a small-caliber firearm. And from behind," Kidahin added, scarcely believing it even now.

"She was a nuclear power systems techmistress. She locked out the control computer and tail-tied the process controllers and electromagnetic emitters to make some kind of static shield. She breached the control room shielding and tapped directly into the dedicated reactor control accumulators. The radiation signal comes from the breach she made," Einstika trilled.

"What is a static shield, and what did she need it for?" the Assaultmistress trilled.

"She succeeded in making a low-power electromagnetic pulse generator. It thumps at a critical frequency and can burn out circuits. She aimed the emitters at the floor, but I do not know why," Einstika sang.

"To keep items or weapons made out of that amber metal alloy from remaining stable in the control room," Kidahin trilled.

"Maybe. Electrical fields cause it to break up into handfuls of wiggly amber grains," Einstika trilled.

"Enough editorializing," the Assaultmistress trilled. "What did you do in the control room?"

"I diverted power from the accumulators, isolated the reactor systems, and restored partial power."

"And after that?" the Assaultmistress pressed as she reached into her combat harness and withdrew a thin pad, a pencil, and began scribbling on the top sheet of paper.

"We backtrailed into a tunnel and found a door on the left. It opens into a transformer room. Inside, another door opens into the back of an intensive care abode. A hundred male bodies covered with skin-rot fungi unlike any I ever saw before lay there. Tialdrin thought it was a quarantine abode because the males were being treated with an antimycotic."

"Neh'tle ke'ne's'tu causes horrible changes in living things," the Assaultmistress trilled in disgust.

"The intensive care healers took shelter in an adjacent room, including a sire cairn of surgery and thirty females. They were all dead, but none of them had any visible wounds. It looked like they just dropped dead. Everything in the room was smashed."

"Suicide?" the Assaultmistress trilled doubtfully.

"No. A mutiny," Einstika interrupted, accidently saying the Delwyn-word.

"A what?" the Assaultmistress trilled sharply.

"Oh, nothing," Einstika evaded. "We turned left and prowled to another door that opened into a large bay. Twelve doors run down the left side and another twelve run down the right."

"How large is this bay?" the Assaultmistress trilled, scribbling rapidly.

"Big. Wide enough for a crane to span the ceiling and roll up and down its length," Kidahin sang.

"The laboratory equipment is the kind found in metallurgy research. I think the Neh'as'anni were analyzing the properties of that amber alloy they were developing," Einstika sang.

The Assaultmistress erased a third of her drawing and drew essentially the same thing but at a much larger scale. She sketched a rough outline of the New Dawn building above the changes.

"Continue," she sang.

"The right corner door opens into a tunnel sloping down onto a ledge. The ledge runs around the perimeter of a vast rectangular quarry pit deep enough to swallow the entire building. A ramp connects the ledge to a small building on the quarry floor. A second ramp on the building roof goes down to the quarry floor. Hundreds of hatches built into the ground surround the building. Radiation there measures in the mid-blue range. The EM field coming from the emitters in the control room are strong enough to reach the floor and interfere with radio reception," Kidahin sang.

"The ground hatches cover mine shafts. A crystal form of the amber alloy covers the sides. Floodlights set at regular intervals light the path. We found a dispensary stocked with antiradiation, vitamins, and amphetamines. Beyond it the shaft widens. Occasional pillars made from the alloy stand in open spaces. I used electricity to dissolve part of one and uncovered the upper third of a male embedded within it. Tialdrin thought the pillar was some kind of novel medical regeneration device," Einstika trilled.

"The male woke up and screamed. That alerted someone wearing golden body armor. She chased us into a secondary shaft. Einstika cut a floodlight power cord and used it to dissolve a hole through the side of the shaft and into an adjacent one. We followed it out through a different floor hatch," Kidahin added.

"Body armor? What body armor?" the Assaultmistress trilled, suddenly alert.

"I do not think it was body armor. No one could wear something as disproportionate to her body as this thing was. Its gait lacked grace and rhythm. It reminded me of something under remote control, a drone of some kind. It transmitted a garbled, flat and toneless sentence over our radios. I thought she was suffering from amusia," Einstika sang.

"People with amusia are psychotic. A voice over the radio? Could it have gone through a scrambler? Did it sound like the A'tayotan Mistress's voice does? Maybe it was telling you to keep out," the Assaultmistress trilled.

"We thought so, too. We recalled to the tunnel, climbed onto the handcar, and rode it to the tunnel entrance."

"You did not take the stairs back to the airlock?" the Assaultmistress trilled.

"No," Kidahin sang.

"Where did you go next?"

"We stepped out onto pavement and looped around the front of New Dawn to a road flanking the left side. Part of the road dropped into a depression covered by debris from a collapsed building. We climbed under it, and I saw the green door on this side of the building as we cleared the rubble," Einstika sang.

The Assaultmistress scribbled a door frame and nodded.

"You entered the building through this door?" she trilled at interrogative tempo.

"Yes. It opens into a pressurized room. A door on the opposite wall opens into a hallway. The hallway runs left about a hundred ells but right only about four. We turned left and walked to the end. The door on the right is welded shut, but the door on the left is the one right behind us," Kidahin sang, snapping her tail at it.

"That adds some perspective. Where did you prowl to from here?"

"We checked the warehouse annex, entered the lift shaft service door, and climbed down thirty ells to a storeroom filled with food sealed in cans."

"Food in cans? Why would anybody put food in cans?" the Assaultmistress trilled doubtfully. "Nevermind, continue."

"A blood trail led us to a door, and we found another door with a taped paper sign calling it a restricted access. The blood trail leads into the cryogenic capsule storage room. We found a desiccated male body on the floor. We also found a sire cairn wearing a hazard suit stuffed into one of the capsules. His head was smashed in," Kidahin trilled.

"They put him in cryogenic storage to keep him alive for later surgery?" the Assaultmistress trilled sharply.

"No. We think the desiccated male was the capsule's original occupant. Someone opened his capsule, threw him out, and shoved the sire cairn in— already dead, most likely," Kidahin trilled in outrage.

"You found only males in those capsules?" the Assaultmistress trilled angrily.

"Yes, but we did not check every capsule," Kidahin trilled.

"The sire cairn wrote a note. It says his occupational association turned against him and that the research should be paused and that the substances are safe," Einstika sang.

"Substances? What substances?" the Assaultmistress trilled.

"He must have meant the auxetic amber alloy in the mines," Kidahin sang.

"I doubt it. I think he meant the cryogenics research and the drugs related to it. His occupational association killed him for experimenting on males," Einstika sang.

"Perhaps, but his death has nothing to do with gaining access to the control room. Continue, Kidahin," the Assaultmistress sang.

"A door beyond the capsules leads into the cryogenic preparation room. We ignored it and backtrailed to a lift shaft inside the food storage area. We found another transformer room near the shaft door. It powers the cryogenics equipment. Einstika flipped some breakers on and others off to turn the lights on and release the electronic locks. We backtrailed to the door with the taped sign. Unlocked, it opens into a lift service shaft and leads into the rear of a nutrition center. Inside, a wide door opens onto a ramp that spirals down to a communal eating hall."

"You unlocked all the doors, Einstika? All of them in the building or just the ones on the cryogenics level?"

"The room distributed power to the cryogenics equipment. I assume breaker boxes there control locks and lights related to critical cryogenic systems, but I do not know," Einstika trilled.

"We entered a large room identified as a recreation center. They built it up from furnished high-relief wood paneling to closely resemble a hollow branch pathway inside of an elleiu tree. They put living plants and even small streams in it, something no elleiu tree has. Craftworker abodes line the walls.

"A right-bearing path remarkably similar to the main path leads up into a tree's vantage splits from there. It leads to a door opening into a large room with a planetarium projector. The left-bearing path goes on up and splits off into a right path further down that leads into the residence abodes. The left path climbs into the command center.

"Keypad locks secure every residence abode. We opened a few and found dead occupants—all of them apparently buhnnie poisoned. The command center pathway opens first into an antechamber. Beyond it we found a reasonable copy of an elleiu tree vantage. Forty-two females sit around it, all dead from buhnnie poisoning. The computer archives are there. We disconnected the hard drive and backtrailed with it until we reached the lift," Kidahin concluded, jerking her tail at the lift across from them.

"And you left the building from here?" the Assaultmistress sang.

"Yes. We took the warehouse ATV and drove through that door," Kidahin sang, pointing her tail at the door they drove through days ago.

The Assaultmistress made several minor changes to her drawing and spread it across a nearby crate.

"These are the paths you took, based on your descriptions. Notice anything odd?"

Kidahin and Einstika squinted at the cluttered crude sketch.

"This is not possible!" Kidahin trilled.

"You think not?" the Assaultmistress trilled a laugh.

"Spirits!" Einstika keened. "The command center is above ground and inside this building?"

"Correct. On the floor above us but on the opposite side is the command center. The floor below it contains the planetarium room. The level below us is food storage."

"The floor above but in the middle of the building contains the residence abodes? The recreation center is below it? We knew the cryogenics and metallurgy lab were underground. How did we not know we climbed above ground and into the building?" Einstika interrupted, sweeping her tail across the drawing.

"Buildings are a rare but necessary eyesore because technology needs them. This building is obscenely large and can contain the entire upper third of an elleiu tree," Kidahin trilled in disgust.

"Indeed," the Assaultmistress sang. "If you could box all the branches with scaffolding and fill the space between branches with abodes and pathways, you could shelter far more than what a single elleiu tree can. You could prowl in such a volume for days."

"We do not have days. We should go. Einstika says she unlocked all the doors," Kidahin sang.

"Only on the cryogenics level, I think. Some of them are welded shut," Einstika protested.

"Shikararro told me as much, so we came prepared," the Assaultmistress trilled. "Cut open all the doors you find on this level," she sang to her subordinate assaultmistresses. She turned and addressed Einstika.

"Go with them. The other side of this hallway opens into the recreation center. You should find the planetarium room beyond it. Find the residence abodes. Two hands will search each abode. You will continue with two hands into the command center and get the computer up and running. Shikararro is sending in portable hard drives formatted to accept data from the computer."

"A few more techmistresses would help," Einstika suggested.

The Assaultmistress ignored her and faced Kidahin.

"You must find a way to the reactor from here," she sang.

"We know the stairs airlock is below New Dawn," Kidahin snarled.

"What about it?" the Assaultmistress trilled impatiently.

"It uses mechanical seals. The pressurized room down the hallway uses mechanical seals, too. Your drawing shows a void between them."

"Check the door down the hall," the Assaultmistress told an assaultstalker.

The assaultstalker left immediately and returned in less than a minute.

"I found a room no bigger than a sleeping nest with a hatch built into the floor. It opens into a stainless steel tube with rungs welded down one side. I saw a hatch on the bottom of the tube," she sang.

The Assaultmistress traced a finger across her drawing and snapped her ears.

"The lower hatch should open into the ceiling of the airlock you took to the stairs. Take two hands and go to the control room and shut the reactor down," she told Kidahin.

"Me?" Kidahin keened. "I am no techmistress. This is Einstika's work."

"No. She must help the healers revive the males still alive. Your green file contains the codes you need. You are our best hope."

"I am your best hope? How am I your best hope?" Kidahin sang.

"You took a lethal dose of radiation and do not have long to live. I am sorry."

Kidahin stared at the Assaultmistress and sighed.

"I suspected as much. The Healer's pheromones conveyed sorrowful helplessness and rage. I—mistook the reason for her rage as my refusal of her treatment."

"If you cannot meet the challenge," the Assaultmistress began.

"I can sit at a control console and type codes from a sheet of paper. This does not mean I can shut the reactor down."

"This building is the lair of neh'tle ke'ne's'tu. The Neh'as'anni believed in their technology and waited too long. Most of La'huaset will die if the core melts into the groundwater."

"I know this," Kidahin trilled as assaultprowlers surrounded and led her down the hallway.

Kidahin stood between iron rails bolted to the concrete floor and waited as the last of the assaultprowlers climbed down the stairs. Whispering echoes brushed her ears.

"Movement in the tunnel," a Warrior's pheromones whispered in her nose.

"No cover on this straight path," the Warrior cursed aloud and drew her sword.

Gunshots echoed down the tunnel.

"The Neh'as'anni are at the tunnel entrance," Kidahin trilled.

"Two hands of shortbow archers hold the transformer room door," an assaultprowler trilled.

"The hands with us will hold the platform while you work on the reactor," the Warrior sang.

Uncertain gunfire echoed behind them. Eyloni did not fight in buildings, in hallways, or in underground tunnels. Firearm usage against any traditionally armed person was heretical, an honor point crime. The Be'atika Senge had outlawed firearms outright soon after the Battle of Withered Trees.

Human attackers would have killed Kidahin and her hands by now, she knew. The Neh'as'anni assault teams used guns as if they were merely improved bows. Delwyn told her firearms prowled tails-entwined with unit tactics, but Eyloni fought as individuals even within hands.

"They will all die. They reject custom by using modern weapons against traditionally armed opponents," the Warrior hissed.

"But why? How can they do this? No honor comes of this," Kidahin trilled.

"Hlorrithin vows to erase New Dawn and the Neh'as'anni from the world for their crimes," the Warrior replied defiantly.

The scene shifted suddenly, warning Kidahin as an explosion rocked the tunnel, followed by attack trills and ricocheting bullets.

"Kidahin, they have broken past the transformer room hands and are heading this way," an assaultmistress keened, grabbed her by the shoulder, and shoved her up the ramp and to the platform door.

"We will hold the door. Go and do what must be done," she sang.

"You cannot hold the platform for long," Kidahin trilled.

"We can. Hurry, and may the spirits prowl with you. *Ma' nako nabi.*"

"*Me nati ka me,*" Kidahin sang softly and rushed through the control room door, stepped over the dead techmistress, sat in the control console seat, opened the green file folder, and spread papers across the blinking status switches.

It took her a minute to find the techmistress's magnetic key card and swipe it across the reader. She typed an access code on the keyboard and waited.

The sounds of combat intensified outside.

The computer displayed a terse green warning.

CORE EXPOSED.

Below the text appeared a graphic of an analog gauge, its needle pointing well into the green scale.

Kidahin picked up a light pen and touched it to the screen.

The computer displayed a menu.

She clicked on the Reactor Status option.

The screen abruptly cleared, and Kidahin froze in dread.

The screen displayed text saying the reactor had executed a panic shutdown days ago. The cooling pumps lacked electricity. The backup generators lacked natural gas to run them. Kidahin already knew this from the last time she was here. She clicked the cooling system option and read until she came across a not-recommended emergency backup.

She tapped the pen to the screen for more information. The backup cooling system drew water from cisterns sunk into the surrounding shallow water table and gravity-fed it into the heat exchanger and out through the dry well.

The computer warned against this procedure except for the most dire of emergencies. A rupture in the heat exchanger would allow contaminated coolant to mix with the water flowing into the drywell and the surrounding environment.

Kidahin clicked on the core status option and waited.

The computer reported the heat exchanger intact, its pump operating from accumulator emergency reserve current, but the coolant was too hot to carry heat away from the core.

A bank of valves in the reactor room controlled cistern flow. Accumulator power was insufficient to open them, but they could be opened manually.

Kidahin clicked on the containment vessel status item and a gauge thermometer appeared. A number highlighted in green flashed on the dial with a black needle hovering hesitantly four marks below it.

"Spirits, the core is less than ten degrees Tail from reaching its melting point!" she keened.

Every remedial option needed electricity, a lot of electricity. But the reserve accumulators barely supplied enough power to flicker a few lights and release simple door locks.

Could she bring the reactor back online and draw enough power to run the pumps and valves? Would the water drop the temperature before the uranium in the core reached its melting point?

No. Thermocouple-like converters charged the accumulators, but main power came from turbine-driven generators. The temperature would jump more than four degrees before the generators even began turning.

Kidahin read through screens of text, found a promising lead, scrolled back, and reread it carefully as a Warrior burst in on her.

"We are being overrun! Lock this door," she sang and fled.

"Spirits," Kidahin snarled as she slammed the door security handle sideways to force the two fist-thick deadbolts into the door frame.

"It does not matter. Only this matters now," she trilled and returned to the console.

She read through the papers in her folder and found a list of door codes. A corresponding list of numbers had been appended to it. The keypad codes for the residence abodes?

"Why put abode door codes in with reactor control protocols? The a'pea A'tayotan mixed the files up," Kidahin keened in fury.

A hollow booming clang startled her. Then a second one, followed by continuous hammering. The Neh'as'anni banging at the platform door meant her defenders were dead.

The concrete facade and heavy metal door would resist wedges and sledgehammers. But if they brought in jackhammers and cutting torches, they could break the door open in a matter of hours.

A number stenciled above the control room door frame caught her eye.

She ignored the constant banging and skipped into the wide hallway and looked above each door.

Numbers marked every door frame. Even the ringing and visibly shaking platform door had a number stenciled above it.

Kidahin ran back into the control room, grabbed a page from the green file folder, and raced back to the platform door.

The banging changed in pitch, a warning that its collapse was imminent.

The number matched a number on the door list, but no door in the antechamber had a keypad.

And welds sealed them shut, so the door codes were useless.

She touched the reactor room door.

"It is hot!" she trilled.

She fingered the weld seam. It felt warm and remarkably smooth. Coppery-gold, the welds stood out against the slate-metal door and frame.

"This is the amber alloy we found in the mines. Einstika called it— auxetic? It shrinks and thickens when hit."

Kidahin grabbed a metal punch and stabbed the weld as hard as she could.

The weld thickened slightly to reinforce the seal.

Kidahin ran to the control room looking for a long electrical cord. Finding only power cords hanging from rack-mounted equipment, she unplugged several of them and ripped out their power cords.

WARNING: CONVERTER LOW VOLTAGE blinked bluely on the console screen.

Did she cause the converter failure by unplugging the instruments? No, the converters fed the accumulators. When they died, so would the lights and the control room electronics.

Kidahin cut off all the plugs but one and stripped the insulation from the exposed wires. She twisted the bare copper wires together again and again to splice together a much longer cord.

She clicked the light pen on the screen again and again until the computer displayed a familiar list of numbers. She clicked on the ones matching those on the sheet of paper.

The computer asked for an authorization code.

She bent over the console keyboard and typed it in.

Nothing happened.

She clicked on the reactor room door number and typed the code listed next to the door number.

REACTOR ROOM DOOR UNLOCKED.
WARNING: RADIATION HAZARD.

Kidahin ignored the green text, plugged the cord into a socket, played it out across the floor to the reactor room door, touched the exposed wires to the weld, and watched the amber seam break up into tiny amber segments and fall to the floor.

She shoved the door open and staggered as a blast of oven-hot air swept over her.

The hammering at the door had stopped, replaced with a low grinding noise. Diamond saws, she guessed. Pieces of concrete fell to the floor.

Nuclear fission was hazardous, so the Neh'as'anni had built this room with simplicity in mind. Ell-wide pipes ran down the opposite wall. All of them terminated into a bank of valves with circular handles.

Kidahin stepped into the baking heat and swooned as it penetrated deeply into her body.

Halfway across the room a wave of nausea struck her. She faltered, slumped to the floor, vomited, and crawled through it to the valve bank.

The grinding at the platform door stopped.

She gripped the handle of the first valve, the hot metal searing her hands.

She turned the valve full open and struggled with the next valve. She opened them all, and as she finished turning the last valve open, she swayed, on the verge of blacking out. She could barely hear the cold subsurface water pouring through the water mains.

The accumulators drained to zero.

The lights dimmed and died.

In the dark and alone, Kidahin heard the metal platform door strike the concrete floor with a metallic thud.

Flashing afterimages filled her vision. The spirits had come to sing her to the Oyya Web.

Then a hand torch blinded her.

Not the spirits, but the Neh'as'anni.

She heard a voice, a familiar one she could not quite place.

A male voice.

"Shikararro said to submit it to my will," Hlorrithin sang in triumph as Kidahin slipped into the eternal Oyya Web of the spirits.

I am at peace. My duty is fulfilled.

Only the spirits of the O'un Tu knew what lay ahead for me.

But the dreams and hopes I knew that day gave me the strength to stand against any evil.

17
RITUAL'S DEEP NEED

A sitting Kidahin opened her eyes as the last vibrant note faded into silence.

She sat cross-legged on the grass, her forearms resting lightly on cramping thighs, her hands cupping the clear sunny violet sky.

But the sun had moved. It was still moving, ever so slightly. How could she see the sun moving across Elleio's sky?

The subtle shifting of several thousand bodies brushed her ears. The sounds drew her wandering mind to the female multitudes sitting around her joined tail-to-thigh. Their combined skin-color patterns and winding seated placement gave them the appearance of leaves sprouting from an elleiu tree branch.

She saw no elleiu trees at all, but she did see spindly ones growing in a sprawling sparse forest all around her. They stood even shorter than arberi trees and sprouted clumpy ugly branches along the upper thirds of their bone-white trunks. Thousands of tightly bundled twigs tipped with overlapping bark-like leaves scarcely longer than her forearm covered the branches. No aerial roots coiled down from those leaf-packed branches. No hollow spaces filled those narrow boughs. No entry boles marred those bone-white trunks. Their bleached smooth bark and yellowish blue-green leaves keened a disorienting wariness in Kidahin's mind, a memory of sickness and death.

"*Bu ta'u wei*," Kidahin muttered in a toneless descant. The Compact of the Ten Tribes of Elleio had put a colony here long ago.

Hunter's Moon came to this world delivering supplies. Soon after he entered standard surveillance orbit Delwyn told her the trees reminded him of creepy pinecones on long sticks.

His scent gave her an idea of what a pinecone was, and she knew him well enough by now to have an idea of what he considered creepy. She agreed with his casual observation and warned him to prowl with care in this forest.

Kidahin glanced at her tail. The last quarter down to the pons remained snugly wrapped around Einstika's thigh. Einstika's tail joined her to the thigh of a Warrior female sitting next to her. Kidahin glanced down and smiled as Tialdrin's pons brushed her right thigh suggestively.

Kidahin shook her head to focus her thoughts on the here and now. She, Tialdrin, Einstika, and a thousand other people formed this one of several hundred branches in a stylized elleiu tree ritual pattern. Their combined pheromones blanketed Singer's Grove with public emotional chatter.

"I am not dead. Thank the spirits," Tialdrin sang softly.

"Of course you are not dead. Although I do admit to some doubt myself after reliving lethal exposure to fission radiation," Kidahin trilled tremulously. She eyed the hideous trees warily. A'pea Delwyn and his lingering scent and its reminder of what the human mind considered creepy.

A pheromonal cue rose above the background scents, and everyone stood up with their tails still entwined. Together they sang in respectful gratitude to the Gracious Mistress of the Singing People for the honor of giving them a place in the Remembrance of the Song of Hlorrithin ritual.

The singing soon ended. With courtesy satisfied, Einstika rubbed the base of her tail and scowled at the alien grass.

"How long did it last?" she trilled, still rubbing.

"An EST week, of course. Your numb tail should tell you as much, even if your empty stomach does not. Or did you somehow eat your fill while wandering through historical scenes in the Oyya Web?" Kidahin sang dryly.

"It feels longer to me," Tialdrin sang. She turned and looked Einstika in the eye. "I kept seeing dead males. I thought they would never go away. You did something wrong, but I do not remember what it was," she added warily.

"I did not!" Einstika snarled and then paused, suddenly uncertain.

"Time is completely subjective in rituals where the singers' metamind creates scenes from the Oyya Web. You know this," Kidahin sang, clearly remembering how she backtrailed through ritual time to send the ATV in the right direction.

Her memory apparently remained intact because her ritual subjective and objective selves merged. But in the corrected ritual reality, the erroneous subjective selves no longer existed for Tialdrin or Einstika.

Scent-linked empathy could sometimes create memories of alternate realities, but the mind was a product of the real world. Memory fragments from Einstika and Tialdrin's subjective selves would backtrail into conscious thought as little more than hazy random glimpses.

"A'pea subjective time, Kidahin. Ritual time does not matter, but historical time does. I saw dead males, dead human males. No one knew about humans in Hlorrithin's time," Einstika trilled unsteadily and then gave a pheromonal frown. "But I stopped seeing them right after we left the New Dawn building," she added.

Tialdrin frowned at a persistent memory and snapped her tail.

"I stopped seeing dead human males the moment I stepped out of the lift shaft and into the warehouse annex. Did you stop seeing them then, too, Kidahin?" she trilled.

"I stopped seeing them when we left New Dawn in the ATV," she sang truthfully.

Einstika felt a gentle tug on her tail, looked up, and flicked an ear in apology at the smiling, patiently waiting Warrior and unwound her tail from the Warrior's thigh.

Free to move more than an ell, Einstika drifted closer to Kidahin, smelling a hint of evasiveness on her scent.

"You lied!" a low and intense voice trilled from behind them.

Kidahin spun at the slander, gave a furious Eldest Huntress and two indignant Warriors the stiff-tail stare, and glared at the accusing Warrior.

"I lied, Mistress Mimiran?" Kidahin trilled heatedly.

"You told me you did not feel any traumatic stress symptoms. I asked if you ever had any dead male flashbacks, and you said no," Mistress of Inner Strength Mimiran trilled softly through gritted teeth.

"I did not lie," Kidahin growled just as softly but defiantly. "I stopped seeing them months ago."

"I did not ask when they stopped. I asked if you saw them ever," Mimiran growled with rising menace.

"You failed to disclose your unfitness to join in such an important ritual as the Song of Hlorrithin. I must report your lapse to the hierarchies," Phelindra trilled in distress as she slid up behind Kidahin.

"I did not lie," Kidahin stammered flatly. "I omitted a tiny detail about my experiences in dealing with a tragedy that happened almost two years ago."

"You failed to appreciate what having unresolved traumatic stress issues might do to your mind. You knew since early adolescence about the male deaths caused by the Neh'as'anni and those clans associating with them. You also knew how much the male deaths on *Londiwe Khoza* were affecting you," Phelindra keened.

"We are guests here. The Bu ta'u wei Gracious Mistress personally extended her invitation through Delwyn asking if some of us wanted a place in this ritual. She extended the honor through him to us and not to us directly," Melkorka keened softly but firmly.

Kidahin leaned back slightly as Melkorka's anger blistered her nose for casting doubts on their Warleader's honor.

"Delwyn is not here?" Kidahin trilled, seeking a distraction. Males were inherently safe, and as vexing as they often were, females always listened to them. A male's mere presence often mediated discord among groups of females.

"Do not think you are getting out of this by waving Delwyn's scent in our noses," Phelindra trilled aggressively.

"But where is he?" Kidahin sang, looking about wildly.

"He was here the whole time. He wore a rebreather because of the high carbon dioxide in the air. We are so proud of him," Melkorka trilled fondly, her severe features softening.

"If he came with you, then why did he leave?" Kidahin trilled.

"He did not come with us because Mistress of Communications Hlindredreda called him back to *Hunter's Moon* as the ritual was ending. She received a priority hyperlink message for him from the Compact Counsel. Delwyn is speaking with Mistress Thelindrallin's communications avatar right now," Phelindra sang.

"Phelindra, Mimiran, Aplilin, and I came here not long after you three killed Shikararro," Melkorka added, her frightful anger rekindling.

"What are you singing about? We did not kill Shikararro," Einstika interrupted.

"We did no such thing," Tialdrin objected as a hazy memory of a wrong turn started casting doubts. She shoved the shadowy figment aside.

"What do you mean by a priority call?" she added curiously.

Mimiran spun on her. "Nothing concerning you. You will return to Health Center and spend the next several weeks reviewing everything in healer records about male deaths causing traumatic stress in females," she trilled with a note of finality.

"When are we leaving this system?" Einstika sang in an attempt to evade Warrior fury.

"You do not escape this matter unscathed," Melkorka trilled impatiently.

"You stand on a brittle branch right now," Mimiran warned. "You made a nonhistorical decision, one contrary to those Einstikalin made, a decision you knew went against a history you have known about since early adolescence. You ignored the singers and strayed from the ritual plot."

"But," Einstika interrupted.

"But nothing! Nobody contradicts scent-linked empathy memory while in remembrance rituals. You always reenact historical scenes as you learned them in the teaching songs and as guided by the singers. You knew Shikararro lived through the Battle of Withered Trees, and yet you killed her anyway," Mimiran trilled.

"I did not. I helped her upload the hard drive files to the A'tayotan. I saw her rejoin her Pathwalker archers before we reentered the Technology Center building!" Einstika keened.

"You have no memory of killing her because we helped Kidahin backtrail into the subjective ritual past. She put you back on the right path. Causality in Oyya Web visions does not follow physical laws. You may remember fragments of the alternate path you three took," Mimiran trilled in disgust.

"But I," Einstika began and paused as Melkorka's demeanor suddenly changed to one of detached delight. Einstika knew of only one person who could cause her pheromones to change so abruptly—Delwyn. Resentment filled Einstika. Why was he not here so she could draw strength from him?

Melkorka stared at Delwyn's holographic image playing across her corneas.

"Melkorka? Aren't they ready yet?" Delwyn snapped.

Melkorka absently twitched an ear to open her commlink.

"They are ready, and they are fine. For now," she trilled menacingly.

"It's not their fault. Not really. I had post-traumatic stress flashbacks for years before your pheromones banished them forever," Delwyn said.

"Forever, as long as you remain among females. Our pheromones restrain the hyperviolent impulses of the male mind," she reminded him.

"Umm-hmm," Delwyn grunted through what sounded suspiciously like a yawn. "We're leaving. Anailiatha is spooling up the jump drive. Trebithia is busy plotting an FTL jump out of this system. The jump clock is already counting down. You have about fifteen—ah, thirty— thirty minutes. You better get up here now unless you'd rather stay behind and enjoy the creepy trees of Bu ta'u wei."

Melkorka snickered to herself. Delwyn habitually thought in human decimal numbers. He certainly knew by now that they counted two legs, two arms, and one tail as their number base: one, two, three, four, ten.

"Our warship goes nowhere without his Mistress of the Ship," she trilled drolly as people began disappearing around her.

The Mistress of Conveyance was already translating people back to the ship? Delwyn was indeed in a hurry.

"What is happening?" Melkorka trilled at interrogative pitch.

"Thelindrallin has asked us on behalf of the Be'atika Senge if we can divert to Earth at our earliest convenience," he said bluntly.

"And did she tell you why?" Melkorka trilled, focusing on his change in tone.

The Be'atika Senge hierarchy decreed the creation of the Compact of the Ten Tribes of Elleio and established the Compact Counsel long ago. The Compact Counsel wielded worldwide governing power on Elleio. Compact warships fought on its behalf, but Eyloni considered warships male persons having autonomy. The Be'atika Senge always asked a warleader to do their bidding. His honor almost always demanded he agree to their requests. Delwyn knew this and understood his place in Elleio's female-dominant society as well as any other male did.

And he certainly would not object to taking *Hunter's Moon* to Earth, if for no other reason than to annoy Captain Judith Arleen Rodgers. For some reason it bothered her to no end that the Society of Hunter's Moon had chosen Delwyn as their Warleader.

"Delwyn?" Melkorka prompted, growing impatient.

"Captain Winters, in his capacity as Coalition Ambassador, asked Thelindrallin to call the Counsel into session. He wants us to pick up Commissioner JoyLynn Labrador-St. Germaine and take her to Tau-1 Gruis. That's the Coalition name for the star where *Londiwe Khoza* was destroyed."

"It will take us months to get there. Why does Coalition Ambassador Alan Dean Winters want us to take this female there?" Melkorka growled, her anger blazing.

Delwyn had an annoying habit of holding back unwelcome news. Close to him, she only needed to smell his scent and empathize with it to find out what he was withholding. But even over the commlink she could tell by his tone that he was enraged.

"She's supposed to meet with a Ni'zakhonii representative. Thelindrallin told me the Ni'zakhonii sent the Coalition a request to negotiate," he snapped in disbelief.

The reptilian Ni'zakhonii ate Eyloni and humans alive—considered them no more than food animals. They had eaten Delwyn's family alive years ago.

Blinding fury overwhelmed Melkorka as the Mistress of Conveyance translated her, Kidahin, and her group back to the ship.

***

Kidahin stepped through the Warleader abode's threshold, hesitated slightly as courtesy required, took a half-step and froze, her path blocked by an immobile and intimidating Comari female.

Kidahin cautiously made respectful eye contact with Lo'sutra'est anni and politely ignored her warning glare.

Delwyn was nowhere in sight.

The Comari seemed both piqued and fatigued, and Kidahin wondered why. Comara often called upon a nearly limitless endurance whenever they thought something threatened their bondmales. But no threat against Delwyn existed aboard their warship or on the surface of Bu ta'u wei. Eyloni evolution and socialization compelled females, regardless of gender phenotype, to relentlessly protect all males.

Had something happened during the week she spent in Singer's Grove?

The mute Comari offered no explanation, not even a terse sign in battle language. Her scent told Kidahin nothing, either. Comara masked their scent when they wanted nobody knowing their emotional state. But Delwyn's human nose barely noticed the food on his plate, so why was Lo'sutra'est anni holding her scent close to her?

"Let her in," Delwyn said and waved Kidahin around the Comari and on into the abode.

The petite, pale, towhead, tailless, and intimidating female glared at Kidahin as she stepped around to Delwyn's side.

Kidahin took pride in her rational thinking. Indeed, she could not help being a supremely rational strategist. Except for a few minor reactively irrational moments she always acted rationally proactive and had done so since birth. Yet every time she caught a whiff of his pheromones, she stumbled into a literal defensiveness.

"What happened to you?" she trilled accusingly, ignoring the Comari's renewed warning glare.

"Nothing happened *to* me," Delwyn stressed and yawned twice.

"You are exhausted. Why?" Kidahin trilled in concern and turned to stare accusingly at the Comari.

"I've been awake for over fifty-five hours. Forget about me. Tell me about you."

Kidahin snapped her head around and glared at him. Telling a female to forget about a male was like telling her to forget about breathing.

"What is there to tell? You already know what happened," Kidahin trilled aggressively.

"Do you really relive historical events as though you are there yourself through pheromonal empathy?" Delwyn asked.

Kidahin hesitated. It was not like Delwyn to ask questions when he already knew the answers. She nodded, wary. He was up to something. Males were strange.

"We often relive the emotions of those who came before us. We become intimately aware of our past in this way," she sang.

"But you have a written history," he said. "I've read a few volumes on La'huaset Tribal continent history myself."

"Of course we have a written history. Reliving historical events is done through ritual empathy. But rituals need a lot of people: the actors who play historical roles, the singers who form the metamind and draw historical scenery from the Oyya Web, and a gracious mistress to set pace, theme, and lead the singers through the plot. You do not need a ritual to read a book," she sang in droll humor.

"I get that. What, then, are the sources for those history books?"

"Eyewitness accounts mostly, but they are often unreliable.

Eyewitnesses tell from a single point of view and fill in gaps with their own guesses and preferences. Ritual reenactments show from multiple pheromonal points of view. Mistresses of Saga often gather in ritual to play out historical roles. After the ritual ends they write what happened to them as they relived the historical event. They collate their experiences and write a unified story."

"So your written history is only as accurate as the pheromonal memories handed down across generations?" Delwyn asked.

"Yes, that is why a gracious mistress brings so many singers into a ritual. Their large numbers keep any outlying hazy memories from corrupting historical accuracy. Scent triggers powerful memories. Remembered emotions sweep us into pheromonal empathy. We remember what we smell perfectly, but not everyone smells the same thing. This is what gives the ritual its perspective," Kidahin sang.

"I get it. Odors can trigger memories in humans, too. But you do this in communally shared mental visions? That sounds like some kind of nose-directed dream control to me."

"Indeed, in a way this is true," Kidahin admitted. "But in ritual, the singers control the scenes and the setting. The people who reenact historical persons use what they learned in teaching songs about the person and the event but are guided by the scenes the singers create through scent-linked empathy."

"But," Delwyn interrupted. "Insignificant actions taken by historical people don't matter. I guess that means ritual actors have some freedom of action as long as they don't stray far from the historical narrative."

"For the most part this is true," Kidahin agreed. "But time flows differently in ritual. It skips over routine events like hours of uneventful travel. A person moves through a historical reenactment ritual like a person reads through scenes in a book. A real danger exists in the ritual when a person prowls between scenes, loses the plot, and gets trapped in self-absorbed loops.

"Think about reading a paragraph in which the content calls out to you. You reread it over and over again, savoring its emotional appeal. You begin to imagine yourself in this scene as if *you* are a character in the story. Through this character you unconsciously subvert the plot and act through scenes you imagine the character moving through indefinitely.

"The Gracious Mistress and her singers focus on keeping the historical plot moving forward. When you read a book the scenes fade away as you turn each page. But if you try to back up and 'reread' earlier scenes in a ritual, *you* risk getting stranded with no way of returning to the continuity of the plot. Think of faded-out ritual scenes as pages ripped out of a book. A reader can skip over the missing pages and read on in a book, but you must move through connecting scenes in a ritual."

"The Wild Mistress," Delwyn murmured softly.

"What about her?" Kidahin wondered.

"I remember—nevermind. Anyway, I visited the tombs of the Heroes of Home before I met with the Be'atika Senge on Na'di Island for the first time. You don't bury your dead, yet all six—eleven—Heroes of Home lay in tombs. It sounded strange to me at the time. I wanted to see Hlorrithin because he was an O'un Tu Clan male, but they said I could not enter the tombs at that time."

"You could not enter Hlorrithin's tomb. You could enter any of the other ten," Kidahin corrected.

"That wasn't how I understood it at the time. Why not Hlorrithin's?"

"His body remains a radiation hazard to this day."

"Oh," Delwyn said and changed the subject.

"So you, Tialdrin, and Einstika assumed the roles of members in an Environmental Interdiction Team. What happened to them?"

"Tialdrinaha was disemboweled on a Neh'as'anni roadside. Einstikalin died from radiation poisoning days after she repaired the cryogenics control electronics so the healers could revive four hundred thirty-four males and one hundred thirty-one Comara. Kidahindrallin died from massive radiation exposure after manually opening the groundwater supply for the reactor. Hlorrithin told Shikararro he believed Kidahindrallin lived long enough to see him enter the reactor room."

"Yes, he did see you," Delwyn said. "And then he manually restarted the reactor, which gave Einstikalin and the healers enough power to revive those still alive in the cryogenic capsules. Then he scrammed the reactor."

"Yes, he lived long enough to hear their cries of gratitude. After ordering all Neh'as'anni technology removed to the A'tayotan for analysis he went to the quarantine abode."

"Where he died in agony," Delwyn said, his eyes tearing. "I remember—I remember Hervorallin telling me about Hlorrithin's Warpact. It punished outlawry. It really wasn't the civil war I thought it was."

"Yes," Kidahin murmured. "His Warpact killed the Neh'as'anni and their allied clans. Every female older than an infant was killed for the honor point crime of causing an ecological disaster and the murder of thousands of males, Comara, and infants."

"And males regardless of age and the infant females with them received sanctuary," Delwyn nodded, remembering when the Wild Mistress had appeared in his own adulthood quest. She forced him to relive a few hours in the life of Fara, an infant male who lived centuries ago.

Kidahin wrapped her tail around his waist and pulled him into her embrace, his cooler body sharpening her focus.

"This is all my fault," she admitted. "The Remembrance of the Song of Hlorrithin is one of our most cherished rituals because it reminds us of Hlorrithin and our duty to take care of our rainforests and one another. We must always remember the sorrow of what the Neh'as'anni did to The People and the sorrow of what The People did to them. My pheromonal presence in the communal metamind corrupted the historical scenes playing through the Oyya Web."

"A natural enough reaction to seeing all those deaths on the *Khoza*. I'm sure Melkorka will consider that. I'll say something to her about it," Delwyn reassured her.

"Males have no say in hierarchy matters. They will resent your interference. I will resent it as well," Kidahin sang forcefully.

"You would?" Delwyn asked, surprised.

Kidahin nodded for the benefit of his poor nose.

"You would insult my honor by suggesting I need a mere male to stand between me and challenging females," she trilled flatly.

"Mere?" Delwyn asked, raising his left eyebrow.

"Do not let male autonomy and your status as our Warleader delude you, Delwyn," Kidahin warned.

"Delwyn?" Mimiran sang over the combat address system. "Is Kidahin with you?"

"She is," he snapped gruffly, resenting Kidahin's reminder that females often considered males little more than errant children.

"I am sorry, Delwyn. Kidahin, see me in Health Center immediately," Mimiran trilled.

"Affirm, Mistress," she sang evenly.

Neutral tone tended to herald ambivalence among Eyloni, Delwyn knew.

"Tell Mimiran to remember what the Territorial Boundaries of Rage and Forgiveness means. The Rite of Forgiveness says she must abandon the social debt. Speaking from experience, I think the Laws of the Clan regarding Remembrance and Continuance apply here because the whole point of the ritual is to remember and learn from history. Besides, the La'huaset Clans' motto says 'What lives shall die. What dies shall live. Strength comes from the spirits, but wisdom comes from experience', and you've certainly had quite an experience."

Kidahin hugged her favorite male, broke the intimate embrace, and ran from the Warleader's abode. It would do her no good to keep Mimiran waiting.

One reason she as huluhar had chosen Delwyn for her society to make their Warleader was that he was brilliant.

But it was not his brilliance alone that mattered most to her.

She sang happily to herself as she danced down forest trails to Health Center.

Aplilin wrapped her tail loosely around Kidahin's waist and on down her tail to her pons.

Kidahin sighed in deeply relaxed pleasure and rolled onto her lover's breasts.

"Feeling better?" Aplilin sang huskily.

"Much better," Kidahin trilled softly.

Kidahin rubbed her nose up and down Aplilin's nose and cheeks. Their pheromone-laced skin oils mingled as their mutual scent-linked empathy lifted them into a higher intimacy.

"Do you feel like talking?" Aplilin sang.

"Mimiran went hard on Tialdrin," Kidahin sang evasively.

"Why? Because she had sponsored Tialdrin for wellnessmistress training?" Aplilin sang curiously.

"That too, but mainly because Tialdrin is our Assault Team-Two wellnessmistress."

"And so she should have known about the flashbacks? Or does Mimiran think Tialdrin knew and said nothing when the Gracious Mistress offered the historical roles to you three?" Aplilin trilled.

"Not my flashbacks, but Tialdrin's. She had them, too, for about a month. She knows more about the subtle effects of traumatic stress and its lingering aspects than the average female. She recognized and dealt with them long ago. Einstika immersed herself in techmistress theory and they went away for her, too. My flashbacks stopped about the same time as hers did," Kidahin sang.

"What did you do about them? You never really talked about them much."

"Mimiran's severe injuries put her in a Health Center regeneration chrysalis for a few months, remember? She was not available, and I never bothered Tialdrin with them. I went to Delwyn instead. We talked about the flashbacks, traumatic stress, and the human variant of it he struggled with until I met him on Ibeetu," Kidahin shyly admitted.

"Me, too," Aplilin confessed.

"You?" Kidahin trilled in surprise.

"Of course. Males are always safe, and I told you long ago how much I like him. His constant complaining, cursing, and going off alone for hours at a time arouse me because I enjoy doing the same things. He is human, and the casualties on the shipwreck were humans. He had the best perspective for helping me deal with them, and he did."

"But?" Kidahin sang. Aplilin's scent told her that she was holding back.

"I try not to think about the deaths in Hlorrithin's time, even now. I refused a place in the remembrance ritual because I knew those dead human males would come for me. Mimiran refused a place for the same reason."

"Mistress of Healers Allohindra told me Mimiran is furious with Tialdrin for ignoring an obvious wellnessmistress duty. She also said to expect Mimiran will insist we get wellness evaluations—all of us in Assault Team-Two," Kidahin sang.

"Really? I do not need or want Mimiran sniffing my pons and asking stupid questions about my feelings," Aplilin trilled flatly.

"She will make Tialdrin do it and evaluate her professional objectivity," Kidahin sang.

"Well, Tialdrin is a wellnessmistress. What should she expect considering how much of an a'pea Mimiran is. What did she say about Einstika?" Aplilin wondered.

"Mimiran says she was not at fault," Kidahin sang.

"But she killed Shikararro," Aplilin trilled angrily.

"Due mostly to my dishonesty," Kidahin sang.

"Mimiran excuses her because of you?" Aplilin growled dangerously.

"Yes, because I did not think reliving the deaths in the ritual could bring those flashbacks back. I should have known better. They drifted through my subconscious mind waiting for something like the deaths in New Dawn to set them on the prowl. The raw emotion they caused altered my pheromones and affected Einstika and Tialdrin through our scent-linked empathy with each other and the singers.

"My primal empathy rating is quite high. I expected to see male deaths in the ritual, but I did not expect to empathize with those deaths and the flashbacks of the deaths we saw on *Londiwe Khoza*. I subconsciously sent visions of those flashbacks out, and they overlaid the historical scenes.

"Einstika and Tialdrin began seeing them, too. They triggered their memories, and their emotions altered their pheromones as well. Our combined scent wove our flashbacks into the historical narrative and pulled us deeper into the altered scenes.

"The changes made us take the wrong turn after we left New Dawn. It sent us down the wrong trail and we found Shikararro too early. Finding her in the wrong place made us suspicious, which led to Einstika killing her. Every time I felt something wrong brushing my tail it would slip away. Only you calling out gave me a liana I could grab onto," Kidahin sang.

"Mimiran knew the minute she smelled your scent what was wrong. She joined in pheromonal empathy with the Gracious Mistress and parted the branches to reach you. It was hard for the Gracious Mistress given how much effort she was spending just to keep Hlorrithin in ritual empathy. We tried several times to reach Tialdrin, Einstika, and you. Forcing a subplot into an established ritual is hard.

"Mimiran said Tialdrin would be the easiest for her to snag because she already knew something was wrong. Einstika just needed a good shove to fall off her branch. But you are headstrong, dear one. For all the guidance Mimiran focused on you, I gave you the motivating presence," Aplilin sang softly.

"Without you I would have wandered through my subconscious mind forever," Kidahin sang.

"I spun you around and down a treacherously unstable trail, but it was the assaultmistress in you who won the victory. You knew what to do all along."

"I knew I was helpless to stop those deaths on *Londiwe Khoza* and the deaths in Hlorrithin's time. I put an unreasonable social debt on Assault Team-Two—even you, Aplilin—for not saving the males on the human shipwreck. I placed an unreasonable honor point debt on myself for failing in leadership because I did not save them, or at least more of them.

"Mimiran says I did all of this unknowingly. She told me to recognize the futility of self-guilt and doubt, set them aside, withhold self-punishment, forget it, and abandon the social debt. Once I forget the offense and abandon the social debt the hierarchies will do the same," Kidahin sang softly.

"You have not yet done this?" Aplilin trilled with a trace of concern.

"It is hard, Aplilin. Doubt and shame led me down false trails. They stopped me from grasping what was happening to us."

"But you did succeed. Twice, in fact. You saved the remaining human shipwreck survivors two years ago and you saved Hlorrithin's mission in the past. Your persistent obligation to duty won out. What did Mimiran recommend to the hierarchies?"

"She told them I held a social grudge against myself for not saving males dead long before we found the shipwreck. If I cannot abandon the self-inflicted honor point debt, Melkorka will charge me with an honor point crime and remove me from the Society of Hunter's Moon."

"What? Why?" Aplilin demanded in sudden trembling fury.

"She thinks those human male deaths exposed a weakness. During my adulthood ceremony I met the spirits. They told me I could not fight beside a male singing on the low ground because I needed to hold the high ground for him."

"The spirits spoke to—you?" Aplilin trilled doubtfully. She thrust her doubt aside violently. Kidahin never made up fireside tales about herself.

"What about it?" she sang cautiously.

"I always thought the male in the Oyya Web vision was Delwyn."

"And now you do not?" Aplilin trilled.

"I never saw him in the vision and the voice was clearly male. You know how adulthood ritual imagery works, Aplilin."

"I know they come from the pheromonal imagery of family females.

I also know this happened a few months before you met Delwyn. What about it?"

"I thought my greatest fulfilling obligation was choosing a new warleader after Kalinn died. After Delwyn became Warleader I thought I could fulfill any obligation no matter what."

"Wait, you think you chose Delwyn because of your adulthood vision and not because he was the best choice? Are you trying to justify that choice now, or are you doubting that choice in the first place?"

"I know he was the best choice. It is my objectivity I doubt, not his fitness," Kidahin admitted.

"We are together, and you know how hard I am to get along with."

Kidahin gave Aplilin the pheromonal scent of a troubled smile.

"You saved me. I thought my adulthood vision meant I was going to save Delwyn. Do not take this wrong, but I always thought he would save me. I should be happy he came to Singer's Grove to check on me."

"He was there all along, but he could not check on you. He did not tell you, did he?" Aplilin trilled into rough laughter.

"Tell me what? What is so funny?"

"It probably slipped his mind. Only the Gracious Mistress and her singers' pheromonal support allowed him to remain awake and alert for an EST week. He probably ate the whole time he was talking to Thelindrallin's communications avatar. He should be asleep by now. I am sure Phelindra and Lo'sutra'est anni are sleeping with him. Lucky them," Aplilin trilled enviously.

"Delwyn was with me the whole time?"

"Spirits, no. The Gracious Mistress granted him the highest honor you can imagine. She insisted he play the part of Hlorrithin!" Aplilin trilled happily.

Kidahin scowled at her lover both physically and empathically. Aplilin stretched the patience of many people. Delwyn did, too. He and the aggressive, muscular Huntress shared a handful of annoying habits and were much alike.

And Kidahin knew she held them both firmly in her grasp.

Aplilin's pheromonal empathy filled Kidahin's nose and exploded into her emotional awareness. Filled with Aplilin's empathic presence, she sang.

Aplilin joined her immediately.

This is the most beautiful day we can remember.
The young spirits left joyful laughter as they flew away.
The males' spirits blessed us with songs we never heard before.
The light they left in their parting was a gift to face the

darkest night that, without doubt, waited for us ahead. We have long lives to live.

We are at peace, our duty is fulfilled.

Only the spirits of the Uahua'asee'a know what lies ahead for us.

But the dreams and hopes we know this day give us the strength to stand against any evil.

ABOUT THE AUTHOR

David Michael Martin graduated from the Ohio Institute of Technology in 1982 and designed PC-integrated laboratory analyzers until 1987. An avid science fiction and fantasy reader, Mr. Martin successfully wrote and told engaging and entertaining stories as a games master for several of the popular fantasy roleplaying game systems appearing today.

Mr. Martin returned to college and pursued his interests in English and the humanities at Ohio University, earning cum laude honors. Mr. Martin continued his English education, taking graduate English courses at Adams State University.

Mr. Martin has over twenty years' experience tutoring adult basic education classes for adult students seeking their G.E.D. diplomas. Mr. Martin currently lives in western Michigan and trains puppies using Karen Pryor clicker training techniques to become guide dogs for the blind.

In Remembrance of Sorrows is his fifth book in the Hunter's Universe saga and continues the second trilogy. The first trilogy features Warleader Delwyn, and the second trilogy features the Eyloni Hunter female Kidahin.